About the author

Göte Nyman is a curiosity-driven innovator and humanist. He has written non-fiction books, including the recent *On the Edge of Human Technology*, and the autobio-inspired *Perceptions of a Camino*. He writes columns and runs an extensive blog series (gotepoem at Wordpress). *Les Demoiselles* is his first major novel.

Göte has an unusual career in science, human technology, innovation and university management, and he has authored numerous scientific articles. Close to his heart is collaboration with the Peace Innovation Laboratory at Stanford, where they aim to promote positive human developments with the support of ICT and networks.

Specializing in vision, brain and imaging quality, Göte loves visual arts and technologies. He enjoys the tranquillity of a distant island cottage; sports and gym have a natural part in his life. Göte was born in Helsinki in 1947 and continues his career as a university professor of psychology.

PERCEPTIONS OF THE LES DEMOISELLES D'AVIGNON

Göte Nyman

PERCEPTIONS OF THE LES DEMOISELLES D'AVIGNON

Vanguard Press

VANGUARD PAPERBACK

A CIP catalogue record for this title is
available from the British Library.

ISBN 978-1-80016-096-5

*Vanguard Press is an imprint of
Pegasus Elliot MacKenzie Publishers Ltd.*
www.pegasuspublishers.com

First Published in 2021

**Vanguard Press
Sheraton House Castle Park
Cambridge England**

Printed & Bound in Great Britain

Dedication

To the memory of

Fergus W. Campbell, my mentor

and

Alec Aalto,

a literary friend

Acknowledgements

Les Demoiselles is almost pure fiction. I have invented the Stanley University to avoid any interpretation that the academic events and sites in the story would refer to real Californian universities, especially Stanford. I love Stanford, its campus and the atmosphere there, which is why I have used its wonderful surroundings and Palo Alto in the story. There is no Helsinki University – I come from the University of Helsinki, Finland. Some real historical events and surroundings are included in the story, but any similarities with real people, institutes and other entities described in the book are coincidental.

I asked Harriet Scott Chessman, a wonderful US writer, a sensitive person and an amazing critic and coach I had met at Stanford, to look at my text and help improve it. I could not have a better supporter and coach. After my *Perceptions of a Camino* book, which she helped me to prepare, she once told me: "Göte, I see another book in you." This is it, Harriet, thank you! I still wanted to have a near-to-final read for the text and asked Marlene Broemer to do it; she did much more than proofreading.

When I had only the general outline of the book, I kept thinking about a time shift in the story and how to tell it in such an eloquent way as it happens in Woodie Allen's charming movie *Midnight in Paris*, where the protagonist simply gets into a historical car and finds himself in the middle of the famous artists of the 1920s. Then in 2016, Professor of Theatre Work, Pauliina Hulkko and Professor Esa Kirkkopelto gave my wife, Kiisa, a present, two tickets to a play in Helsinki: *Go Down, Moses* by Romeo Castellucci. In one of its stage settings the audience could spontaneously and without any effort, immerse into a historical episode, or that's how I felt it. The observation inspired me to a literary solution and I was ready to complete the story. Thank you, Pauliina and Esa!

Soon after the play, I worked with full energy and wrote bravely in my gotepoem blog fiction science – a genre: *"I've understood that it is not wise or respectable professional behavior from a writer to publicly announce that he or she is writing a novel, which will be finished and published by a specific date. So, I will release my book, a novel, on September 9th 2017 in Helsinki, Finland, probably at about 3 p.m."*

The first sentence was wise, wiser than I could imagine. On a serene July evening in 2017, we were enjoying delicious Finnish berries and crepes on a distant island in Lake Saimaa, when I had a stroke in my right carotid artery and a mild paralysis in my left arm. We were 40 kilometres away from the nearest hospital. There was no place for an emergency helicopter to land, and reaching a hospital required a boat trip over the lake and then a 15 kilometre long, narrow, winding sand road through forests, leading to a highway where it was possible to drive faster. It was a story for a novel, my wife Kiisa rally-driving to save me, while I followed the paralysis advance in my fingers and along the left forearm, calling the hospital and explaining the symptoms.

This is the place to express my sincere gratitude to Kiisa again and to thank the amazing Finnish public health care, the people at Mikkeli Central Hospital and the vascular surgery and intensive care at the Helsinki University Hospital. Later, in Helsinki, I found myself lying in the same unit where I had worked in 1970s as a young neuropsychologist, often testing patients like me. The devoted professionals saved my brain and life. The book launch did not take place as intended, and I had to take a break. As an ex-clinical neuropsychologist and brain scientist, I knew how blessed I was, to recover fully with no serious handicaps and able to continue.

Giving the manuscript for someone to read and evaluate is not easy when it's about the first serious novel you have written. I started with an evening story, reading one chapter at a time to Kiisa, and received her unending encouragement. I was ready to show the manuscript to my literary friend, Alec Aalto, whose warm support helped me to continue and be brave with the book. Then in the early summer 2017, in Sicily, visiting a charming countryside villa, up on a hill with an open view to every direction, we were a group of long-time friends having an evening gathering on its beautiful terrace, and I asked Alec with his colourful bass voice and diplomatic aura, to read the first passages of the book to our friends. That was the moment when I felt he breathed a special life into the story and I still feel it there. Especially I remember the comment by my godson, Emil, who was in the audience: "I got hooked on the first paragraphs!" Thank you, my dear friends, for being present with the first episodes of the story.

Having recovered from the stroke I had the courage to ask Satu Lindroos to read the manuscript. We had written a non-fiction book with Satu and Katja Lindroos, and I knew her beautiful, artistic sense of style and critical elegance in her writing from which I had tried to take my own lessons. She commented on the text with her soft and solid emotional wisdom and suggested improvements. I followed her advice and it was time to look for a publisher.

Searching for a publisher can be an adventure, but the welcoming reception by Pegasus Elliot Mackenzie Publishers Ltd, Cambridge, UK made my day. I'm grateful to Vicky Gorry for her kind professional touch and the seamless interaction during the production process.

In order to avoid spoiling the reading experience I have explained some of my sources in the postscript.

Every day I have been astonished by the love and encouragement my wife Kiisa has given me during the writing journey and at the moments of eternal uncertainty. Preparing a fiction story that covers a family history, a university in California, the academia, artists in Paris, and history of science, is like constructing a quilt with complex patterns: I was prepared to leave one and perhaps even more misplaced pieces in it, as "only God is perfect".

In Siuntio, Finland, 20th April, 2021

Göte Nyman

PART I

Chapter 1
The Measure of Everything

Johan Ek stood still and focused, facing a marble plaque at the end of a classic arcade. He had arrived half an hour earlier that morning at the distinctive old building in Paris, and had continued to stare, with the sharp eye of a young physicist, at the rectangular plaque attached to the brownish-gray stone wall at the end of a thirty-meter corridor. He did not move an inch, just stayed there, mesmerized, like a statue from the era when the marble plate had been crafted and celebrated. The plate's surface and edges, under the classical marble shelf, were visibly worn, with a delicate, historical beige tint; it was about forty inches wide and ten inches high, but its width of about one meter attracted Johan's attention.

Like a blond and live version of Rodin's works, motionless but expressive in his prepared-for-something posture, Johan looked ready to embrace the plaque. The passers-by did not disturb him, and he barely noticed them hurrying by in their haste in the gray, foggy and drizzly morning. No one else showed the slightest interest in the modest object of his fascination. Only some women, under their colorful, waving umbrellas, would cast a quick glance and a flash of smile at the serious-looking fellow, dressed in a blue checkered flannel shirt and blue jeans, and who with his fair Nordic looks, had the appearance of a young and vigorous but harmless Viking, with his bright blue eyes and six feet five inches height.

At this precious moment, however, Johan was fully engaged with the plaque and its enlightening and violent history. Had the pedestrians understood its significance in their everyday life and even at their moment of death, they might have stopped to look, at least once in a lifetime. Johan noticed how the end-wall and the arcade spanned a comfortable space, making it a momentary, private and historical art gallery and a shelter from the misty morning rain. The word "METRE" stood boldly in the center of the plaque over a carved double line marked into ten segments.

It was April 4, 2016. Johan had arrived to see the plate at 36, rue de Vaugirard, in the Sixth Arrondissement, opposite the Senate at the *Palais du Luxembourg* and its impressive entrance, a massive, bluish-green, six-meter-high double door of metal, rising high to the arching top. The gate was flanked by two French flags with their blue, white and red colors, the blue European Union flag with its yellow stars hung beside them on both sides of the gate. The familiar words LIBERTÉ, ÉGALITÉ, FRATERNITÉ, in gold capital letters were written there, easy to read, even through the misty rain, and from the place under the archway where the plate was hidden under its small marble shelf.

"It cannot be time alone causing the visible wear on its corners and on the smooth marble surface," he thought; the insight sent a faintly discernible wave of wrinkles onto his forehead. "People just have not been able to keep their hands off it. I wonder how many of them, the uneducated minds, have known this word carved here in marble as the symbol of every possible measure in their world, a measure of all measures. Perhaps touching this plaque has given the word "METRE" a tangible life, a rare form of solidity in a world where every possible ground and measure had been shattering, cultural and physical alike."

Johan leaned slightly forward, extending his hands, as if to measure the width of the plate, slowly and softly touching its ends simultaneously, feeling and enjoying the measure and its delicate forms under the fingertips of his strong hands, caressing the old stone surface. He did not smile; a shadow of worry crossed his face.

Hands still extended, holding the plate at both ends, Johan studied the details of the engraved word and the two thinly carved, horizontal lines on the marble surface just below it. Two small bronze knobs, exactly one meter apart, defined the lines' boundaries.

Only a month ago Johan had worked as a researcher of theoretical physics at the prestigious Stanley University in California, but had come under pressure to quit his job, and had moved, or escaped as he felt it, to Paris. He had now come to visit the Metre, not to marvel at the historical plaque but to find relief from his anxiety and to see one of the places in

Paris his father had incessantly described in his stories after returning from his journeys, either physical or psychological.

Sten Ek, Johan's father, who had passed away four years ago, could disappear for days, without leaving a note to the family, leaving Johan and his mother worried and frightened, not knowing what had happened to him. The Metre had become the first of Sten's compulsions, and often when returning home from his frightening journeys, he would tell its story to an incredulous Johan, explaining how important it had been to see it, to face it and to understand its underlying powers. Johan could never understand why the Metre had so possessed his father, but facing his own troubles at Stanley, he had decided to see it himself, hoping it would help him, somehow.

Johan tried to stand at a distance of about two feet from the Metre, knowing — it was an amusing compulsion of his — that the distance would make every centimeter on the plate correspond roughly to one degree of a visual angle. This habit of immersing himself in the intricate measurements of sight originated in his laboratory, where he used optical instruments and visualizations as a natural part of his everyday tasks. Knowing the angular size of an object makes it possible to calculate the size of its image projected on the retina of a standard person. In real life, as he had often learned from his teasing friends, it did not seem a very rational behavior. "Life may be enormous, but our retinal images are miniscule!" his physicist colleagues used to say, laughing at Johan's excitement. Johan, however, remained enchanted with this capacity of human vision in relation to the grandest objects in nature. The size of the most impressive scenes, the largest paintings, even the latest wide-screens in movie theaters and the breath-taking views of mountain scenery or an enchanting astronomical image of the universe, when projected at the back of the eye, has barely the size of the nail on a large thumb. Johan would often entertain this astonishing insight when, as a physicist, he could admire the amazing power of the human perception system, its ability to use a miniature sensory device like the retina to create everything humans can see and experience as the visual world, its objects and scenes.

Johan took a careful step back from the plate, slowly turning his gaze to the left, curious, to admire the impressive gate rising on the other side of the street, the words *Liberté, Égalité, Fraternité* glimmering in the morning haze. He was slowly drifting away from his immersive state, back to the reality of this Paris morning, when suddenly he saw a thin, light-brown, partly pinkish, transparent, mildly undulating silky fabric rise in front of the entrance to the Jardin, like a graceful, translucent wall. In less than two seconds it covered the entire gate and its jambs, at about one yard from it, extending from the ground to the top of the building. For a moment Johan was confident that he could also discern faint female figures displayed on this dreamlike, soft wall, as a painting. "Is that the *Les Demoiselles*?" was his first amazed reaction. It was one of the few paintings from Picasso's work that Johan had learned to know. He had never seriously studied art history but in the stories his father had told, the painting and the Metre were often interconnected in a compelling way that had attracted his interest. The half-naked female figures in the painting had become familiar to Johan from art books and as a young boy they had always embarrassed him, but he never understood why. Neither could he see any logic behind the mysterious connection between the painting and the Metre.

The vision of the painting on the fabric vanished in a quick, blinding, bright flash. Recovering from the flash, Johan noticed that the fabric remained, hovering in front of the gate and yet the figures had been erased. Next, he saw someone behind the silky screen, a real person, in an urban scene. It was a young man with a moustache and slightly curly dark hair; he was dressed in a black overcoat, standing still behind the fabric. The scene and the man appeared to be from another era, perhaps the 1930s or even earlier, but Johan could not be sure; he could not see enough of the details. But then, a nervous blink of the eyes made Johan's vision disappear and he could only see the massive gate and a drizzling rain, clouding its appearance. He did not doubt his eyes. He had seen something similar before. He spoke silently to himself, scared.

"It's the wall — again! Had father seen this, too?"

Johan sighed deeply; he did not move, staring at the people hurrying by and behind them, the Jardin walls, masked by the drizzle. It was again the plain, massive and historical wall, with its bluish-green and grayish surface, wet from the rain he saw now but deprived of the transient life he had seen there, behind and on the silky screen. Only after a minute or two he could return, slowly, to the marble "METRE." He stood still again in front of the plaque, listening to the echoing footsteps of the people seeking shelter from the rain under the arcade.

Johan started humming the song-mantra he had so often hummed in the last two months, amid the moments of deepest grief. It was always the same section of the classic Eagles piece, "Hotel California". Thinking the words, he hummed it half-silently, the few lines from the beginning, carrying him somewhere far, into a tranquil silence.

He did not understand why this song had such a powerful, calming impact. It made him feel like being "outside the inviting but fatal campfires of life," as a friend used to say, describing Johan's occasional way of behaving like a social outsider, distancing himself from everything and seeking time to be alone. His friends did not know the reasons for this exceptional habit. The song had originally been a favorite of his father's, who used to listen to it and sing along at their home in Finland, the stereo at a disturbingly high volume, making neighbors nervous and often irritated, not only with Sten, but also with Johan and his mother Karin. At first, Johan, could not understand or discern the words properly from his father's blurry humming, and it had been difficult to make any sense of them, but over time he could follow the story in the lyrics and even immerse in their world himself.

Standing at the marble plaque, contemplating the dream vision he had just witnessed, Johan let himself think about his father's troubled life and his own childhood.

Sten had been a gifted student already at school and started studying mathematics and physics at the Helsinki University, but on his third year he enrolled in theology and philosophy. Karin, Johan's mother, had been Sten's long-time girlfriend, the same age as he, but she did not go to the university, and began to work as a secretary at a paper mill. They lived together as a young couple for some time and married in 1986 when they both were twenty-six. From his mother Johan had heard about the first difficult periods of Sten's life. At the beginning of the following year, soon after Johan was born in December 1985, Sten ended up in trouble with his supervisor, a professor of theology. Nobody knew the exact story, but after the incident Sten began to suffer from other conflicts as well, telling stories about the evil and systematically malevolent behaviors of the professors, about their persecution of him and other research students, their forgery of invoices and documents, and their way of spreading evil rumors, especially about Sten. Karin was afraid they were the first signs of his emerging paranoia.

When Johan was two, they moved outside the busy Helsinki to the countryside, ending up in Vihti, which was not far from the paper mill where Karin worked. Vihti was a quiet village-like environment some 30 miles from Helsinki, where they lived in a two-story, 1980s duplex, with a wooden facade of traditional ochre color; a small green, modest garden was in front of the house and a charming pine forest opened behind it. The apartment was spacious enough so that Johan had his own room. It was a perfect environment where the children could play in the surrounding forest in summer and enjoy skating on the nearby lake in winter. Before the teenage years, Johan never wondered why his parents had their own bedrooms.

As Johan grew up, he realized that his mother had decided to make this move to live in Vihti because she had been worried about his father's state of mind. Sten was often restless and explained that his professors were persecuting him and accusing him of misbehavior. Karin constantly worried that Sten was losing his sense of reality entirely.

Karin had thought that the simple and peaceful environment of a rural village could be good for Sten, but it became clear to Johan, even as a small child, that his father was still troubled. Johan grew up understanding that his mother was the only one who could keep a job and support the family. Money was often a worry in the household, because even in Vihti, the cost of living was high.

When Johan was a teenager it was evident that he had inherited his father's looks so much that his best friends used to joke with him about how two faces could be so similar physically, but with totally different expressions. Johan smiled often, responding spontaneously to his friends' comments and stories, sharing their joys and worries. It was a remarkable contrast to his father, whose expressionless face was difficult to interpret. People often had trouble knowing what might lie behind his eyes, or what he would do next. Johan's friends were afraid of his father. When they came to fetch Johan for a game or a sports exercise and his father opened the door, they never entered the house, but just stayed outside, hesitant, even when Sten asked them to come in. Sten could surprise Johan's friends by speaking Swedish to them, as Swedish was his mother tongue, which they did not understand and became even more reserved. Only later as an adult did Johan realize that Sten's Finnish-Swedish background had been an invisible social barrier between himself and his friends, who did not speak Swedish and had very little experience of this small minority in Finland. Even his name, Johan Ek, suggested a Finnish-Swedish background, although he never learned to speak fluent Swedish. It was a strange disconnection between Johan, his father and father's Swedish-speaking friends who would occasionally visit them. Before learning Swedish at school, Johan could not understand what they were talking about. Father never spoke Swedish to Johan.

Sten was born in 1960, the only child of his farmer parents, who were bilingual and both had a Finnish-Swedish background. A clever and fast-learning student, he enjoyed his first two, easy and successful school years in his small home village in northwestern Finland. Then his father left the family, as a total surprise to his wife Elli, when Sten was only eight years old. He and his mother could not take care of the farming and had to rent out the fields to their relatives and try to manage as best they could; Elli took odd jobs in the village and helped the farmers, especially in summer. Life became difficult, and the silent and unspoken shame from the episode came to Sten's dreams and contributed to his growing lack of trust in anybody, a symptom that later grew into paranoia, causing both social and marriage problems. In 1970, when Sten was ten, he and his mother moved to Seinäjoki, a small town not far from the home village. Elli never remarried and worked first as a shop assistant and then, being a hard and skilled worker, she later became a store manager, and life became easier for her and Sten.

When Sten began his studies at the university, he moved to Helsinki and to student housing, hoping to help his mother by taking care of himself. Life became easier when Sten's mother moved to a smaller apartment in Seinäjoki, and Sten met Karin in Helsinki. Over the years, during the difficult times, when Sten's problems grew serious and he needed professional help, Sten and Karin started spontaneously isolating socially and only during major celebrations would they meet Sten's mother Elli and a few friends. Sten lost contact with his mother, who still lived in Seinäjoki, some two hundred and fifty miles from Vihti and he did not know she had suffered from heart problems but never went to see a doctor. In 1988, soon after Sten and Karin were married, Elli, Johan's grandmother, passed away at the age of fifty, due to sudden heart failure. Sten went speechless for three weeks, and only after the funeral was he able to communicate with his wife again. The shock at the loss of his mother, the distressing mistrust, extreme criticism, and pessimistic expectations Sten easily and spontaneously expressed when meeting people made it difficult to build lasting friendships and he remained a loner. Karin did her best to support him and protect Johan, but the family life became broken.

Johan had only vague memories of Sten when grandmother passed away, and he had often wondered how much he could actually remember, having been only three at the time and how much of it was his own imagination colored by the anxious stories his mother used to tell about Sten. From his early teenage years onward, Johan did have vivid memories on how occasionally, for a reason nobody understood, his father could surprise the family and the few friends who would visit them, by becoming a lively, even a jolly companion, for a little while, waving his hands in the air, excited, immersed in a fascinating story he was about to tell. He was an excellent storyteller then. Johan did not know much about the medicine his father was taking — it was never discussed and remained a mystery. He was often puzzled by the impact it had on his father's behavior and especially when he realized that sometimes, this temporary expansiveness and happiness in Sten came when he had *not* taken his daily medicine. Johan understood that the medicine helped contain Sten's anxieties and over-energetic, scary paranoia, yet it also appeared to take away his best emotions and the energy of life.

Once Sten had taken his dose, he returned to his private world, listening to his favorite music, loud, and disconnected from the family. The familiar, comforting music carried Sten somewhere away, far into his personal mystery space, totally out of reach. He would have visions of his dreamlike travels to other places. Only the strange drawings he made after these episodes-told the story of his whereabouts. Johan and his mother would gaze at the drawings, worry and try to understand what Sten had experienced.

The drawings were always the same: four people, men, simply dressed, gathered around an old, decorated well of a village plaza, standing close to each other; they had a feeling of togetherness and the camaraderie of an intimate circle. Their figures were not rich in detail, and the repeating, overlapping traces of the pen were so strong, exaggerated, appearing manic in nature, that it was difficult to identify any of the characters or their natural features. Typically, the drawings would include different perspectives and a mix of viewing angles, sometimes depicting the figures simultaneously and overlapping in the same drawing, making the image bizarre and disorderly in style. In the lower right corner of the paper Sten would typically leave an empty space, but occasionally he drew a small and simple graphical symbol, ⋈, there: the delicate form of the bowtie, floating on the paper as if it did not belong there at all.

Johan would later learn that this bowtie was a historical sign, the signature of his father's family, a rare link to Sten's home and its local history near the coast of the sixty-miles-wide Gulf of Botnia separating Finland and Sweden. Johan became fascinated by the symbol and the family story behind it and had started using it as his own *ex libris* mark, having the habit of signing his most interesting copies of scientific articles with it.

Sten had never explained who the characters in his drawings were and what they were doing there, but occasionally when he was ready to talk about the drawings, he launched into a manic sounding talk, a monotonic sermon, explaining to Johan how dangerous the physical standards and especially the Metre, are to mankind. The young Johan could not understand at all how and why the standards would have anything to do with his father's experiences and the drawings. Later, when he studied theoretical physics, he became aware of the power of standards and constants in physics, noticing how part of the fame of some exceptional physicists carried over generations because of the constants named after them: Boltzmann, Dirac, Planck. Johan would never question these innate elements of physics, but he had not forgotten how

Sten would typically end his sermon about the dangers of standards by telling, almost commanding him, without any further explanation:

"The Metre is the worst of all! Go and see it in Paris! It will open your eyes, too!"

Johan was always curious about this strange command as he thought of it but received no answer to his eager inquiries.

This was how Johan first found out about the Metre and then, much later, got to know the compelling story behind it. This was why he was now standing, mesmerized, in search of personal relief, in front of the historical standard in the Paris morning rain, puzzled by the mystic meaning of the Metre and the plaque, wondering what they had to offer, what did father mean by claiming that 'it would open his eyes, too'. The momentary wall had taken him by surprise evoking anxious memories of his recent encounters. It was his own, private vision, something he had faced before, when desperate at Stanley, in Palo Alto; it had been a most frightening experience. He had never heard his father mention anything like it.

Chapter 2
The Hitchhiker

At the age of fourteen, Johan had accompanied his father, who was then forty and wanted to visit his childhood village, which was just a few kilometers from Vaasa, a small town on the northwestern coast of Finland. They had planned to make what they called a "memory lane trip" together; Johan's father was curious for the first time in twenty years to see where he had been born, and spent the first years of his life. It was a warm day in early June, and Johan's summer holiday from the school had just begun.

Driving there, passing by the smallish town of Seinäjoki where Sten had lived with his mother, Johan noticed how his father first commented on many of the fond memories about Elli, repeatedly mentioning how his mother had always taken good care of him. But then, arriving at Sten's home village some forty miles from Seinäjoki, the comments began to have a disconnected, almost sad tone when he named the people he had known there, or observed the peculiar features of the houses and the narrow, dusty roads. Johan could sense the mixed feelings his father had about his own history. It was in striking contrast to what he told Johan about his strong, intimate and almost inseparable feeling of being connected with the large open grain fields they saw everywhere, the lake with its charming small islands, and the dark, slowly flowing water in the river where he had learned to swim and to catch grayfish. Johan could not understand what his father meant by repeatedly and in great detail describing his paradoxical experience of being personally separated, completely, from the people of the village while being intimately connected with the natural world surrounding it.

It had been a beautiful, warm and bright summer day in June with no wind, clear blue skies; the charming lake shone blue and reflected the images of the few, thin white clouds on its mirror-like surface. The small, forested islands were barely visible in the distance, but made a wide-extending, wavy, greenish forest profile embracing the lake.

They took a morning walk along the lakefront and admired the landscape while Sten told stories about how he and his friends used to swim and fish there until very late, almost midnight, in the summer evenings when the appearance of the water had turned from clean-fresh to dark-brown, almost black. Nights were short.

Johan had never before heard his father use such a soft tone and affectionate expressions about his personal experiences and life history and felt a rare, instant bondage emerge, an enchanting moment without the familiar, everyday fear and uncertainty he had when near his father at home. He was embarrassed to feel tears sliding on his cheek and tried to swipe them away unnoticed.

At lunchtime, they headed toward the cozy, small village hostel, built and renovated from an old, red-ochre country house where they stayed overnight. They were both enchanted by the beauty of the lake and fields, and excited by the lively stories from Sten's childhood. Driving along, they almost hit an old man, perhaps in his eighties, standing in the middle of the dusty sand road, waving towards the oncoming traffic. The man was dressed in a black, creased suit, a bright-white shirt, and a black tie, a black wide-brimmed hat, and wore eyeglasses with brown frames and very thick lenses. He carried a small, worn-out dark-brown briefcase and had an air of calmness, apparently not at all afraid of the cars on the narrow country road. The curious fellow was holding a walking stick in his left, extended, tanned hand, the thumb up. In his right hand, he waved the briefcase, high in the air. To Johan's eyes he had surprisingly dark hair, thick dark eyebrows and a tanned face, something one might get from working long days outside. The man had an original way of making himself utterly visible in this dangerous situation; he was smiling, a kind, wide smile enhancing the marked wrinkles in the corners of his eyes. The fellow was hitchhiking.

Sten had to brake hard to avoid hitting the man, forcing Johan to take a firm hold with both hands on the dashboard to avoid hitting himself against it. The car stopped beside the strange fellow and Sten opened the left window, as the man still stood in the middle of the road. Johan could smell the road dust floating in the air through the open window. Sten addressed the man, leaning out the window, and sounded surprisingly polite to Johan:

"Excuse me, sir, where are you going? I almost hit you; why do you stand there, in such a dangerous place? You could get hurt."

Johan was astonished to notice how calm his father was in the strange and dangerous situation. He spoke in a kind tone, without the slightest sign of nervousness or annoyance. The man stepped closer to the car window. He spoke with a funny local dialect Johan had only rarely heard his father use.

"Hi, boys, you can drive me to the bank. I have to meet the director, but you can wait outside and take me back home then."

Johan did not expect such a blunt request from the man and was even more puzzled by the fact that his father appeared to see nothing peculiar in the situation. Sten had a wide smile on his face, and his bright blue eyes shone, just like during the visit to the lakefront. This cheerful, balanced spirit and appearance were something Johan had not seen in him for a long time at home, and he wondered why he was seeing it now. When his father spoke again, it was with the same funny intonation this villager had used.

"Of course, please step in. I'm Sten Ek, and this is my son Johan; we are just visiting here, but I know where the bank is."

Observing the mystery man in black approaching the car and touching its surface, guiding his careful movements towards the left back door and smoothly entering the back seat, Johan realized their new passenger suffered from visual impairment or could even be blind, but wondered then how the fellow could know there were two men — boys — in the car. He did have eyeglasses, but he behaved like a blind man. Johan didn't say anything; it was an odd enough situation already.

"Are you the son of Johan Ek, the sailor who left his wife Elli and you here and never returned? I heard he died in America. I'm blind, you see; I cannot see you!"

He laughed, continuing so that Sten did not have a chance to answer, "You wonder why I'm wearing eyeglasses, then, don't you? They make me remember how it felt, seeing and looking straight at things. I don't see anything, but I love the feeling of the frame on my nose and ears. It helps me orient, too!"

He paused briefly, so that Johan's father could answer.

"Yes, I'm Sten, and my son's name is a reminder of his grandfather."

"I'm Alex Guldstrand. We are family relatives then: your grandfather's sister and my uncle Eric were married and lived here before moving to America." Johan could not immediately imagine their ages and was puzzled by this family history.

Sten turned the car around, to drive towards the bank, one kilometer ahead in the village center. Alex and Sten started an intense discussion, about people, places and happenings before and during World War II; most of the names were totally unknown to Johan, who remained silent, staring at the road but listening. His father, asking about the local history, became visibly curious and moved to hear about the current situation in the village. The younger generation had moved to the cities to look for jobs, and many had gone to Sweden. The village's future was uncertain.

Johan's father would tell him, later that afternoon, how in the midst of this conversation he had started to remember the family stories about Alex. He described how his mother would discuss or gossip with her friends about this village fool, a friendly but strange local lunatic, not so rare during the times when psychiatric disorders did not typically get any proper medical diagnosis, especially in the countryside, far from urban services. Local people were quick to deliver their own diagnosis, and the village hosted different kinds of fools, a few only, but everyone knew them. Children were typically afraid of these eccentric characters, but for the farmers they were often a useful work force.

In the car, Johan's father smiled as he asked Alex, "How do you know all this, are you a historian?"

"I have collected everything possible related to the local history, but I should find a better place to store all my treasures, as a part of our municipal museum perhaps, if they are interested. I have a nice old warehouse, but I'm quite blind and it's somewhat difficult to find things and store them in good order now. Collecting the historical objects from the houses that still have them is not easy; people have just disposed of beautiful and even rare cultural artifacts they think have no practical value. But I can still see all kinds of things with my hands, and smell them, too, like your deodorants."

He laughed, a heartfelt, raspy laugh, and then surprised Johan by asking if he could touch his face to "see" if he could recognize something familiar in Johan's facial features. Johan blushed, embarrassed, but did not want to disappoint the old man by refusing.

"Yes, of course."

Johan continued to face forward and did not turn his head towards Alex, who moved to the seat behind Johan and extended both of his hands, touching Johan's eyebrows first, then the nose, chin and finally the hairline; he sensed every spot on the face, symmetrically from both sides. The intimate feeling of the rough and strong hands, their robust, dusty smell, a mild scent of tar, was a strange new experience to Johan, whose parents only rarely touched or hugged him. If they did so, it was only briefly, in a distant, absent-feeling manner. Johan had always felt an unexplainable, helpless shame whenever someone surprised him by a spontaneous hug, but now, for a reason he did not understand, the powerful but kind touch of the hands relaxed him. It was not only the physical way Alex stroked his face, searching for the details, that made Johan feel the emotional intensity and commitment transmitted with every small, sensitive movement, but it was also the expression of this person's genuine curiosity and care. Johan felt that Alex was searching for connections to Johan's family history, and his character and inner being.

"No doubt, you are like Johan, your grandfather. He had that same small, rather short but strong boxer-like nose, high forehead and the funny small dip at the back of the head. Are you blond, too? Your smooth hair feels like it? You might lose it one day like your grandfather did, quite early I remember."

Johan blushed. "Yes, I do have blond hair, and I hope to keep it."

"Have you been crying, there are traces of tears on your cheek?"

"It's just dust I got in my eyes," Johan said, and his face became red. He felt Alex's hand on his cheek make a very slight move and Johan could sense him smiling behind his back.

After a few minutes' drive they stopped in front of the bank: a light-green, small, two-story, wooden house, right in the center of the miniscule village.

Sten advised Alex, "Be careful, the bank door and the stairs are on the left of the car."

But Alex had already stepped out of the car from the right, walking around the front of it, waving his hand and walking stick:

"I know the bumps and curves of the road, and the smells, too! I'll be back in a minute."

Alex hurried, almost rushed up the half dozen, knotty, worn-out, wooden stairs, and opened the door to the bank. Observing his behavior, it was impossible to guess he was blind. Johan followed him keenly with his eyes, admiring the old man's agility. He realized that the wooden stairs guided Alex by echoing the sounds of his footsteps, signaling there was nobody else entering or coming out of the bank.

They had to wait for half an hour before Alex came back. Sten had time to explain the background he knew about the Guldstrand family, which had lived only two kilometers from Sten's home, in a classic farmhouse that used to have its own fields for hay and grain, a dozen cows, pigs, horses and hens; this was typical for most of the local farmers. Before either Johan or Sten could get out of the car to help, the arriving Alex had already entered the back seat as smoothly as he had left it.

Alex did not explain why he took so long, he did not apologize in any way, saying only, "I know the ancient and traditional sign of your family; it originates from the time some hundred years ago. I can show it to you, so you can preserve it. Do you know where the Snakefields are, Sten? Drive us there, please!"

"Yes, I remember them, but don't exactly know where they are; I was there only once or twice. There were so many snakes, poisonous vipers, that my grandparents did not want to take me there."

Alex ignored this comment. He simply guided the way, instructing Johan's father in a loud voice from the back seat as if he could see. He was leaning forward from his seat, his head between Sten and Johan, when he explained the reason for family signs in that area.

"The signs date back to the sixteenth century, from which time there are preserved church documents, even here. When people could not write, they used these family symbols to sign contracts and documents; valuable property was often marked with the owner's sign as well."

Alex surprised Sten and Johan again with his accurate instructions, as they drove along the winding, bumpy and narrow forest road for about eight miles to the west. He must have had an inner sense of each meter, because suddenly he spoke up.

"Here! Stop! On the left there should be the old sandy road, leading to the barn. Can you see it? Leave the car here; there are too many stones on the road. We can walk from here."

Johan's father parked the car where the modest, barely visible road to the fields started. Alex was again quick, being the first out of the car, hurrying towards the vast fields. Johan could see there had once been a road, but now brush and small bushes filled in the space. Only if you looked closely could you see the tops of gray stones peeking out from the ground.

"You can walk with me; we should find an old barn somewhere there on the right side of this field."

They followed the hurrying Alex, walking about a hundred yards, when he stopped, waved his hands to the right and towards the ground.

"There should be a ditch here. Can you help me jump over it? Just show me where the edge is."

Johan could not stop smiling and admiring the agile old man, trying to grasp how he could manage like that, blind, without a bit of hesitation or complaint. Johan wondered, "How is that possible, how can one learn such an amazing skill to see and not to see and to learn to live with it? He must have some peculiar, inner measures of his own."

He took Alex by the left arm and guided him to the edge of a ditch, almost three feet deep and two feet wide.

"You're a kind boy!"

Johan did not have time to explain what the ditch was like or to help Alex further, because Alex had already jumped to the other side.

"It should be there, the barn, can you see it? Let's go!"

The barn was only ten yards from the ditch, partly masked by the high-growing, dense bushes. It had six-feet-high walls, a gabled roof made of shingles, and a floor area of about two hundred square feet. The building was made of rounded logs, gray and worn, about six inches thick, and looked to be at least one hundred years old. The barn had a square-form, three by three-foot entrance opening, with no door.

Sten and Johan had not even asked Alex, who had already approached the barn entrance, where he was taking them. Alex had been convincing enough, so they did not doubt his knowledge and motivations.

"Help me step in. There should be a high threshold of three logs here at the door. Is the floor still there?"

They stepped into a high open space, more than ten feet from the floor to the top. "Oh, it's really well preserved!" Alex exclaimed and tested the floor with two energetic jumps. Gazing up, they could discern the firm wooden structures of the classic shingle roof. Johan took careful steps on the dusty, worn, wooden floor, afraid it would break under his weight, but then noticed it did not give way at all and carried their weight well. Johan was amazed by the open slits between the weathered wall logs, which would let the rain and snow come inside. Somehow, though, the barn had survived a hundred summers and winters.

It was a new, puzzling experience for Johan to smell, simultaneously, both the dusty and clean air inside the barn. This perception was enriched by the mix of the hazy white summer light filtered through the narrow slits in the walls. Johan was not sure, but although this barn was bare, he sensed something like a smell of hay or grain in the air. He did not say anything to his father or Alex about this surprising fragrance. It felt like a true time shift to stand there, engaged with the signs of life from one hundred years back, and to imagine people, including children, carrying hay into this barn for drying.

As if his father had heard Johan's thoughts, he said, "There is still a mild fragrance of hay! It's the airflow that does it, covering the walls and the floor with a dust of hay particles; the slits let light in, too."

"Boys, here should be your family sign somewhere. You know, perhaps you remember, Sten, that these fields used to belong to your family. I know they carved the sign here above the door opening, I've seen it, to leave the owner's mark, inside, on the face of the first log, somewhere here, above!"

Alex was eagerly sliding his hand along the gray log surface.

"Here it is!"

Sten and Johan came closer to properly see the sign, but it did not stand out in the shadowy location, where the contrast with the bright light coming through the door opening blinded them. They had to try to touch and feel it, just as Alex did, crowding the log surface with their hands, sliding their hands over it from different directions until they could feel the five inches-wide and two-inches high, carefully carved symbol in the shape of a bowtie: ⋈. They all were quiet, breathing heavily from the excitement. Johan's father sighed: "Johan, this is the symbol of our family; it's meant for us!" Then he became silent, stood still, tears sliding on his cheeks leaving faint gray traces. After the moment of silence, he sighed, wiping his tears away, smiling at Alex:

"It's the only memento I have from my family! You are a treasure, Alex!" Alex did not answer, only kept running his fingertips over the bowtie symbol on the log.

Johan could imagine his father thinking about his grandparents or their parents carving this and celebrating it. Touching the symbol, Johan's father appeared to be making contact with the family members he had entirely lost. Johan wondered if his father was picturing his own father, years ago, hoping that someone, a son or a grandson, would come upon this symbol in the future. It took some time for the young Johan, the teenager, to realize how special the symbol was for him, too.

After returning from the Snakefields, Alex took the travelers — he did not offer them a choice — to see the historical collection he had stored in a large, old, and well-kept barn, nicely situated in the courtyard of the main building, his home. Both buildings had the typical plain style of Finnish country houses: a gabled roof, the color of red ochre, with white window frames outside, perfectly matching with the style and coloring of other buildings surrounding the courtyard: a cowshed, a workshop and a stable with a stall for two horses. By now it had become clear to Johan and Sten that Alex was an amazing, systematic collector, having made it his mission to store and organize the valuable objects of everyday history of the village for the generations to come.

Johan's father told how he now understood why the locals had thought and gossiped about Alex as the village fool. People then were not well-educated, and seeing someone eagerly collect their old and worn-out, everyday things of no practical value, was impossible to understand; it was incompatible with the simple agricultural life and worldview. Typically, the old tools, furniture and other used objects and equipment had been forgotten in a backyard storage and even left outside. What probably had made matters worse among the village people was that Alex had not only collected these cast-offs, but had also recorded compelling stories about the history of the people and the families of the village. For many it was not at all comfortable to hear stories about past fights, marriage problems, babies with an unknown father, inheritance disputes, and other sensitive matters. It was easy to frame Alex as a local fool with a wild imagination.

Alex took Johan's father by the arm and spoke in a soft tone.

"Sten," he said, "I know your home had a long history extending back to the sixteenth century. You might wonder why I don't have any material from it." Sten did not say anything, only nodded with a sad smile to Alex, who continued:

"It's for the simple reason that after your father left and you moved to Seinäjoki with your mother Elli, the new owners got rid of most of the historical objects, and as you know even the house was totally demolished and a new one built in its place!"

"It's sad," was all Sten said, and when Johan was about to express his anger Alex interrupted: "But I have something. I only hope you let me keep it so that I can offer it to the museum one day."

"What is it?" Johan and his father exclaimed simultaneously.

Alex opened the door to a wooden, light-green-painted closet and took out a wooden stick, about one-by-one inches thick, two-feet long, with a carved handle at one end. It was painted brownish-red and had some systematic, regularly spaced markings on one side. Before Johan and his father asked about it, Alex was already explaining:

"Sten, your great-grandfather made this with his own hands. It's a measuring stick as you can see. But notice, it's not a metric stick; instead, it is fifty-nine centimeters and a few millimeters long, the traditional measure we Finns have used before we moved to the metric system. Its origins are in Sweden. If you look carefully, you can see that there are markings for the foot and inches."

Sten surprised Alex and Johan by rushing out, without saying a word, and Johan worried that seeing the stick had been too much for Sten and had triggered one of his frightening fits and the paranoia about the meter standard. He was relieved to see his father coming back with a camera, telling Alex he'd be happy to leave the measuring stick for him, but explained why he would like to take a photo of it:

"The stick reminds me of honest measures; here in my home village it was not a power tool, but a measure of trust. I want to remember it as such."

Alex looked puzzled but did not say anything. Johan knew how important the measures, especially the meter, was for his father, but he did not understand why this measurement stick would be any different from other standards, like the famous meter. It was as if Sten had heard the silent questions Alex and Johan had in their minds when he explained further:

"Alex, as a historian you know, that whoever made this stick — my great-grandfather — he had someone to trust when he copied the measures on this stick. Its story consists of a chain of trust between people. They could be relatives, friends or the officers in the village everyone knew. My great-grandfather trusted this chain whenever he used it to measure objects and things of importance to him." Johan remained silent, when Alex nodded, saying: "You are one in this chain; I do know that there have been misused and forged measures, but this is not one of them."

Sten took several photos of the stick and asked Alex and Johan to pose with it, as if they were members of this chain of trust. The serious atmosphere changed and they all enjoyed the sense of historical trust they could feel together. Coming out from the fascinating private museum, Sten and Johan said goodbye to Alex and thanked him. Johan could see Alex wave at them when they were driving away, back towards the village center and ready to return home.

On their way back, they did not speak much at first, and Johan could see that for Sten the visit was a mix of joy from the chain of trust he experienced with Alex, while at the same time the social distance from the childhood village and its communities was only reinforced. Practically nothing was left of his family history; his home had been torn down, there were no photos, no written descriptions or other documents, nobody had taken care of the historical artefacts that had been even distantly related to the family. Johan realized how Sten's father's escape to the seas had made the family history something that was more natural to forget than to celebrate and conserve. There was practically nothing, but the bowtie sign and the measurement stick.

For Johan the visit revealed, thoroughly, how fragmented his family background was, how problematic his father's life had been. He became aware of the striking similarity between his own and his father's childhood: the difficult histories had made it almost natural for a family to become an isolated and a psychologically closed unit, a unit of private problems. It had happened to Sten when his father disappeared physically and now Johan realized how his own father's occasional psychological escapes, driven by his mental problems, had caused him to disappear too, taking him on strange psychic journeys. For the only child in the family, it did not make much difference whether the father was physically present when he was psychologically absent. As Johan realized all too well, it could make things worse.

From then on, Johan remained sharply aware of his own small family's isolation. He had often wondered about the absence of relatives in their life. Now he realized that all the relatives, including those from Johan's mother's side, stayed away so consistently that Johan had never gotten to know any of them. He became convinced that they were scared of Sten's mental problems, and no doubt ashamed of such a threatening, hidden potential in the family; theirs was an unwelcomed, twisted branch in the family tree. The symbol on the barn wall began to seem like the one sign of a larger extended family that Johan could cling to and then there was the chain of trust in people who had passed away, long ago.

"Where had everyone gone?" he wondered.

This car trip became the last intact series of pleasant episodes Johan would remember of his father, who during the three days of their visit was like a different person; he did not suffer mental pressures or paranoid fits. Immediately upon their return home, it was painful for Johan to observe how quickly difficult times arrived again; it was like the home and its environment were under a spell and had the power to transform Sten the moment they returned. Johan felt an obscure but disturbing guilt for the transformation he saw and could not understand why the pleasant atmosphere and their relationship during the journey were suddenly wiped away and his father moved back into his detached private world.

He could see how some unknown, serious and destructive forces caught his father when he arrived at home and started re-living his anxieties.

Over the next five years, Sten's problems accumulated. The disappearances, not only psychological, fits, and visits to the psychiatric clinic became an everyday routine for Johan and his mother, Karin, to live with; several medicines were tested during and in between the frequent therapy sessions and temporary hospitalizations, but they did not seem to help him.

Strangely, when Sten was temporarily free from his worst psychotic fits and could, repeatedly, with a frightening intensity, tell the stories of his strange journeys to Johan, he never spoke about the bowtie sign. It was as if he had totally forgotten it, but he would sometimes mention "the stick of trust".

Johan did not give up reminding his father that to *him*, the sign had become a personal treasure, a bridge carrying him to their real past and to the living relatives, whoever they were, despite their reluctance to make any connection with Sten or Johan. The sign and the stick were all they had together as a reminder of the family past. Johan wanted to point out the meaning of this to his father; they formed the only solid grounding point to their life and the history they shared.

Occasionally, Sten appeared to have healthy periods, and then he even found some odd jobs. Gradually, however, the–symptoms would worsen and disturb his life almost without a break, making him unable to keep any proper job or to get another one. In one of his janitorial jobs at the university, he got into trouble, claiming he had seen research data manipulated and mistakes being hidden. He suffered from long-lasting depression and found only temporary relief with medication. Within only two years, he could not even take care of his daily routines or hygiene properly.

The pathological condition became worse, and then, despite the shock, it was not a surprise to Johan — he had been afraid of it since his early childhood — Sten passed away in the winter of 2012, at the age of fifty-two, by committing suicide at home. Beside Sten's body, Johan's mother had found the familiar drawing of the men gathered around a well, but there was no text nor explanation. This happened just when

Johan had taken his first steps on his research career at the age of twenty-six and had already moved away from their home in Vihti.

Only two years had passed when Johan's mother Karin followed her husband, just before the Christmas 2014, due to a fast-spreading breast cancer. Johan had finished his doctoral thesis already in autumn, but it had been a difficult time for him, to force himself to work on the dissertation under the unbearable grief, after his mother had gotten worse, being totally alone, with no close relatives who could support him or even know of him.

Chapter 3
Sin in Science

Standing in front of the Metre, still startled by the sudden reappearance of the screen wall, Johan wondered why the lyrics of the song "Hotel California" were now so comforting and meaningful to him. It was as if the words had been imprinted in him, to form a therapeutic-psychological algorithm to help him survive his inner turmoil.

One line especially, as he hummed it, evoked distant images from California, having nothing in common with Paris, but suggesting a willing life as a prisoner, perhaps in a golden cage, if you allow it to happen. Humming this line, mesmerized by the metre plate, Johan had the familiar, eerie feeling of being transported from the present spot, to some other place where he became a total outsider, living — like his father perhaps — far away from the campfires of everything and everybody, even out of reach of his best and dearest friends. The one-liner prison-earworm kept circling in his mind, like a repeating algorithm, reminding him of his problems.

To Johan, the *device,* a striking symbol of it, at least, was the metre. He knew that there would not be any physics without standards and he never doubted them as necessary tools in any science. But now he knew better; he had become aware of the birth of the metric system and the way scientists and politicians worked to define and manipulate standards. It was not only about the tools of science, but also about the power in the scientific communities he had painfully experienced during the last few weeks. Expressing these thoughts and reservations to his colleagues had made him vulnerable as a trustworthy scientist, so much so that he even doubted the rationality of his new attitude.

Johan had never even imagined the meter as a symbol of misconduct in science before his father had started preaching about it. The unbelievable stories were not without an impact and sometimes at the lab Johan could joke with his colleagues about the human nature of the meter and any other measures in science, to challenge their thinking about the foundations of physics. But even then, he would tend to think the stories were father's paranoid ideas, a product of a pathological mind, an uneducated view a real scientist would just ignore and reject. The recent experiences at Stanley had changed this. When Johan met the devastating impact of the powerful elite and establishment in science, he became painfully aware of the possibility of fraud in science and it was impossible to forget his father's warnings. He remembered the chain of trust.

Now one of the original signs of the meter was in front of him, appearing to hold within it the intricate system of all physical measurements, the necessary social conventions, and all the consequences it had to other measures of the world as Johan thoroughly knew and had studied in physics. This perception of the metrical system, and the idea that it shapes and controls practically all aspects of people's lives, had indeed sounded like paranoia to some of the colleagues to whom Johan told about it. He wondered now if they were right.

"It's just metrics," they would say. "It's a good thing. Science depends upon it. The world depends upon it. So what if the physicists got it wrong at first, now it's all corrected. It works! What is your problem?"

Johan went over the history of the metre as he stood transfixed, the line from "Hotel California", of the treacherous device, going through his mind repeatedly. Originally sixteen plates of the Metre standard had been implanted in Paris during the years 1796-97, in various busy, public locations, after the meter as a reference measure had been defined and accepted by the *Académie des Sciences* in 1791. The plates had been prepared for the citizens of the Revolution and the generations to come, for all men to see and learn about the profound and most basic standard of humankind, of everything. They would, from that point on, be immersed in the world of the meter: comparing their own sticks, volumes and other measures against it; checking that they had not been cheated when being taxed or buying land, or buying everyday materials and groceries; they would incorporate this measurement into all sciences and everyday practices. Two of the metre plates had been preserved right up to the present, placed in two public places in Paris, to be visible and touchable since the times of the French Revolution and what Johan considered to be the violent epoch of the Enlightenment. Together, the metre plates were an international symbol of trust. The trouble was, the plates held a measure that had been discovered to be a mistake and based on a fraud.

As a young man, Johan had spent days reading the detailed story of this history of the global standard in *The Measure of All Things* by Ken Alder. It had been his father's suggestion to read it and "learn how we are being cheated by all scientists in all sciences." Sten had never gotten tired of mentioning the fraud, repeating it to Johan, telling him to go and see the real Metre in Paris, as he himself had done. At first, Johan had not understood why it would matter, why he should see it. He had not understood why the Metre had meant so much to his father. Having seen the familiar wall appear today in front of the gate to the Jardin had made him worry about his own tendency to the same illness from which his father had suffered, yet wondering what if his father's visions had been something more than schizophrenia? Johan could sometimes, for a passing moment, think these visions had been something else: a mystery his father had experienced. Could his father's profound skepticism about science — justified by the story of the metric system — have had some basis in reality?

The book by Alder told Johan the story of the brave adventure of the two French *savants*; it impressed and touched him, but it also revealed the human nature of any scientific endeavor and the impact of the crucial scientific mistakes in defining the metre or any other scientific measure, a definition relying on human perception. The tragedy with the metre standard became an existent proof to Johan that a fraud can occur in solving the most profound problems humankind can face.

Johan recited the history to himself. In 1792, two scientists had taken up the task to deliver an accurate distance measure — better than ever before, and to lay foundations for a democratic standard, the meter for everyone on earth and why not even outside the earth, as the participating astronomers could imagine. The measurement endeavor took place in the true spirit of the Revolution, and in the name of Égalité the standard would be based on the circumference of the earth, something that no one owns but that belongs to everyone.

Accomplishing the huge task required a devoted and well-coordinated collaboration in using the best available measurement tools, conducting measurements, and reporting the results. The work demanded absolute trust among the participating scientists. Two brave and ambitious men, Jean Baptiste Joseph Delambre and Pierre François André Méchain, both renowned astronomers, set up to carry the responsibility of measuring the length of two segments of the meridian. One segment, from Paris running north to Dunkirk, was the responsibility of Delambre, while the other segment, running south from Paris to Barcelona, was assigned to Méchain. The measurement arrangement clearly implied that Paris was to remain the spiritual *origo* if not the center of earth and the universe. The savants followed the burdensome triangulation method, using the best visual observation instruments, especially a novel innovation, the repeating circle, designed by Jean-Charles de Borda, an ingenious mechanic.

The repeating circle instrument was used to measure the angular distance between two points of observation, two stars or other objects of interest, such as landmarks, using two optical scopes to target them. It was a clever, early visual measurement device allowing the astronomer to produce during a single session of observation multiple readings of the same target angle between the two objects. The device had an ingenious, built-in, mechanical arrangement, allowing the observer to repeat each angular measurement, so that the perceptual error resulting from a single observation could be averaged out during the measurement session. This brilliant mechanical design was aimed at circumventing the natural human weaknesses in perception: single observations are unreliable.

The purpose of the Delambre-Méchain endeavor was twofold: first, to measure the lengths of the selected meridian segments, and then to use this data as a basis for computing the length of the quadrant from the North Pole to the equator. One ten-millionth of this distance was to become the objective, democratic, and *the* global distance measure, a standard meter "for all people, for all time."

It was physically and mentally a most demanding task, and both scientists, as Johan had discovered in his research, met insurmountable problems during the seven-year journey. They could face aggressive locals ready to kill them on the spot as enemies of the Revolution, even as spies, or for being suspicious representatives of the old Academy of Sciences in France. Sometimes they were met with superstition as people watched them constructing the measurement installations in unusual locations. Their shiny, mysterious instruments of brass and the quirky measurement process itself did not seem to carry the slightest human sense or meaning to those who mistrusted these scientists. It was a mistrust created by both ignorance and the revolutionists' suspicions and beliefs. Méchain even ended up in the middle of the France-Spain war and had to spend years in Spain trying to arrange conditions for his difficult work, and sometimes struggled simply to stay alive.

The tragedy was that Méchain had made a horrendous mistake in his measurements near Barcelona, resulting in a more than 5% discrepancy in measuring the 1.1-mile arc at that post. It was an intolerable mistake and would bias the standard. Méchain knew what he had done, but covered it up, hid it, even manipulated the data and was reluctant to share it with his colleague. There were good reasons, including above all the war between France and Spain, which was why it was practically impossible to return to the measurement site at Mont-Jouy, outside Barcelona, and repeat the measurements, but science accepts no excuses; he had sinned.

Over the years, Méchain kept his secret as best he could from his devoted scientific partner Delambre, suppressing and altering the data where it suited him. As he did this, he introduced a significant error that carried to the definition of the meter itself up to the gates of modern times. The scientific community did not know about this error, and the two scientists were highly celebrated when in 1798 they offered their preliminary results at the first-ever international scientific conference, the International Commission in Paris. Delambre and Méchain had reached the top of their careers. Knowledgeable representatives of selected Western European countries came to Paris to celebrate them, but only from the nations having a friendly or submissive relationship with France. Therefore, the conference was not only a symbol of the infant global science of metrics, it also became a modern rite of injecting politics into science.

While the scientists were still in the process of analyzing the data from Delambre and Méchain, the tangible outcome of the conference was the production of a series of the famous platinum meter-standard bars. One of these, which best matched the computed value became the de facto standard, the Métre des Archives. Ironically, comparing the present-day satellite measurements against the meridian-based standard of the meter shows that the platinum meter was about 0.2 mm short of what is today considered as a meter. In the emerging modern world of science, this was a major error, and for the sciences to come it was a huge mistake based on fraud. Johan would astonish his colleagues by explaining how measuring the distance from Earth to Mars with this standard, the platinum stick, would introduce a discrepancy of tens of thousands of kilometers when compared against the measurements with the current meter standard! The error in the original data was discovered soon after Delambre and Méchain's work was finished, but it did not prevent the use of this standard as the legal meter in France and wherever it was accepted as a measure.

It had taken almost two hundred years to correct Méchain's error. In 1975, the meter standard was re-defined with a modern ambition, so that it would be accurate and reliable enough to concern all the measurements of the whole universe as it is known today: the standard meter became the length of the path traveled by light in a vacuum during a time interval of 1/299,792,458th of a second.

To Johan, who was beginning his career and idealistic about the scientific endeavor, the occurrence of political, personal, national ambitions, and conflicts in defining the most basic ground truth, this had been a major disappointment. Although the scientific community had learned to trust the work behind the metric standard, Johan could not accept this kind of trust. Advancing in his physics studies and learning about all the modern standards and constants used in physics, Johan could not help admiring his father, and wondering how a paranoid schizophrenic like him could be so deranged and so right at the same time. On the rare occasions Johan could joke about this, he would say: "The worst thing happens when a paranoid is right!" He never explained to his friends the origins of the joke.

The awareness of such a complex, human ambition-driven and politically biased process in deriving a scientific truth made the design of scientific standards and everything in measurement-based science appear suspicious to Johan. He knew that there was no alternative; he had to rely on the standards in everything he did in his research, but the awareness of the historical fraud, the possibility of such things happening in science at any time, hovered like a cloud of doubt sometimes as he did his work. Added to this story of measuring space, of course, there was the story of measuring time, and the definition of the second, which had been impossible to do without relying on some form of a distance measure or on tools using a distance measure. Given the mistakes at the heart of this time-space system of measurement, Johan could not see how anyone could believe in a solid ground truth; he was confused. Working with the best scientists did not relieve him from the disturbing knowledge and awareness of the risk for fraud. Not even using the tools that worked well and accurately could change his mind and let him forget the existence of a sin in science.

Méchain died in Valencia, Spain in 1804 and never saw the true impact of his work, but he was saved from a public humiliation. Delambre worked hard to check Méchain's data and did his best to protect his colleague when documenting the history of their measurement journeys and their contribution to the standard.

For a serious young scientist like Johan, educated to trust the inherent ethics and ethos of science, the historical disaster and the deliberate scientific misbehavior was a startling fact, fracturing his identity as a scientist and physicist. He would sometimes ask his physicist colleagues, "Where else have we been cheated, what is the modern version of the meter standard? What is a meter?" He might also say, "Have you heard about the study published in the most prestigious medical journal *Lancet*, with fabricated data, claiming there is a connection between autism and childhood vaccines? It has taken huge resources from scientists who have tried to find out about it; it's all far from real science. And it makes children sick because their parents trust in this kind of false science. How can these researchers do this? What do they trust? Who are they? Do you know there is again an epidemic of measles because people have stopped trusting the science behind vaccinations?"

Johan's research work was not about standards, but he had become seriously puzzled realizing how the measure of distance, the very idea of it in physics, was not only a basic measure of the world, but also a cornerstone of everything else measured or imagined in physics and all other sciences as well. It was an essential foundation of any classic or modern theory of the world and of humans.

Johan knew well how the distance itself had been an object of wonder for theoretical physicists, who observed how quantum states of particles could be almost mystically interdependent over very large distances: Einstein called it the "spooky effect". What especially puzzled Johan when he studied the theories of the spooky effect, was that once the concept of distance is defined and accepted, there is nothing in the physical measures, as they are used and applied in each theory, that would remain unaffected by this critical choice: all measures, experiments and their results will rely on it, for better or worse. In the case of a measurement fraud, a social or political compromise, every physical constant, every variable, every natural law becomes an inherent part of this fraud in science; a lie changes the future of science. It does not even respect the direction of time but biases the history of science as well until the fraudulent source is revealed.

To Johan, it was clear that monumental errors could hide anywhere, unnoticed, and the dominant scientific community would protect itself and pass it over in everything it did, like confederates. In Johan's eyes, Méchain's error had not been a matter of a simple adjustment of the parameters of the length standard, and he could not distance himself from the disturbing thought that it was a pure form of the original sin in science. The fact that science has often corrected itself as had happened in this case was a meager consolation to Johan and the knowledge of it did not wipe away the worry.

Johan had found it impossible to discuss these problems and the way he thought about them with his colleagues, first at Helsinki University and later at Stanley in Palo Alto. It always resulted in a suspicious atmosphere, ridicule or simple neglect; slowly, he realized it was not good for his reputation to take up such an unusual, psychological topic among his talented physicist colleagues. Philosophical considerations were welcome, even wild ones, especially when decorated with a proper name and -ism dropping; it was not rare to listen to and read philosophers and theoretical physicists discussing the nature of quantum mechanics or the possibility of parallel universes. Many of the physicists had indeed studied philosophy and could have degrees in the field as well.

At first, Johan did not believe his colleagues would question his mental status, at least they did not directly comment on it, but it was evident they took his critical stance as an alarming sign of weakness in his scientific thinking. He was never treated badly by his young research colleagues, but their reservation was visible whenever he would deal with the problem that was most natural to him, the question of the power of human perception and how it has contributed to the formation of the most basic measures of physics. It felt like the most fundamental question of physics, underlying any theory of observation. After all, the first physicists had to rely on their senses and perceptual capacities; it was all they had before the instruments.

Nevertheless, for a reason unknown to Johan, taking a perceptual-psychological perspective to physics was a social taboo among the physicists. He had his own, painfully well-founded reasons to know how the word psychology was typically associated with insanity and other spooky, pathological aspects of human behavior, especially so when a theoretical physicist mentioned it.

Some of Johan's colleagues began to avoid such discussions with him, were annoyed by his paranoid attitude, and feared he might one day attack one of them for unethical behavior in science. This surprised Johan, who felt he was only trying to get his colleagues interested in the most important values in science and among the scientists. This happened before Johan had his most painful experiences during his career and which had finally brought him to Paris, to face and touch the symbol his father had seen and touched.

Johan had shared his thoughts about the Metre with Yvonne, a physicist colleague, who had quite recently become a trusted friend, first in California and especially during the last month Johan had spent in Paris. She had not wanted to join Johan to see the historical symbol, as she knew the problems troubling him. Yvonne knew what had happened to Johan at Stanley and she had heard him repeatedly describe his personal anxiety arising from both his recent experiences in academia and the overpowering awareness of the sin in science. As a physicist Yvonne could follow Johan's factual arguments, but she also knew the dark side, the reasons for Johan's distress; she tried to guide him to the open waters of a free scientific mind, as she called it.

Yvonne was only one year younger than Johan; she was born in 1987 in Shanghai from a French father and a Chinese mother. Living and studying in Paris, she had become a charming *Parisienne*, with an impeccable style, not uncommon among the modern, young women there. She had natural, almost bluish-dark, short, straight hair, and simple elegant clothes, often black except when she wore her sports gear. Her face had an oval form with naturally high cheek bones; her brown, slightly Asian eyes, were framed by delicately arching dark eyebrows. Yvonne appeared soft and serious, almost defensive, but when she smiled broadly, and gave herself over to laughter, she became a radiant, delightful character, a true shining light source. On her right eyebrow there was a faintly visible scar and six small dots, the signs left from three stitches. When someone asked about them, her response was simply, "Bike. Bike."

Being only five feet and four inches tall did not undermine her appearance as a sporty, agile young woman, with visibly muscular arms; the subtle feminine muscles contrasted with her overall light bone structure. She had a visibly erect stance, as if she had learned to adopt a powerful upward gaze, chin up, when meeting people, especially men, face-to-face. With Johan she indeed had to do that and from their first meeting she had faced him without the slightest sign of submission. Over an intense discussion, Johan would often notice her personal power and could not help laughing, amused, explaining how *he* felt forced to look up to *her* as a person. Only rarely would she wear high heels. Yvonne had grown strong, both physically and mentally, from her mountain-biking exercises, which she never skipped, even when traveling abroad.

Whenever, over their discussions, Johan started worrying about the untrustworthy nature of science, so vulnerable to fraud and to politics, Yvonne would be on the alert for the first signs of one of his "fits": she would see how Johan would suddenly stop talking, even in the middle of a sentence, remaining silent for a second or two, and then how he would pause in his usual energetic movements, grasping the hair at the back of his head, slowly, as he got ready to face his disturbing state of mind.

When she saw these symptoms for the first time, she felt the pain of helplessness as she watched Johan vanish into his painful world, entering a period of depression that lasted all day. He became silent and distant, almost as if he had become mute. These episodes happened often, and she quickly learned to perceive the conspicuous predictive signs of what was to come: the gloomy state of mind, when Johan continuously and under great anxiety repeated his depressive experiences. Observing the alarming signs Yvonne would immediately interrupt him, early enough, during the short window of silence, before Johan could even take his first deep breath to start the avalanche of worrisome thoughts and comments. Each time she caught him at this point, she would just look up at him, smile, and say, word by word:

"Forget the frauds! It does not matter what a meter is! You should know that. That's history! A definition is a definition and science is derived thinking. We could as well use the *Vitruvian man* and measure his arms, legs, or fingers, or whatever organs we wish to choose as our standards. We can just stick to them, honestly, in everything we do; it's trivial! Stop worrying, you sound like a paranoid maniac! It's not healthy!"

And then she would stop, stand still in front of Johan, looking straight and deep into his eyes, sometimes uttering with a surprisingly low note in her voice, "Forget it, return to your work, find a lab, find a lab!"

She had a peculiar, charming habit of repeating the last words of a phrase whenever she got seriously worried or excited. It was like drilling the message properly into the recipient, but also into herself. Johan had learned the proactive argument she would use every time to interrupt his gloomy tendency, and after he had heard it several times, it had begun to sound humorous, preventing the melancholic slide towards the looming depression. Her intervention became a miniature, compassionate instant of successful therapy for the grateful Johan.

Yvonne spoke excellent English, with only a slight, charming French-like accent. A surprising, contrasting feature in her voice was the high pitch she had adopted in California, where she worked for three years as a research fellow at the Stanley Linear Accelerator Lab (CLASH) lab. It was the kind of female voice often heard there in public places, a distinctly high pitch that carries far, and sounds conspicuously childish to the European ear. It was an amusing mystery to Johan how and why women in Palo Alto used such a sharp, high-pitched voice, but visiting the noisy bars, restaurants, conference receptions, and sports fields, and knowing the competitive atmosphere, he had a good guess at the reason: if a woman kept her voice quiet, she would be out.

Johan could joke with his male friends, but not with Yvonne, despite having only minor experience with the topic, that there were other situations where the highest possible female pitch was no longer the only spontaneous alternative or even a necessity for emotional discharges, and curiously enough, it was during sex, where suddenly the series of OMGs were coded in the widest possible range of audio frequencies. Only sometimes, when Yvonne spoke about important, personal matters or showed her affection and care, did her pitch lower and often surprised Johan by its full, emotionally rich tone.

Yvonne had worked at CLASH studying methods for detailed imaging of atoms and molecules using X-ray lasers. CLASH was explicit in its recruitment principles, appreciating the applicants with variable backgrounds; she had immediately become fascinated with the multi-disciplinary work and the exceptional knowledge and skills of the people there. She got to know application areas in several research fields, where the studies ranged from molecular synthesis to the design of new energy sources. CLASH was a real paradise for any ambitious physicist motivated to make a better world, create solutions for real life and even space conditions, for medicine, and to help build a cleaner environment. Johan knew they did not accept just anyone as a research fellow there.

***

Yvonne was nowhere near him as he stood in the rain, and the noise from the morning traffic took Johan back to the present and his own memories of the recent personal disaster. He remained standing in front of the Metre and considered the events in California that had propelled him on this journey to Paris. He did not know what had been the real fraud in what he was working on, or even if there had been any, but he had reasons to believe that something utterly false, even evil had happened, that people with a malevolent motivation had deliberately hurt him, and were ready to destroy his future as a researcher. Someone had wanted to tarnish his reputation and make his work and future in science impossible. Johan could not overcome his anxiety.

Distressed, recalling the painful experiences and trying to make sense of them, he spun a private, purely psychological scene, like an internal slow motion movie in his mind, with no main characters or events in it, no plot, only an internal, black-blue-gray, murky background everywhere in the scene, the whirling stage pulsating in emotionally dark-colored turbulence, evoking such a continuously deepening, spiral-like, endless anxiety in him that he had to deliberately try to pull himself out from it. Unlike the external wall he had seen only a moment ago, this was his internal state; it was scary, and he wanted to get rid of it. Twisting his head and stamping his feet, waving his hands, he made a physical effort to escape from the frightening psychological corners of his mind, and to feel the real world, the pavement under his feet. He yearned to return to the safe and predictable Newtonian world of cafes and people on errands, happily unaware of anything but what appeared normal and measurable.

Johan hummed the Hotel California mantra again, this time loudly enough to produce echoes from the end-wall of the archway, the story of chambers, knives and feasts.

This momentary fall into the private, mental world had not been a dream and it was not the wall he had seen earlier. This was private, and he was fully awake as he had been when he saw the wall. This state reminded him of the meditation sessions during some of his yoga classes in Palo Alto, but it was a paranoid space in its deepest feelings, with no recognizable characters in it, only himself, alone, immersed in an impersonal, unknown and threatening scene.

It was not the first time Johan had fallen into this murky mental world, into a psychological cave, but the frightful episodes had started occurring only when recalling the recent problem episodes. There was no perceptual logic in the dream-like experience, no persons doing harm to him, no creatures or objects to scare him, but still he was facing an internal, repeated, threatening drama and feelings of an infinite personal tragedy and fear. The only mental images present, the blurry black-blue-

51

gray textured whirls and their black background, were felt rather than seen, and they frightened him more than any person or event could or had ever done. Johan had not been able to come up with any rational explanation for these pure fears. He only knew that they were related to his real world, recent experiences at the lab and to his own research community.

Sometimes, after such a dream-like event or fit, he could imagine how the terrifying emotional content was produced by a powerful generator, a mental program which had been somehow launched a long time ago in his childhood, and it could be applied to his mind at any moment, like an automaton, refreshing the permanently hiding psychological algorithms whenever a pertinent, painful event at home or at the university triggered it. It was like an implanted, ready-to-act, personal processing-virus maintaining his mental suffering, always ready to act, painting the murky mental landscape whenever the life conditions matched its requirements; there were no means to delete the virus. Johan could not imagine a way back to its origin, to change the algorithm. He remained silent, pale and helpless in front of the historical flagstone.

Chapter 4
Color Shadows and Personal Entanglements

Before coming to Paris, Johan had been working at Stanley as a post-doc in theoretical physics and had spent almost a year in the new environment, enjoying the comfortable seasons and especially the long and warm summer. Like any young scientist there, he was living what he felt were the best days ever during his "nascent career", as he often characterized it to his teammates. Johan had loved his research projects in Helsinki, but there was something very Protestant in the way of working there: it was serious and lacked positive feed-back and spontaneity. He had grown up with it and never noticed the atmosphere, particularly, but when he arrived at Stanley, he realized what had been missing.

From the beginning, he dove into his work with full energy and enthusiasm, devoting long hours as a new and eager member of his research group at the Institute of General Physics. He could not get enough of the ambitious and creative atmosphere, where every day brought new inspirations. He had a clear agenda, as a part of his supervisor Professor Carl Roos' project in Helsinki, to demonstrate the success of Roos' model in analyzing particle collisions. The goal was to prove, through simulations at Stanley, that the model and approach developed by Roos could be a feasible alternative to its competitors and become one of the primary models of analysis for the data generated at CERN, the European Organization for Nuclear Research.

Johan's closest research community of about fifty people included unusually skilled scientists, many of whom were young experts on string theory and holography, with a special interest in research on the general theory of relativity. It was both theoretical and empirical work, and aside from his own task, Johan helped the colleagues from other teams with their computational analyses on the massive data sets on collision recordings obtained from CERN.

The huge data masses had indeed been everyday material for the physicist community at Stanley, much before the fashionable term "big data" had ever been introduced to the public. When two protons, coming fast, with a large energy from opposite directions, are made to collide, it is their constituents, the quarks and gluons, that collide and who knows what else. With such an instantaneous energy, a fireworks and dance of particle scatter emerge, and the traces of the generated, different particles are recorded. As Johan and his Stanley colleagues well knew, it was a real puzzle to develop methods to accurately record and model such complex collision moments; different skill sets, and excellent teamwork were required to deal with it.

Johan's team consisted of nine members, and it was not exceptional at Stanley that only two of them were from the USA. Two were women from France, and the others were from Germany, Italy, Switzerland, and China; Johan was the only Nordic. Because of his tall and blond looks they immediately started calling him "The Viking", but on one noisy evening at the sports bar on Ramona Street, Johan educated them. He had to shout to be heard there; it was a typical Friday evening. He roared that Finns did not have very much to do with the Vikings, so he was then, on the spot, named "Pisa", a creative combination of the Leaning Tower of Pisa and the famous international performance test, PISA, for fifteen-year-old students. Finnish kids had gained a reputation for their excellent performance in the test, despite their fame for spending very little time on homework; many believed Finns didn't do any homework at all. Like the Leaning Tower of Pisa, Johan often soared head and shoulders above his colleagues, and had to lean visibly forward and down when talking to them, especially in places like the noisy bar. It could be tricky for him to understand their English, sometimes, unless he ducked his head and listened closely. Pisa was also a friendly pun from the colleagues who were proud to work hard at home, day and night, to remind Johan that, "Here we work long hours and are proud of it!"

Everyone shared a passion for the study of quantum gravity. Many used to joke that "There is serious gravity in the air," some focusing on the presumed event horizon phenomena in black holes, while others worked on the collision data. Indeed, the popular media publicity on these topics, all over the world, had not made their work less appealing.

Sometimes, discussing any of their acute research problems with his multi-skilled friends and colleagues, Johan got a strangely familiar, tickling but distant feeling, that reminded him of his childhood excitement when learning to skate in Finland.

His father Sten had taught him on a lake near their home in southern Finland, in Vihti. He had been about five then and Vihti made a perfect surrounding for children excited about the adventures in the nearby lake where they would learn to swim in summer and skate in winters. Like many of the children there, he learned to hike in the dense forests and along the lake shores.

Later he had loved to spend afternoons and evenings on the ice, often exercising alone, if there was no one playing ice hockey. On a cold winter day in December, he started to make his private, thrilling discoveries about patterns on the ice. He was ten then, and the ice on the lake had just become hard enough to carry a skater; its surface was smooth like a shining mirror with no snow on it yet. He found how he could, by skating, produce imaginative figures on the ice, curves, lines, spirals, even waves and figures of wavy surfaces, something like the 2-D wave graphics his father had shown and demonstrated to him on their computer display. He would fall repeatedly, in trying to produce ever more complex but systematic drawings on the smooth ice surface. As he grew older, he often thought of that day as his first entrance into the world of science, but of course, then, for the ten-year old Johan it was something else: a new kind of game.

After this first experimental skating session, Johan went onto the ice as often as he could. One day he got the idea to make the figures during the daytime, and then, when the winter darkness fell over the lake — already in the late afternoon — and it became difficult to see, he would attempt, in the deepening darkness, to draw, exactly, overlapping them, the same figures on ice as he had done in the daylight. Then he would return early the next morning, before school, with a flashlight — if it was still dark — to compare the two traces of his skating and see how well he had succeeded. Like a young scientist, he would strive to figure out what would be the right way to tell how well he had done. Recalling these experiences, in Palo Alto, as he was immersed in this new teamwork, he thought about how, even as a child, he had been fascinated by the relationship between the model and the reality, to find out how the model predictions matched the observed reality.

Spurred on by the beauty and promise of his ice designs, as long as there was no snow, sometimes in the evening he would fetch several, as many as ten flashlights, to light the scene and to see how accurate he had been in reproducing the skating traces in the dark when trying to memorize the original. Having the flashlights switched on, he got curious, noticing how the light sources produced several, often overlapping shadows of his skating, which inspired him to lay the flashlights out on the ice, like a light fence, to surround his fifty feet diameter skating rink. At first, each light pointed towards the center. Seeing the complex shadow configurations, he became excited, and then tried different geometrical arrangements with the lights: a square, a triangle, a circle, and a random design, so that the shadows produced by the skater would crisscross in various forms and scales, always producing surprising, ever-changing shadow dances on the ice, depending on how he moved on the rink. It felt like a mystery to see how such a simple arrangement created these complex images; all he had to do was to skate as he liked. He even tried attaching the lights high on poles, each one at a different height - with the same, amazing result of a skater's light and shadow show, but in 3-D they were even more dynamic and lively. There was never an audience; it was his private, creative theater. He did not see anything strange or peculiar in this magical research, until he was a young adult and realized that not everyone focused so intently on such things.

Whenever the winter conditions allowed, he continued with the evening sessions. Then at the age of twelve, he was courageous enough to ask, for the first time, someone to join him, a girl for an evening date. Her name was Lumi, and she was from a different class; she was somehow attractive and kind to his eye, blonde and blue-eyed like him, with slightly curly hair, and always nicely dressed. Boys had the habit of making jokes about her hair, yet even though Johan was playing with them, he never joined the teasing; he did not like it. Then once, when escaping the teasing boys again, she stopped, turned around, and pointed her finger at Johan. "You are different!" she had said, and then she had run away again. This was enough to encourage Johan, so that a week later he dared to ask her for a date.

"Would you like to come for a night skate on the lake with me? I have the lights."

To Johan's surprise and delight, Lumi said yes. He set up the lights, and as they began to skate, she was totally fascinated.

"Where did you get this amazing, crazy idea? It's wooonderful!!!"

They skated together until late, trying to form different figures and shadow configurations on the ice, separately and hand-in-hand and doing pirouettes alone or together, until they were so tired that they had to stop to rest.

The girls at school would gossip about his wonderful evening game and its possible true purpose, but the boys did not show any interest, except that it was "sissy". They started calling Johan the "Lighthead". It did not bother him; it was only boys' talk and they never really bullied him. There was a good reason for this: because of the intensive skating exercises, Johan had become a skillful ice hockey player, fast and clever, even unpredictable in his moves, although he was still rather skinny. This was important capital in the boys' world and when he became a member of the school's ice hockey team, he was naturally left in peace. Later, when he was fifteen and his friends had their own hobbies and regular sports activities, he could not get rid of the feeling that in the eyes of his friends he probably appeared to be a bizarre character.

On one evening skate on the lake, at the age of thirteen, Johan had accidentally taken one red-colored flashlight with the white ones. Setting up his usual light rink with white lights and one red one, he noticed how this time, standing or skating in the rink, a surprising, colorful green shadow appeared, in addition to the reddish-grey one and the white background.

"How can there be a green shadow when I use only white and red light? I don't have any green light!" he thought. "How can a shadow have color at all? Isn't a shadow something from which light has been subtracted?" He could not understand at all what was happening there, where the colors came from.

Puzzled by the surprising observation, one evening he tried flashlights with different colors — red, blue, green, and their combinations, and he discovered that he could produce several simultaneous, colored shadows, a wonderful colorful, shadow kaleidoscope on the ice. Still, he did not understand why and how this happened, why was there a shadow with a color he did not have in his lights? Johan decided to ask his father.

At home, he found his father sitting at his desk, focused and immersed in a thick book with large photos of paintings. Johan was reluctant to disturb him, but Sten had noticed his curious looks and hesitation, and wanted to know what the matter was. Johan explained the colored shadows he had seen and was surprised that Sten did not question his observations at all; instead, he told him immediately that he did not have an explanation for the phenomenon, and without saying a word, stood up and went to the bookshelf for help and found two old physics books. Johan stood by his father's side when he searched for an explanation to the color shadow phenomena from the books and became frustrated at not finding any information on it. He put the books aside, sighed and looked at the puzzled Johan:

"This is impossible. Why don't you call the Department of Physics at the university? They should know." Johan was afraid to do that, but his father convinced him that it was the professors' job to know and tell; that's what they got paid for.

"I'll give you the phone number of a professor of applied optics. Just introduce yourself and tell him that you have made a peculiar observation, and would like to know what causes the optical phenomenon you observed. Then thank him after you have heard the explanation. That is important."

The professor who answered the phone call was reluctant to discuss the matter in detail, sounding arrogant as he explained. "There is nothing mystical about it; it's a simple sum of different, complex spectra from your light sources. Besides, the ice can be a diffuse reflector, and can have several reflecting and interfering layers depending on the winter conditions. Was there water on the ice? Was there still some evening light on the sky? Anything can appear by having such a complex combination of light sources and reflecting surfaces. Are you sure you know what color exactly your flashlights are sending? It's trivial; the colors you see there are a sum of the wavelengths of your light sources;

the ice surface and the lighting arrangement together just make it less self-evident. There is nothing new in it."

Johan thanked him, but did not understand the logic of the professor's explanation at all, and the problem continued to bother him so much that he asked his father to search the internet for a more precise answer. Sten was visibly irritated by the professor's attitude and vague response, commenting to Johan:

"It's again one of those 'I-know-it-all-but-won't-tell' wizards; I thought he would be different, but no. I'll see what I can find."

After various trials and tedious searching, Sten became excited when he found an online document from a visual scientist offering a trustworthy explanation. It was in English, but easy enough to translate and explain to the eager Johan who was delighted to see his father in such a good mood. They moved to the living room and sat side by side on the couch to read.

Johan and Sten learned that the colored shadows are not physical in nature; they are pure visual, experiential and even relative phenomena. There was no simple physical explanation to the colored shadows since they were produced by the visual system of the observer. In fact, an observer with peculiar visual system characteristics of color vision must be assumed to explain the phenomenon. They learned that when a colored light is used together with a white light source to light an object in a scene, the colored shadow occurs where the white light plus the colored one is forming the background to which the observer's eyes adapt.

This is how Johan understood it. A white and a red light source are used together, from different directions, to light a scene with one object, like a skater, in it. When at first, only the white light is shone on the ice where the skater does not obstruct it, the scene will have a natural appearance, lit by a uniform white light, and the ice appears white to the observer. A skater on that scene will then produce a normal grayish shadow. When an additional colored light, like red, from a slightly different direction is then switched on, it adds red to the white everywhere in the scene where the skater does not obstruct it. As a result, this original white only background is now white+red, but the observer's visual system adapts quickly to this new combination of colors, and it becomes the new color reference for the observer, who perceives it as mildly pinkish white. It is a matter of sensory and intelligent adaptation of the human observer, so natural and an everyday phenomenon that people do not normally notice any color changes in their living environments where the lighting conditions change, even dramatically. When shadows are formed by the white and red light sources, surprising colors appear.

It took Johan by surprise to notice that when he moved on the ice, lit by the white and the red source, two different shadows were formed of him. In the place where the shadow was cast from the white source, the shadow was reddish-gray, but surprisingly, in the place where the shadow was cast from the red source, he saw a green shadow!

The explanation the visual scientist had offered in the document was the following: the shadow means that light has been subtracted from the location on which it is cast. Red-colored light is subtracted when the object is in front of the red light source, which makes a full shadow. When the surrounding part of the scene where this shadow falls is lit by white+red, and appears only mildly reddish white to the observer, then the shadow has much less red than its immediate surroundings: the shadow produced by the red light is then seen as green, the opposite color, the color opponent, to red. The same thing would happen for any pure white surface when red is subtracted from some part of it — which makes the part look green. It is a visual phenomenon that cannot be explained by physics only. This was a surprise to Johan. He realized that colors are not seen "objectively"; color perception is relative.

Excited about his observations, Johan continued his evening experiments on the ice, with variable color configurations. He discovered the same color-shadow and opponent color phenomena for other colors: white, yellow and blue, in a similar situation. The complex explanation made sense to Johan, but it remained a mystery how human vision made this happen. Neither could his father explain how the visual system works in such situations. It was Johan's first realization that it is one thing to describe the laws of a phenomenon like gravity and another to explain what in fact is going on, what the mechanisms are that produce it. Then he continued wondering what if similar phenomena occur for every human sense, for hearing and skin senses, perhaps olfaction or any other natural phenomena? He never heard of such phenomena at his physics lectures, but thought that perhaps they would be explained later at his high school classes.

Johan's father could not help him solve the wonderful puzzles more than they found from the internet, but he would tap Johan on the shoulder, smile at him and explain, as he walked around the room:

"Now you know how color shadows are formed, but the next step is to find out why! But there is more to it if you noticed! The article mentioned Albers the famous painter who has done wonderful experiments by making beautiful color contrasts visible in his paintings! This is where science and art meet; remember that!"

Sten was full of energy, eyes shining, but then he would, abruptly, return to his desk and his book, remain silent for several minutes, stare at the painting photos, and smile. He did not explain his thoughts to Johan, but Johan realized that his father was proud of him and excited.

Encouraged by his father and the color experiences, Johan began to search for art works where similar phenomena occur. He read about Albers, whose works demonstrated color contrast phenomena, colors interacting, in a way similar to what Johan had created on the ice, the colored shadows, and for which the physics professor he contacted did not offer any explanation Johan would have understood. During his physics studies, often when the theory of relativity was introduced, he would remember Albers, his own color shadow experiments, and the relativity of color, as he would think about it.

Working with his team at Stanley, Johan remembered his youthful enthusiasm on the skating rink with the test lights. The scientific work was psychologically very similar in its immersive pleasures and delights, despite the many daily routines like studying, analyzing and running the model simulations he had as an assignment from Helsinki. Living in California, he found it natural to think about his collaborative work as a form of surfing with his colleagues on the leading edge of the wave of human knowledge, facing new puzzles, often surprises, learning, measuring, running novel experiments and then learning more, together. This sense of community reminded him of his skating forays with Lumi. It was so much better to be with others than isolated and on his own. He wished his father could have had just such a community, as he might not have developed the bitterness and woundedness he felt at the hands of his scientific community.

Johan was devoted to help produce better than ever and useful predictions for the collision data. The work had a close connection with CLASH, where the teams could meet, sometimes at their weekly lunch seminars; some of them were open to anyone. Whenever someone had an interesting and relevant topic to introduce or a novel problem to present, there were the best audiences in the world. Johan learned early that his colleagues listened to anyone who had a reasonable or even revolutionary *physical* question to present, and they encouraged each other to find out more. He was utterly excited about his work, every day, never alone; it was easy to get help and support from the participants, in solving any difficult problems.

The relaxed but serious gatherings were somewhat of a surprise to Johan, who had learned to live in the closed and sometimes even hostile world of tricky relationships between the Finnish laboratories. In Helsinki he could hear some of his colleagues call their competing research groups their "enemies" and had even heard a rumor of how the colleagues working just one floor below his own lab called his work on the string theory a *thong project*, referring to the two exceptionally charming young women with whom Johan worked at the lab. It was a local form of harassment not directed toward the women, but toward him; he had not been at all prepared to find such attitudes in academia.

The topic of quantum gravity had become a real media attractor, first after the huge interest in the search for the Higgs particle and then the detection of the gravitational waves. Johan was at home with the methods used and the new findings, but despite the simple graphic explanations of these phenomena in the media, he had learned early that it was impossible for him to explain, deep down, to his non-physicist friends why the quantum gravitation was such a wonderful and inspiring topic to him. It was not only about the ambitious search for a theory and empirical proof for the most fundamental questions like what mass, lack of mass, and gravitation are. He was convinced that the best physicists not only worked with serious physical problems, but also tried to learn about the deepest spiritual problems he could ever imagine for mankind: what are space and time? From where does the underlying metric for all that come? Are the same laws true everywhere in the universe, and if not, why not? And why are we made to live in a curved space, which we describe with our mathematical tools? Physicists might well ask, "Are our tools all there are?"

It had been impossible to share these thoughts with non-physicist friends, but it had come as a major surprise to him, a serious disappointment, to discover that even his physicist colleagues in Finland had their own, obscure reasons to oppose his deepest spiritual views. For the Helsinki laboratory and its scientific community, such spiritual considerations — the "cloud department" as they jokingly called it — were just too much. The local physics intelligentsia led the popular discourse on the quantum world and the universe. Johan could only wonder at their limitations, as he contemplated their mantra: "We trust objective data only. The human observer is not our problem and we do not need a God. Spirituality is for the uneducated mind, a cognitive illusion." Atheism and cognitive anti-spiritualism had been on the rise in the Nordic countries, since his childhood, and so it was in Finland. To Johan it appeared that a side effect of this "objective" development was to neglect or forget about the fundamental, spiritual human factors, both at the lab and in the power politics of science.

Johan was not religious, but he could not call himself an atheist either; he was confused about spiritual matters, but eager to talk about them as one aspect of science. For him, thinking about space could not be purely rational without considering all the possible descriptions and theories of space, including, of course, how it should be measured, what the Metre is, the grounding measure underlying everything, and hence, what is the role of the observer and the role of the scientific communities that trust in human senses?

In Helsinki, Johan had often found himself teasing his colleagues, asking them, "What if instead of us humans, frogs had been the scientists? What if frogs had had the capacity of the human brain but having the typical frog eyes and started doing frog physics. What would their Metre be? The frog scientists' problem would be that nobody in the frog community could see a metre stick even in front of their yes, even if it was made of frog-platinum. They would not see a food that does not move even if they were starving. The frogs have movement-sensitive eyes that see only moving or flashing objects: i.e., bugs. For them, there would be no use of the expensive platinum Metres, unless they were moved, waved around or flashed on and off in front of them, all the time. The frogs would desperately need a bug-Metre to measure their universe and perhaps a frog theory of relativity, for that matter. So, what is a Metre, in the universe of aliens?"

Johan thought he sounded to his Finnish colleagues as if he were joking, yet he had been serious; it was just that, to human physicists, the very notion of perception through another creature's eyes made no sense. This question of the primary importance of subjective vision and perception, in all of science was exactly the philosophical question which did not leave Johan in peace. During the first year of his doctoral studies, he would spontaneously take it up in any conversation at lab, over dinner, even in seminars, but his straightforward physicist friends were very blunt about the questions they saw as useless no-brainers, far-fetched, ill-defined, Donald Duck problems, not worth considering in the real and serious world of science. They would make fun of Johan.

"You have a slight problem there, you see, we are not frogs!" someone could exclaim when a French lab colleague happened to be present. It did not help when Johan took up Kant, citing that philosopher's powerful and ground-forming view, which Johan had learned by heart:

Without community, each perception of an appearance in space is broken off from every other, and the chain of empirical representations — i.e. experience — would have to start all over again with each new object, with its immediate predecessor having not the least connection with it or being temporally related to it.

"This is exactly what has happened in the way the metre was defined, it's about the chain of trust" Johan would say, trying to challenge his teammates.

Getting frustrated, he would continue, "Frog communities would have their ways; we have ours. A Kant-frog could not agree with the human Kant. For Kant aliens our metre would be a nightmare; they could not even begin to discuss science and its metrics with us!"

The aversion towards the problem he introduced was evident; it was not any of the few logical counter-arguments from his colleagues that puzzled him; rather, there was an undefined, personal component in them, a sense of spiritual closure, defining what was considered a proper and practical way to approach and deal with physical problems. When Johan tried to move outside the closure, he appeared to them either suspicious or simply stupid.

"Talk to the psychologists," his Finnish colleagues would say, "and let us know when they have accomplished something that works in the quantum world or even in the object world!"

There was no use continuing the argument, and he found it impossible to connect his deepest thoughts with his colleagues' work. Still, he felt that the two worlds, the physical and the spiritual, were destined to be forever and inseparably interconnected. The experience of the disturbing intellectual closure made him sometimes feel like being an outsider among the colleagues and vivid images of his father's desperate experiences at the University came to his mind, making him question his own views. He remembered that his father had moved from mathematics and physics to studying theology and philosophy.

Trying to find any relevant articles on this unwelcome topic of the spiritual within physics, he came across an unpublished research article on the internet, describing a model where the quantum mechanical (QM) knowledge and theory — not the everyday, real world or the Newtonian one — is taken as the ground truth of everything. According to the author, the concepts and perceptions of everyday reality, everyday truths, the world as it is perceived and the way people sense themselves, must be made compatible with what is known in QM. If this compatibility cannot be perfectly achieved, then it is only too bad for everyday conceptions of the world. In these considerations, Johan saw QM to be closer to the concept of God than the earthly ground.

Johan often thought about the fact that ancient people, who came up with their own early practical ways of measuring the world, could not have known that all their measurement sticks would have something to do with quantum mechanics. He understood that the scientists working before the construction of the Metre, had followed even earlier scientists of Egypt and the Indus Valley, with their own measuring tools. It had not been their fault that such a human urge to measure and quantify the world had led to this ousting of the spiritual.

PART II

Chapter 5
Epi Café and Wolle

In California, the spontaneous and energetic atmosphere at the lab encouraged Johan to introduce his frog-physics thinking to his new colleagues and teammates, hoping to receive more an open-minded or theoretically invigorating reception and comments on his brainteaser than had happened in Finland. However, even there, amidst friendly and clever fellow researchers, he could not inspire anyone to get exited or show the slightest amount of interest. Johan had the disturbing feeling that, for reasons unknown to him, his colleagues did not *want to* see the frog problem as an introduction to the theory of a general observer, something that did not exist in theoretical physics.-Having tried it a few times, he began to feel like a bad comedian in front of a silent, even annoyed audience. Once, in the same spirit as the frog story, he teased his American colleagues with a humorous—reformulation of the Gettysburg Address: *"Metre is the measure of the people, has been created by the people, is meant for the people and will not perish from the earth, but has probably already perished from the rest of the universe."*

"Interestingly," he would continue, "when we, as humans, take the quantum mechanical knowledge as the ground truth of everything in our physical world, we take quite a leap of faith. Certainly, the frog physicists or aliens would not take the same leap. In this sense, our QM reality as we see it today is the modern version of existential grief, nothing more."

"But this leap, it works! Your spirit doesn't!" his colleagues would exclaim. "Why do you think the atom bomb is not only a spiritual puff?"

It was clear to Johan that it was way too much and simply annoying to disturb the "real" world of the physicists with his spiritual questions, or even with his questions about the subjectivity of perception. As an uncomfortable side effect, when seeing their reaction, Johan realized the frog story was insulting to the two French QM specialists at the lab. He learned quickly to keep his amateur-philosophical considerations to himself, and even joking about the topic did not feel right.

Johan turned to working on the problems assigned to him by his supervisors in Helsinki and at Stanley, trying his best to prepare and document his data to the research community in Helsinki. He cheerfully shrugged off his Stanley colleagues' refusal to discuss the frog problem and began to call his own work ethic his personal way of Kantian-Kuhnian life at the lab. He was glad to notice that his colleagues were more receptive to this and could even smile at his reference to Kuhn, the famous physicist-philosopher, who saw science as an unpredictable series of paradigm shifts, with unavoidable social forces moving the whole system back and forth, the dominant truth at each historical moment being but an outcome of a consensus of the scientific community. He had seen how such a social-scientific power movement could dominate and conquer a whole seven-floor department in Helsinki and he had a feeling that his colleagues at Stanley were not unaware of these forces at their own lab. At his home university, Johan had tried to find a way to have one foot close to a suitable "Kuhn" camp, even as he privately held more to "Kant", whom he imagined had enjoyed his frog problem. Being a representative of a different mode of thinking, working on the novel and emerging string theory in modern physics, made him a puzzling theoretician, who did not seem to belong to any paradigm camp at the department. Johan did not understand why some colleagues in Helsinki had tried to ridicule his work by calling his approach as "thong theory"; he could only assume it had something to do with the Kuhnian camp phenomena.

Paradoxically, it was exactly his excelling in string theory and its complex problems in describing the essence of matter, his exceptional mathematical skills and having a recent, recognized publication in the field that made Johan a promising young researcher outside his own physics lab. He became a perfect candidate for a post-doc at Stanley and a competent representative of his supervisor, Professor Roos, who had earlier conducted his doctoral studies at the General Physics Institute there. With his support Johan received an invitation from Stanley and sufficient funding from the Civil Fund in Finland for his first year at Stanley, with the option to renew it for another year. The second and even the third year was almost without exception guaranteed for a researcher who could demonstrate real progress, according to the research plan presented to the Fund. Johan began his work already in the winter of 2015 in Helsinki and was ready to continue it, without a break, at Stanley.

Johan accepted the grant, without paying much attention to the fact, a matter of simple practicality and a hovering ghost of Kuhn, that in the scientific world, the young generation of students and post-docs must work on topics that have originally made their supervisors prominent, sometimes even famous stars within the relatively small social circles of specific research fields. The best of the best of the supervisors had made breakthroughs and introduced promising research data and theories which have attracted a large enough community of colleagues to join forces and benefit from it. Large teams and research networks have become a necessity in modern physics. This was the case of Roos as well, and Johan was delighted to receive his post-doc funding for one year at Stanley and the option to continue. He was ready and eager to take the responsibility to test the feasibility of the Roos model on the data sets now available to the research group in California. For Johan, Stanley was a special kind of a social ground truth within the scientific community; to be welcomed and accepted there, in one of the best universities in the world, offered relief from the constraints and disturbing attitudes he had experienced in Helsinki. April 2015 was his starting date.

"This is the way science works," he thought. "May the best models and theories win and prevail!" He was full of enthusiasm to find and join a new research community and to make his best contribution to the everlasting circle of knowledge creation. It was a win-win situation for him and his supervisor: Johan would get a recognized kick-start for his career at a top university and find a new life and invigorating environment, and Roos would gain more fame and perhaps even a better position in the competition for the scarce resources and rare academic awards at home.

Stanley campus and the Silicon Valley environment do not constitute a peculiar world-class science ecosystem only. From the start, Johan perceived the whole area as an ongoing, continuous technological, social-economic, fast-paced experiment, inviting anyone with novel, relevant ideas and initiatives to join and contribute. Then there was the money; no one underestimated its significance, given the economic realities of living, working and beginning something new, an innovation or a research project, but money was happily not the talk of the day. Of course, Johan realized that money could become important if resources were to dry up, and it always became a subject of conversation when someone received substantial funding, but overall, the working culture of Silicon Valley, for Johan, was lively, collaborative and full of hope.

It was practically impossible to find even a miniscule cafeteria or a bar in Palo Alto where Johan would not meet people with similar passions and excitement, although in totally different fields of expertise. Going for a pizza could turn into an unexpected chance to learn about the latest in x-ray crystallography (which you may not even fully understand, but it was not your fault) or hear about the innovations for global peace with technology. Unlike in Helsinki, where he often had his lunch alone, it had become a natural habit for Johan to join colleagues and their friends and go for an early dinner at a sushi bar, pizzeria, Thai or a Chinese restaurant.

On one such outing with his colleagues at Epi Café, a smallish restaurant and cafeteria on University Avenue, Johan had met Wolfgang Kron, Wolle, a post-doc student like him, from Freiburg, Germany and who worked at CLASH. He did not have the looks of a typical, casual and introverted nerd in Silicon Valley, but rather of a vigorous version of a hippie: slim, with reddish, curly, slightly messy-appearing hair covering his ears and a mildly reddish-pale color of his face. Wolle was blue eyed like Johan, but he was not tall, perhaps about five foot nine, and he wore beige jeans, soft leather shoes and a long shirt with color stripes. At first when arriving in Palo Alto, Johan would wear a suit or sports jacket but soon, observing his colleagues, he learned that it was typically over dressing, and he got used to wearing t-shirts, often with some blue, gray and white colors, a one-colored sweater, standard jeans and running shoes; it was a comfortable outfit for any weather. At their first meeting, Johan had noticed Wolle's exceptionally good posture and his agile but smooth movements among the crowd, when he greeted Johan and took the chair at the table.

Johan had become fond of Epi, sensing how every time he was there for a lunch or dinner with his colleagues or friends, even for a beer or a frothy latte by himself, something novel, peculiar and interesting came up. It was as if the place fed his creative thinking, even with its modest style and plain environment, and its standard but good menu, which included simple food from salads to steaks. "Perhaps it's the welcoming atmosphere, the sense of the ideal spirit of Silicon Valley, or just the friendly people serving, welcoming and remembering the guests," he thought. Sometimes Johan wondered if it was the other way around so that it was he and his colleagues who made the place such an inspiring place to visit.

"Welcome again! Where have you been? We have not seen you for some time! Beer?"

Only rarely could he hear this welcome in Helsinki and felt a spontaneous gratitude for the gesture, the kind reception. Johan was exceptionally sensitive to the gentle atmosphere that made him relax and feel free from the worry and responsibility he had learned at home, when the unpredictability of his father's behavior often spawned an atmosphere of uncertainty, even subconscious, ever-present fear.

Johan was not alone with his special relationship with Epi. One Wednesday night, having an intense exchange of ideas with Wolle on how to best organize the collaboration between different labs around the world, each with their own cultural peculiarities, an elegant young Asian-looking, but English-speaking, couple who had arrived there for a dinner, seated at their own table but close to them, broke the ongoing intense discussions Wolle and Johan were having, by standing up, glancing quickly around, smiling at Johan and Wolle, and started a modern dance to the swing music playing in the background. They moved in an astonishingly expressive style, with smooth turns and graceful posture in the small space between the tables, chairs and among the delighted customers. A moment of art was born. When they finished their beautiful duet, everyone smiled and applauded; then it was something else again, the inspirational atmosphere prevailed and elevated people and their thinking.

Johan could not help staring at the couple, trying to see what it was in this happy couple that made them create such a wonderful scene in front of the small audience; he waved his thanks at them and turned to Wolle, joking and admiring the dance.

"Wow! What a wonderful entanglement, a real one."

Wolle nodded, remained seated but made a slight turn of his upper body, opening his arms and making a bow to thank the couple, and said to Johan, "They have a classic background; its written all over them."

Johan did not ask for a clarification but wondered why Wolle, a physicist, would know about a classic background in dance.

On their first visit at Epi, Wolle had surprised Johan with his excellent and detailed knowledge of the preliminary model that Roos had put forward and on which Johan was now working. But that was not all. Wolle had earlier participated in the design and building of the measurement instruments at CERN. This was nothing new at Stanley; Johan had learned to expect people to know a lot there, to have a most peculiar background, as the young diamonds in the world of science, business or technology.

A further surprise came two weeks later that confirmed Johan's first observations about the couple dancing at Epi, when Wolle described his career as a professional ballet dancer at the Bolshoi Ballet in Moscow; he said he had also finished his doctoral studies at the university there but had decided to end his professional career and continue his physics studies at the time the new manager at Bolshoi was attacked and burning acid was thrown on his face, blinding him in one eye.

"Institutes are the same, they can dig the worst out of people. Nobody knows exactly what happened at Bolshoi, even after the attacker, a guy, one of its best dancers, was caught. Not very different from what happened in US figure skating some years ago. Did you know about that? I'm afraid, at its worst, science is no different; I just cannot watch it and do nothing!" He continued, and Johan could see signs of excitement on Wolle's face when he added: "And I am not alone in my desire to join with others in the international community, to fight such ugliness when I can."

This puzzled Johan, who was full of optimistic energy and admired the Stanley community. He did not know how to react to Wolle's surprising comment and what he meant by not being able to only watch something negative happening. He wondered who those others in the international community were that Wolle had mentioned. Johan did not want to ask about it and spoil the inspiring and creative aura they had at Epi, discussing science. They changed the topic and shared their personal experiences when, as young scientists, entering the world of science, they had plunged into the excitement and disappointments, the monumental challenges ahead and the continuous pressure and motivation to learn more. Johan eventually forgot Wolle's odd comments.

Chapter 6
Career Collisions

The reason for working on the proton collision model, the assignment Johan had at Stanley, was that by improving the prediction model of the collision outcome, new phenomena might become identifiable (or could be guessed) better than before. Succeeding in this would be a sign of progress and significant improvement; the research community would receive it with applause. When Johan had started his research work in Helsinki, it had come as a real surprise to him that a quantum-mechanically unique and true or near-perfect solution to collider data prediction was not even in the horizon of research and instead, various ways, including complex statistical simulations and others had been developed to "model" the enchanting collision event and its consequences.

To Johan, at first as a student, it was like talking about nature's quantum phenomena by using a fairy tale as a metaphor — the models appeared to be so far from reality. What could a simulation tell about the essence of nature? Is it only a fairy tale that seems to work? Mathematically and technically, it may be fine, but what is the real thing, the objects of life, protons interacting in the collision?

So many questions were and remained unknown, that he had come up with a favorite expression to describe his astonishment: "Nobody, not even the best brains in the world, knows what the quantum world is actually made of — in detail."

When talking to his non-physicist friends he would continue and tease them with the fairy-tale-like, but real, concepts used in his research field: "We do not know how the pale and colorless hadrons actually have been built from the colorful quarks. Besides, we don't have the faintest empirically based idea about how this wonderful design came about in the first place!"

While his colleagues took such a statement as a fact — a problematic one, yet true — it made his non-professional friends stare at him in silence and amazement, as if they were listening to a shaman or a comedian talking, unable to know what to believe; finally, they did not know whether they were amused by a mystery story or by an enchanting fairy tale. Johan would observe the astounded faces; his friends were like the best possible audience any wannabe new age guru would dream of meeting when trying to convince potential followers that they have amazing auras around them and above their heads. Recognizing the reactions, Johan saw the manipulative power the knowledge of theoretical physics gave to him. He felt that it was not right to talk about the true nature of the world out there, about our own essence as part of it, in such difficult terms to an audience who could not present any real counter arguments. He remained puzzled how to continue without a shared and honest ground for a reasonable discussion. A sip of guilt and shame bothered him when he realized that he was about to join the elite of science. Was there any way for him to explain the assumed, underlying mechanisms of a natural phenomenon to someone who doesn't understand what it is he tries to explain — the quantum mechanical ground truth of us and the world?

"We are no less quantum creatures than the rest of the world, but I'm not convinced at all that quantum mechanics is enough to understand us and the universe" was the frequent sighing comment from Johan to his friends, trying to convince them that if quantum mechanics, instead of classical physics, is taken as the solid ground truth of all knowledge and for all men, it is no less challenging a problem, with its own psychology of power, than measuring the segments of the meridian during the French Revolution. Johan became quickly aware that his friends and colleagues knew nothing about the meridian expedition, either.

The knowledge of quantum mechanics did not relieve Johan from what he felt to be the unavoidable inferiority complex of humankind, knowing that we are but an insignificant part of the universe, not different from other materials there. He started thinking that perhaps it was just the knowledge of a theoretical physicist, not of psychologists, for example, that is required for understanding how limited the current research tools are in revealing the true nature of the world — and man.

This awareness had been one of the reasons he got so excited about QM — how necessary it was to understand QM as a basis for everything while at the same time realizing how inept the existing theoretical models are in predicting even the simplest particle behaviors and their observed properties in the collisions, perhaps even with the increasing power in producing proton collisions, typically measured in teraelectronvolts (TeV), 'tera' meaning simply twelve zeros. Johan had noticed how there was a pride in the mystery his physicist colleagues seemed to enjoy when mentioning these huge power numbers as if the tossing around of such numbers increased the scientists' own personal power.

He used to enjoy and share with his physicist friends what he had read from a hilarious MIT article, which celebrated the eternal human inferiority complex, as he called it. In the News article, physicist Jennifer Chu had described the huge 13TeV power of the collision energy at CERN, with which the physicist had worked. She explained how the energy in this immense system was actually only about the same amount used by a flying mosquito! But *"when that energy is packed into a single proton, less than a trillionth the size of a mosquito, that particle's energy density becomes enormous."* Every new perspective on QM had made Johan even more curious and uncertain. The powers were not immense at all in the scale of the universe, but they could be made such by dwarfing the scale.

***

One of the meetings with Wolle at Epi Café, in September 2015, became different. After some everyday chat on CLASH rumors and happenings, Wolle's appearance changed. He became quiet, looking anxious, unlike his usually joyful appearance when making the first jokes of the evening, about the latest news from the Large Hadron Collider at CERN. He quickly took up the Roos model and its ability to predict the collision data. Wolle said that he had started to wonder why the promising model Johan was working on was expected to beat the existing ones with such a large margin — there was a rumor that it would drop the error probability of a false detection by half, while it also would manage well with other performance measures. If this were true, it would be a significant contribution to improve the possibilities of finding novel particles, and to recognize their dynamic character.

The Roos method Johan was to use for the collision data modeling was based on statistical simulation, a method based on random number generation, just like some other popular models, of which Johan was fully aware of — and of their underlying assumptions and potential weaknesses, at least so he thought. There was stimulating competition in the air, a need to improve the accuracy of the methods. At MIT they had, for some time already, taken a different approach and tested a novel, empirical way to deal with the particle collision data. It was part of the competition to produce the best and most feasible model — and to receive the acceptance and respect of the physicist community.

As Johan well knew, in this search for new particles there lurks the risk of misinterpreting the collision data, and the research community cannot afford too many mistakes, which easily triggered media sensations and false claims of a new astonishing particle being found. A wave of doubt and blunt questions would always arise, from the innovation journalists first, but what could be even more problematic, also from the academy itself and from the various funding organizations: "Why throw so much money in this guessing game, when other sciences suffer from the devastating cuts?" A couple of false alarms could kill research funding more effectively than one economic downturn — a well-known PR fact among physicists.

Yet here was Wolle looking Johan straight in the eyes, without the slightest smile, as he raised a question Johan could not have anticipated, one that collided with the trust Johan held in his supervisor's model.

Speaking slowly, almost whispering, as if making sure they would not be heard, dropping one word at a time, Wolle said, "I've come to think there is something fishy with the Roos package, its parameter use, and the programming code it uses. Are you sure that it has been fairly tested against its best competitors? I have not seen any such data. Why don't they conduct fair comparisons with the best methods available? Are you sure they have not discarded data that could show its problems?"

Such an unfair and unethical procedure was unimaginable to Johan. Wolle's open accusation upset him.

"It's not finished yet," Johan quickly said, puzzled, "so the real tests will come later, but what do you mean? You cannot mean there would be something intentionally suspicious behind its testing? That does not sound rational or a comment from a trusted friend? Besides, I'm working with the method, too, remember?"

Wolle took a deep sigh, straightened up his already good posture, and started again, now fast, but in a soft voice, without an interruption.

"I have gone through all the publications from your Helsinki team, every preliminary conference paper included, and found the discussion where a major improvement in the model performance was suggested, but not proven or demonstrated yet; the one test run at the end of 2014 was not properly described. I understood that Peter Jason knows about their work and is even collaborating with Roos. I could not find any confirmation of the model's performance by other teams, not yet at least. I can understand that, it will take time. But neither could I find a testable explanation on what could lead to such high hopes of its performance. I assume that with successful parametrization and some retuning it could be possible, but everything about it appears disturbingly fuzzy to me." He looked earnestly into Johan's eyes. "You do know I have also worked with one model using similar simulation methods, and the approach is not new to me? I also know how complex and slow this work is. I became curious first and then suspicious. I just wanted to look into its details, surely you understand that? I have not contacted Roos or Peter, yet. Thought to ask you first."

Now it was Johan's turn to be silent and slow. He could not find the words for almost a minute, as he moved the vegetables on the plate with his fork, pushing them back and forth nervously, before he could start. He could not eat.

"Why would there be something suspicious or hidden, even a fraud? What exactly do you mean? It's serious work they started, much before I joined the team there. I don't like this at all."

He blushed, profoundly and painfully offended for the first time during his Silicon Valley visit. He felt an automatic pressure to defend the Helsinki team's work, as if it were his own, to represent the model and the work behind it. It took some time to realize and wonder why he felt responsible for how the Roos model was discussed and treated. He had become defensive.

"It would be an impudent and stupid thing to do if the Helsinki team knew there was something wrong with the model. I cannot imagine anyone doing that, it's just impossible. Roos would be caught as soon as the model is tested seriously against the others and the results publicized. It would certainly hurt his reputation; there is no way he would take that risk. Even my own work could undermine his work if there is something fishy in it, something I don't know. Why would he send me here with a disaster on my hands?"

"Well, I don't know the background, and many of the details are obscure to me. You have seen how slowly these things progress, and it's just one of several models we use. Not too many papers are published where serious comparisons are systematically made. Competition can be hard and unfair, but I cannot understand where these exceptional expectations come from. I just don't get it. Besides, this is not the most important topic in physics, but it should be trustworthy, otherwise we all lose and waste precious time trying to figure it out."

"No way that someone would do anything wrong, not on purpose in this!"

Johan's strict comment ended the discussion, but he was left with an uncomfortable feeling after noticing Wolle did not trust in what he was doing. The automatic reaction was to carry the burden and take a serious look at the model history, to talk with Roos about it. He was worried, but he didn't want Wolle to know how worried he was.

Wolle was not smiling when he said, "Fair enough. I hope I'm not causing you trouble with this. But it is important also for you, Johan. I will not mention this to anybody before I hear from you. Maybe I'm wrong. Maybe. I hope I'm wrong. Please don't mention my name to anybody before that, not to Roos and even less to Peter — ok? I don't want to get into trouble here either."

Johan nodded, and said a muted "OK. You can trust me in this."

Wolle left, still looking reserved, avoiding eye contact, waving a hesitant goodbye to Johan, who stayed there at Epi, alone for an hour, without touching his food. An anxious after-effect hit him: could there be truth in Wolle's words? He tried to imagine what it was Wolle had hinted at: was there something else, something he did not know of that he had missed? Was someone behind the suspicion? Could a malevolent rumor have been started by a competitor? Why? Who could it be? Wolle was extremely competent in what he did, always, he could not have made a mistake with a topic he knew so well.

That night Johan could not sleep, as distressing topics, incessantly alternating, kept whirling in his mind, keeping him agitated and awake: the model's components and potential loopholes, questioning his own work, thinking about the colleagues in Helsinki, the whole process he was now participating in at Stanley. Johan knew the overall structure and properties of the model, but it was not his work, not in every detail; there had been several contributors working on it. It would be a huge, extra job even to try to go through its whole history.

He stayed awake planning a way to present the story to Roos, whom he knew as a hothead and extra sensitive about his personal reputation, always searching for opportunities for success and fame. Many of the colleagues of Roos gossiped it was the major driving force in anything he did. At the first hours of the morning, Johan could not wait any longer and decided to make a call, immediately, to Roos, to explain what Wolle had asked. It was still early afternoon in Helsinki, and it was the second time during his visit Johan had called him. Ordinarily, they used Skype and email.

"Hi, Calle, It's Johan here."

"Hi, Johan, I'm surprised you're using the phone; great to hear from you, how are your projects going? Enjoying California and the sun?"

"Yes, nothing to complain about the weather here. Everything is fine and I'm enjoying it immensely. It's a great team and all the facilities are just excellent, as I've told you. But I have a specific question, it's a bit sensitive but I hope you can help me with it."

"Oh, what is it?"

Johan sensed that the tone of Roos' question sounded like he was not only curious, but already suspicious. He made a deep sigh and took a short break before answering.

"I've been asked if our model has been already tested in a fair comparison situation with other competing models, Monte Carlos and others. I could not immediately answer and wondered if there are already some simulation runs and data, I'm not aware of. They would like to see the material and the test data having the promising outcome you described in the latest abstract."

"They — who?"

"A colleague of mine from here who worked at CERN with similar methods and instrumentation; knows the stuff really well, works for CLASH now."

"CERN?" He sounded alarmed. "Who is he?"

"I'm sorry, but I cannot tell. I promised."

"So, you want me to give you our confidential data, what we have under preparation, and you would then offer it to someone I don't know, is that it?

"No, no. I don't see it that way. I hope you can trust me; it's only about confirming the performance of the model or what you already know about it. I think it would be good for its reputation, too. Of course, it is important to me, too. I want to be as open as possible with my colleagues here. I was a bit ashamed that I was not able to fully explain what you might have already done. There is no risk; I fully trust the person."

"But you don't want to be open with me?"

"Well, I promised my colleague, when asked, not to disclose the person's identity yet. What do you suggest? Can you send me any links then, public even, to relevant documents if there are any I don't already have, something that is accessible?"

"You have them all. There is nothing secret or hidden."

"But my colleague explained that it was impossible to find detailed enough comparison data from the available publications and it would have been especially interesting to see something of the expected performance improvement, based on the 2014 tests. Is there something special in it, something I have not seen or don't know?"

"I don't want to talk about this unless I know to whom I'm talking."

Roos sounded aggressive, talking with a louder voice, almost shouting, making Johan even more worried; he had seen that kind of behavior before. He tried to remain calm, to continue without losing his own temper. If he did that, there would be no end to it, as he knew from the earlier experiences with Roos.

"If you have unpublished data on any test runs, anything useful to me, could you please send it so that I can just look at the materials. I don't need to tell about the runs or data in detail, it's enough that I can see everything relevant, OK?"

"So you don't trust us either, what we do here in Helsinki? You want to check that we are not crooks?"

"Sorry, I don't mean it that way."

"What do you mean then?"

It was getting hopeless to Johan; he tried to stay calm.

"Is there a way you could confirm that there are no problems or new challenges in the testing? Of course I trust you, I just want to be able to tell this to my colleague. I'm worried I'll give a bad impression if I cannot properly defend our approach. I thought I knew it well enough."

"Fuck you! Now listen to me, you can tell the guy to fly here at his own cost and see for himself! Who is he to doubt us? And if you want to continue there just stick to what you are supposed to do. You know that your funding is only one year at a time and it must be continued for the next year — next month is the deadline. Don't mess it up!"

It was straightforward, impudent blackmail. Johan felt a wave of anxiety as his hands started sweating and trembling. When he spoke again, his voice sounded oddly harsh:

"I'm sorry you take it like that, Calle, I just don't know what to do with this. I was hoping you would understand and help with it."

Roos hung up without saying a word.

At home, Johan did not sleep a minute, feeling the adrenaline rushing in his whole body. Memories of his father's desperate fits flashed on and off in his mind, the paranoid stories about falsified data and persecution at the university intervened his worrying about the way Roos had threatened him. His hands were shaking uncontrollably, he walked restlessly around the small one-bedroom apartment, bumping into its modest furniture, cursing, and then accidentally knocking an empty beer glass from the small kitchen table, breaking it into shards of glass.

The funding from the Finnish Civil Fund had originally been awarded for two and even three years at best, and until now Johan had been fairly certain he would receive new funding for his second year. His application for a second year was due in a month, at the end of October, and Johan already had the application ready, in good detail, describing all his activities and achievements. Everything was well documented, including his participation in writing research manuscripts with his Stanley colleagues. It had looked exceptionally good to Johan, who had felt proud of the list of articles in preparation; it had been a productive, fruitful year for him.

All of this looked uncertain to Johan now, however. The hint of blackmail in his conversation with Roos was a shock; he had never before experienced anything like it during his time in the academia. He could not understand what Roos' threat meant, trying to conjecture whether it was only aggressive talk, a personal worry, or something real, which could undermine Johan's present work. He decided to see his Principal Investigator, PI Peter Jason, his Stanley professor who was the 'guardian angel' and whose signature guaranteed the work and living there, to ask for his advice and a letter of recommendation, which could be included in Johan's application to the Fund. A supporting letter from the famous Stanley scholar should do it.

Next day at the lab was difficult. Johan was tired, going through all the documents he had about their model and then repeatedly making small mistakes in the simulation runs, getting irritated by this baffling difficulty. Could there be something really wrong with this model? He did not join his teammates' lively discussions and then even refused the lunch they used to have together; later his colleagues threw worried glances at him, when they heard he would not come to the dinner, either. Johan did not notice the surprised looks and the raised eyebrows of his teammates; he was too worried to pay any attention to his surroundings.

Johan called Wolle and told him about Roos. He went silent for a while, and when Johan suggested they meet immediately he refused, explaining it was bad timing and he had so much do right now. Johan noticed Wolle was reluctant to talk about the matter at all, and only after he had repeated his plea to meet did Wolle promise to arrange a time by the end of the week. Wolle's refusal was an uncomfortable surprise to Johan, who could not understand his behavior and what could be so urgent for Wolle. Sitting alone at his small lab desk, Johan was totally confused; now also Wolle made him nervous and worried. He had an eerie feeling, when he finally realized the teammates had somehow been observing him from a distance and avoiding eye contact. It was Tuesday evening.

Chapter 7
Physics and Death

Johan was in a difficult situation economically and had no extra savings to cover his living expenses in California. His father had been practically unemployed for long periods, having had only a couple of odd jobs with a low salary, causing a long-term, pressing economic crisis in the family. Ever since he was a teenager and even as a student, Johan had tried his best to help, but during his studies in Helsinki he had his own living costs in the expensive city and with the modest income he had as a research aide, he had not been able to do much.

For Johan's mother, Karin, life had not been easy. Sten's accumulating expenses from supporting and taking care of him, the therapy and the medicine had made her chronically worried about their economic future. She had arranged the sale of their apartment and had convinced Sten they should move to a cheaper flat. This was when she had rented the flat in a nice duplex in Vihti, some thirty miles from Helsinki, early before Johan started his school. It was far from the university campuses near Helsinki where Sten had managed to get a temporary job as a janitor, but they had peaceful rural surroundings. She had hoped this move would help Sten find peace, far away from the social life of academia, which often seemed to trigger his fits of anxiety and frustration. Over the years even the scarce money had been spent, but Johan never suffered from the modest way of living in Vihti; he had not even noticed their meager economic resources. He had simply been happy at school, which was easy for him, yet this positive change could not bring Sten calmness for long. Karin and Johan tiptoed around Sten, who had become increasingly distant and troubled.

Early one dark Monday morning in November 2012, alone at home, Sten had shot himself. Johan did not even know they had a gun in the house. He had left only a drawing as his last note; there was no writing in it; it was just another version of the group of men Johan and his mother had seen in his drawings. At first Johan was too shocked to look at the mound of drawings Sten had sketched. It took Johan a month after the funeral to go into his father's study and open the portfolio with all these drawings, each one so similar. It was then that he noticed for the first time something significant about Sten's last piece: how instead of the four men usually depicted, in the last drawing there were five, one of them about to take his own place among the group, his hand resting on the shoulder of one of the other men. The men were drawn with very strong, overlapping and repeating lines, so that it was impossible to recognize any details hinting to their background or profession. There was something in the style of these sketches that caught his attention; the modest park where they had gathered around a well hinted at a time in the past, in a city maybe; it could have been an old park scene from an old European city like Paris. The theme made painful sense: father had imagined joining this friendly band, which had become so dear to him, and more important than Johan and his mother. It was impossible to understand why.

The suicide was a terrible experience for Karin, who had found her dead husband when returning home from work. It was late in the evening and Johan was in Helsinki. She never recovered from the shocking episode, the scene and everything related to it. She tried to explain the unexplainable to Johan, talked to the police, and discussed everything with Sten's therapist and medical personnel. She had to manage Sten's estate, sort through his personal belongings, organize the funeral, all while wrestling with her guilt. Life was hard for her. She became silent and even though she still worked as a secretary, living was not easy. Karin did have friends, but she never asked for their help or accepted anything offered. Johan realized it was impossible for her to suddenly abandon her role as a wife and mother, responsible for her husband and her son, to become a vulnerable person herself, in need of support and love. She had learned to live in isolation with Sten.

When her breast cancer was diagnosed in September 2013, it had already spread to her lungs and liver. In the middle of all the suffering and anxiety from Sten's suicide, she had not had the energy to go to her regular medical checkups, even when her breathing had become difficult, and Johan had arranged an invitation to a clinic where the costs would have been minimal. She did not go there. Finally, Johan took her to a doctor, who was upset to notice her bad condition. The first results from the tests and tomography were alarming, indicating the situation was already critical; the cancer had spread fast and aggressively, and even with the available treatments her prognosis was not good.

Johan had been terrified to see how Karin, without the slightest sign of fight to survive, no color of life left in her, followed her husband almost willingly, to somewhere or nowhere, as Johan thought of it, barely one year after the cancer was detected. There was nothing he could do, just be there, and help her over the difficult and helpless last moments of her everyday life and then towards the slow and silent end at the hospital. She did not say goodbye, and died in her sleep one afternoon in December 2014, when Johan had come to visit amid the first signs of the emerging winter. It was impossible for Johan to understand how she could perish so quickly, leave their shared world, in total silence, and escape into a merciful, eternal sleep.

Johan had no religious beliefs and when someone asked him, he would often give his mystical comment: "I trust only quanta and entanglement, even when I cannot see them." It had been the strangest experience for him, to stare at his mother lying pale and dead in the hospital bed, to feel the presence of her invisible, personal after-effect, the dear mother, a spirit, memory, or something he could not understand or explain in his sorrow. He had no way to avoid feeling her presence. Even more startling was to see her dead body. She now appeared to be a total stranger, not from this world, forcing Johan to wonder about the great mystery of death. "Why don't our physical bodies talk to each other, but the souls do?" he thought, as he sat by her bedside. "Why is there nothing left in the body to make me see this dead body as my mother?"

Johan could not resist thinking it was only her soul, the awareness of it, that mattered. He could not imagine any better way to express the scary, new insight, that there was no bond — no entanglement, in terms of physics — between his and his mother's bodies; even touching her did not carry the feeling of life or death. The physical connection was now meaningless, but something, in the form of the awareness, more than a memory image, kept the souls connected. It was a true "spiritual spooky effect", as Johan thought of it that day and afterward. He could not imagine a better way to express his feeling of a mystical connection with something that was not material in nature.

Johan faced the utmost loneliness while sensing the presence of someone, his mother, or something he could not explain. The grief was about the soul and the spirit, not about the physical body, an experience he could not express in words. He had never believed there was anything like a soul in man, but it was exactly the presence of the soul of his mother that he felt and was with him, the only thing left. He had not experienced anything like this when his father had died, but now even the soul of his father, or something he could not explain, joined the shared presence.

For Johan, the physicist, the paradox was the dead body; it was real in the world of any physical theories and even measurements, but still to him, as a human, it was nothing. The soul was real in his mind; it had not escaped the world; for a devoted physicist it was imperative to think the phenomenon must exist somewhere as a tangible entity. "How else could I experience its presence?" he thought when his grief permitted a momentary rational thought.

During the worst time of suffering, in the hospital and at the funeral, Johan was scared, scared of the painful thoughts and mysteries, scared of his total inability to explain where these black, overpowering feelings of total uncertainty, their unavoidable realness, came from. When alone at home, his father's terrible psychotic-paranoid seizures and the loud, mechanical talk about the living and the dead rushed vividly into his mind. He remembered how during the worst psychotic, out-of-this-world episodes, Sten seemed to enjoy his private world; it was as if he lived among the dead and the living at the same time, and it did not bother him at all. This had terrified Johan and his mother.

During the funeral ceremonies in the church, when people, a few invited relatives and friends, were singing the psalms, he started silently humming his melody of grief, sobbing. It was the first time he had ever sung the song "Hotel California", so familiar to him, unaware of the suspicious looks from the funeral guests. He kept repeating the part of the song his father used to sing, painting a paradoxical way to leave this world and remain its prisoner forever.

Chapter 8
From Darkness to Light and Back

In February 2015 Johan had received his post-doc funding from the Civil Fund, for the first one-year period to work in Helsinki and then at Stanley, where he moved in March 2015. He had no reason to stay in Helsinki and hoped the new life would keep him busy and focused, and push his grief to the background, to slowly fade away or at least become easier to bear.

Moving to California was no simple process with the exhaustive bureaucratic paperwork, from getting the right type of visa and insurance to going through all the conditions for the eligibility of living there, committing to the extensive conditions by Stanley, finding proper furniture and other necessities, not least the internet connection. The arrangements took all Johan's spare time and energy; he was relieved to finally move in to live on the campus, in a small one-room "standard studio" with a kitchenette, only a few blocks from the central campus.

The flat was expensive, with its 2,500 dollars per month rent, with all the amenities included; it was more expensive than in Helsinki, but an extra fund he received from his supervisor Roos' project guaranteed a reasonable coverage for both the apartment and the travel costs. It was simple living economically, but it did not bother him; used to simple, frugal life during his studies and his childhood, it felt almost extravagant in the wonderful academic environment of his first year in California.

***

On Wednesday, October 7th 2015, when he had already worked seven months at Stanley, Johan prepared an outline for a letter to the Civil Fund; he would ask his PI Peter to write in support of the application; he hoped the Fund would guarantee a continuation of the funding for the next one-year period, starting in the following year, from February 2016.

Then he prepared an email to Roos, still troubled by the last phone call, trying to be careful in his expressions and emphasize the good and fair motivations behind his questions. He was hesitant to send it, however, as he wanted to make sure there was no way Wolle would, even accidentally, get into trouble.

As Johan thought this through, he decided to talk to Wolle first and then called him in the afternoon, asking for the permission to reveal his identity to Roos, but Wolle just said "no" in a very firm tone, with no explanations; he sounded somewhat aggressive. Johan was again struck by the disturbing thought that he might lose the funding if Roos was serious about his threat. He had no plan B.

Johan was too tired to work, and it was already six p.m. when he forced himself to go out, to escape his anxiety. Entering his favorite place, Epi, on University Avenue, he tried to find a quiet table by the wall where he could be alone. Usually, he did not drink much and was practically never drunk, even in the company of his fun-loving colleagues, some of whom could be sick as dogs the next morning. He sat on one of the high chairs by the wall, scarcely looking around, not talking to anybody and ordered a beer from the waiter, who recognized him and with whom he exchanged a few words. But as often happened in Palo Alto, a fellow customer, a man, standing on his right, perhaps in his sixties, with remarkably curly, gray hair, approached him, smiling.

"Hi, I couldn't help listening to you talking to the waiter; I noticed you have an interesting accent. I suppose you are from Finland; there is something typically Swedish in it, I mean you have a Swedish accent."

Johan turned to him to comment on the accurate observation and to correct the mistake about the Swedish language, when to his astonishment, another guest, a young woman who had been sitting at a table behind Johan, joined, practically jumped into the conversation, between the man and Johan, timing her entrance perfectly, just when Johan was about to make his comment. It was Yvonne as Johan would later learn, a charming Asian-looking woman. She stepped closer, her shoulders almost touching Johan when she teased the man in a friendly manner.

"Can you guess where I come from?" she asked the fellow, and then she gave a short demonstration of accent by describing the people she saw at the café.

The immediate diagnosis was: "Well, you are French, no doubt, but you must have learned a specific version of Chinese as a kid, somewhere near Shanghai would be my educated guess."

"How, for heaven's sake, can you do that? Or do you judge on the basis of what we look like?"

The man gave a kind laugh, "No, no! Hi, I'm Patrick."

He shook hands with Yvonne first and then Johan, who stood up to greet him; they both introduced themselves.

"I'm here every year to give a course on English pronunciation. The Asians especially — and many from India — find it useful, perhaps necessary. You can guess I have an endless job here, but I do have some background in Europe and even Finland; that's why I was curious about your accent, Johan. My original research topic was the Baltic language family, an inspiring and compelling theme, linguistically."

A humorous and enthusiastic discussion began; Patrick explained in detail and with his funny mouth-tongue movement demonstrations — he was a marvelous imitator of different accents — how he taught the students to recognize their own accents from the way they used the lips, tongue and mouth in pronunciation, and then taught them how to change this to get rid of the specific features of their accent that could impair communication. Johan described his Finnish-Swedish background: his mother was a Finn and he did not learn to speak Swedish, but his father had a Finnish-Swedish background. Then Yvonne described her childhood in Shanghai, living in the French quarter there, about her Chinese mother and the problems this kind of a marriage created for the family. She told touching stories about how the whole city area was now undergoing a major social and structural transformation, with only some old people brave enough to protest. The lively discussion and the shared, two-cultures background with Yvonne made Johan feel better and for a while he forgot his dark thoughts.

When Patrick had to leave, Johan was glad to stay at Epi with Yvonne and offered her a chair at his table. He had become spontaneously interested in her and her background, but immediately when Patrick left, she somehow changed her stance, turning silent, less responsive to Johan's eager questions about her life and reasons to be at Stanley. The only thing Johan learned was that she worked at CLASH.

"Are you OK?" he asked. But she remained distant, did not look straight at Johan, and then just stood up, abruptly, ready to leave.

"I'm sorry I have to go, I still have something at the lab; it cannot wait, it cannot wait. It was nice to meet you!"

Before Johan could utter a word, she was gone, and he could only follow her with his eyes, as she half-ran through the crowd and the tables, like a skilled dancer in the fully packed café.

Johan was disappointed, but the friendly discussion had been a kind and needed break, a wake-up to him, to rediscover his lost energy, and to begin thinking how to get things straight with Roos. He moved to a quieter place near the back corner of Epi, where he could think about his situation undisturbed. Slowly he ended up deciding to call Roos once more. He found new courage, thinking: "Why wait and be nervous and uncertain about what is going to happen next?" It was only eight p.m. in California, still too early in Finland, so he made up his mind to wait, to stay at Epi, enjoy a beer or two before the call. Even in the distant corner, every now and then Johan was joined by a talkative customer and met friendly approaches by men and women there, which kept him in good humor. It was not easy to stay alone and sad in Palo Alto cafés and bars.

At ten p.m. he left, walked towards Hamilton Street, where it was less noisy than in the still rather busy University Avenue, and sat down on a park bench where he could talk on his cell phone in peace and privacy. The evening was mildly warm and comfortable, with a faint sense of the coming, fresh, slightly chilly night. He called Roos, who answered immediately.

"Calle here, hi, Johan. You are early today or late there. Have you been drinking?"

"Why no, I was just waiting, so that you would be awake there. I'd still like to talk about the system and how to inform my colleague here. I asked about it, but I still cannot reveal the identity of the person, but you will probably be contacted sooner or later. I hope you understand."

"I'm a bit busy now, and have to rush to an early meeting, but don't worry about this. I suggest you just stay calm; don't talk about this any more to your colleague; we can be in touch later; there is no problem with this. I could have a chat with him or her when possible. By the way, is the source a he or a she? You never revealed that."

"Cannot say. But that sounds reasonable; I will speed up my own work, and continue with the model, as we decided. I'm so glad and relieved you understand this; sorry about the trouble. I just try to be as open as possible. I've prepared my application to the Civil Fund and will ask for a letter of recommendation from Peter. I believe that should guarantee my continuation."

"Nobody has better credentials and outcome than you, especially with the Stanley connection. Besides, I'm the vice chair of the review board there, and although I cannot interfere with the process, I can at least make sure your application will be fairly evaluated and treated. You are the best candidate from our department and your progress has been remarkable. I have to go now, bye!"

Johan was uncertain about Roos, at first, wondering why he now sounded so supportive, reasonable and friendly, but then he slowly relaxed. "Perhaps I should have been more careful in how I presented the problem to him?" he thought. He remained on the bench, enjoying the soft evening breeze, and became gradually almost euphoric. On the way home, he started planning the next steps in his project and decided to apologize, first thing in the morning, to his colleagues for his bad mood during the last two days.

At eight in the morning, he went to see his teammates, who were already busy working in the open space they shared at the Institute. Entering the room, remaining standing by the door, Johan clapped his hands to get their attention.

"Guys, and you two wonderful ladies! You know I love you, but I've been behaving like a jerk during the last few days. Please forgive me! I've had a difficult time, and I've been almost desperate about the continuation of my research funding. I thought I could lose you and our collaboration." Johan got an uncomfortable feeling for having said "I love you" to his colleagues; for a Finn it is very unusual behavior and at the lab such an expression among colleagues was never heard. He did not understand why, but having said it made him feel recovered.

Their response was, at first, alarmingly reserved to Johan's eyes, but then Marie the younger of the two French researchers, stood and approached him, smiling, and hugged him.

"I know your melancholic Nordic mind. Don't worry. I believe I can say for all of us, you are forgiven! Except that next time, when you've got the confirmation about the funding, you get a round of *salmiakkikossu* for all of us!"

Johan smiled at her way to pronounce the Finnish word *salmiakkikossu*, tapped her lightly on the shoulder and was so relieved with the good turn of the events, the chance to apologize, and Marie's kind words that he almost failed to notice the sluggish reaction by his other teammates, who smiled, but did not show much enthusiasm.

"Glad that you respect my national drink, Marie! Will do. I'll find a way to get a bottle of it here; it's a Finnish treasure. And if I cannot get it, I'll visit the pharmacy for the salty licorice and mix it here with genuine Finnish vodka, *Kossu* as we call it! You won't survive it!"

Now he saw smiles as some of his colleagues greeted him, with a wave of a hand, a "can't wait", "welcome aboard", or just "arrrggh!" Johan felt totally relieved, stayed by the door for a while, watching them get back to work again. He was happy to see his busy and focused colleagues engaged in their mutual project. After a moment he walked to his desk and sat down.

"Let's work; thank you so much, guys. I love you!" This time he did not feel any shame for what he knew would have been a misplaced emotional expression in Finland.

Johan had tears of gratitude and happiness in his eyes. He made an inner effort to ignore the silence among the colleagues that had new shades of gray in it. He had to wait for a while to be able to open his laptop and begin working.

First, he sent the outline email to Peter, as he felt much better, even confident. The last months had been very efficient: the work with his colleagues had led to two manuscripts for articles and three abstracts for scientific meetings and conferences. Putting all this into the recommendation letter outline felt good and empowering; he had done more than he had suggested in the first application to the Civil Fund.

On Friday, he finally met Wolle over a lunch at Epi and immediately told him what Roos had said.

"You can be in touch with him any time," Johan said warmly. "Just call him; he will be delighted and will provide the info you need. He was a bit worried the other day, when I couldn't reveal your identity to him, not even your gender, but it's fine now. I should have been more careful not to upset him. I hope I don't have to worry about this any more and can continue with the model."

Johan could not interpret Wolle, who remained expressionless and did not say yes or no to a possible call to Roos. Johan sensed something was missing from or obstructing their typically spontaneous, direct, and fun connection and communication. He felt as if an extremely thin, silky window or translucent screen had fallen between them, suspending their mutual trust. "Perhaps it is only this awkward problem," he thought.

They spent a comfortable lunch there, Johan trying actively to re-boot their friendship and trust. They discussed the availability of the new collision data they were supposed to receive from CERN, and then wondered what the analysis process would be like and what their role would be. They did not return to Roos or the model issue, and Johan was glad to notice that Wolle slowly regained his typical, energetic, and enthusiastic tone in communicating and expressing himself. They left Epi in good spirits; Wolle took his bike, sat on the saddle, ready to pedal to the lab.

Before leaving he gazed at Johan, softly tilting his head, and commented, in his familiar philosophical style, looking pensive, "You know, Johan, how the unknown forces in the universe are a problem and an unending inspiration for us. The unknown forces in the scientific community are but a problem, nothing more. Take care!" he pedaled off, leaving Johan puzzled, a mild wave of uncertainty disturbing his sense of relief.

* * *

Days went by and the application deadline at the end of October, approached. Luckily, electronic delivery was enough for the Civil Fund; Johan did not trust the speed of snail mail. This was not a place to take any risks with his computer system either, and when there was still one week left, and he had not received a response from Peter, he decided to call him. He felt somewhat worried, but ready to hear an explanation that Peter had so much digital "paperwork" to do.

"Hi, this is Johan, I hope I'm not disturbing you too much. I just wanted to check that you got my request for the letter of recommendation. I prepared the outline to save you time.

"I have it ready," Peter said. "You've done an excellent job during your stay, Johan, there is no doubt about that. I've already talked to your colleagues here earlier and they all seemed to support you, even appreciate your skills. I have not talked to Roos yet, but I'll send my recommendation directly to him and he can then forward it to the board of the Civil Fund. I understand that he's a member of the review committee, so you should be able to make it. I understand it's more a standard procedure to get a continuation?"

"Yes, it is. Thank you so much; you cannot imagine how grateful I am for this! Then it is just a matter of waiting."

When they finished the call, Johan felt reborn, back in the good and welcoming universe. All the worries were behind him; Roos had calmed down, the resume and application to the Fund was just excellent, he had the support of one of the most prestigious scientists at Stanley. He knew it was normal practice to continue the funding if the applicant showed real progress and had accomplished what had been represented in the original application. His situation couldn't be better. Nothing could go wrong.

***

Three months passed quickly. It was already January and Johan did not think much about the application, continuing his work as before; he was excited and full of energy, and even worked over the Christmas holiday, helping his colleagues in their analyses and participating in the completion of the manuscripts. He had also kept his promise and run a series of new simulations on the Roos model software he had received from Helsinki and carefully kept Roos informed online with the work. He had tested a large set of parameters and the plan was to continue with a thorough, preliminary comparison with four other models frequently used in collision data analysis.

Johan had recovered his original enthusiasm and trust in his career's future. He gained extra energy and even joined his colleagues who invited him to try yoga lessons in Palo Alto. On weekends he took long bike trips and walks in the nearby hills, mostly alone, as he had time to think about his recent past and a new future. In the Skype talks with his Finnish colleagues, he would tease them by describing vividly his walks in the warm afternoons, crowded café terraces, and the smell of the fresh dusk in the green parks. It was dark and cold, and not much snow in the southern parts of Finland to reflect the meager sunlight.

Then on the 1st February, early Monday morning in 2016, Johan was on his way to work on Sand Hill Road, walking towards CLASH to meet Wolle, when he got a phone call from his Finnish colleague, Siiri, with whom he had worked as a graduate student in Helsinki. It was a surprise call; Johan had not heard from her for months. The last time he had heard news of her she was working in Helsinki.

Siiri had become a close friend of Johan's despite, and perhaps even because of, her peculiar character. A devoted hacker, with a strange combination of style and original punk, she was tall for a woman, six feet, slim, blonde, and blue-eyed like Johan. He had never seen a blonde using such extremely white makeup that made her face look like she was straight from a revue in a Hamburg night club from the 1930s. She was a white-white-blond, but with a visibly healthy and energetic appearance. Johan knew she was beautiful in a most natural, almost classic Finnish way, if she would ever allow anyone to see her like that, without her white makeup and dark eye liner.

Johan had once spent a night with her. One evening after a long day of work at the lab, they had ended up at her home for a late evening snack and some delicious Italian red wine, Boca from Piedmont. The next morning, waking up in the same bed, Johan had smiled at her as she was just waking up, naked; it was the first and only time Johan had seen her completely without the makeup, almost unrecognizable, plain beautiful. Gazing at her, he had felt on the edge of seriously falling in love with her, but instead of describing his feelings immediately, he had tried to make a good joke out of her transformation.

"Who are you? Did I make love to this beauty? Where is Siiri? Who is she?" he laughed, trying to hug her.

She did not feel at ease with the joke at all, however. She immediately became agitated, turned her back abruptly, did not say a word and then sprang naked off the bed.

"I'm sorry! I hope I did not hurt your feelings!" Johan shouted after her when she escaped to the bathroom; she returned after ten minutes, in her red morning gown, a full white makeup on, and looked exactly as she had the previous evening, but with a grave face now; all the smiles, excitement, and pleasure had been wiped from her expression. Johan asked her what the matter was, but never received an answer; she behaved like nothing had happened and it was a new day of work ahead; she told Johan to leave and go home.

Siiri never wanted to continue the affair after their spontaneous night together. Johan could not revive their relationship or find out why she felt so reluctant; she did not want to talk about it. Over time they somehow restored their friendship, still aware of their ambiguous history, yet never mentioned it; they behaved almost, but not quite, as if nothing had happened between them. She left the university to work in Espoo, a suburb near Helsinki, for a major ICT company that specialized in security threats.

Siiri did not have a habit of engaging in small talk, and now she dove in bluntly.

"Hello, Johan. It's Siiri. I found out from the Civil Fund that you had submitted an application to continue your work there. Do you know that you will not get it?"

Johan panicked. The delight of hearing her voice was swept away; he could not even greet her.

"What do you mean, how can you know that? The decisions have not been even published yet?"

"Never mind; that's how it is. I thought you'd like to know."

"Are you absolutely sure?"

"Yes."

She remained silent on the phone and Johan could only hear her nervous tapping of a table or something with a pen or her fingernails. His mind was already flying wild and low with dark thoughts: "What has happened? Is that true? How can I continue here if it is true? I must check it, but I cannot do it before the decisions have been published. I have to call Roos."

"I'm sorry, Siiri, I'm in serious trouble. Are you absolutely, I mean absolutely, sure? There is no way I can live here without the money!"

"Yes. Yes."

"I must hang up now and call Roos. Are you one hundred percent sure of this?"

"More than that. I have money if you need it."

"Thank you, Siiri, but no thank you, I have to deal with this somehow. Can I call you back another time?"

"No need to do that. Bye." She hung up.

Continuing his walk, now unusually slowly, along the sidewalk, Johan felt shocked. He stopped every now and then, blind to the beautiful morning sunshine, passively watching the cars passing along Sand Hill Road. He could not find a proper way to react to Siiri's hacked finding. He was sure she had learned the information by hacking; he knew Siiri could do it. The pressure was too much, and he could not just wait to see what had happened. He had learned to trust and never to doubt what Siiri said; she could remain secretive about herself, but she never spoke lightly and without a purpose about anything.

Johan decided to call Roos, who did not answer; Johan knew it was evening in Finland, but he did not give up, and tried three times without a response. Then on the fourth try Roos answered. Johan stepped aside from the sidewalk, found a quiet place under a chestnut tree, and went straight to the matter.

"Do you know why I didn't get the continuation to my funding?"

"How can you know that? It's not public yet."

"I just know."

"Is this another secret operation of yours?"

"I just want to know what has happened."

"You must know, I'm not allowed to talk to you about this before it's public. What I can say is, there was nothing I could do; you had clearly the best application of all the candidates, and they moved you into a special group outside the normal one; it was open to everyone applying. I was one hundred percent sure you would make it there, and it would have been a better deal for you. Something must have gone wrong. It was a tough competition, tougher than I could expect. I know nothing about it."

"So, I don't have research money from this March on?"

Roos remained silent.

The situation was slowly dawning on Johan. He felt as if he was completely losing control of something; the feeling was devastating, like the sudden attack of a high fever. His funding money would be barely enough for two more months of living expenses, and then nothing, no income. If he could not continue at Stanley, he should reserve something for the return ticket and then for living in Finland. To get any other funding would take at least half a year and he would have to find a job somewhere; there was no fast track to get research money in Finland. It was an economic catastrophe ahead if he would only wait, and not only that, but a break, a failure in his career. Before Johan could continue the talk, Roos hung up, without saying a word.

The situation was now so serious that Johan did not care any more if Roos would lose his temper. He quickly called again to ask if Roos had any project money to cover Johan's costs. Johan hoped this could be possible, because he often had more than enough extra funds on hand to cover emergencies like this one.

Roos sounded annoyed. "This is no time to talk. It's late evening here; you should know that. And no, I don't have extra money, unfortunately. Everything I have is already reserved or fixed for my researchers and assistants. It is not even enough. Bye." He hung up again.

Johan remained standing under the tree for almost half an hour without moving; he was just thinking. He could not stop trembling and feeling cold, as if he was having a premonition of something even worse happening. Then he began a slow walk, stopping every now and then, trying to calm down, but it was impossible. He had to sit down on a park bench, hesitating and wondering if he should call Peter Jason and ask for his advice or help. Johan stood up and dialed his number while his hands trembled.

Peter sounded unusually reserved.

Without any small talk, Peter, too just started, "There is something strange going on with your work and your communication. I don't like it. I understood from Roos that you have some suspicious associates here. Is that true? You do know that any conduct that might violate our principles can cost you your right to work here, not only for now, but also in the future. This is serious, believe me!"

"There is absolutely nothing wrong. It is just scientific interaction, nothing exceptional, life as usual. I have done nothing wrong. What did he tell you?"

"I cannot say, but I trust him. I've known him for years. He's worried."

"I don't get it! Suddenly I have no research money and then there are even rumors about my behavior that I cannot prove to be false, not on the spot anyway. I have no idea what these rumors are! What can I do?"

"How did you get to know about the Civil Fund decision from Finland? Roos told me it is not public yet; it's supposed to be secured and classified until published, which will take place after three weeks. How can you have access to the decision? Who are you working with behind our backs?" Johan realized Roos had already been immediately in touch with Peter, while he had been trying to recover from the shock, but he was too nervous to ask for an explanation.

"I have nothing to hide."

Now Johan's voice broke again, and his hands kept shaking, as he realized the hopeless, cul-de-sac of his situation. No way to go. It was Roos' word against his, and he did not have a chance to get his own message through. Johan tried to remain composed and be careful in his expressions. An image of his father Sten flashed briefly through his mind, the way he used to quote the Eagles song, by putting a cold-sounding stress on the words heaven and hell, when talking about his problems at the university.

"I hope I can continue as usual. I'll try to find funding elsewhere."

"We will come back to you; there is something I want to make very clear to you. I cannot talk to you now, but you will hear from us."

Johan tried to respond, but Peter had already hung up.

Peter's last words "You will hear from us" shook Johan. He had never heard such a formal expression from anyone, especially from a colleague or a supervisor; it sounded like an explicit threat. He remembered how his father had talked about the accusations against him at the university; he imitated the people who accused him, with a monotonic, almost metallic-sounding formal tone. To Johan, it had sounded paranoid then.

Peter left Johan in a state of total, helpless confusion, standing alone on the sidewalk. He realized he could not immediately contact the Fund to find out what had gone wrong and why, because he was not supposed to have this information about the decision yet. He stared blankly at the winding pavement ahead of him, running between the trees and bushes, opposite the Stanley Mall. A few cyclists passed by him; he was unable to move, as if caught by a sudden fit of catatonia. When he finally took the first hesitant step, blindly in the bike lane, someone almost hit him, waking him up, shouting something to Johan and ringing the bicycle's bell. Slowly Johan started walking towards CLASH, up along Sand Hill Road. He was already tired and exhausted. Finally, he entered the entrance hall to meet Wolle, who would come and fetch him.

Showing his CLASH ID badge at the check-in gate, the security lady, a young, nice looking Latina with strong make-up and shining dark hair, gestured to him to stay there. She threw a sharp, steady look at him; she was serious.

"Sir, I'm sorry but your ID is not valid. It's been cancelled, only a few moments ago."

Johan blushed in embarrassment and tried to explain, "But it's been OK for almost a year already with no problems."

He saw Wolle standing further away, behind the security gate. His stance, as he positioned himself partly sideways to Johan, chin up, disclosed an explicit unwillingness to help or intervene in any way. Wolle remained distant, appearing like a stranger, an outsider to Johan's painful and embarrassing situation; there was a peculiar sign of a misplaced curiosity on his face, which Johan could not read. Johan waved at him but did not get any response; Wolle just stood there as if he were waiting for something to happen. Johan could not understand his indifferent attitude.

"What is the problem?" Johan asked the woman. "Has it expired? Should I renew it? Can I do something? A colleague is waiting for me there."

"You better leave, sir! There is nothing I can do. We have a security alert on you; you have no entrance here! So please, if you don't leave immediately, I will have to call the guards!"

Johan knew enough of the local practices in these matters not to stay there a second more. Desperate, he gazed at Wolle, who remained distant, standing behind the gates. Johan tried once more to gesture to him, but he just stood there, did not show any intention, or even an interest to move. It was impossible for Johan to understand why he behaved like that.

Johan rushed out and started slowly walking down the Sand Hill Road, by the shopping center on the right, and to the railroad crossing. He felt devastated, with no idea why he had suddenly ended up in such a mess. He imagined Roos behind it all but could not understand why and how. Who wanted to harm him so much, with such a blunt and viciously real intent to hurt him, to destroy his life and reputation here? It could not be a misunderstanding only. There was no other person responsible than Roos, but why? "Why?" filled and conquered his mind, with no answer to the rush of painful questions.

"I must talk to Roos seriously and clear things up." Johan was talking to himself when he reached the railroad crossing at the end of Sand Hill Road and near the park where the Stanley symbol, The Tower, made of redwood, stood high for the eager tourists to see. Like any scholar there, Johan knew the Stanley slogan "Climb the tower!" and laughed bitterly. This morning it really felt as if the tower was casting a threatening shadow over him, and soon would fall on top of-him.

The barrier gate across the train tracks had been lowered to stop the car traffic; several cyclists and a few pedestrians were waiting to cross. The Caltrain approached from the right, from the Palo Alto station. Johan could already hear its rumbling sound, a peculiar, monumental noise, too massive for any man-made vehicle, sounding more as if it originated from a huge steel factory on wheels than from a comfortable train. The Caltrain added its ear-splitting whistle to the noise as it approached the crossing. There had been several accidents along the tracks; the train had crashed into cars, or into people who placed themselves in the train's path. A train of that size, going at that speed, simply could not stop even if the train driver were to see someone on the rails.

The Caltrain flew past Johan. He felt the mechanical low-frequency, shaking vibrations under his feet, and heard the high-pitched screeches, the smell of oil and dust sweeping over his face, all this in a perfect synchrony with the powerful motion, the smells, the smooth bed of air the locomotive was pushing aside, and then, the core, its piercing, powerful chorus of metallic sounds. It was a wonderful synchrony, a multi-sensory symphony with a destructive harmony. As the monster of noise hurtled on and vanished to the horizon, Johan welcomed the fast return to the blessed silence and peace. As often happened, a car he had not noticed, beside the hurricane of the train, started up, surprising him with its sounds like soft music or the purr of a kitten.

Johan crossed the railroad immediately after the train. He did not even wait for the barrier to rise properly, and did not turn his gaze to the other, opposite direction for another possible arriving monster, speeding towards Palo Alto. He was on a waking dream walk along Alma Street and then turned left onto University Avenue, walking along it, passing by Epi on the other side of the street. It felt like a totally wrong time to go there now. Johan sat down on a bench, trying to calm his mind, to find control and free himself from the crushing and humiliating experiences, to figure out what he was going through. Only when grasping his hair in despair, leaning down against his knees, a fraction of a second before closing his eyes to dive into the blessed darkness, did he notice a shabby-looking man beside him, on his right, tanned, with a reddish, long beard, unkempt, but not dirty, observing him.

With a surprisingly bright look in his eyes, the bearded man said, "Sit down and relax, you look tired and frightened. What's the matter?"

Johan did not react, eyes closed now; he did not have the energy.

Slowly, after a few minutes or an hour — it was impossible to know — Johan became aware of his surroundings again. He opened his eyes and remembered having seen this shabby but bright-eyed fellow several times, often with similar-looking friends, sitting on this bench, watching the passers-by, even sleeping there or near the wall. Sometimes the man had a handwritten, cardboard sign that said: "Help me, I lost my job, have no place to stay!" The man did not look like a drunk or a junkie at all, and yet he appeared to have no home.

It was not rare to see people like that in Palo Alto, spending their days and early evenings on the benches, and at night sleeping wherever they could rest without being disturbed or pushed away by the guards and the police. Johan had never seen the police treat these poor fellows aggressively, and for a short moment wondered why they behaved like that, without the traditional power role of the militant police in the US. He recalled the inexorable attitude of the security guard at CLASH.

Visiting the Palo Alto shops and the pleasant restaurants in University Avenue, Johan had never gotten used to the disturbing feeling he had of an unexpected contrast: the immersive, welcoming spirit of Silicon Valley everywhere, with its creative, optimistic promise, and the deepest human misery painting the same scene with shadows of grief. Especially in the evening it became an unsettling reality, like the feeling arising when, having walked out of a movie theater after a captivating drama, you are startled by the presence of the real world outside the show in which you have just been immersed. Johan felt that he had been catapulted out of a safe, friendly world, where he had a position, a community and money, into this other, much more sober reality. It was as if a veil had been lifted from his eyes, and he now could see what was on the other side; he could see it, not just see it from a distance, but experience it as a place he now inhabited.

Sitting on the bench beside the homeless person, Johan remembered the days — just earlier this week, in fact! — when the festive streetlights would go on, wrapped around the trees, and when shop windows would glitter and invite him to daydream about all the beautiful and expensive items. He had felt part of this culture of wealth and expansiveness, filled with young people, some of them looking like casual tourists and some like a combination of nerds and businessmen. He too had been one of the groups spilling out of the bars and restaurants, and passing by the shabby fellows, mostly men, but sometimes also women. Then, like all the smiling, chatting people around him, he would perceive, face, meet or try to avoid these people in need. Quite a few would give a dollar bill, or even more to help them and help themselves to survive the biting reality that could break their sense of happiness and security, causing the pain of seeing reality. It had remained a mystery to Johan, why these poor people were there, what had happened to them and what were they expecting to happen in their lives there? He had never had the courage to ask them, and now he felt as if he had crossed over to their side.

Johan was a true child of the welfare system in Finland, where the beggars were not Finnish, but were real outsiders, who came from Romania, Bulgaria and other Eastern European countries. The locals in the Nordic countries know how to receive state support for housing and living, and for health care unless they have serious mental or other problems that prevent their rational behavior. It is like a golden caste system: a person is either born a Nordic or not, and lives the consequences.

Johan did not feel uncomfortable to stay there with the man on the bench.

"I'm fine, I just..." and then he became silent again, closing his eyes and not saying a word more.

The man let him be in peace, alone in his thoughts, and only when Johan started humming one of his verses of grief, did the bearded fellow turn to Johan with a curious look of understanding in his eyes. He touched Johan lightly on his right shoulder, smiling a soft, longing smile.

Johan Ek had no idea what to do next. There was no solution at hand, no shimmering light for him; he spent the whole evening, helpless, with the shabby guy, who was like a welcome partner in grief: unable to find a way out, no escape anywhere, not knowing what would hit him next; unable to talk to the man. At about eleven p.m. he started back home.

Chapter 9
Closing Doors

Johan could not sleep well, and before seven the next morning, tired and exhausted, he started to his office at the physics lab near the Oval, the magnificent entrance to Stanley at the end of Palm Drive. Approaching the lab building, he saw that no one was around or arriving. It was still too early. He tried to open the entrance door with his key card, but it did not work. A guard appeared, a man he had gotten to know rather well during his stay there.

The guard looked serious, but not aggressive as he said, "You have a security issue, Johan; you must know that. They have disabled your card. I'm really sorry, but I have to ask you to leave. You can come and fetch your documents and other personal materials from me later when we arrange a time for it. I can help you. I need to accompany you then. Please be careful! Please leave."

The guard showed unexpected compassion, the way he talked and gestured to Johan; he was acting kindly. For a moment it puzzled Johan, who realized the guard could have taken the normal harsh attitude, without the slightest sign that the matter could be negotiable, or that there would be help or support available. A hard approach was familiar in science research areas nowadays, with all the threats in the air, but for some reason this guard acted more humanely. For a second Johan wondered why, but then his sickening feeling took him again. The humiliating situation was complete. He had experienced it at CLASH, but did not expect this to happen here, immediately and at his own lab and place of work. He turned his back to the guard and broke down, tears leaving visible traces on his cheeks as he slowly walked away, dragging his feet in a way he never did. He wanted to find a place to rest and stay, and looked around randomly, as if scanning for help.

"Take care! I'm sorry about this!" the guard shouted after Johan, who was already heading towards the Oval. Arriving there, he fell on the ground, and laid on the lawn, still damp after the night, near the shining red roses planted there. He smelled their early-morning, sweet fragrance; they seemed to remind him of everything wonderful he was about to lose. He was startled, and noticed that it was impossible for him to enjoy the beauty surrounding him, now that he had no security and his life was shattered and future unknown.

He lay there for an hour, unable to think of any solution, losing a sense of time; the future and past were mixed up. The pain of embarrassment and fear were too much, yet the sun was rising, warm; his time did not stop, and the fast, impersonal flow of time began to hurt him, as he felt forced to live in a world of inescapable disaster.

Finally, he took his mobile phone, and tried to connect to the Stanley net for emails, but even that did not work, and after three tries in vain he knew his internet permission at Stanley had been cancelled as well. He still had an internet connection provided by an operator and the phone worked, to Johan's relief. He called Wolle to ask for help, to find out what was going on, but Wolle did not answer. Then Johan tried his teammates, each one of them separately, with the same frustrating result: no answer to his calls. He knew they must have seen his incoming caller ID. "They are totally cutting me out," he thought, "both physically and virtually."

In that moment, a potential new threat hit him: what about his housing? Remembering a comment by Peter, he became seriously scared, jumped up, and almost ran, hurrying home, sweating. He was relieved to open the doors and enter his studio. Nothing had been touched, but there was a paper form on the table. Someone had been there.

You have been reported by your Principal Investigator as guilty of misconduct involving illegal intrusion into a computer network and the disclosure of confidential research information to a third party. Signing the housing contract, you committed to our rules that in the case of misconduct violating the rights of others, your occupancy can be immediately terminated. This termination includes your right to future housing at Stanley. You have one day (24 hours) to empty your studio, remove your belongings, and leave the keys in the office. If you fail to obey this order, your belongings will be removed by our personnel at your expense. You can get more information about this decision and its further processing from your Principal Investigator, Professor Peter Jason.

Johan was terrified. He did not even look at the signature and the Stanley logo under the text. The situation was impossible. He just had to move. He had some money to survive for a while, but he did not have access to the lab where he had some books, all his work documents, and his computer accessories. Peter was his only influential connection, and it was necessary to meet with him. It was already noon when Peter answered his desperate call. He sounded reserved, even annoyed.

"We can meet somewhere on campus," Peter said, "in a quiet place where there are not too many people around. Let's see, outside the Art Center, its main entrance. I'll be there at one p.m. Bring your ID card with you."

Peter arrived there after Johan, and was casual, but monotonic in his way of telling him the disturbing news.

"There is a good reason, I mean there is no doubt about it, none whatsoever, to suspect you have used our computer systems for an illegal intrusion into a foreign database. We have a reliable source and proof that the system has indeed been hacked. We also know, without a doubt, you have shared, without permission, detailed knowledge about the preliminary theoretical model with an anonymous person and by doing this you have compromised our work with Professor Roos. This is serious; you should understand that, and it's more than enough to terminate our contract with you and take away all your privileges, including the housing. You can be glad that we have not made it a police matter, yet. Please hand me your Stanley ID card."

Johan listened to Peter's talk, thinking it sounded like he had learned it by heart. Johan was tired and drained; he had no energy for aggression or resistance and handed over the card to Peter.

"This is insane. Why are you doing this to me? I have not hacked anything, and the person I talked to about the model works at CLASH."

"How did you get access to the classified Fund data then? Roos was explicit about it. I have it documented."

"I did not do it."

"Well, who did it then?"

"I cannot say."

"But you know?"

"Yes, but I had nothing to do with it."

"That is hard to believe. It's about your application. Why would an outsider hack it? It's going to be hard for you to prove your innocence, if you have nothing more to tell. Even if there is an outsider, you are as guilty as whoever he is. Misconduct is misconduct. Why did you disclose the preliminary data about our model to an outsider?" Johan noticed that it was "their" model now, but he did not comment on this change of ownership.

"I didn't, and it was not an outsider, as I already told you. The person is a colleague and works at CLASH. I did not help in any way. My colleague just searched through open and publicly available sources; any scientist could present the same questions if there are reasons to ask for more information about the model. It's science and ethics, for God's sake!"

"But it was not published yet, there was no detailed data available in the publications. You knew we have worked hard on it, me and Roos. You have put our reputation at risk!"

"I don't see it that way at all. I didn't do anything like that! Has Roos been making all these accusations? How can he prove that?"

"He played a recording from your phone calls, where you admitted the connection but refused to disclose it to him. It cannot be used as evidence, but it is enough for me. You don't have a chance in this situation. It's your mistake!"

Peter was becoming visibly nervous: his face was nearly white, and he sounded aggressive, as he waved his hands in the air and then used such a loud voice that the museum visitors threw nervous looks at him.

"How can I prove that I'm not guilty of what you say?"

"I wouldn't try if I were you. Our lawyers will get you, and it will be both painful and expensive for you. You'll be in jail in no time. Besides, Roos has already sent a letter to some thirty of your faculty members in Helsinki and told them that he will ask the ethics committee there to begin a process against you!"

Johan felt as if Peter had struck him. The news about a letter to the influential faculty members of his university, tarnishing his reputation, was unimaginable. Fearing he would faint on the spot, he turned his back on Peter and left, without saying goodbye; he could not remain there any more. There was no reason to argue with Peter, in any case. Clearly Roos was the one behind it all, and Peter as Roos' long-time friend and academic colleague had chosen to follow. They would never let him loose. He kept thinking a way to save himself. "Should I reveal Wolle and Siiri? What would follow then? I'd still be guilty and we'll all suffer the consequences. I cannot betray them!"

It was barely past one in the afternoon and almost the early hours in Finland, but he was too nervous to wait. He called Roos, who answered immediately, shouting, "What the hell do you think you are doing, calling me at this hour! Haven't you caused enough damage already?"

Johan tried to interrupt. "I heard from Peter that you have sent a letter to the faculty members, about me. Is it true?"

Roos continued shouting, "You'll see when the process starts. Ask the office to send you a copy!"

He hung up.

Johan was devastated. It was another blow that made him tremble; he felt a thrumming pulse in his chest and his blood pressure grinding in his temples. Unsure about what to do, he began to wander around the campus. He found himself entering the Stanley student center and walking up to the cafeteria, but just when he was about to sit down and rest there, he realized that the studio must be emptied, and he had no place to store his belongings.

Returning home, he began nervously packing, but had to stop every five minutes to take a deep breath. He could not help thinking about the faculty letter and its possible contents. It was worse than losing the funding. He could use his mobile phone and its internet connection and send an email from his Gmail account to the faculty office in Helsinki, to ask for a copy of the letter, but it would probably take several hours before they would send it. There was nothing he could do immediately to find relief from the terrifying, looming disaster.

Two suitcases and a backpack were all he had; he had nothing else in which he could put all his clothes and other belongings. He found a public self-storage unit from the net and took a taxi there. It was cheap and did not require a credit card; he was relieved to be able to use cash. Then he returned to the empty studio, sat down on the floor, breathing heavily, unable to formulate any coherent plan to get out of this strange trap. He did not know how to proceed at Stanley to get help; there were no documents to begin anything, to find legal advice. His own situation was compromised because of Siiri's hacking. In Helsinki he would have known whom to approach, but it was a different world now, and he was scared of any possible legal processes, knowing what they cost in the US and how problematic they could be.

Roos, Wolle and Siiri were whirling in his mind, over and over. It was impossible even to try to get rid of this baffling–circle. He kept imagining what actions he could take, going over the possibilities in a repetitious, painful circle of frustration. Disclosing Siiri would harm her, perhaps even destroy her professional life. It would not help anyway, having himself used the illegal information and being stupid enough to reveal it to Roos. It was plainly evident that if he could not get things right, his whole academic career would be over, just as his father's had been.

Finally, accepting the fact that he had no place to stay, he decided to look for housing somewhere outside Stanley's strangling and far-reaching grip, somewhere he would be safe from the devastating grasp that extended everywhere on the campus. He had no idea where to go, and tried again calling his teammates for help, but after several attempts, when no one answered, he finally gave up. "They are scared or just minding their own business," he thought. He remembered Wolle's comments on the Bolshoi and the true nature of institutions how they "dig the worst out of people."

It was a most profound personal disappointment to notice how, at the moment of need, his colleagues and friends suddenly disappeared, totally, as if they had never existed. Certainly, they did not appear to care. With them he had shared his passion for science, enjoyed the demanding work, lived in the intense atmosphere, shared in the accomplishments, all the while admiring their wonderful skills and assuming, without ever saying it aloud, that they would help each other in the case of serious problems, even when facing personal troubles. Johan had the uneasy feeling that he had been unable to match his own emotional hopes with the reality of work and work relationships.

"This is not real; it is something else. But what is it, why don't they care, how can they refuse to be in touch with me? How can they just watch me being destroyed? They must know I've been honest in my actions? Have I been blind or just an idealistic idiot? Have I done something wrong? Why am I left so alone with this? How can a scientific community act like this? Why doesn't anyone help?"

The avalanche of terrible, endless thoughts was too much, triggering new waves of gloomy anxiety and images of the ill fate awaiting him. He could not stay still, and had to go out to walk, to walk, not to think, somewhere outside the distressing campus.

Chapter 10
A Thin Wall

It was already early evening. But Johan did not know exactly what time it was; time had no meaning. He only knew that it was not dark yet, when he started wandering along and around University Avenue, realizing how everything there that used to be a source of joy and excitement had now turned into an irritating, ironic world of superficial fun and enjoyment. It was greed and arrogance with style he saw everywhere, smiling dog-eating-dog, nothing, nobody to trust. The visible joy and loud excitement of the restaurant goers and bar-hoppers made him suffer a kind of sickness and sense of loss. The frustration was overpowering, as all his wonderful images and motivation that had carried him at the lab and at Stanley, now had vanished.

He passed by the familiar homeless guy sitting on his bench, who asked him, "How are you, any better?"

Johan did not answer, just continued his dead walk. He started towards Alma Street, where it was silent and dark, less like the cheerful Silicon Valley atmosphere on University Avenue. He arrived at the park near the railroad crossing, where Alma Street has turned into Palo Alto Avenue. For the second time, he decided to look at the Tower, he felt an unexpected urge to touch it.

In the daytime, the sun's rays were blocked by the dense branches of the trees around the Tower. Later in the afternoon, when the air cooled, the massive tree trunks and the Tower still radiated the summer warmth, a welcoming soft wall of summer heat. Standing there for several minutes made Johan feel better, as if vitalized by the spirit of the trees and the Tower, the shadows, and the fresh, warm air around the tree trunks. He stayed in the park for almost an hour, too exhausted to view or read any of the stories and historical timelines about El Palo Alto, which means "the tall stick" in Spanish, depicted on the information boards there.

As dusk began to fall, the place started feeling strange, almost alien to him. Surprised by the quickly falling evening darkness, he walked back towards the railroad crossing, where the boom barrier had started lowering again in front of him, and he moved to the narrow passage on the right leading over the rails. The Caltrain passed by with its familiar noise, window lights flashing in front of his eyes, in the warm dark evening. The poles were raised up and the cars prepared to cross the rails.

Johan did not move but started scrutinizing the boom barrier, its red and white stripes, high up, and the separate gates and railings for the pedestrians. He continued peacefully walking around, not crossing the rails, apparently without a visible purpose, stopping and touching the pedestrian gate, its metal handrail, near the narrow passage, testing its solidity. He walked back towards the park and stopped by the El Palo Alto Park sign, as if listening to something.

The alarm sounded again, warning of the approaching Caltrain. Johan saw and heard the boom barrier lowering down, walked back to the passage, near the rails, and stopped there near the base of the pole. It was dream walking; he did not even try to see if there was anyone around, he only stayed there, standing still, sensing how pale he must look. When the massive train noise was audibly approaching from his right, from the Menlo Park direction, he took one slow, deliberate step towards the rails, remained standing there for a while, the train approaching, its engine sounds growing stronger, the front lights and cabin window lights already flashing in the distance, clearly visible, the vibrations of the ground tickling his feet as if encouraging him to take one more step. He took another step and was on the first, the nearest rail, ready for one more step.

Johan could not know what hit him. It happened fast, like a flash of lightning he could only hear but not see. First, he felt a faint, silky-thin, brownish and transparent wall separating him from the rails, but he still felt caught by the presence of the mechanical, immersive noise from the train. It was a sound like one coming from short-circuited electric wires; he could smell, almost taste it. His everyday self and being, fell apart, in its entirety. All this happened too abruptly for him to perceive anything coherent, or to understand how he lost his logical senses and perceptions, and fell over. He felt a momentary, sharp thud against his chest. He rolled on the ground, stopped by a railing near the pedestrian's gate. A thick, soft wall of warm air, generated by the gigantic train, swept over him.

He found himself lying on the ground, on his back, not able to figure out what his position was, how to stand up, or whether to use his hands or legs first. He had lost his sense of balance and orientation. The train was gone, and the silence fell again. It was quiet.

Leaning his elbows against the ground, he tried to stand up. About fifteen feet away, he saw someone lying still on the narrow, asphalt sidewalk leading to the park. It was a small figure, dressed in black biker gear, with a biking helmet on, lying face down, the right cheek against the asphalt, and the left hand firmly holding the handlebar of the bike, feet tightly on the pedals as if they were there on purpose. The bike frame was twisted; the red, rear light flickered in the dark. As Johan stood up carefully, he supported himself on the pedestrian gate bar, and was surprised to notice he could move. He did not even feel dizzy when taking a few tentative steps towards the figure, a young woman with blood on her right cheek and covering the right eye; half of her face was covered with blood. When Johan tried to move her, she whispered something that he could not understand, sounding like Chinese. "I have to get her to a hospital!" Johan said aloud. Now he got scared. "Where is my phone? I'll call an ambulance!" He did not know where to call and looked around nervously for a car or a taxi so he could get her help.

The woman, slowly regained consciousness, turned over towards Johan, and said in a feeble voice: "My right eye is full of blood, I can't see!"

A car coming from the direction of Palo Alto stopped, and the owner offered to help, but when Johan asked him to drive them to the emergency clinic, he refused.

"No, no, call 911! They will come and help you!"

Johan did not understand what he meant, and got angry, and shouted with no control:

"No way! I want to get her to a hospital! Now!"

It was dark already and the driver, looked frightened, hesitated, but finally agreed to help her into his car. Johan climbed in after her. They started towards the Stanley Hospital Emergency Clinic.

Only in the back seat of the car did Johan become calm enough to take a good look at her as she rested against him. He realized, with surprise, that it was Yvonne, the woman he had met at Epi three months ago, but he had never seen her since. He did not want to tell her that he recognized her, though, not then. He scrutinized her eye carefully, trying to figure out what had happened to it. She pushed Johan's hand away forcefully, and tried to rub the blood away, but Johan took her hand firmly and stopped her.

"Wait until we get to the hospital. Don't make it worse by rubbing it, please! You'll just infect it."

Astonished to see how calm she appeared, Johan worried that she might be suffering from a concussion or even worse.

Then she surprised him even more, when she uttered in a soft, faint voice, "I recognized you! I recognized you!"

Johan did not understand why she was saying that. "How? What?" he was thinking, and before she had explained it more, they had arrived at the hospital entrance.

Someone brought a stretcher with wheels and a nurse helped Yvonne to lie down on it, so she could wheel her to the Emergency Room. Johan had no idea how to behave there, to get her immediately to the emergency care, and tried to go straight towards the reception desk, to pass by the guard, and ask for help, proceeding directly the way he would have done in a hospital at home in Helsinki. The guard stopped him.

"Please go through the metal detector! Do you have guns or knives or any other arms on you? Please empty your pockets!"

Johan was startled, as if waking up from a nightmare.

"What? No, of course I don't have arms."

"Please proceed!"

Nobody was queuing for the desk and Johan sat down in front of a young receptionist, dressed in a green nurse outfit, and he explained the situation to her. She listened attentively and did not interrupt Johan's story. When he had finished, she asked the routine questions.

"What is her name? Are you a family member? Does she have any insurance or a valid credit card?"

Johan couldn't believe what he had just heard. He wanted to shout, "First you check to see if I have a gun, and then you want her money!

How about care? How about just taking care of her? She has hurt her head and she is bleeding!"

Johan had gone through enough setbacks, however, so he tried to remain calm and in control. In a careful, quiet voice he told the receptionist to talk to Yvonne. He could not say he had a Stanley ID.

"I don't actually know her. We are just friends."

He sighed, taking a deep breath. The receptionist looked at him, suspicious.

"Was there any violence involved?"

"No, it was a bike accident!" Johan said quickly, as he immediately felt a disturbing guilt, as if he had something to hide or defend. The nurse stood up and disappeared into the first Emergency Room behind gray curtains. After five minutes, she returned and waved to Johan as she reported:

"She's from Stanley and everything — the insurance and all — is OK. She asked for you, the tall, blond guy, to visit her. She did not say your name?"

The receptionist remained serious, looking at Johan with mistrust: Johan realized she expected him to give his name, but he said nothing.

"You have to wait here first. A doctor is attending her, and then she will be taken to be examined. We don't know how long it will take. She does not know your name?" Johan remained silent for a moment, afraid to give his name.

"We are just friends and colleagues. I'll wait here, no matter how long it takes."

The style and atmosphere of the waiting room was totally different from what Johan was used to at home, and what he had experienced when waiting for his father in the psychiatric clinic or from a therapy session at the local health care center. He had never gone through a metal detector at a hospital, and only once or twice had he seen a guard in such a building. Only a hospital in the large city of Helsinki would have a guard, who would typically remain in the background and at ease, if visible at all. Neither had Johan ever walked in carpeted hospital hallways; he was accustomed to a more uniform, minimalistic space, where all surfaces were flat and easy to clean. It was a mystery to him, why such a visible difference existed, and he felt slightly uncomfortable thinking about what might hide within the thick carpets, since patients came and went over them all day and night, with every possible, individual germ.

Johan sat down in a comfortable leather chair in a distant corner of the waiting room. He was tired and puzzled by what exactly had happened at the railway crossing, and what Yvonne had meant by her comment, "I recognized you." He was worried about her eye and already felt guilty about it, despite not knowing what exactly had happened. Johan had not wanted to ask Yvonne anything during their drive to the hospital. He had been too frightened and in mild shock himself. It was difficult to recall the details of the sudden, scary episode. He only remembered the massive presence of the Caltrain and wondered whether the blow he had felt had been an accident or something else. He did not dare to think he had been suicidal, but images floating in his mind of his father's funeral made him uneasy and aware of that possibility. He tried to remember every detail of how he had stood under the Tower in El Palo Alto Park, and how he had then gotten to the railroad crossing. He wondered where Yvonne had come from and what had happened to her. All the worries about his career and funding had suddenly been pushed aside, as if they had been moved, or shifted in time. He did not give a first thought to them, and instead focused on trying to figure out what had caused Yvonne's accident; was it just a coincidence that she fell with her bike there or was it something else, he wondered. Johan had forgotten his own pain.

Waiting for the medical information from Yvonne, Johan had time to think about his own situation. He recalled his depressed feelings and the thoughts about suicide, but could not be sure whether he, in fact, did take, or even intended to take the final step and fall under the train. It was all too fuzzy to think about, and memory images of his father continued to flash through his mind: first he saw his pale and anxious appearance, like a gloomy black and white photograph, and then suddenly, he had a glimpse of his excited father when they visited the barn with Alex and saw the family symbol, and the measurement stick.

Johan had a vague memory of something separating him from the rail, a thin, brownish-gray, silky screen or a curtain undulating with a beautiful, harmonious, and familiar waveform, with its powerful, pulsating center sending first its circular, smooth radial waves towards the screen edges and then making the whole screen wave like a sheet hanging on a clothesline to dry in the wind. It was a most conspicuous contrast between the beauty of the screen and his devastating innermost feelings. He remembered trying to push it, to touch it, or experiencing something that was like touching but not quite; it was more like a wind caressing his arms, a mystic feeling he could not explain to himself. He had a vague feeling there were human figures, as in a painting, on the thin screen. Then the flash-like episode was over in a couple of seconds and the next thing he knew, he had been lying on the ground, but how and why? Something had hit him on the chest, but what?

Closing his eyes and resting in the comfortable chair, forgetting the hospital environment, he discovered that he could now remember the weird, unusual flow of thoughts, his mental scenes, a few seconds before he fell or was thrown down. He had been imagining the most monumental, human collision of life and death, with a grandeur that dwarfs any proton-to-proton collision. He had momentarily pictured the essence of a human collision, the death of a human being — himself — impossible to model even with the best equipment and simulation tools he knew. They were tools that could imitate, on a microscopic scale, the physical crushing of the skull, the brain, the individual neurons and their interconnecting pathways being ripped apart, all the metabolites with them, their electro-chemical momentary states changing, the supporting structures of the cells thrown into disorder, everything living being transformed into an irrecoverable mass, with no purpose, except death and decomposition. He remembered the puzzling, mystic moment at his mother's death bed.

Momentarily, he became aware of how the disappearing order of life, the loss of the necessary sequencing of cells and structures composing the human body remains a mystery, upon death, not unlike the unknown ingredients of a proton disappearing in a collision. The everyday, meaningful composition of the living organism is lost forever, but because the true nature of the detailed order in human life is not known, it is not possible to know what exactly is lost by the collision and at the final moment of death. To Johan, for a second, the crushing of a human skull, his own, and the brain protected by it, did not appear at all different from the problem of proton-to-proton collision he had so intensively studied.

In the waiting room, he continued pondering this odd, new insight. He could not help taking the familiar and safe approach of a physicist, the way he had when working with the collision data: if there is no perfect model to accurately predict how different elements of a proton or a human system will be scattered in a collision, and what basic elements are involved, it is impossible to understand what happens in the collision. To the ignorant observer it is an ill-defined mess where the collision outcome is a banal massacre of the particles or men, a macabre episode of two masses, destructively meeting each other, nothing more. Death as not-life or life as not-death are simple to recognize, but the process of the death-inducing collision remains impossible to follow in every detail.

All this Johan contemplated while waiting for status information about Yvonne, but after a while he hesitated, wondering if all these ideas about human collision and scattering were pure imagination, or a result of his mild shock, a way to survive the emotional suffering. The terrible Stanley sequence of events rose to his awareness again, but it was a strange, paradoxical experience to notice that they did not bother him any more. He remembered a result of a study he had heard about a patient suffering from an intolerable pain, who was treated with a lobotomy in the 1940s: after the operation, when the patient had been asked if the pain was still there, the relieved comment was: "Yes, it is, it has not changed at all, but it does not bother me any more." Johan had sometimes teased his friends with this trivia, which totally confused them. Now he knew it could be possible to experience the same pain, yet interpret or perceive it as small, light, and distant. He still could not understand why this was so, or why this phenomenon worked, yet he could see now that it did.

Four hours had passed, and every now and then Johan went to the desk to ask the receptionist for any information, but she could only tell him that the doctors were still examining Yvonne, even though her brain and whole-body scans had already been done. An hour more had passed when a nurse came from the examination room and asked for Johan by his first name.

"Mr. Johan, Ms. Bonett asked for you to come and see her for a moment. She's been sedated and is very tired."

It was the first time Johan had heard Yvonne's family name mentioned.

The nurse continued explaining the situation as she walked with Johan towards the room where Yvonne lay.

"She was lucky, the blood on her face is only from her forehead just on the eyebrow, it bled heavily, and she now has three stitches there," she said. "The skin around her eye is swollen, but she will recover. Her helmet was broken from the inside, but there were no signs of brain or other damage, besides the cut on her eyebrow. The helmet saved her, but it is a small wonder how she could fall like that, hit her head very hard, but have no fractures in her hands or legs, nor visible bruises on her body. There were only some signs of a mild concussion and scratches. She needs to rest for a couple of days at least. She's been extremely lucky, or just blessed. Please come with me."

Yvonne was lying on a bed, in a light-blue hospital gown; gray curtains separated her bed from the others. Entering Yvonne's compartment, Johan could hear another nurse talking to a patient behind the curtain, trying to speak Spanish to her with little success. The nurse accompanying Johan offered him a chair, so he could sit beside Yvonne. It felt strangely intimate to be so close to her, even at the same eye-level, beside her bed, to see every detail on her face. She was pale, and the bandage covered her right eye. Yvonne turned her head slowly right to better see Johan with her left eye:

"Ouch, my neck hurts a bit," she said, and then, smiling faintly she asked Johan, "Are you OK?"

The question took Johan totally by surprise. He could not stop a sudden flood of tears and covered his eyes with the back of his left hand to conceal his reaction. Lowering his right hand lightly on Yvonne's right hand, still covering his eyes with his left hand, he felt shy, realizing he had not touched her like that before. He felt awkward hiding his eyes and slowly laid his left hand on Yvonne's bed.

"How are you feeling? Are you in pain? Don't even think about me now."

Yvonne remained silent, touching the patch of gauze covering her right eye as if to make sure she could still see.

"I know how to fall with a bike!" She tried to smile, but then grinned in pain, sighed and continued, "I don't have anyone to take me home from here. I must call my father, but he's in Paris. Could you be so kind as to help me get home with a taxi when they let me out? They said I could leave in an hour or so. They just have some insurance paperwork to take care of. I live on the campus; I have a small studio there, near the Student Center."

"Of course! I live close by there. I'll wait for you here in the lobby. I can fetch your bike too; it's still there near the crossing. It has had some damage, as you can guess."

She smiled, whispering, "I'm OK, I'm OK."

They did not talk much, only about her bruises and the examinations. It was a new experience for Johan to look Yvonne straight in the eye, to be so close to her. She returned a calm, soft gaze. During the intimate and peaceful discussion, Johan sensed his embarrassment fade away, allowing a new connection between them. A swift and fast bond was emerging, the way people can sometimes create such closeness when it is seriously needed, when there is no time to interact and tune into each other, no time for a rational check of honesty or a reliance on past experiences. Despite this new bond, however, Johan still did not know Yvonne at all, and could not yet ask what had happened at the crossing. He decided his questions about her puzzling accident and recovery could wait.

After some fifteen minutes, the nurse peeked through the curtain opening; she smiled and gestured to Johan that it was time to leave. He touched Yvonne's hand softly to say a soft goodbye and left. On their way out, the nurse told Johan to come back in two hours.

Johan was exhausted, took a seat in the waiting room and fell immediately asleep, waking up only when the receptionist tapped him on the shoulder, saying, "Ms. Bonett will need someone to take her home; she said you offered to do that. Are you OK? Can we trust you to escort her safely home?"

Johan was disoriented, waking up in a hospital environment. He had a spontaneous reaction, a habit from waiting for his father in the hospital.

He answered in Finnish, "*Ilman muuta, taisin hieman nukahtaa.*" He blushed, realizing the mistake, and said, "Of course, I'm sorry, I was just saying I fell into a deep sleep."

The nurse looked him in the eyes, a sharp gaze, evaluating him, not smiling.

"Please be careful; she needs your help. I will go and get her. I trust you."

When the nurse returned with Yvonne, who sat in a wheelchair, Johan rose from his chair, and hurried to meet her outside the emergency room exit door, where she stood up. He was astonished by the energy of her walk, the way she came towards him, agile, as if nothing had happened. She moved quickly with surprising power, a wide smile on her face though a patch covered her right eye. She carried her helmet in her left hand and was dressed in her biking gear.

Johan was startled by the change in her appearance and rushed towards her to help. He took her by the right arm, gently taking the helmet from her.

"Let me help you. You have to be careful now. You never know about possible after-effects."

"I got some nice drugs to help me," she said, laughing.

Johan could smell her light, sweet perfume that the antiseptic hospital fragrance had not been able to completely erase.

Chapter 11
A String Emerging

The sun was already rising when Johan and Yvonne stepped into a taxi and drove to the quiet campus, only two blocks from Johan's house. While he paid the taxi driver, Yvonne was already out of the car ahead of both him and the driver, who was willing to help. Without thinking about it, Johan had used his credit card. At the front door to her building, she waited for Johan, and as soon as he came inside, she rushed upstairs, to the third floor. Johan followed as quickly as he could, although he felt weary from such a long night at the hospital.

Yvonne had a small, two-room studio with a kitchenette like Johan's and a single bed in the living room. In the other room, there was a small office desk with a Mac and some familiar-looking articles spread all over it. The simple appearance of the furniture and the textiles, together with the lack of any bright colors, reminded Johan of Nordic minimalism rather than French or Chinese style. The place looked like a perfect hub for an enthusiastic scientist.

Two large posters caught Johan's eye: one showed a mountain biker on a dangerously narrow mountain road. Johan had seen an amazing YouTube video on that famous bike route. Such a bicycling adventure was all about risk, skill, and courage. The other poster was a classic black and white midnight scene of the Eiffel Tower, but for some reason, Yvonne had turned it upside down. The tower was fully lit, as if for a celebration, and there was a text in French he could not understand; he had never studied French. In one corner of the living room, he noticed a modest bookshelf, with a dozen books, and a golden statue of a sitting Buddha on top of it.

Yvonne began to prepare tea for them, but then suddenly went pale and sat down on the bed, as she asked Johan to continue.

"Can you please prepare some tea for us? I don't feel so well, just feel a bit dizzy. I have not eaten much today — I mean yesterday. I must rest awhile. There's some Jasmine tea in the can on the table. It would be good for you, too. Have you eaten anything?"

Johan was again surprised and confused by her caring about him and tried make a joke.

"Please don't worry about me; it makes me worried!"

He did not understand what she meant by the comment about the tea being good for him. Then he noticed how pale and fragile she looked, lying on her bed. She looked anxious, too.

Johan asked, "Do you have anyone to take care of you here for a few days?"

"Not right now," she murmured with a soft, low voice.

Johan remained quiet for a moment, gazing at her, trying to think of what to say and how to explain his own difficult situation. After a while, he decided to be fully open with her and take the risk that she might be upset about what she would hear.

"I got kicked out of my apartment. Right now, I have no place to stay overnight or for any other night, for that matter. I don't want to bother you with this; I just don't know where I'll be staying, but I will help you with everything you need. Oh, and the bike, I'll fetch it tomorrow, I mean today."

"I'm sorry," Yvonne said. "I'm too tired to talk about that now. Why don't we talk it over tomorrow when I'm better? You could just stay here overnight. I have an extra mattress, very primitive, I'm afraid. You can find it in the closet there. You can sleep in my office room and help me with food and things, then find yourself a place to stay, and I will kick you out when I'm OK again. It could be as early as tomorrow."

"Well, it's more complicated than that, but if you trust me to stay here, I'd be ever so grateful for it. But please don't tell anybody, especially at Stanley, or to the housing staff, about my staying here. I'm in serious trouble. I assure you, I have done nothing wrong. It's just a terrible mess."

Yvonne had started to close her eyes as he spoke, and by the time Johan had heated the water and found cups and tea bags, she was already asleep. He wondered if she had heard his story. Putting the tea things away, he quietly prepared his bed on the floor. Without taking a shower or brushing his teeth, he fell immediately into sleep.

Johan did not sleep well and was up when Yvonne was still asleep, and he immediately remembered the letter Roos had sent to the faculty. Hands trembling, he opened his Gmail on his cell phone. Instantly he saw the letter from the Chair of his faculty in Helsinki. The letter was short, addressed to *"Distinguished Colleagues,"* with the subject: *"A misconduct, possibly involving a criminal hacking of confidential funding information by Dr. Johan Ek."*

The letter explained the suspected hacking, claiming that Johan had admitted it in a phone call with Calle Roos, of which a recording existed. After a few colorful repetitions of the accusation, it ended with the sentence: *"I hereby inform you of my intent to initiate a process whereby the ethical committee of the university will begin an investigation on the matter and then in due time decide on the consequences for misconduct. This letter has been sent to the colleagues listed below."* The names of thirty-one faculty members at Helsinki University were listed at the end of the letter.

At first Johan felt struck by this blow, and he could not find his breath. More quickly than the day before, though, he was able to gain his balance. Although his hands still trembled, he carefully re-read the letter several times, after which he was convinced that he would be questioned and prosecuted soon in Helsinki, perhaps even at Stanley too. There was no doubt about Roos' intention. He wanted to hurt Johan and nothing would stop that now, Johan thought. Everyone receiving the letter at the faculty would assume he was guilty. He put the phone away and opened the door to the living room, where Yvonne was still asleep. Watching her pale face, observing the swollen, right temple and the bandage, listening to her deep breathing, he sighed and almost completely forgot the letter.

There was practically no food in Yvonne's fridge or in the cupboards. Johan took the keys and went out to shop for lunch and breakfast, but decided to fetch the bike first, worrying it might have been taken away already. It was a longish walk there and he was relieved to see the bike resting against a tree trunk. Walking back with a broken bike in the fresh air, the mystery events at the rail crossing and images of Yvonne made him forget Roos for a while. He left the bike in the stairways and started towards the grocery shop when he was struck by a sudden feeling of being observed and followed; he took a few extra energetic steps to abolish the disturbing feeling of guilt and worry. In addition to the basic groceries, he bought a bottle of Japanese whisky and a pack of beer. The cashier, a young girl, smiled at him, lifting her eyebrows; it was only ten a.m.

Returning, he found Yvonne still in bed, but awake, complaining about her neck and back pains.

"I knew the pains would get me first in the morning. I've had them before after falling in a competition. I have some painkillers to help, but it feels like I have to take it easy for a day or two. Is that OK for you, if I might need some help?"

Johan was making the tea. He had found croissants, still warm, and now he prepared a plate of fruits and vegetables. He was hungry, and despite the threatening letter, he was relaxing.

Turning to Yvonne, he said, "Do you want to join me for a heavy-duty Spanish omelet?"

"No, thank you, I'm fine with something light, a yogurt and some fruit; maybe you noticed I live with a thin diet: no meat, and I'm careful with the carbs."

Johan smiled warmly at her and nodded. "Of course," he said, aware once again that he did not know Yvonne at all.

When they were seated at the small kitchen table and Yvonne had found a comfortable posture that did not cause pain, Johan started explaining what had happened at the crossing. For the first time, although he had guessed something like it at the hospital, Johan felt almost positive that Yvonne had saved his life. He did not yet feel ready, however, to confess — even to himself — the possibility that he had been ready to step under the train.

Yvonne told him that she had been on the other side of the crossing, coming from Sand Hill Road and along Palo Alto Avenue to the crossing. She had been waiting there for the red light to change, and had noticed Johan, on the other side, walking restlessly from the park towards the pedestrian gate, and then behaving at the gate like a dream-walker, continuing over the first rail. She had realized at once that something was wrong. The crossing was well lit, and she could recognize Johan, as she remembered him from the Epi.

She heard the train coming from her left, from the Menlo Park direction, and made the quick decision to hurry against the red light, to warn him. Cars honked at her when she took a quick turn around the end of the lowered boom barrier there, hurrying to Johan's side of the crossing. Seeing and hearing the train arriving, she had to bike as fast as she could towards the train and to Johan, who already stood over the first rail, where nothing prevented him from stepping under the train. She shouted at him, but the noise from the approaching train was too loud, so she sped along the rails with all her skill and power, took a smooth curve right, over the rails, towards Johan. She lifted her right elbow to hit him hard, just before the train would have done it. Johan took a couple of hasty, unbalanced steps back, before he fell down; she passed by Johan, falling on her right, taking a good grip of the bike handles, pushed her legs tightly together, and braking, kept both her feet on the pedals as she fell over onto the narrow, asphalt passage leading to the park. She remembered falling, but the impact on her right eyebrow was only a fragmented memory of a thump and a flash of light in her eyes. The first thing she remembered was Johan trying to talk to her. She did not know where she was.

"I was surprised at the hospital that I could remember so many details of the incident. Perhaps the helmet protected me from a serious concussion and a memory loss."

"Did you speak Chinese?

Yvonne laughed a little. "That's possible, I don't remember; it's my second, actually my first language. I learned it in Shanghai."

"Where did you learn to bike that that? Have you had accidents before?"

"In Shanghai biking was natural and necessary, everyone had a bike. If you ever go there and try biking, you understand what I mean. We lived in a Chinese-French community where my French friends were mountain bikers. There I learned how to fall and learned some special French from them, too."

Johan continued, "I'm from a bilingual family too! I speak Finnish, but my father was Swedish-speaking, and only later learned proper Finnish, which took the dominant role at home. My mother did not speak Swedish, and I never learned it either, before I studied it at school I mean.

131

My father was a schizophrenic, so later it was often difficult to talk with him in any language, Swedish included, especially when I was already at the university. Sorry, this sounds macabre, but it's true."

They continued sharing their life stories and Johan found out about Yvonne's work at CLASH and her plan to return to Paris next month, where she would work at a high-energy physics laboratory.

Johan tried to explain his acute situation as best he could, but he felt awkward and easily became emotional. He had to stop every now and then to calm down, looking at Yvonne for possible signs of her reservation, to see how she would relate to his strange story and situation. Seeing her swollen forehead and the bandage over her eye, listening to her weak voice, he discovered that he felt less worried about his own problems.

"You are worried about me, Johan. Don't be. I checked your background already when I left Epi, from the lab visitors and Google and all. I know quite a lot about you. You have written a beautiful story about how you learned to love math and physics by skating. It was in Finnish, in a magazine, and you even received an award for it. It must be an exceptionally beautiful story in its original form. I used the latest version of Google translate and could get a reasonable feel for it."

"Nothing can be hidden any more, except for some dirty games in the system!" Johan smiled, relieved, realizing her interest in him. He looked more closely at her and raised his eyebrows in a question.

"You ran away from me at Epi."

Yvonne shrugged and gave Johan a mysterious smile. "Something like that."

Then they had a lengthy conversation; Yvonne rested every now and then. She fell asleep for an hour, and when she woke up she asked Johan to stay there for a couple of days and to be careful not to be seen with her or living there. Johan was glad and grateful to have a place to rest and try to recover from the shocks he had lived through in the couple of days. He was tired but at the same time curiously light-hearted because of the sudden development of this new relationship with Yvonne.

It was like a fresh, emerging friendship in the middle of chaos. It was something new and promising he could not quite figure out. He was grateful to Yvonne, who had been brave to save him, but also surprisingly thorough in the way she had made her background checks about him. Johan decided to spend his time at the apartment as long as she needed help, and when Yvonne would start working again at the lab after a five-day rest, he'd find a place to be alone, go through the events, and prepare for what was to come.

He did not need to continue the planning for long. On the following day, Yvonne suggested, "You can stay here as long as you need to find an apartment. Don't worry!"

"Thank you! You are an angel! That sounds wonderful. I just don't know if I have the money to stay here in California. Let's see."

He could not bring himself to confess to Yvonne that there was no way he could stay in California. He worried that he barely had enough money to pay for groceries in the coming weeks.

Then one evening when Yvonne had recovered and started working again, she returned from CLASH with a message from Wolle. She had just been leaving CLASH with her new mountain bike, adjusting its handlebar, when someone she did not know kneeled right next to her in the row of bikes, doing something with his bike and at the same time talking quietly to Yvonne.

"We have something to share, Yvonne," this person had said. "I'm a friend of Johan's. I cannot talk here, but please tell him I want to meet him in San Francisco, at the Opera house, this Friday at six p.m. near the entrance to the Lost and Found in the North Lobby. Do you have that? I cannot send any messages to him. Just tell him please to trust me on this! He's in trouble."

Yvonne said, "And then he stood up, walked to another bike, and pedaled away!"

Johan and Yvonne talked about the strange episode and the message until late in the evening. It was Tuesday, and Johan had time to think about whether it was a trap or something even more evil than had already happened. Was this a new "trouble" facing Johan, and what could it be? The last time he had seen Wolle, at CLASH, it had been impossible to read his face at all; it had even felt as if he was somehow involved with the catastrophe. Johan could not dismiss his fear and distrust.

Yvonne asked about their relationship, Wolle's background, and especially about Russia. She said to Johan that she felt puzzled, but not surprised, about his history and talents as a dancer. After Johan had told her about his inspiring talks with Wolle at Epi, the fun and friendship he had experienced with him, and about Wolle's cautious way of dealing with the model problem, she encouraged Johan to go to San Francisco to talk with Wolle again.

"You have to meet him. He trusts you. Do you understand? Why else would he have approached me in such secrecy? He took a risk. Just go there, go there!"

Johan was confused by her eagerness in encouraging him to meet Wolle, despite the risks. He had seen how benevolent Yvonne could be even when her own situation was bad, and he assumed that this same generous attitude was reflected in this, too. "She seems like a hopeless idealist, but what if she's right in this case?" he thought. He did not want to challenge Yvonne with his reservations.

It had been a long time since Johan could rely on someone advising him like that. Receiving the mindful support from Yvonne was difficult and triggered a looming guilt in him. "Perhaps it was the accident that created the sudden bond between us," he thought. It was a new experience of personal support and care, something he had not felt for years. His father had lived in his own worlds, and his mother had struggled under her family and personal burden. This recent experience with Roos and his team at Stanley had thrown him back into isolation. The emotionally cold nature of academia had made people unable or unwilling to support him when he desperately had needed it.

Thinking of all this, he was moved and startled by Yvonne's kindness. Trying to prevent a flow of tears, he avoided Yvonne's eyes. He wanted to hug her, but he could not.

Yvonne did not wait, but embraced Johan gently, in silence, a frail touch; then it was over. A warm wave of relief and joy rushed through Johan's body. He decided to meet Wolle. The "Lost and Found" sounded just like a place Wolle would suggest to meet.

Chapter 12
Wolle

To Johan, the San Francisco Opera house appeared monumental. Its entrances and the inside structure, its festive architecture reminded him more of Paris than of any Californian design. As Johan came inside the building, and walked into the North Lobby, looking for the Lost and Found, Wolle surprised him, stepping out of a shadow, and humorously approached him in the style of a Bournonville ballet dancer, with his arms low in front of his body, moving gracefully and precisely.

Johan could not help smiling as he exclaimed, "What is that? You look like a star from a circus!" Johan had only once visited a ballet performance.

"You should know better and more! There is a marvelous Finnish opera singer, Karita Mattila, performing here, and Mikko Nissinen, one of the principal dancers of the ballet here, was a Finn. I heard of him in Russia. He was a tremendous success here, too; your real roots are in a mystic, musical nation. You should know!"

Johan did not know either of these famous Finnish figures. He had been living like a laboratory rat for several years already, as he often characterized himself when friends like Wolle used to tease him for not knowing any modern rock and pop music either. Wolle's welcoming line and performance were familiar, a code Johan recognized, a code of friendship he was relieved to receive.

Wolle returned to his normal posture and continued, "Let's find a less glorious place to talk. You don't have to go far to see the realities of life here; it matches better with your situation." Johan took the harsh joke as gesture of friendship but wanted to know what had happened between them.

"I'm sorry to say this, Wolle, but I've been utterly disappointed by your behavior. I thought we were friends and I could trust you."

Johan started to say more, but Wolle shook his head and interrupted him.

"Let's walk and talk somewhere else."

"What's going on? Why have you been so secretive and distant? You behave like there was a Russian agent or someone after us or at least between us. Why doesn't anybody answer my calls? I've been totally cut out from the community!"

They did not have to walk far, towards Union Square, for Johan to forget his own problems again. He could not avoid seeing the homeless people they passed, feeling the personal burden, a peculiar kind of a Nordic responsibility for what he saw, all the signs of the grim life in San Francisco, not far from the prestigious opera and its audiences. There were young men among the homeless, evidently on drugs, mostly black people. Some of the older men and women were carrying their plastic bags and dirty backpacks full of mysterious stuff; men were standing on the street corners, often in small groups, perhaps in their teams of poverty, doing whatever they might have to do to survive. Much as Johan sympathized with these people, he was still suspicious of them. It was impossible to know what was there, or how much that might be dangerous or frightening behind each sad appearance. The uncomfortable reaction he had was a measure of how safe a place this area of San Francisco was for a Stanley fellow to talk about anything, with no risk of being spotted by any colleagues.

Wolle started a long monologue, as if defending himself, and Johan listened, trying to understand.

"I've seen this happen before. Someone high enough on the academic ladder, for one reason or another, starts spreading rumors. Now it's about a claimed unethical behavior — yours — of sharing classified information, stealing ideas, and misusing research money, even possible espionage. Nobody in *your* team talks about it openly — they have seen you and the way you work and behave every day — but they hear hints of it from others, repeatedly, perhaps even from their supervisors or faculty people and from colleagues who might not even know you, but who have become the innocent message carriers. It is impossible to resist the false stories initiated by such closed circles. You don't know where to interfere and there is no counter-force; most of the colleagues simply don't know the truth, and even if your teammates cared, they are helpless.

I've heard people talking about you having stolen a research idea from your PI and sharing it with an unknown third party. They don't know it's me they're talking about. I've heard Peter has already approached the responsible Dean to start a process against you. Perhaps they're doing the same in Finland. I don't know the practices there. Nobody knows exactly what factual information or proof, if any, they have on you to make their case. But that's not the point. You are a marked man; you don't have a chance to make it. I have no idea why they have started such harsh, even violent moves against you. You can try to defend yourself, but how would you do it? By revealing me? I would be forced to deny everything. And remember, many of our colleagues know we're friends, so I'm not the first one to whom they tell these stories. You can imagine what is going on."

"Why can't we just tell it like it is, about your fair inquiries and our discussions? Document it all, carefully, perhaps even write a research paper on it?"

"It's not about what has really happened. It's more that, for some reason, something we don't know, they want to get rid of you and the risk they see now. It's become a power game. They want to make sure Roos' reputation will not be tarnished. It would be bad for Peter's standing too, so he and Roos have a shared interest. It's possible that Peter does not know about the problem, but I don't think so; this is too serious now. Surely, you know they are long-time family friends, Peter and Roos? My guess is there is something, a serious problem perhaps with the model, and they don't want it to come up. It may well be one reason for their sudden and harsh action: they are afraid of something and nervous; they will clean the case by keeping your mouth shut and then they just continue as before or start anew if needed. They will lose nothing. Nothing has happened so far. It was just a coincidence that I became so interested in it, and I had my own reasons. It was your bad luck."

Johan felt muted by the gloomy analysis and did not know what to say. He saw Wolle becoming pale, as he continued to defend himself.

"Remember, I worked and studied in Moscow. What do you think my chances are against them if they start making even the slightest claims that I might have secret connections in Russia? In today's atmosphere in the US? I'm just a poor post-doc fellow like you, but with the suspicious history at a Russian university and even a ballet dancer, for God's sake."

This was the vulnerable Wolle talking; he was sharing a part of himself that Johan had not seen or heard before, a worried and anxious post-doc, like himself. Johan began to understand the extreme reservations Wolle had shown. Today, he was still hoping that, together with Wolle, he could clarify the situation with Roos and Peter by documenting the case carefully. Maybe Wolle could describe what it was about the model he wanted to know and why, and then Johan could just go and present this question to the relevant people or even to the ethical committee if there were one. It should be a scientifically well-founded case; however, he did not know who to approach.

"What if we prepare our case with care," Johan said, "get someone, a physicist colleague, to support us, and then invite Roos and Peter to deal with it? If and when the ethics committee starts looking at this, we would have a well-documented case at hand. We must be heard, and our views considered before any real process can be initiated to formally accuse us or me. Peter and Roos might even reconsider, if they see that we will reveal everything as openly as possible?"

"Think again: they are already blaming you, and I'm the next one on the list. The Dean has the words of Peter and Roos, at a minimum, against us. It would not be the first time they will have trusting or politically clever colleagues who will immediately join to support them. There is already a rumor of your unstable mental background, your paranoia about frauds in science, the problems of your father, and your strange ideas about the meter." Johan felt sudden pain on his chest hearing Wolle mention his father.

"How can they take up my father, too? Why?" Wolle did not answer but continued.

"Not only that, they can spread any rumors even in Finland, and you'll end up in a perfect trap there, too."

"Roos already did that, sent dozens of letters of accusation to the faculty members."

Wolle stared at him, frowning.

"Well, what else is news," he said. Taking a deep breath and shrugging, he continued. "If they start that process, for how long do you think it will last? Furthermore, what can you endure? Look at the Stanley guidelines on this. It's complicated and time consuming. Six months, a year? In case of serious legal stuff, what do you think it will cost you here in the US? Do you have the money? I know you don't. The Dean can deal with you as an emergency case to run through the process as fast as possible and he has real power. You can barely support yourself for the next month here, right?"

Johan listened to Wolle, speechless. Wolle's words were like waves crashing around his head; he felt he was swimming without a way to find land. He remembered the encounter with the massive, crushing power of the approaching Caltrain; stepping in front of it would have meant certain death. Now it was about career collision.

"I've seen this happen before," Wolle went on, "at another university. Take this case as a warning: a doctoral student — a case like yours — was accused of a scientific fraud. After a one-year process, he was finally declared innocent beyond the slightest doubt, but before the end of the process, he had already been kicked out from the department and what was worse, he had become so exhausted, afraid, his reputation tarnished and stressed that he simply did not have the will and courage to continue the fight. Besides, how could he have recovered his position at their project after that with the professor who was after him and to continue working with him as if nothing had happened? No way. It does not work like that in academia. There was no way for the poor fellow to get justice. It was an impossible, lose-lose game, so he left the university and never returned. And imagine this: even when he was officially declared innocent, nobody, no colleague, no department officials, nobody reacted, to clear his reputation. The professor and his colleagues just continued publicly accusing him of fraud and unethical behavior. His academic reputation was destroyed forever. Simple as that! You need to consider: do you have the mental stamina to go through this? Knowing your history, I do not think you can take the risk."

They stopped at a street corner, near a small, shabby grocery store, out of words both, for a moment, when a young black guy, with plastic

139

bags in both of his hands, approached, stopping in front of them. Johan felt he came too close. The young man observed them both, tilting his head in a strange way, so that Johan got worried and nervous about what he might do next.

The man asked Johan, "I have not been eating well lately, but what I dream of now is a cold beer. Can you spare me five bucks to get one or two?"

Johan was amused and relieved by the straightforward wish, and without comment he gave the fellow a five-dollar bill. He did not know whether to cry or smile; it was more than a sad story. The timing could not have been better for him to rethink his own situation. The man thanked him profusely. Perhaps he had learned that over-the-top gratitude was the right strategy with guys that looked like them. It made Johan feel he had done something to relieve his Nordic guilt, but grew aware of how significant a fraction of his savings that five-dollar bill had been.

They continued, without uttering a word, towards Union Square, and the change in the social environment came abruptly, like the bright light from the morning sun, social and economic in nature. They stopped in front of the Hilton Hotel, observing busy men in black coats and blue suits; there were only a few women, jumping out of taxis or Ubers, some wearing conference badges, their gazes immediately fixed on the entrance door, even through the door windows and inside the lobby, as if they were searching for something of importance and purpose there. Only on a rare occasion did someone look at the door attendant or the porter in the eyes and smile. Smiles were usually reserved for the opposite sex or someone smartly dressed, often with a collage of conference badges communicating his or her role at the occasion.

Conferences and business meetings had conquered the major hotels. This polished hyper professionalization was nothing new in Johan's and Wolle's world, despite their own modest lifestyle as academics, but they were no match for the glittering business representatives and their glamorous colleagues swarming this affluent part of San Francisco. The two friends became more attentive to their surroundings as they continued the discussion, approaching the hotel entrance. Johan was the first to break the silence.

"I don't want to submit to the injustice, Wolle, but I'm scared and afraid you are right. It's impossible to guess what will happen to me if I start a serious process, a fight. I must try to stop them somehow, though. I cannot vanish, not just like that. If I run away and disappear, I'll be in worse trouble; it would be like admitting I've done something wrong. Here in this country, I'm a total outsider, practically helpless. This sounds paradoxical, but remembering the poor fellow we just saw — I'm just like him. I'm in academia, but like him, I don't have any safety net. When signing the contract here, in my worst dreams I couldn't have thought about this, to need money to legally defend myself. I was only thinking about possible physical damages and accidents when arranging my insurance deal, and that I might be robbed in the US. This is worse; it's an academic robbery."

Johan started to relax as he talked, and he felt a rise in spirits as he joked, "They leave the clothes I have on me, but they steal my wallet and my brain!"

Johan went on, "I'm still confused about your role, though, Wolle. Why did you want to meet me now? I appreciate your warnings, but you practically suggest I give up to these crooks. Do you mean I should quit science, too? I'm confused."

"I wanted to warn you — if you start playing their game you will most certainly be kicked out from science, at least from any universities. They will put the fraud label on you. But what I mean is, don't throw gasoline on the fire now! Stay silent, don't fight them, find another place to work as soon as possible. Stanley and Helsinki are just two options. There are others. But don't start wrestling with them now. It will destroy you!"

Suddenly, Johan stopped walking when he realized how right Wolle was. It was against his nature to give up, but he knew he had to — at least for now. Wolle turned to him and took a firm grip on Johan's shoulders.

"In Freiburg," Wolle said, laughing, "I knew a guy who had a university background, but had decided to become a farmer and he got a huge pig farm. He had a saying, which he claimed was based on his own experiences at the university: "Don't start wrestling with the pigs in a puddle of shit. You only get dirty, and the pigs just love it!"

This hilarious vision triggered a heartfelt laugh from both. After a while, recovering from the laughter, Wolle surprised Johan.

"Talk to Yvonne!" he said.

Johan was startled. "Do you know Yvonne?"

"No, not personally, we have only met at CLASH, but I know of her and her activities. She's a promising scientist and has an excellent network."

Johan was still confused and surprised about the connection between the two, feeling a nip of undefined jealousy, but he was delighted about the chance to revive this trusted friendship with Wolle, to reboot their relationship. He suggested they enter the lobby bar of the Hilton and celebrate their reunion with a glass of beer.

"Let's go in, I've been there a couple of times at a conference; there's a nice, busy bar beyond the lobby."

At the bar Wolle lifted his beer glass to Johan, and then he waved it in the air, to indicate the well-heeled people all around them.

"Look at these people," he said. "There's a scientific conference going on here, perhaps several hundreds of attendees from all over the world. They are forced to travel a long way to come here, from China, Brazil, even Finland to meet their best colleagues and to see and hear what wonderful things they are studying and developing right now—if those colleagues are ready to disclose it. Often, they are not before they have published their data. Surely you know it yourself. The first thing you'd ask when you meet a colleague at a bar like this is: 'What are you working on?' They may tell you or they may not, and some may even enjoy leading you astray. Most probably they will not tell the exact truth, especially if they have something promising going on, something that could bring them value and fame. They don't want to share the expected glory with any outsiders, at least not before they have benefitted from it. They want to be the first ones to announce a new finding. It's more important than sharing it with as many colleagues as possible and as soon as possible. The whole system is extremely slow, driven by such ambition and the greed for fame, and research money, of course. It's got a very bad signal-to-noise ratio, and it's wasting human time and talent. It's insane! Don't you agree, Johan?"

Johan looked at Wolle, puzzled. He wondered why he was speaking like this. They had never touched on this subject before.

"I don't think it's that bad, Wolle. At least the scientists meet here and give talks and write articles. They are all open to criticism here. It's a perfectly rational and fair way to share scientific knowledge and keep the standards high. Besides, it's open to anyone."

Wolle became agitated. "Yes, if you have travel money and money to work on a project. Yes, if you work to build your supervisor's reputation. Yes, if your professors want to support your funding applications. Yes, if you don't have enemies like Roos and Peter! But if you are alone and think differently, even with the brightest idea, you don't have a chance. It does not matter how great your ideas are, not in tens of years anyway."

He paused, sipping the wheat beer from his tall glass. Soon he continued.

"Besides, they interact within their own closed circles or clubs. Look around! You don't have to be an anthropologist or a social psychologist to notice the closed groups even here. That's where the definition of good science, peer circle building, takes place; it does not happen in the heavens! There is no Jesus of science. Some call this behavior, politely, a paradigm. To me, it seems like a waste of time!"

Wolle was unusually excited about his criticism of the professional scientific world, but Johan couldn't resist testing, even teasing, him further.

"Well, why do you work at CLASH then? Why do you write your articles and visit the conferences, even the workshops at Stanley? You are actually supporting the system you criticize!"

"I'm a member of the scientific community and remain so, yes. But that's not everything. To me, science is the most important movement of mankind, and we should promote that, not the fame of the ambitious and often sick and greedy individuals. It's not simple, but I'm not passive. I try to change the system!"

"What do you mean?"

Wolle scanned the bar as if making sure no one was listening to them. Johan was surprised to see Wolle's, unusually fragile posture, since he usually had such grace and style. He seemed very nervous. He turned to Johan:

"This all will change, and it has to change if we want to make sure science becomes possible for everyone on earth. The fame game of the elite must be broken, and I know it's possible." Then he became silent, staring Johan, serious, before continuing, his forehead had deep wrinkles:

"Sorry to bother you with this, I'll tell you more later. Let's go out and walk back to the Opera. I have my car there. I'll tell you one day, but now is not the time. You have enough troubles on your shoulders already."

"You cannot avoid answering just like that!"

"Well, record my brain then; the truth must be there somewhere!" Wolle laughed, stretched, and stood up, waving to Johan to follow.

On the way towards the Opera, Johan could not help watching the homeless men and women, young and old alike, sitting on the street together, talking to each other, some lying asleep or unconscious, everyone with shabby looks and many of them extremely dirty. Wolle could tell by the worried look on Johan's face that the scene had an impact on him.

"Perceiving them, do you now see what I mean by claiming that science is the number one movement of mankind? The politicians will do nothing about this. These poor people on the street may well die here; it's the invariant part of the American dream, which is out of their reach."

Johan did not know what to say.

They entered the small corner shop they had seen earlier, to get the groceries Johan had promised to take to Yvonne. The same young, black guy they had met before greeted Johan inside the shop.

"Thanks for the beers! Do you have another five bucks to spare?"

He had a wide smile on his face, revealing his rotten teeth and the dark holes left by the missing ones. To Johan's eyes the man had an aura of intelligence and humor, so strong that he was ready to ask him something he had never dared to ask the men living on University Avenue.

"What has happened to you? Why are you on the street?"

The man became very serious. A sharp flash in his eyes disturbed Johan, but he did not try to avoid the man's intense gaze.

"I had a firm and I made bad, very bad investments. It was not about the money, but about the people who were my partners. They started fighting in the company and we failed our customers. It did not take long, and we went down. My partners managed to save their own money, by getting out sooner, but I tried to get the last buck and lost. I had no insurance or anything. I drank too much, but I'm OK now."

"What were you producing, or was it a service of some kind?"

"It was a digital learning and collaboration app, three years ago, a really novel and special system. My clients thought it was revolutionary. But it's too late now."

Johan was surprised by the articulate and professional manner the fellow told his story. He did not look sad at all, as if he had told it so many times that he did not care; it was history now. Johan was curious and continued asking the man about the overall details of his firm and the technology they had used; the fellow's way of speaking about his firm convinced Johan he was not being fooled. It took only a few phrases and descriptions of the system to fully convince Johan of the young man's genuine knowledge. He was not a fake.

"Are you trying to get out of the streets, seriously, I mean?"

"Sometimes, yes, but not right now; I'm fine with my friends here and begging. I collect bottles and I've found shops that donate food to my friends and me instead of throwing it away. You know, there's a firm that asks people who move to donate their food they don't take with them, and I can help those in worse trouble than I am. I have something simple to do and I might try back again one day, but it is difficult. Look at me, you know!"

Johan shook hands with him, saying, "I'm Johan. I work — or, worked — at Stanley. Made some bad investments in people there, too, and at home. I don't have any money on me right now, but is there a place I could send a few dollars, to help you?"

"Thank you. I'm Don Mayer. I still have a mailbox; I'll write it down for you. Why would you help me, though?"

Johan asked for a pen and paper from the shopkeeper, an old, gray-haired man who had silently followed their discussion and handed them straight to Don. Don wrote the address and gave the wrinkled note back to Johan.

"It's a long story," said Johan. "I'd just like to start again when I'm better off. Your app is not my field, but I'd like to help."

They left the store, Don's comment ringing in Johan's ears: "You're a strange chap, but thank you, some Viking Jesus you are!"

Walking towards the Opera, Johan turned to Wolle and said, with a sad smile, "I got your point. I mean, I must find a way out, try to see other opportunities, like the guy we just met. He was helping his poor friends. My problem is I really don't know the life outside the science communities." Wolle did not say anything, only continued his quiet walk with Johan.

It was early evening when they arrived back at Stanley and Wolle parked in front of Yvonne's apartment, once more instructing Johan to remain passive in his current situation, not to start an open struggle with Roos and Peter.

Finally, he turned in his seat towards Johan, serious, a calm and composed look on his face, and said, "I have learned to know you as a true scientist; don't give up on that; you are a good man; there are always alternatives. Listen to Yvonne and remember the pigs!"

Then he hugged Johan and tapped him on the shoulder as a sign of goodbye.

"I'll keep in touch!" he said.

Johan was moved; he could only quickly utter his own "goodbye" as he stepped out of the car. He leaned down to look soberly into Wolle's eyes through the car window, but Wolle looked serious again as he waved and drove off.

Chapter 13
The Story of Wax

Johan was surprised to meet Yvonne at home. She was resting but had already recovered enough to continue working on the outline of her manuscript on x-ray crystallography of some virus Johan did not know much about. She was visibly happy to see Johan, but immediately noticed his serious looks.

"What has happened? You look pale. Was it about Wolle?"

"No, no, we had a wonderful, remarkable meeting, but it felt so bad to see the homeless people in San Francisco. I even talked to one of them, a sad story to hear, although the guy seemed to be somehow OK. I want to help him when I can; I've got his contact info. My troubles are small by comparison."

Yvonne was silent for a moment and Johan thought he saw a tear on her left cheek when she stood up from the desk and approached Johan. She said,

"I know, I know. I've seen it in Shanghai, even in Paris. It's global. We should do something about it everywhere."

She changed the topic, trying to cheer Johan up.

"Let's play house, and have a proper dinner. I've prepared some green salad with figs and oranges and some nice spices in the dressing. There is some wine for you too. I think I'm not ready for it yet. You can prepare the chicken breasts."

She came close to Johan to face him. She did not touch him, but just stood there, calm and smiling, until Johan felt awkward about the intimate situation and began to unpack the grocery bags.

Johan cut the chicken, and prepared it using pepper and salt and some spices unknown to him, but that Yvonne suggested, warning him to use them sparingly.

Then Johan began to relate all his troubles, telling the whole story in detail, from the first encounters with Wolle, to his phone call with Siiri, who let him know that his second year would not be funded. He told Yvonne everything, right up to being kicked out of his apartment, and wandering through Palo Alto, ending up at Caltrain, when he sensed the strange curtain floating in front of him. Yvonne had saved him, and today he had had another touching event: the meeting with Wolle. As Johan talked about Wolle, however, he began to feel gloomy again; he told Yvonne how Wolle had advised him to stay passive and see if Roos and Peter would give up or at least let him find work elsewhere.

"What if I can't find a new position, though?" Johan asked, raising his gaze from the chicken already sizzling in the pan, but again before continuing his gloomy comments, Yvonne interrupted him:

"They cannot prevent you from everything. They may harm you, but they are just playing. They are not as powerful as you think! They can't kill your brain. It's a power game, a game." Then she surprised Johan, by lightly touching his right arm. "Who is Siiri, by the way? Why did she help you?"

Johan blushed; he had a sudden flash of memories about the intimate night with Siiri. He had told Yvonne about the hacking, but he was sure he had not mentioned Siiri's name and wondered how Yvonne had discovered Siiri's involvement.

"She's a friend and a colleague. I don't know, I don't have a faintest idea why she did that. Sorry, I don't want to burden you with this, sorry."

Yvonne laughed.

"A good friend, I see! You are totally red in the face!"

She continued to laugh heartily. It was the first time Johan had heard her fully relaxed, lovely laughter, which matched her surprisingly low voice and wide smile so well. Yvonne rubbed the top of her head with both hands.

"Ohh, it hurts to laugh, sorry!"

Johan could not say anything; he just looked at her with a somewhat nervous but attentive gaze, trying to remain serious, but then he burst into laughter too. Johan prepared the chicken and then put it in the oven to bake. They sat down on the couch, still laughing, waiting for the chicken to be ready, every now and then gazing at each other. Yvonne was the first to recover from the laughter.

"Johan, I agree with Wolle's suggestions to you. If Peter and Roos can avoid it, I think, they will not do it, start the whole process for real, the inquiry and a possible investigation. They will need strong evidence and the faculty people must interview you and other witnesses. Nothing serious has happened yet, only that they risk their own reputation if they continue and fail. If you start openly telling what you and Wolle have been up to, everything about it will be documented. For them the easiest way out is that they scare you, and you just leave Stanley, let it be, disappear and let them win this round. Besides, what can you lose? You'll find work somewhere else and if they force the Dean to initiate an inquiry, there is nothing you can do anyway. Waiting and suffering here is the worst thing you can do. You must take care of yourself. Only that matters."

"I don't know. They have started the process in Helsinki already."

Yvonne turned to look right into his eyes.

"Why don't you join me and come to Paris? I'm leaving in three weeks. I can introduce you to the people there at my lab. Who knows what can be done? It's easy to arrange a guest accommodation for a few weeks; it's not expensive, and you can meet my colleagues. They are French, and they don't buy everything that happens here in this community or in Helsinki, for that matter. I have good connections and can write to them about you. Now is a good time. Nothing has happened yet. It's a slow process."

Johan did not know what to say. The idea of leaving Stanley was painful and made him uncertain, but he had his own reasons to think about Paris, about the way his father had confided in Johan about his experiences there. Paris held a different kind of attraction, something he had never told anybody.

"I will sleep on this. I don't know how to thank you enough for your offer, and besides, you saved my life. I never imagined I would ever need someone to save me. It makes me feel so embarrassed, like a small child. I will think about Paris. I love your offer."

It was already late and Yvonne's "goodnight" was the sign for Johan to go to his mattress. She was tired and still needed time to recover.

Johan was awake early the next morning. He tried to be quiet, and prepare a full breakfast with green tea, a selection of cheeses, warm croissants, raspberry jam, and a fruit salad he loved. He used to experiment with the salad, and now wanted to create a harmony between the colors and tastes of the fruits, filling the bottom of the glass bowl with thin slices of mango, then layers of blackberries, banana and kiwi, and finally decorating the top with carefully cut, extremely thin slices of fresh strawberries, arranged in the form of a hexagon. He finished it with a minuscule, purple violet in the middle.

Yvonne woke up, and joined him after a quick shower, smiling as she admired the breakfast setting. Johan was still standing by the kitchen table when she surprised him by stepping on the nearest chair and giving him a quick kiss on the top of his head.

"Nothing is impossible. Don't forget that! Thank you!"

Johan blushed, and only after a while could he look her in the eyes again.

"I have a strange story to tell you, about Paris, and why I've been so passionate about it for years, what especially puzzles me, but also scares me. It's about my father, who was an art enthusiast and could not get enough of the paintings and painters from the early 1900s, their lives and work in Paris. He loved Picasso and Braque; he called them the gods of Cubism."

He paused for a while, sighing.

"My father — his name was Sten, but I never, never called him by that name, I don't know why — well, he suffered from what seemed like a serious, paranoid-depressive schizophrenia and could, for days, live in these closed-from-us worlds, sometimes also physically, just disappearing for days, occasionally for a week or two so that we sometimes had to send the police after him, typically with no result and then he just returned. To me he could then tell something about his journey. We knew he had a substantial risk for suicide and he often threatened it when desperate. As a child, I was constantly afraid he would take his own life. I stayed awake all night, waiting, and I had frequently had nightmares about death. It was in one of my dreams that I saw, for the first time, these strange, undulating curtains or walls, like the one I saw at the crossing. They are not real walls, but they feel like it."

Yvonne did not say anything; she looked very serious. Johan was so immersed in his own history that he did not notice a tear running down her left cheek.

"Then every time father would return, it was a paradoxical relief and delight to me, and I did not know how to be angry with him for the torment and suffering he caused, especially when I was a young kid. I was always glad he returned safe and alive. He was a kind man. He would return from his journeys as if nothing special had happened and sometimes he would begin to vividly describe his experiences to me, but he never told these stories to my mother. If she happened to be around, he would remain silent."

Yvonne nodded, and said with a very low voice: "I understand, I understand." Then she remained quiet again.

"Sometime in the mid-1980s, when my father was only fifteen or sixteen, he had visited what he described as a small wax museum in Paris. I don't know if it still exists in the same place. It was somewhere near Sacré Coeur. Ever since then it was a serious compulsion to him, to visit Paris and especially the museum, which now is — perhaps it was that already then, I don't know — the Musée Grévin. Later, as a kid, I remember my friends, their families, visiting Spain and Italy for the sun, to enjoy the warm weather, to swim and relax on the beach. We never did that. Once, I think I was eight or nine then, when we could afford it, we made a family trip to Paris, where he would take mother and me to the wax museum and stay there for two hours or more; we called it the wax trip. It was no fun for me and I never told anyone about it, even my closest friends. For some reason, perhaps it was my father's mania about it that made me ashamed of it."

Johan continued, "I've never visited Grévin since. I know that famous artists have had their wax-versions there, perhaps even today: Toulouse Lautrec, Gauguin, Cézanne, even Van Gogh, I think. My father often mentioned Hemingway, whom he admired, but he did not like Van Gogh who, according to him, was 'a sick and unreliable fellow'. Father would repeat his vivid stories about how he felt there in the wax world. He said he could really live there; it was not a mere museum to him. I could not comprehend what he meant by that. Later and recently, I've been wondering if Van Gogh had something to do with his suicide; they both used a pistol, while Hemingway used a rifle."

Yvonne looked frightened, saying: "This must have been terrible time for you, to listen to the scary stories about the suicides. You were too young to understand that it could become a reality in your family, too."

Johan remained silent for a moment and then continued. "Somehow, I got used to it and learned how to be afraid, every day. But then, here is the remarkable thing: I remember his stories almost exactly, word-by-word as he used to tell me, dozens of times, but later, always the same formulation, typically when recovering from his attacks, he would say: '*In the wax museum, I am safe. It is the purest enjoyment to live there. It is real; there is care; nobody threatens me; they don't have evil plans for me, and many of them love me there. My tomorrow is the problem.*'"

Yvonne had listened to Johan in silence, appearing serious, every now and then commenting or nodding. Occasionally, she nervously touched the eye bandage over her right eyebrow. Johan observed her doing that and wondered what she might be thinking but did not want to ask her. He paused for a while as if again trying to understand the world of Sten's stories. It was his turn now to be in such a terrible situation, under the threat of people trying to hurt him. Yet, unlike his father, Johan had no other world to which he could escape. Johan looked earnestly at Yvonne.

"He would go on and on, and as a child I would just listen, trying to understand. '*Life is just astonishing there,*' he would say. He'd say he found it difficult to believe, but it was true. He would say it in exactly these words: it was '*truer than anything here at home. Of course, I know they are made of wax, it's a wax museum, for Heaven's sake, but it's exactly the reason why their wax-life does not interfere with me. They do me no harm. It's real people who are dangerous, artists and scientists alike. There is only the thin wall. There is wonderful life among the wax figures.*'"

Then Johan tried to explain his response to his father's stories. This aspect was hard, because it involved his own sense of responsibility for his father, and his childhood fear of discovering the wall in his own life.

"I still remember his stories in every minor detail; I've heard them dozens of times. I was always afraid of them and ashamed, which is probably why I remember them in such detail, word-for-word. It's been an ever-present emotional burden to me. The wall frightens me."

Yvonne nodded, and touched Johan's arm lightly, to show she was listening.

"I've never forgotten this," Johan said, "especially his story about what it was like to be transported, immersed in the wax-world. I couldn't understand what he meant. It was something about a smoke screen, a curtain or a mesh, usually invisible to him and to us — as he said — and that it blocked our perceptions of the other, better world. He told me that at first, he could make the wall transparent by touching it properly, exactly with a certain state of mind and perception, but when he started seeing something peculiar, like human figures, there on the screen, the wall somehow opened to him. It sounds insane and it probably was, as he was indeed a schizophrenic."

Johan continued in a more scientific voice. "It was not about a wormhole for moving in space-time as we physicists imagine it. He described it as an interface between different human time-spaces. To me they seem like Hugh Everett's worlds — you know him — the idea that there are parallel worlds, but which do not allow moving from one world to another. The life in these parallel worlds is such that each world consists of a series of choices, choice after choice, and each choice is irrevocable, and then the next choice and the next one. There is no way back or across the worlds; everything possible is happening all the time. Each journey in these parallel worlds has its own future, too. But my father would always come back, at least until he died. How strange it is to say this."

Now Johan saw Yvonne dry the tears on her left cheek. She tried carefully to dry the eye under the patch covering the right eye and her eyebrow.

"Of course, I thought they were his hallucinations, the grandiose confabulations of a sick man, but there was something fascinating in his stories." Johan continued, now a bit relieved, "He really did feel he lived there, in the wax world, leading an almost full life if I understood it right, almost but not quite, as he mysteriously used to say, living beyond the screen, with the artists who welcomed him. I have no idea how long he spent *there*. It could have been only seconds, minutes or even hours." Johan tried to make a joke. "He had to eat, anyway, and wax does not work that way."

Yvonne did not smile at his joke, but remained serious, silent.

"But Father also said he could not talk to them, the wax people, about everything. I did not understand what that meant, but when I asked, 'What do you really talk about there, with them?' he just waved his hands in front of him, like pointing to something ahead of him or us. I did not understand it."

Johan looked at Yvonne again, hoping she could understand all that he was saying.

"At the crossing where you saved me, for a moment, I think I had an experience of something similar to his curtain or wall. It was a scary episode. I lost control somehow."

Yvonne smiled lightly, commenting, "You are exhausted, Johan, with so many threatening experiences, no proper sleep and wandering around Palo Alto. Had I lived through such a terrible setback, a series of them, so many disappointments in such a brief time, I would be seeing Chinese movies everywhere."

"I hope it is so, but my father's experiences really intrigue me. If I come to Paris with you, I must visit the wax museum. I'm ready for it now, even curious. Perhaps it is the same one, I don't know. I've been thinking about it often and for some reason, especially last night. I'd like to join you to Paris, but how can I?"

PART III

Chapter 14
Calls in Paris

Four weeks after their discussion, at the end of the second week of March, 2016 Johan arrived in Paris. Yvonne had traveled earlier than planned and had already been there for two weeks. She had arranged a room for Johan in a guesthouse in what sounded like a research community, and had even managed to get a one-month coverage for his rent, with the condition that he give three talks about any of his favorite topics in the recent developments of string theory. The audience would be a class of French doctoral students, an easy and energizing task.

Entering his new home on the Left Bank, in the Fifth Arrondissement of Paris, on rue des Ursulines, Johan was greeted by a man in his fifties, offering to carry his luggage and show him the premises, at Villa Gay-Lussac, a charming, quiet and modernized, four-story building located behind the buildings at rue des Ursulines. From the outset, it appeared like any well-kept block house and inside it had several, modest apartments; only a few were meant for larger families, offered to scientists, innovators, and technologists at a different phase of their career from post docs to professors and chief officers of technology. In addition to the apartments, the building had three cozy seminar rooms, a modest library and a rather large breakfast room where breakfast was served every day. The founders of the Villa had quickly learned how valuable such a gathering place could be for their visitors. Many of them praised the times when at breakfast they could meet brilliant and skilled scientists or engineers from around the world, and from any discipline, with whom they could have inspiring discussions over breakfast. It was an exceptional hub where curious minds could meet.

"Welcome to Villa Gay-Lussac; we are glad to have you as our guest. I'm Bernard. There are other theoretical physicists living here, too; I hope you will enjoy their company. They are in different fields from yours, but everyone here has an interesting background. You might know that many of our visitors work with companies and in academia. Two of them are specialists on the mathematics of the string theory, applying it to different problems, not only to quantum gravity as you do."

Johan was surprised by the knowledge the person carrying his bags had; he had assumed the fellow was simply the caretaker of the Villa.

"Nice to meet you, Bernard, but how do you know my field?"

"We saw the documents and it was easy to see that you are working with string theory and quantum gravity, and some recent work on CERN proton-to-proton collision data, if I understood right? You are not alone with these topics here!"

Climbing up the stairs to the third floor, following Bernard, Johan felt a rush of excitement about this new home. Bernard continued to talk in such a friendly and trusting way, as they walked up together, that Johan could not find a suitable moment to ask for an explanation of his excellent knowledge. Johan was startled by the comments on the collision data, especially since he had worked on the CERN data only at Stanley, and had not yet published his research yet. He imagined Yvonne might have been the source, but he did not bother to ask for details; however, he was happy to get into his room. Bernard did not stay to wait for a tip, but only wished him welcome.

"Enjoy!"

This new, temporary home was a total, unexpected relief for Johan. Before even starting to unpack he fell on the couch and stayed there, observing the nice, clean modern flat with one bedroom, a cozy living room, a small kitchenette and its table; it was everything he would need. The move had been smooth, as if nobody had resisted it, and he was welcome there. It was a strange feeling after the total disaster and all the obstructions he had met in everything he had tried to do at Stanley. He had not yet heard anything from Helsinki. It was a mystery why it had been so easy for Yvonne to find the place. He knew she was always extremely effective, but Johan felt sure that she could not have done it alone; someone had to be favorable to him, somehow. The Villa could not be open to just anyone.

He called Yvonne to tell her he had arrived and to ask if he could meet her as soon as possible. She was very busy and promised to be in touch after a few days. Johan was disappointed and surprised that she did not have time to see him immediately, and wondered what could be so important to her.

In California, Johan had been alone in the apartment after Yvonne had left for Paris. They had only a simple farewell dinner, knowing they would meet soon, but Yvonne was so busy with her moving that they did not have much chance for talk or further planning of Johan's visit. The idea was simple and promising to Johan: Yvonne would arrange a place for him to stay, probably at a visiting scholars' premises that she knew.

Soon after she left, Johan had started to feel inundated by his father's stories about Paris. His memories of these stories had kept him half awake at nights, with vivid, colorful visuals hovering in front of his closed eyes. He could recall, almost hear, word-for-word, his father's passionate warning: "The Metre tells it all, the frauds that spoil you if you don't resist, the games that strangle you; go and see it for yourself!" He had vivid dreams, almost every night.

The story his father told about Delambre and Méchain, and his own recent experiences at Stanley came to the dreams and the disturbing historical events were painfully mixed with his own reality; he could not figure out why his father's words kept commanding him so forcefully. He recognized his dream-visions as lucid dreams, feeling all too real and rich in detail. Restless, alternating between the states of being awake and asleep, he had remembered the warning from his father's psychiatrist and had felt frightened about following in his father's path. The doctor had explained how Sten had a tendency for lucid dreaming, and that there was a possible link between such peculiar forms of dreaming and the ensuing psychotic states. He had said that the borderline between wakefulness and dreaming could become fuzzy and sometimes seriously disturb the sense of reality.

Now in Paris, Johan knew, in his best rational mind, that he could try to live like a free man, having spent his time like a prisoner at Stanley after all that happened there. He was recovering and could even make a joke of it, telling Yvonne on the phone how he had gone through a real first-person prison experiment. Lying on his back on the couch, lazy, observing the high, classically decorated pinkish ceiling, Johan started humming his song of grief, trying to relax but the dark side of the lyrics kept haunting him.

He decided to see the Metre of his father's story. Maybe if he could see it for himself, he could start to figure out how to live free of "masters" and injustice. He hoped he could find a way out of this feeling of academic imprisonment that still found a home inside him. He had escaped Stanley's "social prison", but he wondered if he could find a way out of the mental prison inside his mind.

Johan quickly discovered that the Villa Gay-Lussac was meant for international researchers. It was a charming place to stay and a lively community, in a well-kept modernized building, in a most exciting, historical environment of Paris.

Johan had read about the encouraging mission of the place as *"a home and creative hub for innovative scientists, technologists, business people and all creative minds. A place to make a healthy and beautiful future happen."* It sounded like an unusual mission to him, having experienced the reluctance of Finnish academia to seriously consider these different worlds as supporting and complementing each other. At his home university in Finland, they had been treated like Everett's perfectly exclusive parallel worlds, without a chance to travel from one world to another, from businesses to academia. Political talk about "collaboration" was frequent and admired, but only rare daredevils had found the forbidden wormholes between these different worlds and survived the journey. He decided to find out why the Villa was so dedicated to supporting a mutual relationship between universities and business.

The Villa and its location, were the best environments in Paris Johan could have dreamed of, close to many university departments, and of course, the University Pierre and Marie Curie, UPMC, even the Curie Museum, and within walking distance of Notre-Dame and Jardin du Luxenbourg. He had not forgotten the wax museum, but the most enchanting, nearby academic attraction was Collège de France, the place where Einstein had given his famous talk on the Theory of Relativity. The lecture had taken place on Friday the 31st of March at five p.m. in 1922, ninety-five years before, in Amphitheatre VIII with prominent academics and other curious people present.

It was no accident that Johan remembered Einstein's talk in such exceptional detail. He had carefully read and studied the story by a journalist, who had been present on the occasion, writing about it and the atmosphere of the peculiar meeting. This journalist had commented ironically on the audience for Einstein's talk: "There were truly very few famous actresses or high-society ladies, in this gathering of dignitaries whose compressibility was put to such harsh trial." Johan had imagined that it must have been a crowded meeting, uncomfortable, perhaps for the non-scientist elite.

Johan had memorized the intriguing facts ever since he first read the story and the philosophical-physical impact of the meeting. Not only did Einstein's Theory of Relativity awaken the physicists, it made some theoretical physicists and mathematicians lose their temper, and it seriously irritated a couple of dominant philosophers of that time; indeed, some of their conceptions of time now met a tougher test than ever before. No wonder then that many of the philosophers and journalists just discounted Einstein or made fun of him in their comments and writings. The gathering had significant, unforeseen, indirect consequences.

During his first week at the Villa, Johan had no engagements and he did not meet Yvonne, who only once called him to say that she was still busy. Johan had time to study and read the scientific journals he had missed during the conflict at Stanley, and had soon updated his knowledge on the latest works relevant to him.

Being in Paris, he began to visit art museums, too. He had looked at art very little in his life, yet now, surrounded by such beautiful paintings at the Louvre and the Musée d'Orsay, he found himself increasingly curious about the mathematics of art, especially in the famous works by Picasso, something his father had often mentioned. Johan wondered if his father's stories about Picasso's paintings held more than psychotic dreaming, and could help Johan now, in ways he could not yet know.

The famous work *Les Demoiselles d'Avignon* had, in fact, been Sten's favorite topic in the arts. Describing it, his eyes had shone, and he had smiled, describing how the simultaneous and opposing perspectives in the painting opened their doors to him: "I could see different worlds at the same time, in a way it is impossible to see otherwise. The doors were wide open, begging me to enter, but which one to choose?" It had been impossible for Johan to understand what his father had meant by the open doors, yet now he felt the urge to understand this phenomenon that had so delighted his father.

At home Johan's family had owned a large poster of *Les Demoiselles*. It had been an embarrassing surprise to the teenage Johan, at first, to learn that it had originally been named *The Brothel of Avignon on Avinyó Street in Barcelona*. His father had mentioned this matter-of-factly, and yet as soon as Johan had understood that these five figures in the painting were actually five prostitutes, each one in a curious, sensuous and partly unnatural posture, he had experienced a strangely sexual, fuzzy excitement and shame whenever he had gazed at the image. Despite this embarrassment, he had sensed the open invitation of the women in the painting, their call to enter the world of art, making him even more uncomfortable and curious.

Johan had already embarked upon his study of mathematics at the university when, staring at the painting on the living room wall at home and reading about its history, he had started to comprehend that the famous painting was not only about whores. Just as his father had tried to articulate, this image offered a novel and creative representation of its characters and their backgrounds, based on a complex analysis and simultaneous depiction of different geometrical viewpoints. It was an unusual combination of art and mathematics that had given Sten such joy. Johan had started to see how the painting was meant to shake and disturb anyone used to classic and realistic art forms, and how perhaps even the questionable content served that purpose.

Alone in his new home and study at the Villa, looking at the photos he found of this painting, Johan had time to study it carefully. He felt moved by its power to question people's habits of perception and thought. To his modern theoretical physicist's mindset, it was not difficult to imagine why it had been challenging to position such a work with the multiple perspectives and even the fourth dimension in the classic art scene. Indeed, reading up on this subject now, he learned that Picasso's *Les Demoiselles* had been a teasing problem to the art critics and to many of the artists at that time, and of course it had been too much for most viewers, who used to enjoy paintings describing what they thought of as the one and only real world. Johan could now understand such views as blind realism, not much different from the trust in the classical Newtonian physics.

For the mathematical mind, it was easy to admire the conceptual novelty of *Les Demoiselles*, a truly astonishing work. Having free time in Paris now, Johan could, for the first time, make a sincere effort to learn about this kind of art, trying to understand how Picasso — the artist, not a mathematician — had ended up creating such a wonderful, revolutionary style. It was no surprise then to learn the art historical fact that it was in exactly this painting where Picasso transformed painting to something beyond photography and the classic representation of reality.

There was one more surprise waiting for Johan, when he studied the representation of the fourth dimension in arts. Arthur I. Miller's scholarly work *Einstein and Picasso* struck Johan so powerfully that he felt it could have been written directly for him, personally. He was immediately overwhelmed to realize how the worlds of classical mechanics and figurative arts had been transformed by these two geniuses, practically at the same time in history and by two men who had never met each other. Johan's first thought was that there must have been a kind of a human-cultural bond between them, even something like entanglement and the spooky effect in quantum physics. He became painfully aware how little he knew about cultural history and the arts.

Johan knew, in full detail, what Einstein had done and accomplished, when all that had happened. He knew the exact years, dates and places; however, Picasso was a mystery. Reading the book by Miller, he could, for the first time, relate the two geniuses in a way possible for a physicist to understand. When Einstein gave his speech in 1922 about relativity at the Collège de France, not far from the Villa, Picasso had lived in Paris, too, although he had already finished the revolutionary *Les Demoiselles* in 1907, at the time when Einstein had begun to develop his theory of general relativity. Johan was baffled by the amazing coincidences and realized he had no words or even basic concepts to formulate his own thoughts about the overlapping transformations in art and physics. He was helpless in trying to relate the two transformative developments. It was a problem of several magnitudes more difficult than any of those he had met in the analysis of proton-to-proton collisions.

The insight was a humiliating and inspiring experience, to realize his own professional and personal limits in trying to figure out how the sciences and visual arts could interact, or were entangled, as he formulated it in his physicist's thoughts. His first and the only serious encounter with visual arts and artists had been when reading about the colored shadows he had observed and admired on the nightly skating rink as a young boy. The fond memories from the late winter nights on the frozen lake reminded Johan of his present situation. He felt as if he were skating now on fresh, untouched, mirror-like new ice in the dark, eagerly waiting for tomorrow, to see what he had accomplished.

One more joyful realization for Johan was that the Institute of Henri Poincaré was within walking distance from the Villa. From the history of modern physics, Johan knew Poincaré well. Among the great achievements of this famous mathematician and theoretical physicist was that he had been among the first, perhaps *the* first, to suggest the existence of gravitational waves.

Studying the life of Picasso, Johan had found out about a mysterious link between Poincaré and Picasso: a mathematician in the first few years of the twentieth century — an admirer of Poincaré — had also known and admired Picasso. This mathematician had given informal lectures about the fourth dimension to Picasso and his friends, and in this way had carried and translated, or possibly transformed, Poincaré's early ideas in a form that Picasso may then have used for his inspiration.

Johan had been enthusiastic to learn how an artist would seriously study and consider four-dimensional geometry for his own painting style, and even make several fascinating sketches and drawings of it, all this happening at the same time that Einstein was writing his masterpieces on time, space and gravity. It was an exciting thought that Picasso had so early made the fourth dimension available to people admiring his work.

Johan's research into the history of art brought him to a less rosy insight, however. He could see that the artist's world was not so different from what he knew about the dark side of the sciences. Picasso had not had an easy time with his novel approach, what came to be called Cubism. His revolutionary creativity had triggered devastating counterforces that hurt not only him, but also infected his friends and colleagues as the forces were social in nature, almost like a deadly disease. Together they had had to face the arrogant, purist opposition. Johan could imagine how at that time the concept of three-dimensional, ordered, and rational space must have been a holy property of the universe: touch it and even worse, twist and bend it, and a person could end up in trouble with the elite of science and the arts.

A week in Paris had passed; Johan had organized his life a bit and was grateful for Yvonne's help, as he only knew a few words of French. The days went by fast, as he adjusted to his new life and living conditions. He would not call this adjustment "therapy", but he became aware of the therapeutic effects of building a life at such a healthy distance from his recent problems and pains.

Johan wanted to describe to Yvonne his new excitement and enthusiasm about Picasso, art and physics, and this new home she had helped him find. In Palo Alto he had felt uncomfortable to talk to Yvonne about his real interest in art; he had felt it was too far from the world of physics and too near the problems of his father. He longed to have the chance to see Yvonne again soon at a museum, or even just at a café, and to talk about all of these new inspirations.

It was Monday morning when Yvonne finally called him and said she was free. They decided to have lunch, and Yvonne suggested they meet and celebrate with champagne at Les Ursulines, a traditional, modest brasserie, next to the Villa, on the corner of rue Gay-Lussac and rue des Ursulines. Gay-Lussac, born in 1778, had been a famous physicist and chemist every student had heard of at school. Living in the Villa now and navigating among the street names referring to historical French heroes and celebrities, was to Johan like joining a dense network of physical and symbolic signs and names, pointing to the magnificent European history of science.

This was in striking contrast to Palo Alto and Stanley, where the street names so directly and in a downright manner reflected American history and the heroes of capitalism. It was rare to see names of any of the prominent European scientists there. Street names like Lagunita, Panama and Serra at Stanley had their stories to tell in the US, but they did not resonate with Johan's own academic history or his European identity. Still, the Jobs Computer Science Hall, Bezos buildings, even Volvo Building with its Nordic background on the Stanley campus had their immediate impact, with the same local-historical power as Villa Gay-Lussac now showed Johan in Paris.

Waiting outside the brasserie, Johan saw Yvonne, at a distance, approaching in a hurry with her energetic stride along rue des Ursulines. As she came closer, he could see her broad smile. She came straight without hesitation to hug Johan, firmly, her hands on his shoulders, eyes shining.

"I'm so happy for you, for this new opportunity! Here — in Paris!" she exclaimed.

Johan gave her a big smile as he took her by the hand and led her to the entrance door.

Inside a waiter, a young man in his early thirties perhaps, welcomed them from behind the bar desk. He was immersed in reading a thick book on his lap, but he stood up eagerly, and hastily put the book aside when they entered. Curious about his behavior, Johan caught a quick glimpse of the cover of this book and saw that it was a recent and advanced university book on modern physics, a book he knew well in English, and one he did not expect to see in this context. He looked at Yvonne, lifting his eyebrows as a sign of admiration, and made his guess.

"He's probably a doctoral student here somewhere, working part time. Who knows? Maybe I will meet him in another context."

Les Ursulines was a traditional Parisian café-bistro-brasserie that had its entrance at the street corner. Less than twenty, small reddish-brown wooden tables crowded the cozy space, while a few paintings and posters decorated the walls. The large windows offered views of the streets. A small separate bar area invited people for a quick lunch or instant celebration with wine. The back wall was lined with a row of couches with violet-brown, slightly worn, leatherette covers. Only two couples were enjoying their early lunches, and two other waiters, a younger one and an older man, were immersed in a conversation at one of the side tables.

Johan asked for a quiet table. The waiter took them to a corner table at the back of the café. Sitting down, they ordered two glasses of champagne, and the waiter suggested that they test the house champagne, which he then brought immediately, showing the bottle and describing its origins from Ludes. Johan did not want to reveal his ignorance of champagnes. He did not know where Ludes was.

Relaxing at the table, facing the smiling Yvonne, Johan began to eagerly describe his acclimatization; he said he was already beginning to feel like a European in Paris, even after such a short time. He was excited, hands waving in the air, just as he had often been in Palo Alto. Then suddenly, he turned serious, and explained how he had enjoyed Stanley immensely. As he thought about it, he felt that even the terrible encounters there had not abolished the best of his memories and inspirations; the pain and frustration had originated from only a few people, not from the place and they could not erase its meaning to him. From the first days at Stanley, he had felt like an enchanted and welcomed outsider, one among the many, like anyone from India, or from other Asian and European countries. It had not bothered him at all to have no real, local connection there.

"I knew I was an invited and accepted member of the Stanley community, a respected, perhaps even a close colleague at the lab and the department, but then again not, as I immediately experienced when the problems arose. It was painful, a serious disappointment, a breaking point in my committed idealism. It initiated a new kind of disbelief in me and I cannot get rid of it even now. It's like a vibrating, separating wall between them and me. I was never before so acutely aware of the personal distances, and I had taken it for granted without ever thinking about it. I had thought I would get support in times of trouble. The lack of support broke me."

Yvonne, possibly hoping to divert Johan from his thoughts about Stanley, changed the subject, as she leaned across the narrow table towards Johan.

"Johan," she said, "I'm confused by the story you told me, in Palo Alto, about the wax museum here in Paris, and the way your father experienced it. Then there is your imagining of a wall, between you and the Caltrain. There is so much I would like to understand about you, Johan! Do you still think about that image of a wall, and what it means to you?"

Johan was startled. "Why do you ask that? The wall was scary and real, to me at least; it's not a fairy tale at all and it's not a physical wall; it's more like a nightmare."

"What is the *wall*, then, the silky, opaque curtain you always refer to? Is it only a metaphor, an illusion? Or something real to you? Are there people behind it? I just cannot understand it. It sounds frightening to me."

"I don't know, but seeing or experiencing it was very real, more than just perceiving something. I was so aware of its presence that it became somehow tangible to me. It has happened a few times now and it's always the same, even in different situations. It makes me remember what my father told me about the scientific fraud behind the Metre. He used to say: 'How can you not see it? There is a wall hiding the truth from you, why can't you see through it?' Of course, I knew it was his paranoia. But then at the rail crossing, the first time I saw the wall myself, it was the most devastating experience, a very realistic one. It was a wall between this life and something else. I was not only sensing or perceiving it, and neither did I *see* it in the sense we see *things*. The awareness pierced my whole body, so that I became able to see through the screen, as if it was a channel to another world, but still not to death, to something different, somehow visible. It felt like two parallel worlds; I cannot explain it. Only Everett's parallel worlds and the story of Tuonela in our national epic *Kalevala* come to my mind now. But this was no river of death."

Then he smiled. Yvonne had succeeded in interrupting his depressive slide and he was full of energy again.

"I did not see any angels or devils there, if that's what you mean, but there were some kinds of Gestalts I could experience, but not see in detail, clearly familiar characters or objects but I don't know why.

"What do you mean by 'Gestalts' there?" I know it's a kind of a philosophical concept, a German one?"

"It simply means seeing the whole of something, something more than the sum of its details. It is not possible to explain the perceived whole by a simple sum, or even a weighed sum of the visible details. The wall was something like that; I'm not sure about all of its details. Haven't you ever have experienced anything like that, even in your dreams?"

"Never. What is that *Kalevala* story, the Tuonela, then?"

Johan smiled, "Your French accent sounds almost erotic when you pronounce 'Tuonela'. It's the place for the dead in our national epos *Kalevala*. You make it sound like an invitation to a charming Parisian night club!"

Yvonne was not annoyed by the comment, and smiled at Johan, even flirtatiously, but then became serious again.

"You sound like a new age prophet talking. You should do

something about that before it sucks and kills you. You should talk to a shrink."

"I've seen enough of them, believe me, treating my father. No way! They make things worse."

"Do you know that we are building a magnetic stimulator system at the lab with the hospital? It's used for treating depression by stimulating the brain at certain locations. We call it transcranial magnetic stimulation, or TMS for short. Surely you know the method? It is known to work on serious depression. We have neuropsychologists and neurologists working with us, who know how to use it in therapy."

"Yes, I do know it, even too well, and I'm not depressed, I'm just too exhausted and confused. I need time to recover."

"But you just cannot go on living with your walls, Johan. I feel that you must forget them. If you cannot forget them, and you don't like shrinks, then why not take the wall by its horns and go to Grévin, to see for yourself and get rid of the illusion and your strange imaginings?"

Johan laughed at Yvonne's image of taking the wall by the horns.

"The wax museum here?"

"Yes."

Johan was quiet for a while, remembering the boring visit as a kid to the museum, years before with his father. Later he had become intrigued by it; he was not afraid of the place where the wax figures appeared like animations in 3D, nothing more. They were dead dolls, not interesting in any way. Now he grew uncertain, whether Grévin would be the best place to visit first.

"Do you know the meter standard still exists here in Paris and not only in a museum? I could start from the Metre. It feels safer and it's somehow related to the wall. My father used to talk about them both and he did actually visit the Metre, to see and touch it. For him, touching it was mysteriously significant. He would vividly describe how it seemed to melt away and vanish when he found just the right way to contact it. It was always a bizarre story. One of the original metre signs is close by here on the Northern side of Le Jardin du Luxembourg, only a fifteen-minute walk. I know, this sounds pure new age, and yes, my father was crazy, but I feel like I must go and see it for myself. Do you want to come with me?"

"No way, the whole thing is too creepy to me!"

"Well, visiting those places is better than shooting at my precious brain with haphazard magnetic fields! The physicists have no idea of what I have in my brain, but they are encouraged by the psychologists, who are ignorant as to what the magnetic gun will do, *in situ* as they so eloquently say, to my precious brain cells and everything surrounding and feeding them. The 'situ' just happens to be me. It's a modern form of witchcraft, and even better, an innovative knife to perform lobotomy, using magnetic fields instead of steel; it's nice and comfortable, they just push a button and don't need to hold a scalpel in hand and to see blood flowing, tissues incised. They should stick to rats and bunnies. Sorry about the irony here, but I've seen enough of these so-called psychologists attacking my father. I'll want to keep my precious *situ* untouched!"

Yvonne shook her head, a little sadly.

"Can you understand this, Yvonne? I have to go forward, solve the painful puzzles. They are more important than any of the career problems. This is about myself as a person, about my identity as a scientist and as the son of Sten and Karin, living with the history of my father."

"Well," Yvonne said slowly. "This sounds worse than your stories about the *Kalevala*! I cannot see how you would benefit from the fight with the wax-people and even with your father. You should build your own life, my friend! It is just insane. If I were you, I'd try to get rid of the nightmares and replace them with something healthier. Forget them, forget them!"

Johan gazed at Yvonne's earnest, impassioned face. He smiled and touched both her hands, yet inwardly. It was the first time Johan realized he had not asked about Yvonne and her life at all. He blushed.

"I have been talking about me and my problems all the time and you keep listening and supporting me. I have been stupid and selfish and not asked about your life once. I do care, but I've been lost. Can we talk about you? I want to learn to know you, I mean really know you!"

"We can do that but not now. Go to see your Metre."

When Johan was about to repeat his request, Yvonne interrupted him already before he had time to utter anything and said with her familiar low voice:

"Go! Go!"

Johan decided to see the Metre but not in a hurry. Now he grew curious, in a new way, about Yvonne.

Chapter 15
Marble, Metre and Wax

Johan had been standing silent, like a statue, for an hour staring at the Metre standard at 36, rue de Vaugirard. The brisk morning rain reminded him of the historical invariances of things that don't change over generations. The effect of the rain on people and the Metre had remained the same during their histories, with only a little variation. He felt silly standing there, as if he expected something extraordinary to happen, something like what had happened to his father, at least in his imagination. Still, Johan had grown anxious, as if something uncontrollable could happen to him right on this spot.

The flash-like glimpse of the brownish, silky-thin wall on the opposite side of the street had worried him, but he dared to look straight at the wall again. He wanted to face it, not to turn his gaze away, whatever it was and whatever might hide behind it. The silky wall had vanished. He hurried across the street, in the drizzling rain, to study the massive metal gate more closely, to touch and caress it. When he softly touched the grey, painted, and slightly rusted metal surface, with both hands flat on it, as if listening to it with his hands, an armed guard approached fast, asking or commanding something in French. Johan did not understand his words but realized he must look like an insane tourist there, caressing a metal gate, in a city still in mourning after violent terrorist attacks. Of course, the police must be worried about any suspicious actions. Johan remembered the embarrassing meetings with the guards in Palo Alto.

Then suddenly, his hands started shaking uncontrollably, and a flash of a scene opened in front of his eyes, lit by something reminding him of the color of a blue laser light, its tint familiar, but somehow distorted by a greenish, even muddy hue, lighting the whole scene uniformly in front of him. There was nobody in the scene, there was no wall, only something eerie and scary and the mud-green-blue, intense color painting the whole visual space in front of him. He felt it was pure visual experience without any visible objects. The emotions from the encounter with the guard at CLASH and then from the railway crossing in Palo Alto startled him and he could not escape from a keen feeling of anxiety.

He could barely mutter to the guard, "Sorry, sorry, I was just interested in this."

The guard looked at him, suspicious, his right hand resting on the gun on the belt, as he gestured aggressively with his other hand, explicit enough to make it clear to Johan that he should get out of there. He started walking, rushed back to the other side of the street, in the intensifying rain, hands still shaking. He found a small café, Le Renoir, open, and he entered, sat down by the window to observe the gate from a distance, ordered a continental breakfast and sighed. It was tranquil in the classic Parisian-style café; the old red-tile walls reminded him of the warm and cozy colors of the country houses of his childhood in Finland. His anxiety slipped away and he stayed there for more than an hour, recovering, going through the visions he had seen, and staring at the massive gate and the guard who every now and then stepped into the rain from somewhere Johan could not see, as if making sure the stranger would not reappear. Johan could not understand what the visions were that he had encountered at the gate: that flash, that muddy and indeterminate sense of a scene — and he had seen people behind the wall. "I must see the wax people, whatever happens," he said quietly. He started humming the Eagles song again. The lady with brown hair, wearing an apron with red-brown stripes, standing at the bar, probably the owner of the place and in her fifties, as Johan thought, looked at him, but she did not say anything, just tilted her head sideways, left and right, slowly.

The rain had stopped. It was not yet noon when Johan left the cafeteria, thanking the lady, in English, for the breakfast and for her understanding. She nodded back, answering, with a soft smile: "The garden is a place for peace and art. The gate doesn't do justice to the Jardin behind it!"

Johan headed towards the wax museum, a vivid memory of the wall and the startling flash of light he had just encountered by the gate, whirling in his mind.

Musée Grévin is located at Boulevard Montmartre, near its crossing with rue Montmartre, in the middle of a classic boulevard scene in Paris, with avant-garde shops and busy restaurants and terraces on both sides. Arriving there, Johan saw eager tourists walking, talking, and standing everywhere. The entrance to the museum looked like a gate to a luxurious cave, with somewhat Chinese nuances; it had a red, marble-like, gold-decorated, magnificent frame and the text *Cabinet Fantastique, Palais des Mirages*, written on the three-meter-high entrance arch. Johan's father had never mentioned this museum's architecture and the interior lay-out; to him this architecture had been apparently less important than the wax world, a world of trust, containing the characters and the wall invisible to others. To Sten, in fact, Johan realized now, it had never been a museum; it had been a tangible, kind and caring world.

Johan stopped in front of the entrance to peer at its detailed decorations, lifting his gaze towards the golden relief above it, two women holding the sign with "Grévin" on it, and then turned back to follow the crowd passing by. The pavement was wide; no one rushed past or bumped into fellow pedestrians or tourists standing in their way. There was no queue to the museum and nobody seemed to be in a hurry. Many of the simple restaurants near Grévin seemed more appealing to passers-by than the wax world.

Entering the wax museum entrance reminded Johan of an enchanting cave of adventures. Having bought the ticket, he headed toward the stairs, which began between two full-sized women figures dressed something like belly dancers, both appearing very real. For a second Johan thought about the *Les Demoiselles* painting and the inviting prostitutes there. These female charmers appeared more like ancient guards than welcoming hostesses to Johan, who still felt the after-effect of agitation and anxiety from his mysterious fit at the Luxembourg gate and the encounter with the guard.

Taking the first steps up the stairs, excited and nervous, embraced by the guardian women on his left and right, he had recovered enough to smile at himself, remembering the Stanley experiences and thinking: "Damn it, I've developed a neurotic fear of guards!"

On the first floor, the soft red carpet was enough to frame a gentle and safe time-shift in his mind, a better reality, and a welcoming feeling of going somewhere, back in time, far away and detached from his personal problems. A light show had already launched the museum tour in a grand entrance hall with mirrors scattered everywhere in the gold-decorated room; it looked like an infinite labyrinth, with colorful lights sweeping over the space and zig-zagging between the mirrors. Johan was not interested in *this* light show at all, and waited impatiently for the flashing lights, the echoing circus-like voices, and the uncomfortably noisy music to end. To Johan it was a futile, artificial replacement for what he felt to be the real history: the famous, historical figures waiting somewhere inside. He sensed the call from the wax-people who would not threaten but perhaps — perhaps — welcome him in some way he could not yet imagine.

To Johan, it looked like the museum had been designed as a maze, which would prevent the visitor from seeing several wax figures from different historical epochs and places at the same time and in the same place. Instead, figures of the same era were grouped together, along a maze-like design, so that Johan realized one had a sense of walking through a charming, undulating form of space-time, where each visitor, moving from one historical wax-figure and its situation to another, and then sliding on the space-time surface, along a tangible wormhole — the museum corridor — could visit the world of the next figure. In doing so, as Johan perceived, the visitor would distort the space-time with the impact of his or her own personal history, which was carried along like an aura. Each new instant of meeting with these historical characters was stabilized when the visitor remained in front of a chosen wax figure, to observe it, to adapt and think, while totally losing the sense of personal time and space. Only the future was out of reach there.

The first wax-character Johan met was Salvador Dali. He wore a dark suit and a black cylinder hat, as he stood by a statue of a Roman emperor, perhaps Caesar. Johan was puzzled by this arrangement, which did not match his theory of the space-time design of the museum. In his mind the emperor and Dali had nothing, no space-time in common. The wax-Dali did not inspire Johan, who noticed the hazy, unfocused gaze of the artist: his eyes showed no energy, something Johan would never have expected from Dali, known for his passionate, imaginative, out-of-this-world paintings and sculptures.

Standing in front of Dali, Johan remembered a story of a mystic experience from a scientific imaging conference his senior colleague, a vision scientist, had attended. It had been in 1984 in Cambridge, at the European Conference on Visual Perception, ECVP for short. A typical talk had been given in one of the classic lecture halls in Cambridge, to an audience consisting of the leading visual scientists from all over the world, especially Europe. When the participating researchers registered for the conference, several months beforehand they were requested to outline the work they had already done and describe what they were planning to present at the meeting. Typically, this was accomplished in the form of a short summary introducing the theory and methods used and the main results. The summaries could then be offered to the participants before the conference started.

One of the studies presented at Cambridge was on the visual processing of images, like faces and landscapes and a prominent researcher from Germany had used an artistic portrait of Dali as one of the test images, which were manipulated by his image processing algorithms. For this talk, the German researcher had chosen to use a painting by the Austrian photo artist Gottfried Helnwein; it was a painting titled *Salvatore brennt, 1981*, in which Dali's head is in colorful flames.

Soon after this paper had been given at the 1984 conference, a *New York Times* article had appeared, reporting fresh news that Salvador Dali, the real person, had been in a fire, suffering burns to his right leg. The members of the conference were astonished to discover this coincidence. The test photo the researchers had used in their experiments at least half a year before the conference and then shown to the scientists at ECVP, was like a premonition of what was to happen to Dali.

This story had often intrigued Johan. At the conference, the coincidence was vividly discussed in the evenings and at the conference bar, but then totally forgotten, and it remained only a historical curiosity. Yet Johan could not help thinking of the notion that the past and future could be connected, a possibility that theoretical physicists did not deny, but were not too eager to speculate about, at least in public. Similarly, at the wax museum he was facing the mix of past and present.

One of Dali's famous works had fascinated Johan: the 1931 painting *The Persistence of Memory*, with the deformed clocks, which one of his colleagues had used in his lecture. To Johan, as to many of his physicist colleagues, the strange clocks, which appear soft and melting, represented a concrete, tangible folding and twisting of space-time. After he heard this story of the 1984 conference, Johan had continued to wonder whether there could be a mystery link between Dali's way of playing with space-time and the astonishing coincidence.

Johan could not explain his fascination and had even felt shame over such new-age thoughts, but every now and then he would tell the story to his physicist colleagues, who happened to mention time travel, and speculate about the wormhole concept. Nobody was seriously interested in hearing about the Dali coincidence, even though it had happened in front of the scientists' eyes. To most physicists, this had just been an accidental, rare event like the trace of a single photon, with no explanation, even no need to explain it. It could be simply lightly dismissed as "the Dali phenomenon". Sceptics enjoyed making fun of Johan's thoughts and questioning on this topic.

"But you do know how to model the photon flow?" was Johan's comment to the those who were reluctant. No one was interested in continuing the discussion about the burning Dali; photons were another matter.

Having examined the wax Dali with curiosity, hoping to see something welcoming in it, Johan was disappointed. "This Dali is not from this world. He's lost! He's real and pure wax and only that," Johan thought to himself, remembering his father's story about the kindness of the wax people. He moved away from Dali, sliding slowly far from the soulless copy, towards the next one, a well-tanned, bald Pablo Picasso, perhaps in his fifties, with a bit of thin gray hair on his temples. Picasso sat on a simple chair, turned around 180 degrees, facing the passing museum guests, as he rested his right hand and arm lightly on its backrest. He looked grave and agile, even slightly suspicious or aggressive, with no signs of a smile on his face, as he sat there, dressed in his typical, striped white shirt with narrow, dark stripes and no collar. Near Picasso, a wax figure of Rodin was working on a block of something white, marble perhaps, with a hammer and chisel.

Both artists were lit by a bright white light, but even under the dazzling lighting Johan was sure he saw a different, shining light emanating from Picasso's face. Rodin was not at all impressive to Johan; the famous sculptor, known for his dynamic human statues, appeared rather static, even though he was about to hit the chisel with the hammer. Rodin remained psychologically in the background.

To Johan, the shine on Picasso's face appeared as if it originated from a real light source, located somewhere around Picasso's eyes and forehead, above the eyebrows and spreading towards the temples. Picasso's informal way of sitting on the chair made the artist easy to approach, even though the gaze failed to hide the sense of anxiety and passion, the presence of a critical intelligence that both invited Johan and forbid his approach.

Johan became increasingly curious and eager to take a closer look at the artist. He felt almost as if he were being called closer by this figure. At first, he did not understand why he had this urge, but then it struck him that it had been similar in his relationship with his father, especially when Sten had suffered the schizophrenic fits. His father too had had the same, conflicted appearance on his face and in his gestures, suggesting both an invitation and a warning. It had been this sense of conflict that had caused Johan's friends to feel afraid to approach Sten, when for Johan it had felt only natural to witness the two sides of his father's character. It had been his love for his father in trouble and pain that had made Johan approach him, just as it was now spontaneous and natural to approach and admire this wax figure Picasso. "This is not the wax artist like Dali, not at all, this is almost alive," Johan said to himself.

As Johan took his first eager and willing steps toward Picasso, to get close to him, a sudden flash emerged and a wide screen or a curtain, about 2.5 meters high and wide swung into his vision. It was the wall again, with its silky, opaque, brownish fabric, appearing from somewhere, out of nothing, as if it had fallen from the ceiling, to spread in front of Johan's eyes. Like a movie screen, but transparent, between him and Picasso, who sat behind the left edge of the screen, this shimmering sheet had a delicate, faint, almost foggy, colored version of *Les Demoiselles d'Avignon* painted on it; it was so faint that it was barely visible and transparent. This screen did not have the powerful appearance of the undulating pattern that he had seen at the rail crossing; it was instead like a harmoniously, gently undulating bed sheet hung up on a clothesline to dry outside in a fresh, mathematically kind wind, as Johan imagined, producing smooth-soft waveforms on the sheet. He could see through the wall's kaleidoscopic, geometrical nature. Picasso was clearly and vividly visible behind the sheet, his tanned skin color, and the details of his facial expression still clear, but his whole figure was being transformed in a strange, sharp-edged, geometric manner.

Johan took careful, slow steps along the curtain. His full attention was captured by the observation of how the appearance of Picasso changed when he walked alongside the screen. On the left side of the curtain the artist was already somehow slightly unnatural, deformed in his upper body, the other arm, not the one resting on the chair, but his left free hand, extending up and left, towards the wall, as if trying to open a narrow passage in the curtain. Walking towards its rightmost edge, stopping in the middle, Johan saw Picasso transforming again and being twisted in a most unnatural fashion, his head turning around 180 degrees, hands and legs disoriented, the body geometry becoming fully unrealistic and adopting forms and composition simply impossible in real life. Reaching the rightmost edge of the wall, Johan noticed how Picasso's appearance had changed from an older man towards a youngster with thick, dark hair. It was a simultaneous transformation of both time and space, a warp in the wall.

Unlike at the railway crossing in Palo Alto, Johan felt that everything was natural and not unpleasant or surprising; he eagerly, without the slightest hesitation, continued to scrutinize the scene opening in front of his eyes. He continued to walk back and forth in front of the wall, like a true experimenter, to see the repeating transformations. Suddenly, he realized what these various transformations of Picasso's figure were about: the changing geometry of the wall and the way he now saw Picasso from different directions was the same as depicted in *Les Demoiselles*, only now it was Picasso alone he saw, and not the women behind the Les Demoiselles screen, undergoing the transformations in time and space. The sheet could now be seen as a magical version of a work of art; it offered the same curtains, opening into its space, as in the original painting!

Picasso's unnaturally long, extended left hand indeed made an opening or a door to the wall, in the wall's upper-left corner. It looked bizarre, but the feeling it produced was that of a welcoming gesture and invitation. In the upper-right corner, Picasso did the same with both of his hands. The narrow spaces, the painted openings looked like genuine doors, inviting and real. "What is this, what is going on? Is this just my imagination?" Johan thought. "Do these openings have any meaning at all? Is this what my father saw? Should I choose one of the openings? Am I losing my mind?"

The worried thoughts did not stop or prevent Johan from looking closer; he became agitated to find out more. Then he took a quick, decisive step towards the wider opening in the wall, on the right from where Picasso sat, towards the faintly visible back of the rightmost, barely visible Demoiselles woman in the painting, and for a reason he did not know or even think about, he reached down to the lower right corner, when something hit him. He lost consciousness, and fell to the ground, partly through the wall. The last thought he had, just before falling, was to shout: "I'm coming through, I'm from your future!" But something choked him and prevented him from uttering the hasty words. He experienced a brownish-pink, colored but pure brightness, no dreams or visions, no scene of a dream, simply an empty but lively mental space where normally his dreams would flourish and make up his other reality in sleep, yet this was not sleep.

PART IV

Chapter 16
Beyond the Wall

Opening his eyes, Johan did not feel as if he had just woken up or regained consciousness; he felt as if he had awoken into a fresh and vivid orientation to a new day, in a compelling but familiar place, a world he had known somehow much earlier in his life. He found himself sitting on a brownish, painted wooden floor, here and there marked by odd drops of every possible color of paint. The floor shone in the bright sunlight coming through the dusty windows, which gave the light a slightly bluish tint.

Johan realized it was still daytime. Everything seemed familiar in its meaning and purpose, but different from what he was used to. He remained sitting on the wooden floor, hands around his knees, gazing around the room to find out where he was. He noticed the greenish-gray, shabby walls crowded with oil paintings, hand-written pinned papers of different colors and colored textures. Near one of the walls, a large, worn-out sofa with a velvet cover gave the room a cozy feeling. The old wooden furniture consisted of three simple chairs with woven rope as seats and a worn-out table piled high with drawings, paintbrushes and glass jars with various colors of paint powder in them. The metal jars and wooden boxes attached on the walls made Johan doubt his eyes and wonder if he was indeed only dreaming.

The room had not been cleaned for some time and he sensed a hovering odor of trash, urine, and turpentine. It left no doubt: the place was an atelier. A dozen paintings of different sizes rested against the wall behind the large stand; the painting sides were turned toward the wall, hiding their subjects and themes. A door, closed now, painted to look like a window, led to another room.

Johan felt at home here. He had no burning need to ask what had happened, and there was no one around to ask. Everything had taken place naturally, like any pure and perfect transformation. As he knew from mathematics, a perfect transformation was an operation which maintained everything in the original function, but resulted in a new form of being, with nothing lost. In the best of cases its inverse version can recover the original without the slightest loss. For Johan, the strange, comforting feeling carried an intriguing possibility and distant hope for a perfect return. He was confused, though, being aware of the conflict of his sensations, understanding he *should be* worried or even in shock, as he was totally lost while at the same time felt at home. He did not start worrying about it, however. Something unknown made him blissfully carefree about the future.

Johan felt at ease, sitting on the floor, in the middle of the room, behind a high and wide wooden easel that had been set in the middle of the room. He remained there for a few minutes, observing the space around him and then stood up, slowly, to see it properly, with no feeling of dizziness or any weakness, and walked around the easel, to see the painting on it. He did not have enough time to look at it, only noticed it was *Les Demoiselles d'Avignon*, when a young man, perhaps in his thirties, with dark hair and a neat and stylish appearance, moving carefully as if planning his every step, entered the room. He was dressed in a blue sweater with straight white trousers and a blazer, clothes that did not match at all the overall disorder and mix of styles in the room.

Johan tried to introduce himself to the man by a spontaneous "Hi…" to explain what had happened, but something stopped him, making him unable to say what he had intended.

The approaching man greeted Johan like old friends would do, surprising him with a warm and quick hug. Johan was astonished to realize he did not have the usual awkward reaction, the need to step back, when a man hugged him; this felt natural and welcome, but he did not understand why.

"Welcome again to the Bateau-Lavoir and Butte, Johan, what a joy to see you alive! Where have you been? We have not seen you for a long while! So much has happened, and you left us in grief. We thought you were dead! You do look different! What on earth has happened to you? You look as if you had seen a ghost or maybe Pablo's latest insane works. He's much better off now than when you left; remember, he had barely money for food and a proper place to sleep. Had Max not been there, I don't know what would have happened to him. Max gave him money from the little he had."

Johan did not know the man and did not know who Max was. He wondered how the happy fellow could know his name.

The man continued, with a kind smile, like a friend to a friend, relaxed, delighted, and spontaneous, ready to move on.

Johan tried once more to explain what had happened in the wax museum.

"Grévin, I was visiting the wax museum..." but after the word Grévin, he could not finish the sentence. Something stopped him again, almost violently. Johan sensed a burning shame and burden, unknown in origin and difficult to grasp, but with an absolute power over him and his will. This bafflement of his language felt uncomfortable and irrational, like descriptions of the famous perception-psychological *Stroop effect*, where the viewer can clearly see and read a text like "red", "green", or "blue", but cannot, or has difficulties in naming the color of the ink by which the word has been written: for example, the perceptual difficulty arising when a word like "red" is written in green ink.

The man frowned and bent toward Johan. "Yes?" he asked. "You were saying?"

Johan felt a soft stroke of guilt for being there and for causing this person to wonder and worry. He tried again, nervously aware he was about to make a fool of himself.

"I came to Paris to work on..." He tried again to finish the sentence, but the words would not come; he could not say what he meant. It was impossible to explain what he was doing in Paris. He got nervous and could feel himself blushing. What was happening to him? Had he lost his speech? Was this an aphasic attack or what? Could this have been something his father had gone through?

He tried once more.

"Hi, I'm Johan, a physicist," he said, relieved that he had found the right words.

The man looked at Johan, curious and mildly annoyed.

"Of course you are, you are not an artist, that we certainly know!" He laughed, tapping Johan on the back.

The comment was meant to be a joke, but Johan had no idea what it was about. Then he was astonished to realize that the man must have been speaking French, and yet somehow Johan could understand him without any effort, like in a dream! He had no explanation for it and was trying to figure this out when the man continued the friendly conversation.

"We have been introduced already, even spent some time together here. Do you really not remember? I'm Maurice, are you sick, Johan? It was here we met for the first time. What has happened to you? You made us almost crazy with the metre. Are you OK? I'm so glad to see you again. Have you forgotten it all? You do look like someone in Pablo's portraits. But you are hurting my ego by not remembering me!"

Johan blushed again and tried to think where he was, how he had arrived there, what did the man mean by Bateau-Lavoir and Butte, who this Maurice was, could he be the mathematician he had just read about? But he was too afraid to ask and fail again, to sound like a confused neurotic or an impolite friend. He decided to find out later what had happened. Now he did not know what day it was, although clearly it would soon be afternoon; the sun was shining through the grimy windows that looked as if they had been painted blue. Gazing out through the window, he had a view to a modest garden and sensed summer in the air; there were leaves in the trees. "Perhaps it's not April any more; it's not too cold in the room and the sun is high up," was his first thought. "This must be Paris somewhere, in any case."

Curious to take a better look at the painting, Johan walked closer to the large canvas, which covered most of his visual field in the room; it was indeed *Les Demoiselles*. Instead of the diluted colors he'd seen on the wall only a moment ago, this canvas was fully alive, smelling of fresh oil paints and charged with feminine, almost arrogant energy, the women returning the curious gaze of the viewer. The painting was dominated by the harmonious, inviting reddish colors of the human female skin, the unnatural, but nevertheless sensuous body forms and postures, the multiple, simultaneous perspectives. Johan could not resist the urge, the overpowering curiosity and the irresistible, tickling sexual drive to go and touch this painting and to see its details. Immediately he also felt spontaneous shame emerge, but it did not stop him from scrutinizing the artwork in every detail. He noticed the two openings he had discovered earlier, amid the painted curtains, on the left and right in the painting, exactly as they had appeared in the shimmering screen at the Musée Grévin, where *Les Demoiselles* had been only faintly visible. He got curious to look at the lower right corner, what had been the cause of the irresistible call there, and scrutinized the strange-looking woman figure, with her peculiar features, sitting there on the floor. The wax-Picasso he had seen during the encounter at Grévin had been vivid and sharp in its strange and continuously transforming details, reminding of the unnatural appearance of the sitting woman.

Johan turned to Maurice. "When was this painting finished? Seems like it's taken a lot of work?"

Maurice shrugged. "It's been like that only for a few days now, but I'm not sure it's finished yet. It became a monumental struggle and pain for Pablo, who almost went crazy working on it. He gave me a hard time too and made me suffer. I did not make it any easier to him, explaining all the mathematics about the four dimensions. I even drew plane projections of a four-dimensional geometrical creature for him to help his thinking, but he just got mad and wild, wanted to put all the different perspectives into the same painting, simultaneously. He's an artist, for God's sake! Give him an idea of a concept and he runs wild, twisting and turning it around and upside down, even transforming it while I must fulfill my boring duty as a mathematician: to be accurate and explicit. It's not the easiest combination!"

Johan knew now he had met Maurice Princet, le mathématicien du cubisme he had read about, but he could not figure out how Maurice knew him. Maurice continued, as if to confirm Johan's thoughts:

"You know, I'm a mathematician and an actuary. A clerk really, trying to help rich people keep their money and even make more of it. I'm not too proud of that, as you know, not with *these* people here in the Butte, but hope I can inspire the artists."

Maurice smiled, putting his hand on Johan's left shoulder, while contemplating the painting with him.

"What are you looking for in it, Johan? Pablo calls it *Le Bordel d'Avignon*; it does not sound like a proper title. Who could buy a painting with a title like that?"

"This must be Paris and nineteen hundred something?"

"The painting, you mean? No, it's from Barcelona, a brothel. Oh, do you mean here? Have you indeed lost your mind! Of course, this is Paris, how can you wonder about that? What's the matter with you, seriously?"

"I come from..." and again Johan was unable say it, to finish what he was thinking. "I'm a bit confused and tired. What year is it?"

"Even that! It's 1907, for Heaven's sake, if it helps you. You've lost your marbles on the way. Have you taken ill or is it just some pills? Pablo will be back soon with wine and bread. We'll escape to Au Lapin to get some more wine and something proper to eat. It should wake you up. He has some money now."

To Johan's amazement, Pablo Picasso himself arrived at that moment. As in the Musée Grévin, after the transformation, he seemed to be in his late twenties, about the same age as Johan. Pablo's conspicuous, thick, darkish hair had a side part on the right, and he was dressed in faded, black shorts and a white t-shirt, stained by several colors of paint. He did not utter a word to Johan, threw only a quick, sharp glimpse at him, as if frightened, but only for a second and then an angry look in his black-brown eyes. After the initial, hesitant moment he did not even look at Johan. He just passed by, practically pushing him aside, without saying a word. He threw two baguettes on the sofa, dropped a paper bag full of groceries and two wine bottles in a corner, and stepped in front of Johan, turning his back to him and masking Johan's view of the painting. For a minute or two, Pablo gazed at *Les Demoiselles* with both hands on his waist. Against the large painting he looked astonishingly small to Johan, almost like a pygmy.

"Without you, Maurice, I would have lost my mind, totally, with my blessed whores! Thanks to you, this is my way of showing my gratitude to them. I still don't understand it all, but this is how I have come to see them now. I don't think we should talk about this work any more, ever."

Johan left Pablo standing there and sat down on the sofa, still curious about the painting. He was getting hungry, as he looked at the baguettes and the wine bottles in the corner.

"Could I have a glass of wine, please?"

Maurice smiled, nodded, and offered three mugs to him and then knelt down in the corner to reach for a bottle of red wine Pablo had brought. There was no label on the bottle. He gestured to Johan to go ahead with the baguette.

Maurice took the jugs from Johan, cleaned them with his handkerchief, poured wine and handed one to Johan and then to Pablo who looked annoyed, and did not join them on the sofa. Maurice sat down beside Johan, sighing, lifting his mug like saluting to Pablo first and then to Johan and then turned to look at Johan straight in the eyes, sad.

"I've had a difficult time with my wife again. We only got married a short while ago and it seems she is leaving me already. I come here every now and then to forget the pain, and talk about more inspiring topics, but it's difficult, I cannot forget her strange attitude. I hate the feeling! I don't know what to do! That painting does not help me."

Johan felt embarrassed to listen to Maurice, to see his eyes in tears. It was an unexpected, intimate, personal matter, but he did not know what Maurice meant. He talked to Johan as if to an old friend who should know about him and his marriage.

Pablo interfered, waving his mug high in the air in frustration:

"You are too weak with women, grow up!"

"I'm sorry to hear that," Johan could only say, trying to alleviate Pablo's harsh comment, wondering what had happened, and why Maurice was so open to him.

A moment of silence ensued, and Johan had to force himself to remain serious observing the two men with their empty and worn white-blue metal mugs. He broke off a piece of baguette for Maurice, and poured some wine into his mug, and then stood up to fill Pablo's mug. Pablo did not respond to the friendly gesture, however; he did not even look at Johan and instead appeared upset with him for a reason Johan did not understand. He decided to let it be for the moment, sat down and continued the chat with Maurice.

"I've had my own problems, at Stanley. I've been seriously hurt. My reputation is gone as a scientist. I have no idea why I've been treated like that. I cannot go back. That's why I'm now in Paris, hoping to have some peace here for my lab work."

"You had these problems before, I know, in Helsinki, but isn't that a newly founded university in America? I've heard from Poincaré about it."

"How can you know... No, it's..." Johan tried to ask about Maurice's comment on Helsinki and then to explain that Stanley had had a long history already, but again the same force stopped him. He did not understand at all what was happening to his speech, worrying he might have a brain problem developing.

"Stanley is a wonderful place to work and... we have data from..." This time he could not utter the word "data" or even continue describing his work at all. Maurice, still traces of teardrops on his cheeks, comforted Johan.

"Paris is different. We have our own scientific and especially philosophical disputes and struggles here. Nothing significant happens in America and nobody here really cares what they do there in arts and sciences. You are a free man here. Helsinki and Stanley do not exist to us, as simple as that. Come on, I'll show you my projection drawings on the desk, they've given me some headaches. It's good for me too, finally having someone around again who understands my research."

Pablo did not join their discussion and started walking around the easel, every now and then stopping to view it from different angles.

Maurice and Johan stood up from the couch and moved to two creaky wooden chairs, near the door, starting an intense conversation about the various sketches of the 2D projections Maurice had drawn. Johan cheered up, realizing he could discuss any subjects in 4-dimensional geometry without any of the speech disturbances he had experienced even with the simplest stories he had tried to tell, about his personal life. Maurice explained the logic of the simultaneous, different perspectives in the *Demoiselles* or "The Whores and the Brothel" as he described it, getting excited and energized again.

Maurice lowered his voice when he made jokes about Pablo and his friends, who he said often ended up arguing about the relationship between the worlds of the paintings and the real world. He explained how he used to tease them by claiming that they all lived in a world of projection, a modern version of Plato's cave. When he explained this by using 4-dimensional worlds and objects and their 2D projections as examples, they all had problems grasping the mathematical descriptions of the complicated drawings. Sometimes Pablo would throw the sketches around the atelier or the small room at Au Lapin in frustration. He always came back to him, though, saying, "Please explain it again, I have some ideas already!"

Now Pablo interfered; he had apparently been listening to their talk but did not want to show it:

"The problem with you, Maurice, among other things, women for example, is that you don't know how to imagine worlds you don't have formulas for. I can do whatever I know to be true, but you spend your little life trying to learn new formulas!" Then he started walking around the easel again, and clearly did not expect a comment from either Maurice or Johan, who smiled at each other.

Johan got curious about Maurice's motivations and eagerness to help Pablo and be involved. It was difficult to see what a mathematician would gain from his contributions to an artist. He moved his chair closer to Maurice and tried to speak low now, almost whispering to avoid irritating Pablo.

"Why do you do this? I mean, you put so much effort in explaining the mathematics to your artist friends. Why? And he talks to you like that." Maurice didn't lower his voice at all.

"That is a weird question from you! We've gone through this several times. Look at the whores! I know your mathematical mind is excited about their postures and invitation, but you should see what is possible, not only your closed formulas, and then you might get it!" Johan did not understand the pun at all.

Maurice continued, having recovered his energy, "It's not only that I introduce math to them, to the artists here. They do whatever they like with it, with what I tell them. I have no control over them. I could never have come up with anything like the whores, whatever math I would have used. Besides, I've never visited *them, the brothel I mean!*"

Maurice put a funny stress on "them", throwing a quick glance at Johan.

"It's their way of seeing the world, I mean Pablo's and Braque's, to make it visible, what they see inside their heads. It's like the Plato cave really, only that they are free and inspired to imagine whatever might be outside there, outside the cave, even things that don't match with the shadows. With the best of my imagination, I could not do that. I'm bound by my equations and the shadows make my only available material; it's my empiricism. You see?"

"I've never worked with artists, but what you claim is that your artist friends don't care about any of the details or laws of what you explain. They do what they want, and you can only wait and see what comes out of it. Is that it?"

"Why do you say 'your'? They are your friends, too. Don't get me wrong! They do care about the way mathematics works in nature. I've seen it dozens of times and so have you. Remember? It's not mechanistic care; it's spiritual and creative. They take seriously what I explain, and they get inspired, sometimes like crazy. They care in a most profound sense, but they don't have any responsibility to do exactly as I tell them, no matter how good a mathematician I might be. I can be serious about my own stuff, but to them it is just a window or door to something novel, not only a shadow, something they see but I don't. If all goes well, they come up with something novel and strange, and if it doesn't, well…" He gave his usual graceful shrug. "I can only try to open the door to my artist friends, but I cannot enter!"

Johan was excited about the way Maurice explained his contribution to the artworks, and he remembered vividly the explanation the physics professor had given to his query about the colored shadows. The professor had been mistaken about the physics of the phenomenon, and he had tried to make Johan adopt the same false, exact physical explanation. That professor's stubborn and blind approach had been opposite to what Maurice was now saying about his way of inspiring the artists.

"I find that puzzling as a physicist," Johan said, trying carefully to use expressions which would not be blocked by the disturbing, muted force. "It's like you let something loose that you don't understand or control at all. You don't even have a probable means to predict or follow what will happen as a result of your advice. How can you then know what you encourage to happen? It can be anything, a waste of time and wasted artistic energy."

"I can't know. That's just the point, and don't forget yourself when you helped Pablo last time! Besides, it's more complicated than that. I'm the outsider. I don't have any artistic skills, and all I can do is to offer my mathematician's views and practices, those I've learned from Poincaré.

I try my best to hand them to Pablo and his friends, and doing exactly this makes me happy. It's as simple as that! I gain no professional fame from it, but I'm delighted, feeling privileged to offer my insights. I must confess that sometimes I'm proud of myself, but I say that only to myself."

Maurice was shining and seemed to forget his marital misery, full of life again.

"I'm just a clerk," he said. "To tell you the truth, I don't need to gain anything in this world. I have my salary, while these guys have lived like poor rats of art, especially when they started —at least, this is how the art critics and the establishment treated them. I enjoy seeing my rational mathematics turn into something unexpected and different, creative, even problematic art, something I could never do. Often, I think how lucky I've been to find someone like Pablo to work with, to contribute to his endeavors, being able to offer him what I have, my value. There is no way to know where it leads, if anywhere. Nevertheless, I *know,* I just know, it is the best I can do, to invest my soul in this purpose. What do I get from it? Well, think about this, Johan, what if I didn't have this chance; what would my life be then? Waiting for some sort of a final reward, other than the money I make, and then what? Die waiting? Now I get my reward every time Pablo tries something new after we have exchanged ideas. It does not matter whether he succeeds or not. And I'm not alone, there are other clerks like me, people outside the elite arts and academia, joining our circles. We just want to be part of something new being born, contributing, but not forcing anything."

Johan was confused about the reference to his past and to his earlier role as a friend, but he did not dare to try asking about it, afraid to be struck mute again. He decided to remain quiet, to see what happened next and to learn on the way. The generosity and devotion Maurice showed to the artists moved him. Maurice's approach contrasted remarkably with the way science in his own world had been organized: from the early science career on, everyone had to compete for personal promotion, rewards, awards, and fame. It was a hard game and there could be no future without success. You were encouraged to join the already best leagues of science.

Johan was struck by the way Maurice respected the freedom of the artists to interpret anything, to freely contradict any exact scientific laws and knowledge he provided to them. He could not envision what his own role could ever be in contributing to the arts in this way, yet he felt such a stirring within him, reviving his lifelong love of colors and sensations, his aesthetic and emotional response to the world. Johan's early skating experiences with the colored shadows came flashing back to him, reminding him of the power of curiosity and persistent experimentation, even when his theoretical knowledge had been thin. He remembered how it had not been possible to rely on traditional or even modern school-book optics knowledge to explain the emergence of the colored shadows: a most simple visual phenomenon.

Knowledge of another domain, of human perception was necessary. He had been annoyed by the straightforward way physicists often explained the world. It was not the explanations that bothered him — he knew them well — but it was the unspoken implication that by continuing the same physical approach, all relevant problems could be solved. Looking at *Les Demoiselles,* Johan had experienced the same enchanting excitement he had with the color shadows.

Johan had become so immersed in thought that Maurice had to practically wake him up.

"Are you here at all? You seem like you're floating in another world!"

Johan was alert again, being careful not to mute himself. "I'm fine. I have something to learn here."

Pablo had been standing in front of the *Les Demoiselles* and exclaimed to Johan: "Indeed you do!"

Realizing Pablo had been following their discussion all the time, Johan tried introducing another, safe topic to Maurice. "My friend, there is nothing to be ashamed of, being a mathematician or a clerk. Have you heard about Einstein?"

"I've heard Poincaré mention him in relation to something strange, a 'theory of relativity' he called it, and the hypothesis that the motion of clocks dilates their time. It sounded insane at first, but there was something truly fascinating about it. His ideas caused a massive dispute at the lab and the guy, Einstein, I heard, is indeed also a clerk like me, working in a patent office in Switzerland. He's kind of an existence proof, a proof that it is possible to be both a clerk and a scientist, simultaneously, an anomaly though, that such creatures can indeed survive, even prosper in science, that science can flourish outside of academia and its rites. It takes only pen, paper, and an imaginative brain, just like here with the arts and our poor artists!"

Johan was inspired again and stood up, standing in front of Maurice he tried spontaneously, forgetting his present world and the muting force, to explain how Einstein's theory of relativity had had massive experimental support and it worked even in everyday practice, and had been applied in the computations implemented in GPS systems, but it was impossible. He could only start these observations to Maurice.

"Experiments with..." He tried to say "atom clocks" but could not.

They both remained silent for a while, Johan looking nervously around, searching for any correct or possible words and Maurice looking at him, his eyes full of questions. Finally, Johan realized that it was impossible for him to talk about the future of anything directly related to these people in his own past! "Of course!" he thought, but then he became confused again, as he tried to understand why this was so, or whether this was just a weird dream or delusion? He decided to express his enthusiasm about Maurice's thoughts, through talking about the present time — 1907 — only.

Johan sat down, trying to relax. "I'm puzzled. You combine something well-defined and systematic, like your knowledge of the 4D geometry and the projections. But then you let your artist friend Pablo go wild and do whatever he wants and play with what you have offered. You never know what comes out of it. It can even be impossible for you to understand or accept what they then do with the knowledge you provide, and their art can be full of contradictions and misunderstandings. And still, there is something fascinating in it, an open window somewhere, unknown. But do you ever see works from Pablo you can immediately understand, even love and admire, after he has misused all your advice?"

"Yes, I do," Maurice said. "I often do, and I'm astonished. I'd be careful with the word 'misuse' here, you know. Sometimes I've been thinking I am the one misusing the knowledge I have."

He laughed heartily, and Johan joined in, adding, "I've never seen this kind of fuzzy, almost insane collaboration, or should I call it non-methodical interaction! You combine anything in art and science. But what worries me is, it seems you give way to the art and don't worry about the scientific discipline? Is that it? You do that on purpose?!"

"It's difficult to explain. You have to see it for yourself."

"It can't be easy! I mean, what about the systematics? How can you learn anything by running around wild with crazy ideas?"

"It's not easy. But no, running wildly does not mean we don't learn all the time. We both do, Pablo and me. Just wait and see! You have seen how hard they work, Pablo and his artist friends."

Pablo had been quiet in the background, every now and then interrupting the ongoing discussion, but not saying anything or getting engaged with them. However, Johan had observed his interest grow.

Chapter 17
Au Lapin Agile

Suddenly, Pablo rushed to the door, threw a quick, sharp glance at Johan, and waved his hand as a sign to leave, shouting on his way, "Enough talk! Lunch at Au Lapin!"

He started out, and Maurice and Johan jumped up from their chairs, as if obeying the command of a general, and followed him, exchanging smiles and funny looks. On their way, Johan stopped, abruptly, at the front door of the Bateau, opening to a small plaza. He was startled, and gazed around in amazement as he realized he was indeed in old Paris. He did not have time to scrutinize the surrounding houses and the few people he saw passing by, when Maurice interrupted his wondering and took him by the arm as they hurried to follow Pablo.

"Where is this?" he asked Maurice. "Where are we going?"

"Why do you ask? You've been there before. Are you OK?"

Johan did not know what to say. He still had no memory of any visit to this place and was embarrassed that he repeatedly made Maurice wonder what was wrong with him. He thought perhaps Maurice and Pablo were mistaking him for someone else, but decided to remain calm and not ask for an explanation, yet.

"Sorry, I'm a bit lost, don't worry!"

"I can see that! Try to get a hold of yourself! It's the place only a few minutes from here, up the hill from the square and then down, don't you remember? It's there on your right, near the Saint-Vincent Cemetery, not far from Sacré Coeur! We will walk there; it's a somewhat questionable district, but safe for us, and Pablo is at home there."

They walked, almost ran, after Pablo, who hurried surprisingly fast uphill and then along the narrow streets, crossing the surrounding, open building lots, small untidy parks, and shabby wooden huts; they even passed by a smallish vineyard. On the way, Pablo stopped to greet a young redhaired woman, perhaps in her twenties, in full makeup, dressed in a long bright-green skirt, and carrying a basket full of laundry. Even from a distance, Johan could see the sad look on her face as Pablo tapped her on the shoulder, as if to comfort her. He seemed to be saying a few words to her that Johan could not hear. By the time Johan and Maurice had reached the girl, Pablo had already continued his fast pace down the hill road. She had been crying, but Johan did not have the courage to ask her what the matter was, and only greeted the charming, sad young woman. Maurice greeted her too and threw a quick glance at Johan, tilting his head slightly as a sign of compassion, but he did not comment on her.

Johan felt uncomfortable, but soon forgot the incident. He felt strangely at ease with the scenery, as he and Maurice continued their short walk. Everything was new but historical to him. There were no sidewalks and no rush, and he could take his time, curious to observe men and women, young and old, on their daily duties and routines, carrying their bags or baskets; the men typically wore a black jacket and often a white shirt. The women wore long skirts, and some had an apron which practically swept the dusty ground. Children were playing on the streets and the few horse carriages were the only traffic. Occasionally, he saw men and women pushing their carts loaded with wooden boxes, perhaps to the shops or the marketplace. He saw similar boxes piled against the walls of houses and shops near empty carts.

Walking down the hill, they approached the Lapin Agile along a dusty gravel road, in a grubby housing landscape where a few small buildings were scattered here and there, each one surrounded by a wildly growing small patch of grass. The small terrace of the Lapin lay along one side of the modest, two-story stone building, with a few tables near the orange-pink painted wall, and a rough fence made of rugged logs surrounding the front entrance and the house corners. A dozen people, both men and women, sat outside at the terrace tables, enjoying the afternoon sunshine. Some of them greeted Maurice, or waved at him, smiling. Johan thought he saw some of the clients waving at him, too. Men were typically dressed in dark jackets, wearing black brimmed hats; not many had white ones. A few women had combed their hair nicely up and around their heads, and one of them wore an elegant, beige color, wide-brim hat with red ribbons. An old man carried a guitar, and a cello player was taking a nap by one of the terrace tables, holding tight his cello, like a jealous boy with a new girlfriend. It was already past lunch time.

Johan paused to admire the vista — the breathtaking beauty of Paris. He spotted a car parked in the middle of a road, the only one he had seen, a black cabriolet, with typical large wheels and no doors. He was eager to go and see the details of this historical car, but he overcame his curiosity and decided to stay with Maurice and Pablo at the Lapin.

Looking more closely at the customers here, he realized that he could not judge the background of any of these men or women; their clothing did not tell him much. Some appeared rather modest, even poor, with smudged faces, while a well-dressed man clearly stood out from the crowd, just as Maurice did with his personal, neat style. The place had a true atmosphere of arts and artists, mingling naturally with simple workers. Some people in the crowd showed the signs of heavy drinking with their swollen, red faces.

The cozy atmosphere of the interior welcomed them at the door, in a kind, shabby, but comfortable way. The air was filled with a sweet and bitter smell, and dense smoke from tobacco. Johan could not help making the comparison inwardly: "If I were at home in Finland, this place would be considered dirty by any human standards, and a serious health risk!" However, he remained curious to stay and observe the busy comings and goings and the inviting atmosphere.

For a moment Johan and Maurice stayed by the door and observed the modest room. Johan was puzzled by the spontaneous feeling of being welcome here, a feeling he could not explain. Pablo had already made a conquest of a table, with space for Johan and Maurice, and was eagerly, with intense, vivid eye contact, talking to a young, dark-haired, smiling woman with heavy makeup, dressed in black. Johan saw them flirting and guessed they knew each other well.

The space inside was dark; not much light entered through the small, dirty windows and curtains. The brownish, wooden walls of the main room were covered with posters and several wood carvings. Paintings of various styles and techniques, oil, graphics and watercolor, decorated the walls, and even a large full-size statue had a dominant post, standing in one of the corners. Maurice moved to the table, but Johan stayed by the doorway, quiet, every now and then giving way to the busy customers and the young waitress who rushed in or out.

Pablo was a naturally dominant figure in the scene. Johan could tell from the way he was received by the clients and the guy, probably the owner, behind the bar. Pablo filled up the small space with his charisma. Johan had totally forgotten his own clothing, the jeans and the blue checkered flannel shirt, and how they might appear in the eyes of the clientele here, but he was relieved to notice that no one seemed interested in his clothing or personal style. He remained worried about how to talk to the people and explain himself, what constraints could appear in any possible discussions, what was it he could talk about, and what was impossible or perhaps mysteriously forbidden to him.

Johan thought again about his capacity to speak French now, as if it were his mother tongue. He could not, in every detail, discern the elements of the language or tell what exactly, phonetically, it was he heard, but he could clearly and without hesitation understand it. He could easily communicate with whomever addressed him, too. It was like thinking without the awareness of speaking, something he had only experienced in dreams.

At the Lapin, Johan did not hear anyone use his first name, not even those who greeted him. Only Maurice called him Johan. It was all a mystery, but he just accepted it, trying to cope with it. Perhaps somehow, he would later understand what all this was about. This new confusion reminded him of the uncertainty he always felt when thinking deeply about his own work and what he thought about the possible but hypothetical existence of unknown particles, contributing to the results of his collision experiments. He could remain confident that they were there, the unknown creatures, and some definite laws must govern their behavior, even if it was not possible to know them, to perceive them yet, and still, it was reasonable to continue observing, measuring and quantifying them, to learn more. The sudden visit to the Butte felt no different than this, and Johan decided to accept the mystery of his new situation. Still standing by the doorway, he made up his mind to be as open as possible, and if necessary, to try to share his personal problems with these new — or were they old? — friends.

Pablo, Maurice, and the dark-haired women were leaning across the table, towards each other, forming a living, closed triangle, engaged in a vivid chit-chat. Johan joined them, took a chair and sat down beside Maurice, trying to make eye contact with Pablo and his lovely companion. Without introducing himself, Johan interrupted them, which made them turn their attention to him. The woman introduced herself as Helen, although something in the way she spoke told Johan this was not her real name. Inspired by his strange situation, without excuses, Johan offered his own topic to the discussion, something he had been thinking about when standing by the door, hesitating to join the group.

"You know *carpe diem*, meaning 'seize the moment', 'don't worry about the future', the famous quotation from the Roman poet Horace?"

Johan was glad to receive a bright smile and open look from the young woman. Pablo did not smile, but glanced at him suspiciously, eyes gleaming; it was the familiar sharp gaze again.

"So, what?" Picasso said sharply. This was the first time he had spoken directly to Johan, expecting his comment. "Is there something new in it? Isn't it our everyday life? A true artist cannot worry about the future. He'd be impotent doing that, worth nothing! History is all important but not to be followed exactly! It's there for us to discover which rules to break and how to do it! *Carpe diem* is just a false-artist's absurdity! How could you, with your blind *carpe diem*, know how to break any rules if you don't have any idea of your own history?"

Johan was not surprised by Pablo's clever and blunt comment. He paused before continuing, as if preparing Picasso himself for a surprise.

"Well, actually, I meant the purest possible version of a *carpe diem* state. Imagine you are in a state where you not only avoid thinking about tomorrow and worrying about the future, but it is impossible for you to refer to it, impossible to talk about it, about anything the future may bring! You'd be totally free from the accusation by Horace that many of us cannot live and cherish the precious present moment. I think Horace was not ambitious enough in his demand, you see. Imagine this: you do have a real future, and you may even know every detail of it, but you are denied from referring to it directly in anything you do or say."

He turned his gaze to each of his companions, one at a time, and continued.

"You can have any of the best and tested knowledge of the future world, a conviction, but there is no way you can share this knowledge with anyone else. You are like a muted God, without a voice or even pen and paper. Because of this, you will be aware of an unspoken future history as well, a history still to come, yet you cannot use it in anything you do, say, or even paint today. You are forbidden to refer to it. You know you have this knowledge, but there is no way to use it in anything you do in this world, and you are doomed to live, *a true carpe diem life!* The only way to survive such a life, a curious mental state, is not to care, to do what you know is right, but you are alone with your conviction. Can you imagine someone surviving that and living like a mute in the face of a future only he knows? What kind of life would that be?"

Everyone was quiet. Johan was surprised to notice even Pablo remained wordless. A moment of confusion was born. Pablo stared at Johan deep in his eyes, his gaze slightly softening, and Johan could sense that his words had made an impact. He knew, too, that he had spoken like a maniac. Then he saw the powerful fire return into Pablo's gaze, the direct and flaming look, ready for confrontation.

It was Maurice, however, who broke the silence.

"Now you are back and yourself again, Johan! But I don't get that! We all have a future, some know it better, some don't have the slightest hunch about it, and some like Pablo just don't care. He works and loves his women!"

They all laughed heartily, looking at each other with smiles. Johan noticed again the charming smile and twinkle in Helen's eyes. Pablo continued, now in a soft, kind and surprisingly fragile tone.

"Johan, you know me. My history is the necessary pain I have to carry with me and so is yours. I have lost a friend, Carles. You never met him, but even painting him dead did not relieve me from the suffering and the history. The pain became worse when I saw my own paintings about him. I could not color him away, to extinguish my anguish. I had no tools for *that*. But I know it is possible and I know there is another future I sense, without this pain, but I don't want to think about it now. Thinking destroys my senses. I know it from experience, having seen how most of my colleagues are afraid of the future and so are the critics and dealers. They talk and write about it but when they see it in front of their eyes, they become scared and withdraw! You should have heard what the dealers at the Bateau had to say; they made jokes about my whore painting. I had no words to explain it to them; they were blind to the time windows in it. I must have appeared like a total fool, an insane dream walker to them. I still don't have the words to describe its essence, but I know! I know *you* understand part of it!"

Johan did not know what Pablo meant by referring to him and to their history, how he "knew" him. He was moved by the way Pablo had addressed him now, with a kind tone and appearance, different from what he had seen at the Bateau. Pablo nodded at Maurice.

"Maurice has taught me that not only in my imagination, but also in my works I can fly in his fourth dimension of the universe. You can call it time and the future if you like. Nothing stops me, whatever the real nature of such a dimension, be it forward or backward in time, or some strange aspect of space or whatever, I don't want to fix my future. It's not there!" He pointed with both his both forefingers, like shooting with a revolver, to the darkest corner in the restaurant and then turned back to Johan.

"Besides, I don't think it's time where I fly for that matter. You can call it time if you so desire, but I don't know what it is. It is something to be re-understood and to be created anew. Fixing my future in time would make me an unhappy creature, with only one future, there in the back corner, that's it, and then the stupid death. How do you create anything novel if you move like a brainless train on rails?! I go wherever my any-dimensional journey takes me! Why don't you join the journey, too? Why worry? Or is it the disease of academics you suffer from? That's how it sounded to me last time before you disappeared!"

Johan was startled by Pablo's comment on his disappearance, realizing he knew something about his background. It was a matter of trust now and Johan decided to take the risk and be open with his eager listeners, wondering how he could avoid the mysterious muting by his own future knowledge.

"I have something you don't, please believe me. I'm not insane when I talk about *carpe diem*. It's all about my future past, which has terrified me, seriously." He tried to say "at Stanley and in Helsinki" but couldn't and tried to hide his confusion. "Maybe you don't understand what is my future past, but it is there. My career as a scientist is under threat and someone is trying to kill my future. I almost ended up…"

He tried to say, "killing myself," but became suddenly and forcefully muted, unable to finish his sentence. After an obvious pause, which again made Pablo scrutinize Johan suspiciously, with his burning gaze, Johan tried again.

"I'm desperate, I just want to work on science, physics. That's what I love and hope to do!"

Johan sighed loudly. The images of his time as a beginning research student came vividly to his mind. Suddenly, he recalled the disturbing feelings he had had, when discussing a difficult physics problem or an approach, new to him, with his teachers or other academics, the feeling of being uneducated in the specific topic and how it often felt like being a total outsider, even stupid. Typically, nobody among his student and researcher colleagues apparently wanted to help him to understand the problem, to learn about it; quite the contrary, as if they had been competing for the fame that understanding something provided. Often it seemed like some of the colleagues and even teachers had wanted to make him and other students of physics look stupid by blocking any easy way towards a solution, to understand the problem at hand. This made it impossible to join the ongoing conversation for real. Only later, after some years of studying, he had realized it was a power game. He remained quiet, as he remembered the calls to Calle and the cruel threats from Peter. The familiar anxiety was about to take him over, he was approaching a threatening *cul de sac*, when he realized he was out of the world where his suffering had any meaning. Then he remembered the care from Yvonne and he started shivering, feeling cold.

Helen had noticed Johan's sudden, anxious silence. Leaning across the table, touching both of his hands, she looked at Johan with compassion. Pablo, however, returned to his blunt style.

"That's pure nonsense! Either you live and work or you worry yourself dead! I painted Carles and did not stay passive and weeping. OK, it hurt, it still does, and I cry my eyes out, but I try to do something. You should do the same! Besides, we all have our future pasts, I can imagine a thousand of them for myself and even for you if you want. It does not look good with that stance and attitude; I can do it right now, even paint it if you so wish, just to make you alive again! It was enough that you left us, without a word! Don't paint yourself into a corner!"

For the first time after his entrance to this world, Johan started feeling nervous and sick to his stomach, not being able to say what exactly he meant and had on his mind, what he knew had happened, how he suffered, and what seriously bothered him. What moved him and troubled him was not only the piercing pain from this new existence in a strange world, whatever this existence was: a dream, an attack of schizophrenia or something else, serious, and unknown. It was not only the fact that he could not be himself and contribute creatively to the discussions, when everything about his future knowledge was being forbidden in the arguments and storytelling. It was also the unexpected, simple compassion that moved him, the care he felt from the kind Maurice and the agitated Pablo, even from Helen whom he barely knew. It was too much.

Maurice spoke up, touching his shoulder gently.

"Johan, you are with friends here. Nobody wants to harm you. Remember, we welcomed you, and nothing has changed, not even after your disappearance. Besides, we don't know your future history or whatever you call it, well enough to seriously hurt you, to make you suffer and feel pain in the way a hopeless, desperate man can feel pain. I mean me!"

Friendly laughter erupted again, but Johan did not understand why it was such a good joke. He had observed how touched and worried Maurice was by his wife's negligence. Pablo poured a large glass full of red wine for Johan, winking at him, and smiling. Something had changed in his attitude, without Johan understanding what it was. He remembered his father's words: "I am safe there. It is the purest enjoyment to live there, it is real, there is care, nobody threatens me, they don't have evil plans for me and many of them love me there."

It was exactly what he sensed, and this kind reception by his friends overwhelmed him. Trying to cover his face with both hands, Johan could not prevent tears from flowing. Helen and Maurice stood up and came close to him; even Pablo hurried around the table, hugging Johan powerfully as Helen kissed him on the forehead. When Johan started trembling and sobbing, Pablo took him by the hand, slapped him softly on the top of his head.

Turning to Helen, he said, "You need a woman now, Johan! Helen is the best I know. I've seen how she has looked at your Nordic-blond charm. Take him upstairs, Helen!"

Helen was shining, ready and immediately on her way. Taking Johan by the hand, trying to make him stand up, playing with him and smiling, she coaxed him, but with little response from the shaken Johan. When he finally pulled himself together again and stood up, nervous and blushing, he looked at Helen. Grinning, he hugged her as he whispered in her ear, afraid that others might hear.

"You are so kind and lovely, and I'm the fool who cannot receive your gift. Forgive me!"

The men noticed Johan's reluctance and sat down, smiling and laughing, but Helen remained standing beside Johan, her left hand on his right shoulder. They looked at each other; Helen gazed into his eyes, with a soft and warm look. Pablo was following them keenly, looking at each of them, alternately, and making a funny gesture by rolling his eyes and tilting his head. He shrugged, remained quiet for a few seconds, and then in a loud voice ordered food and more wine for the whole party, not bothering to ask what anyone wanted.

Chapter 18
Moments of Compassion

It was early evening, and the sun was shining orange on the horizon, as they left the Lapin; everyone more than slightly tipsy. Johan walked a few meters behind Maurice and Pablo, who were engaged in an intense argument, shouting every now and then; Pablo did not pay any attention to Johan, who could hear the repeating themes about the four dimensions, their projections and the simultaneous perspectives. He did not want to get lost in the darkness and stayed close to them.

Helen had kissed Johan goodbye, whispering, "You can find me any time here. I'd love to get to know you better! Bye!" Then she moved away, as she had quickly found another lively group of men. Johan was puzzled by her kind approach.

Maurice looked back, every now and then, as if making sure Johan was following them. It was getting dark and only a few gas lights had been lit. Further away, uphill, Johan saw feeble house lights, guiding them back towards Pablo's atelier. The walk from the *Lapin* on the dark, steep street made Johan exhausted and his leg muscles hurt, but somehow this weariness and pain were not uncomfortable; quite the contrary. Johan began to talk to himself again.

"This is unreal, but it is not a dream. The familiar sensation of strain in my legs and body, my lungs and the beating heart are real, the warm touch of the kiss. I've never dreamed of being tipsy like this, and if this is schizophrenia, then it is a new kind of fun!"

He smiled to himself, taking energetic steps, one at a time, feeling like he was climbing a small mountain, breathing heavily, learning about his new reality.

"I can even test my sense of presence and my being in a real world by moving faster or slower, shifting my left and right foot, sensing the gravel under my feet when I so wish, taking a deep breath, and I know I'm here, somehow, in control of my own body and thoughts, not floating around like under drugs, in a wild dream or as a helpless traveler in the private universe of a psychotic. It is like one, full and continuous life."

He stopped to rest, breathing, observing Pablo and Maurice hurry towards the hilltop, with a surprising pace and agility, and disappear behind a house corner. He laughed at his own poor physical condition and shouted after them when they were no longer visible: "Over space and time, I have no physical power to match you!"

Johan did not know at all what he should do now. He had no home there, no place to stay, but his friends did not seem to worry; they did not even ask him about it, behaving as if everything was as it should be. Johan remembered the frequent comments about their shared past and was confused, wondering why they had such memories of him and why they had expressed such kindness, a powerful, touching care for him. "There has to be a history behind all this, a history I don't know."

Exhausted, Johan tried to hurry-to reach his friends, and after two hundred meters rise, he walked briskly down the other side of the hill towards the plaza where the atelier was located. It was still fifty meters to the house and too dark to see its details, but to Johan it appeared as a murky, modest hut. He was amused to notice the energetic zigzag walk of Pablo and Maurice, but quickly he realized that he could not walk straight either, trying to avoid the trees and low-hanging branches that were difficult to see in the dark. Careful in his steps, he approached the Place Ravignan, where only one feeble gaslight and a few candles in house windows provided faint visibility and made the uninviting buildings appear even more repulsive, dark, and dirty. The atelier house, where he had found himself with Pablo and Maurice, the Bateau Lavoir had a simple one-story facade, but as he later learned, it had something of a style of genuine laundry boat as its name hinted: stranded and lost.

A man in his thirties — as far as Johan could tell in the dark — came to meet Pablo and Maurice. As Johan caught up with them, he saw that this man looked naturally powerful and physical in his appearance, with a strong nose and a slightly protruding chin; he wore a black suit, white shirt and bright blue bowtie. As Maurice and Pablo walked to the door of the Bateau, continuing their chat, the man approached and greeted Johan, introducing himself as if he too knew Johan.

"Hello again, you beautiful Viking giant, I'm Guillaume!

Remember? Apollinaire is my adopted family name! We met here, is it already two or three years ago? I'm a poet and the critic of all the critics!"

Once more Johan was puzzled, although he was getting used to the surprise acquaintances and common histories, and was glad to be received in such a friendly and welcoming manner. He decided to do the same.

"Hello, Guillaume, we come from the Lapin where we had a most inspiring discussion on the future of artists. You would have enjoyed it!"

"I have not given up despising the current bourgeois art spreading its disease all over France and killing the best poets and artists of Paris. The blind art politicians are playing their games here. The Louvre is their worst entertainer and the galleries, they exist only as their fields of glory and repression! Pablo will take them by a fatal surprise, just wait and see!"

Johan was amused by Guillaume's pompous and dandy-like manners, but immediately liked the fellow, who appeared open and without reservations, friendly in his approach, behaving as if he was talking to a good old friend who knew what he meant. Guillaume showed a lively and good sense of humor, too.

"Last time we met you were looking really bad, worse than our poorest progressive artists here, as if under hostile drugs, talking like a crazy man. Do you remember anything of it? You were under a spell, incessantly telling us about secret walls and the insane fraud in science. You even forced us to follow you to see the Metre, the symbol of all the scientific betrayals as you said. I'll never forget it! It was four o'clock in the morning, for Heaven's sake, after a heavy, heavy night, when we walked there obediently with you and then back without you, ten kilometers it must have been, drunk as pigs, of course!"

Then he continued, in a loud voice echoing across the buildings that surrounded the small, dark plaza, "There we all stood, all four of us, like drunken statues, you and me, Pablo and Maurice in front of the marble plate, understanding nothing. It was near the Palais du Luxembourg; you lectured us like a maniac about the fraud behind 'the metre'. And that was all you wanted to show us, just the plate and the fraud at four o'clock in the morning! You got Pablo hilariously excited about it and on the way home, it was his turn to torment us with the twisted ideas he got from your preaching!"

Johan stared at Guillaume and interrupted his long but amusing story.

"The story of the metre is haunting me too. It's because Méchain made his mistakes that have carried to the physics of..." He tried to mention modern times, having forgotten where he was, and then he simply stood there, muted, gazing at Guillaume dumbly, as if gasping for air. He seemed so distressed that Guillaume started tapping him on the back.

"Breathe in, my friend, breathe out!" After a brief embarrassing moment, Johan was ready to try again.

"The metre is a monarch and a despot; it defines everything you can do in art, science and engineering, even what you can think of and imagine."

Guillaume nodded, hugged Johan, and got excited again.

"Yes, yes! You made Pablo curious; you helped him to think of something new, and he has not forgotten it! It was like medicine against the art critics! They are the cheaters hiding in their salons. They suffocate the true artists!"

Guillaume waved his hands high in the air, walking nervously around Johan, who had to turn around to follow and listen to him.

"Coming back from the Metre, Pablo was possessed and could not stop explaining his new insights. We had no chance to add anything to his blabbering; he just continued, on and on without a break, making us tired with the passionate monologue about how everything is possible and how we can change everything in the arts and sciences, and nothing can stop us. How we don't need the politically distorted meter sticks which have been constructed to fool us, to make their designers famous and rich. Pablo was seriously drunk, but it all made some sense. At least to me it did, although I think he carried some drugs in his pockets. It was all your fault!"

Johan liked Guillaume's sincere and enthusiastic talk and tried desperately to figure out what it was about, what had happened and why Guillaume thought he had been involved. Even if he had been there with Pablo and Maurice, there were no memory traces left, nothing to remember. It was a disturbing mystery not to recall anything about what

Guillaume was so vividly telling, while these ideas about the Meter were precisely what he had been thinking of and telling his friends in Helsinki and at Stanley. "It's like my father talking" was all he could think, the only rational explanation he could imagine for his strange situation. Guillaume stopped in front of Johan, facing him at such a close distance that Johan felt uncomfortable looking him in the eyes.

"Then we realized you did not follow us! Pablo went back alone to see if you were still enchanted by the Metre but did not find you. It was not the first time you had disappeared like that, but this time it was for almost three years, for God's sake! I'm glad and astonished you are alive and home again. Where have you been? You have not changed at all!"

Guillaume did not wait for an answer, just continued walking slowly around Johan, waving his hands like a black swan in the night. Johan could not avoid a sense of guilt, even though he had no idea why he felt it.

"Pablo took it very hard that you did not return," Guillaume went on. "He was depressed for a week. It was extraordinary for him to be like that. You know, he's changed women without a blink of his eye. If someone hurts him or mistreats him, he just leaves him or her. I believe your vanishing reminded him of the loss of his Spanish friend, Carles Casagemas. Carles shot himself in despair some years ago in Barcelona. Did you know that?"

Johan had never heard this story about Carles, although Pablo had mentioned him. He just shook his head and remained silent.

"Together with him, Pablo had moved to Paris, where they started their difficult life as independent, beginning artists. Male friends, especially artists and poets, have a special place in Pablo's private world, as you know, but even I cannot understand why the bond is so strong. I do love him, he's my dear friend, but still, it's a mystery to me. It could all be about his father, I don't know. Pablo cannot handle emotional losses; they are devastating to him. Go and see the paintings of the dead Carles; they tell it all. I think he tries to avoid the pain of separation at any cost. The paintings are agonizing to look at. Even I get upset when I go too near them. It's almost like Pablo's sorrow at the death of Carles was infectious! I'm sure you know all this, my friend! You could see for yourself how Carles' death affected Pablo."

Johan was amazed by what he heard; from Guillaume's way of telling these stories, he was apparently convinced that Johan had been present for all of this history that Johan himself could not at all recall, or had never actually experienced. His father's stories came repeatedly to his mind. "It could be my father that Guillaume is talking about, not me. Why don't they see the difference, both Maurice and Pablo? What on earth is this? What is going on?"

There was no well-founded, rational, or even irrational explanation to the mystery, and Johan grew increasingly curious about "his" previous life in Paris. He had no idea how and when exactly all this had happened. He only knew the story of the Metre and what father had said and drawn. There was no doubt that Pablo and Guillaume saw him as Johan, but talked about something that could have happened to Sten, who had been dead for almost four years. "Is it possible that they had lived with him, in one way or another?"

There was only one rational explanation, a physical one, he could imagine and rely on, remembering the theory of multiple universes by his favorite physicist, Hugh Everett, and he spoke to himself: "Everything that can happen, happens." It sounded totally unbelievable. The looming, pathological alternative did not leave him, and he kept thinking: "What if I'm following Sten? A schizophrenic with serious delusions? Why don't I feel like one then, disarrayed? Well, actually, I don't know what it feels like to be a schizophrenic, unless it is this, the easy and safe living in another world, disconnected from the real future, from the one and only reality, as most scientists think about it? Only when I try to talk about my real worlds, what I see and experience, I get into trouble." Johan could not grasp why the thought of being mentally ill did not disturb him and then he remembered how Sten would talk about his experiences in the kind world without the slightest sign of anxiety in his voice and tone.

Everett, the famous physicist, was from Johan's own future history and because of that, he knew it was not possible to find a straightforward way to ask Guillaume about Everett's theories of time. He could not even present the simplest of questions: "Are you sure it was me, perhaps he only looked like me? Perhaps he was my father?" That would mean that he would have to explain his coming from the future, just as his father had probably done, or tried to do.

In any case, Johan wanted to know what his friends here knew about "his" life here, in this world, and he was eager and curious again, forgetting all his reservations, as he asked Guillaume, "What if it was…" intending to say, "my father there at the Metre." The muting stopped him, however, and left him gaping as if he was being suffocated. Guillaume gazed at him, puzzled and worried, again tapping him on the back.

"You look like you've got a fishbone in your throat, or just lost a loved one!" He remained standing in front of Johan, observing him carefully, then laying his hands softly on Johan's shoulders and shaking him gently. "Wake up, my friend!"

Johan did not know how to react. Sighing, he said, "I wish I knew the difference between being awake and fully asleep!"

Johan felt as if he had plunged into imagining his father's painful life. It was as if the boundaries between his father and himself had become porous and dissolved. His distress appeared to be his father's distress, yet it was impossible to share this knowledge or any acute questions concerning it, with anyone. In the middle of the confusion, he sensed the looming paranoia, being afraid of losing or having already lost his mind. "How could I know or find out I'm not having the worst form of delusion?" he thought.

At the same time, he was comfortably aware of being a welcomed, cared for member of the team, with Pablo and Maurice and now with Guillaume; although he did not know what his role was with these figures; nevertheless, the experience of care was genuine and strong.

Guillaume joined Pablo and Maurice, leaving Johan alone, standing by a lamp post, where he could follow their intense discussion.

For a moment, observing the three men from the distance, Johan had an alarming sensation of observing them from a different dimension, not as himself, but as his father, even thinking about them as a natural part of his life. Johan was afraid of losing his ability to differentiate, to perceive the differences between his own real life, his father's life, and this new life he had now entered.

Soon Johan was glad to see Guillaume approaching, hands on his waist, visibly drunk, but serious.

"Maurice claims you understand the fourth dimension as well as he does. Is that true?"

Johan did not answer immediately, convinced that he should formulate any comments so that the muting would not get him again. To make his speaking safe, he decided to talk about the present objects and events and touch only on topics they had already covered at the atelier and the *Lapin*.

"Why do you ask?"

"Pablo has always praised Maurice for helping him to come to grips with the idea of the fourth dimension and to try to express it in the *Brothel* painting. Maurice is curious to know what you think of the *Brothel* and its dimensions."

"Well, I do know that painting. There is something peculiar in the way the women are seen there, in different, simultaneous perspectives, as if inviting all of us from our own decent worlds to approach them, the women of the brothel. You can take that as a fourth dimension if you like, a secret door to enter the forbidden world, at least in the painting, which is right now in Pablo's atelier."

He felt it wise not to mention anything about his own experience at Grévin.

"What do you think about the style then, the perspective shown in the *Brothel?* We have followed its birth pains closely, and to me it has become the beginning of a revolution, doing exactly what you told us there when we were facing the Metre. I just did not understand it then. It makes all the measures of the classic arts, even physics, which you understand better than I do, look like ridiculous copies of the assumed, banal reality. How do we know what reality is? We just construct it with our measures. We let our priests and shamans in science construct it for us without questioning them! Pablo is starting a war against this, in the arts. He will lay down the foundations for a new human, even a universal metrics, and it is not only visual! He's not alone; there are physicists doing the same, if I can believe what Maurice has told me, and indeed I do. Poincaré has been preaching it to his students at the Sorbonne!"

Guillaume turned back to join Maurice and Pablo again, leaving Johan alone in the dark.

Johan was learning to pre-think what to say, what he could try to say and how, knowing Guillaume was right. He did not have enough knowledge of art history to be able to tell what exactly would happen in the world of modern arts, and soon, but the future of the *Brothel* painting he knew. Johan again felt shame for being so unknowledgeable about art, a shame mixed with the painful memory of his father's stories about *Les Demoiselles,* the *Brothel.* Johan was eager to explain to his friends how the painting was not only a work of art for him, but also a real physical door to this world, beyond his comprehension, but nevertheless a fact. He felt the familiar symptoms of the muting before even trying to vocalize his carefully formulated, academic thought.

In his mind, he started to formulate his insights. "The *Brothel* is an existence proof of mystic, emergent powers of art and mathematics working together, in parallel! An artist like Pablo can carry us far away, free from the bounded reality. Scientists are just slow at trying."

In spite of the muting of this unspoken idea, this formulation inspired him. The muting had become simply a fact of this new life.

"Science is science," he said to himself. "We just take the basic assumptions and proceed from there, systematically. It should work here, too, without any reference to the future history."

A new idea occurred to him, however; he imagined an unexpected ethical problem: wouldn't discussing science with his new friends, without mentioning what he knew about the future, be unfair, like playing a chess game with them, using hidden guidance from an artificial intelligence system with the best problem-solving capability in the world? Wouldn't this be cheating, hiding something essential? The spontaneous, natural motivation to avoid such unethical behavior in this historical world towards his companions was a revelation to Johan, a sign of how deeply he was immersing himself in this place. He recalled how his father had tried to convince him of the other, good, and caring reality beyond their everyday life. Now Johan had reason to think the call to join this other world was framed by ethics and a sense of fairness, too. He felt bitterly reminded of the lack of these qualities in his recent academic life.

Johan took a few careful steps in the darkness and found a comfortable tree trunk to lean against, to sense the shelter provided by the dense branches above his head. There he could feel how the tree provided a connection, a secure and organic bridge between the two realities, the present one and his rational reality which now was the future. He wondered if he would unlearn and forget all his precious knowledge and skills, for which he had struggled for years at school, at the university and in the labs. Where would such an un-learning development lead him? Was it only a new language, a new way of intellectual being, he had to learn, and was it progression or regression? It was difficult to believe it would lead to something new and transformational.

Johan's worry had begun to grow again when Guillaume found him under the tree. Interrupting his lonely thoughts, breaking the silence, he extended a candle in his hand close to Johan's face, and touched him on the shoulder.

"You seem like you're in need of care and cover!" He shouted at Maurice and Pablo, "I'm leaving you fellows now. I have to rest and prepare a critique for *Le Matin*! Take care of Johan!"

He lifted the candle close to his lips and shouted, so powerfully that the airflow extinguished the weak flame, "Burn down the Louvre!"

Then he walked away into the darkness.

Pablo and Maurice continued their intense conversation, but Johan decided to remain at a distance. He wondered why it was so important for Guillaume to repeatedly blame the Louvre, to make fun of it and treat it like a disgraceful symbol of the establishment in the arts. Guillaume's sarcasm was in uncomfortable contrast to the kind and warm attitude he showed to Johan.

Standing alone in the darkness, reflecting on Guillame's passionate talk, Johan realized that Pablo had already, before the physicists had done it, started the revolution in practice, breaking the rules of traditional arts and sciences with his artistic imagination and tools; to Pablo there was no "objective *metre*" to constrain his thinking.

It was getting late, but the door to the Bateau was still wide open, and Johan stayed alone for almost an hour, following with curiosity what kind of people, typically a couple, entered the house and came out from it. The rule was simple: men and women went in and men typically stayed inside while women came out. It was not difficult to guess what the traffic was about. Pablo seemed to know all the women passing by, greeting them, addressing the young women in a kind tone, with a good humor and laughter. Maurice and Pablo did not seem to be in any hurry, but when Johan finally approached them and mentioned he was getting tired, Maurice agreed with him.

"Time to get some rest! I feel dizzy; I have not slept properly for two days. I'll find a corner in the flat, Pablo, and sleep there; Johan can stay in his own miniature room. You will be making noises all night anyway!"

Pablo was immersed in his own thoughts and only nodded, glancing briefly at Johan.

The invitation to spend the night in "his own room" was an unexpected offer to Johan, who had already become worried about where he could sleep. He did not reveal his astonishment, but instead followed Maurice, who lit a candle when entering the Bateau and walked ahead of Johan, down a dozen stairs to the ground floor. The wooden floor of the small hallway was made of wide, rough planks that gave way slightly under his step, and made creaking sounds. The floor and stairs were covered with sand and gravel, and they had to move carefully in the darkness.

"I'll check to make sure your door is not locked. We have not used it too much since you were here last time. It's been our emergency hideaway, you know."

Maurice smiled at Johan, his white teeth shining in the candlelight. Having observed the nightly traffic to and from the Bateau had made it clear to Johan what kind of emergencies they might have had there.

A narrow, less than twenty inches wide door made of rough boards led to a small, narrow space, not a proper room. One bed, a luxury in this residence, was wedged in there with a small table next to it, leaving practically no room for walking around the bed. This tiny room had no window and no light. By the door there was an empty metal pail, a primitive, rusty version of a chamber pot. Maurice lit another candle and left it on the small table. The uncomfortable odor of human waste was already familiar to Johan, something he had noticed in the atelier and then in the streets to and from the Lapin. Three narrow wooden shelves on the wall held two books and a pile of yellowish-brown paper sheets with some charcoal drawings on them; they were difficult to see in the dim, flickering light from the candles. The walls were almost fully covered by sketches of human figures. Johan could tell that they were rich in detail, and probably black and white, yet they were difficult to see. It was like parts of a whole figural setting had been scattered on the walls.

The darkness prevented Johan from studying the large sketch attached to the ceiling, above the bed. The artwork had been put there to be visible to anyone lying on the bed. A caricature version of the *Brothel* painting had been drawn or painted on the pillow, but it was too dark to see its details. Maurice was leaving, laughing at Johan.

"There's an inspiring place for you, to rest your head! Good night!"

Johan sat on the bed and touched the pillow, smiling. He heard Maurice curse on his way in the hall, possibly looking for a place to sleep. Every now and then Johan heard heavy footsteps, someone entering the Bateau, and occasionally he paid attention to the all too informative noise of the pails being used. He had only the candlelight, deciding to wait for the morning to get to know his room. After using his own pail, tilting his head over the primitive conditions, he fell on the bed and extinguished the candle with a careful puff, too tired to listen to the characteristic sounds of the house, or be afraid to fall asleep in his new, unknown world. He had no idea what his dreams might bring and how the morning would open, where he would wake up, but he did not worry. He knew he was among friends.

Just before falling into a deep sleep, he was puzzled by the sense of a soft-bright scene he saw or more like experienced in front of his mind's eye, a scene which immediately vanished when he opened his eyes, but which always came back, unchanged, when his eyes were closed. "Strange how the light is different in this vision," he thought. "The scene had no shadows or shades of gray; it's just filled with pure light everywhere, coming from all directions like a kind of a haze. It's like a light of my mind, everywhere."

He smiled, tired, sliding into a comfortable, relaxed sleep. He had not felt this tranquil and trusting for many days.

Chapter 19
A Morning at the Bateau

Johan woke up in the dark room, confused and sensing — almost seeing — the presence of the familiar bright, widely open mental scene, the same he had enjoyed before falling asleep. In the dark he could see the pure whiteness with his eyes open, still unaware where he was. He tried to remember what had happened and orient himself.

As soon as he started trying to remember, however, the relaxed trust of the previous evening faded away and a devastating wave of anxiety, the fear he had experienced at Stanley, was about to conquer his thoughts again. There was Peter threatening to sue him and Roos acting in cold blood with the faculty members. There was the inviting wall of death at the railroad crossing. He was waking up into a world of fear, scared to the bones. It was too much again like a multi-layered nightmare, as if waking up into an unknown time and place, having totally forgotten. But now he knew where he had been yesterday and how he had arrived in this strange bed and he was now waking up.

He had a vivid memory flash of Yvonne smiling at him, just when he jumped up from the bed, nervous and agitated, automatically choosing his right side, as he used to do in his own apartment at Stanley. He could not see anything in the darkness and hit his head on the wall, hard, became even more confused, climbed out of the bed at its other end, rushed to where he thought the door was and then kicked sharply, with his bare right foot, what appeared to be a metal bucket. He did not spill all its stinking contents on the floor, but got a cool shower of drops of liquid on his feet. Opening the door, he let a few light rays from the corridor find their way into the room. As he looked at the modest, narrow closet, he remembered it was Paris now, in 1907, not a nightmare and he was standing in the corridor with his feet wet.

The confusion was now complete, a mixture of the frightening memories of Stanley, the wax people, and the time travel to Paris. He had no mental means and resources to explain to himself what this was about. Was it dreaming or was it real life? What had happened? Was this a new day? Everything seemed and felt impossible, but there he was, at the Bateau, experiencing the unavoidable touch of the new reality: pee on his feet.

The memories of his father came vividly to his mind and he took hold of them: the stories Sten had told, the world he had described and kept drawing, again and again. Finally realizing where he was, Johan could not see any real difference between the two worlds: his present being, his mental state, and that of his father's. He wondered again, as he had the day before, if he was on the verge of losing his mind, or had already done so, and was now following his father's mental journey to a place where no one could trace him and grasp the essence of this rich and fascinating, yet unnerving journey. Realizing the parallels with his father's state of mind, Johan felt frightened. He was living in his own, disconnected universe, which not a soul could share. Everett's multiple universes did not offer the slightest comfort: the parallel universes Everett had described were totally disconnected. Even in theory, there was no way to move from one to another and back.

Standing confused in the corridor, Johan found himself in total silence; he did not hear any sounds from the other apartments or from the hidden corners of the Bateau. He had no idea what time it was. Possibly Pablo had worked all night and Johan had been too sound asleep to be disturbed by the sounds of Pablo's steps, or his energetic mixing of colors in the glass jars.

He was staring at his dirty feet, disgusted, when Maurice came rushing down from somewhere upstairs, fully and neatly dressed, smiling at him.

"What on earth are these thumping sounds and the rattle? Are you having nightmares or what? I thought it was Pablo's cats, but the noise was so loud."

Maurice started laughing, pointing at the bucket Johan had taken out from his room, and then he stared at Johan's wet feet.

"Well, that is certainly not my idea of a wet dream! You better clean the floor and your feet, uhh, what a smell, even according to the Bateau standards! You cannot hide behind your scientific explanations for what has happened; the disgusting phenomenology is enough. Sorry, Johan!"

Maurice was in a good mood as he started back upstairs where the entrance door was.

"Come out, I'll fetch some water. You can clean the floor and go outside to wash your feet in the fresh air. I'm not going to do it for you, however noble that would be." He continued his merry laughter. "It's already eleven o'clock. Pablo took my bed only two hours ago and I've been upstairs drawing some imaginative versions of our *team*. I've used the same perspective concept as in *The Brothel Women*. I'll show them to you and Pablo later. You probably noticed Pablo has attached an older sketch on the ceiling. He did it when you disappeared, and it's been there ever since. It's not about the wonderful women from Avignon, but instead of a family; it could be some of us, you included. They are harlequins." He waved his hand, in a casual manner, pointing at Johan's "room", as if there was nothing mysterious about it, and rushed away to get a water bucket.

Johan climbed upstairs, opened the Bateau door to the plaza, and stepped out into a beautiful, sunny morning. "It must be almost noon already, it's definitely summer," he thought. He felt so relieved to experience the remarkable contrast to his dark wake-up moment that he almost forgot his wet feet. The spill from the bucket, its smell in the darkness, had made him feel as if he had been falling deep down into the cellars of his soul, when suddenly the fear had been wiped away at the moment Maurice appeared. Now Johan was healthy again, embracing the new, but manageable, reality. He pulled off his trousers to wash them, wondering what weekday it might be. As Johan sat down on the already warm, wooden entrance stairs of the Bateau, Maurice returned from the well of the plaza, carrying a bucket of water and a small piece of soap. Smiling, Johan started to slowly wash his feet and trousers, observing the modest environment and the miniscule square, as he sat there in his white underwear. None of the men and women hurrying by seemed to take notice of him. They were busy with their daily errands. Johan realized it was not Saturday or Sunday. Then he noticed the well from which Maurice had fetched the water. Johan was thoroughly startled, noticing its familiar features he remembered from his father's drawings. He remained silent for a while, did not move and thought: "This must be my father's hidden world!" Maurice had been standing behind Johan and tapped him softly on the top of his head: "I think your feet expect some treatment; wake up!"

Johan forgot the well and continued cleaning his feet. This washing episode triggered a familiar, permissive feeling he had experienced in the sauna at home, as a small boy. It was an experience every Finnish boy learns, the way of being naked with and under the eyes of the parents first, and then later with male friends and finally again with the new family, a wife and children, a chain of practices carried across generations. As he finished washing his feet on the stairs of the Bateau, he imagined the way he had done it, sitting on a dock by a lake in Finland, when visiting a summer cottage. Feeling the spontaneous approval or the calming ignorance from the passersby here, as he sat on the steps half naked, he let his associations flow, his thoughts jumping from one idea to another, freely, as he tried to find a way to frame his being at the Bateau.

"This place, the Bateau, has a peculiar personality," he thought to himself. "It's closed but also welcoming. It's a circle of artists and other original characters, like the clientele at the Lapin. It does not know an easy life; it's not even beautiful; it's dirty. Strangely enough, though, it is not so far from what the sauna is to the family and friends and to most Finns. Except that sauna is clean and pure, often a charming hut, small, too, a symbol of the purity of the body and the trust of the mind. Life at the Bateau looks dirty, even disreputable, but it welcomes art and creativity. No doubt many non-Nordics, especially Americans, might be suspicious about what goes on in a sauna. And still, there is the ether of invitation in the air, the encouragement to join in the way friends are invited to a sauna. But a person must know and follow the code.

Washing his feet, Johan pondered the code of the Bateau. He had no idea what it might be and thought, "At Stanley I would have been arrested for behaving like this, in my underwear, in a public place. I'd be in jail in no time."

Closing his eyes, Johan turned his face towards the bright, warm sunshine, and tried to recall what had happened to him. "It cannot be April, although how could I know it for certain? It is definitely Paris in 1907." He recalled the unexpected compassion and care he had experienced from his new friends. He opened his eyes and smiled, while observing two young boys perhaps seven or eight, running after a ball.

He accepted it as a mysterious fact that he had landed in the midst of an unquestionable, shared reality, shared with his father, enjoyable and completely different from his own everyday world. The experience launched a wonderful, tickling flow of energy and he joked to Maurice who had remained behind him, smiling as he watched his extremely careful cleaning maneuvers.

Johan laughed aloud, turning towards Maurice, pre-thinking how to talk to him without getting muted.

"You see, Maurice, what I have on my feet is not the worst attack I have experienced; I've seen shit in science!"

Maurice turned to get back in.

"The sun is shining, forget that!"

Johan became aware of his mental-historical brake activating, immediately realizing it was impossible to explain the analogy he had just used. "Maurice has a sharp eye, he must see me as a real question mark, an outlier, a mystery man, without words in the most elementary conversations, but then able to express ideas about the four-dimensional geometry. I must sound like a book of forbidden phrases, continuously avoiding certain words and expressions!" Johan did not know how to deal with the disconcerting thought. Maurice sat down beside him and patted his shoulder in a friendly way.

The overwhelming, kind reception by his friends, the intense, comradely discussions and emotionally loaded interactions, the surprising honesty and care he had felt on the previous day, at the Lapin and at the Bateau, all this added up to something he had now lost in the academia. He was surprised to realize how strong an impact only one day had had on him.

Again, Johan thought about Yvonne. The first thing he felt was the guilt; he remembered how worried they had been at home when father had disappeared. He wondered what Yvonne must be going through right now, if he had somehow disappeared. She must have been tremendously worried, and he knew she would not quit searching for him. Johan had no knowledge or even an educated guess about the time scale of his possible absence. It could be seconds or years. When he closed his eyes to enjoy the sunshine, an intimate sense of Yvonne's presence surrounded him, the inexplicable care and kindness and her friendly, smiling face came close to his, lips almost touching, as he sensed the warmth and inviting fragrance of her perfume and skin. It was a feeling of utmost intimacy and closeness.

Johan was startled and surprised by the enchanting, transient imagery, a trick of his mindful associations and emotional self, a message from his own true but private future. He did indeed feel seriously fond of Yvonne, even if he had had no previous experiences of a meaningful, physical closeness like that with her.

He wanted to find out how much real time had already passed, how much he had spent with the "wax" people, beyond the *Les Demoiselles* wall doors. Johan's father could sometimes disappear for weeks and when returning, behaving as if he had not been away at all, sharing the endless stories with Johan and explaining the meaning of the curious drawings to him. Johan knew how he would sound when and if he could return to Yvonne and tell a truthful story of where he had been and what had happened.

The memories of his father and Yvonne opened the gates of anxiety again. He realized how any expression of his deepest, most personal feelings and affections were forbidden in the present time, in Paris. There was no way to share the *real* worries and fascinations with his closest friends now. As a teenager Johan had learned to spend time alone, in his own imaginary worlds, like during the long and lonely evenings on the skating rink, without a pressing need to share the exciting experiences with someone. His solitude had been voluntary. This time, however, it was a forcible prohibition against revealing his personal future and his future history, the future of his present community. This prohibition isolated him and prevented from sharing the most intimate hopes, thoughts and wishes. It involved a form of aphasia for his future true reality and for the future unknown of his friends. "How could I live like this? My friends here are happy to live their lives and appear unknowing to me, but they are unknowing only when I'm the reference. They make the future happen and I know it is significant what they do and launch. They can't know how the future will unfold, however, and I cannot tell. I'm forced to live here with them, pretending I don't know. It's even worse than pure neglect and agnosia, a blindness of the brain. What kind of life can that be?"

Johan carefully dried his feet, enjoying the feel of the fresh towel and the sunshine on his toes. Slowly, he began to rise out of the hopeless maze of his desperate thoughts.

Johan hung up his jeans outside to dry on a rope between two trees and returned to his modest room. This time he left the door open to the corridor, so that he could see the artwork on the ceiling. Lying on the bed, he observed the painting, a sketch with a square form, three feet by three feet, drawn with both charcoal and oil paints. It was not attached directly above the pillow, but almost two feet towards the end of the bed, so that it was comfortable and relaxing to observe.

Johan could now see that the base of the painting had been lowered from the ceiling by a wooden board, just wide enough to guarantee that the line of sight of the observer on the bed, his head comfortably resting on the pillow, would be almost perpendicular to the surface of the artwork. Johan had not noticed this peculiar arrangement in the darkness and when rushing out from the room. He wondered if it had been Maurice, with his mathematical compulsion, who had made sure the perspective proportions of the drawing would not be distorted by the viewing angle.

The sketch had been drawn with a few expressive strokes of charcoal, perhaps less than a dozen of them for each of the several figures, smoothly curved, something Johan had seen in Pablo's other works, especially in the numerous sketches of Les Demoiselles. Various shades of blue and rose had been added to it later, roughly overlapping the charcoal-drawn lines.

This was a portrait of a peculiar kind of traveling circus people, a family disconnected, though everyone was serious in expression and posture. There was a son, near his twenties perhaps, dressed in a classically colored jester's outfit, and his two younger brothers, and a young ballerina sister. The father was standing close to them, appearing strong but overweight. Together they formed a physically compact, but psychologically loose team. The mother was seated farther away and looked distant. Johan noticed that the son, standing beside the father, had been depicted in an unnatural position, with a strangely extending hand, reminiscent of the twisted perspectives in *Les Demoiselles*. Everyone in the painting was visibly disconnected from everyone else and from the landscape. The characters appeared not to be bound at all to the earth under their feet, as if ready to move, to be transported somewhere. Or maybe they had just arrived, prepared for the unexpected. Johan noticed something peculiar about the mother's hat: it appeared to float in the air.

Johan stayed in the bed for almost an hour, trying to grasp the essence of the artwork, thinking: "An artist from my own time, painting the feelings of the first astronauts on Mars, could make it look like this. The arrivals are alone, as I am here right now. Maybe this is the message in it, but why is it above the bed? There is no safe infrastructure anywhere in the desert-like landscape. They wear special dresses, as if they are ready for a performance, each with his or her own role, ready to move any time. They have only each other, especially when uncertain about the future and their destiny. In the painting, they are an unhappy team. It would be dangerous on Mars and on earth for that matter. Psychologically, a team on Mars would be different, strong, and caring. But my God, looking at this, I see my own present situation, only that I have friends here." For a passing moment, he wondered who had been lying in the bed before, who had seen the same scenery and recognized its melancholic feeling. Then he remembered Maurice mentioning that Pablo had put it there, but why? For whom had the painting been positioned like that? For father?"

Clearly the painting emphasized the sense of loneliness and disconnection someone would feel, lying on the bed, the way it was now affecting Johan, who continued his observations: "There is nobody to help them and even a desperate message sent of an accident or disaster on Mars would take several minutes to reach anyone on the earth." It was not much different from what Johan felt, continuing his pondering: "All the knowledge of mankind would be available to them, but not when needed, only within the future of several minutes. And still, these circus performers would be in a better position than I am, knowing that knowledge is on its way towards them; it is only a matter of being prepared for the delay. I don't have that luxury."

Something strange soon caught Johan's eye: the presence of barely visible, thin lines, drawn with ink, behind the mother, following her outline on her left. Then on her right side, some fuzzy lines or gray strips formed either a shadow of the mother figure or even a faint ghost behind her, almost totally, but not quite, hiding behind her back. To Johan it appeared that there was a figure hiding behind the mother, wearing the hat that at first sight had seemed to float above the mother's head. Johan could not imagine Pablo producing something like that, accidentally, and was puzzled: "Why didn't I ever study art history? Everything seems like a mystery to me now! I don't even know how they actually, with their artist's tools, produce these wonderful pieces of art."

He smiled to himself, at the wonder of it, and drifted off to sleep.

When he woke up, Pablo was already making noises and moving about in his atelier upstairs and Johan heard a dog barking.

Maurice came to greet him, but this time looking so sad that Johan had to ask, "What has happened? You keep suffering from your lost love?"

Maurice did not even try to hide his tears, as he sat down beside Johan, who hugged him, with the deepest compassion, automatically trying to soothe him by describing a promising future:

"If only... you would know..."

He could not get further than "only", when the familiar force strangled the sentence, leaving him totally helpless and frustrated, not being able to support his anxious friend with words. He could only hug him and show his care. For the first time in his life, he was hugging a man, soothing him without words, tears flowing down his cheeks, too, unable to know which one of them needed the closeness most. He gazed at the circus figures on the ceiling, noticing their lonely appearance and the psychological distance between family members. He and Maurice sat on the bed together for five minutes. Not a word was exchanged.

Finally, Maurice stood up, wiping his tears, smiling faintly, and pointing at the ceiling.

"You still haven't got enough of the family?"

Johan did not know what to say, trying to avoid the muting. After careful consideration, he asked, "Do you have any other versions of this sketch? I'd like to compare them. There is something that disturbs me in this one."

Maurice smiled faintly. "Pablo's works seem to do that to

227

everybody, but yes, there is one on the shelf. I put it there just before you disappeared. It's a slightly smaller version of that *Les Saltimbanques*, but it's accurate."

He stood up on the bed to reach for a pile of yellowish papers from the top shelf and spread one of them out on the bed.

"There is not enough light here. Let's go out, or to Pablo's atelier."

On the way out, they met Pablo, who eagerly asked what they were doing with the sketch.

"I got curious about some thin and fuzzy lines of ink drawn on the version attached to the ceiling," Johan said. "It's something behind the mother figure. They appear somehow strange or even extra lines that don't fit with the style, like they don't belong there at all."

Pablo fell into a spontaneous laugh, tapping Johan on the left shoulder.

"Well, indeed, they are extra, since you drew them there, on one of the sketches of the *Saltimbanques*! Don't you remember, or were you so drunk? I put it on the ceiling to remind you of that every day!"

Johan was totally confused. He assumed this drunk friend of Picasso's, who had added to this sketch, had to be his father.

Pablo clapped Johan on the shoulder and added, "We had something of a quarrel, every time you got tipsy at Au Lapin, don't you remember? You would start arguing that the empty space in the family and the hat on the mother's head "demanded" something. And yes, you used the word "demand" when explaining to me that you wanted to contribute to it; you the master artist! Imagine, you correcting my work! You were bragging that it's not the first time you had corrected an artist's bad painting if you could see something wrong or missing in it, if the work demanded something better. It felt so funny to see an amateur artist, I mean you are not even an amateur master, perfecting my work. It was like giving a paintbrush to a monkey, so I thought why not, nobody has done that before; it would be art history; just do it on the sketch but don't touch the original one. If one day you can afford to buy the original you are free to do that, too! I won't give any discount, though!" Pablo was enjoying the memory, laughing from his heart, and rolling his eyes.

Maurice laughed too as he said to Johan, "I remember how bad you sometimes felt, talking about that work. It was not the hat alone, was it?"

Johan did not know what to say, but he had a flashback to his father's strangest habit of "improving" the few oil paintings they had at home, explaining to him and Karin how the artist had missed something important, some detail, or had misused colors or distorted an important feature. It bothered his father so much that he had felt compelled to correct it. Typically, Sten would use oil paints and did not seem to spoil the artworks. Johan had been so ashamed of the unusual behavior that he had not dared to tell anybody about what he thought of as a pathological, but, in a strange way, creative behavior. Later his father's schizophrenic history did not make things any easier, and at home they took this "fixing" of the paintings as one of the serious signs of psychotic compulsion. Curiously enough, however, Johan had never seen his father make visible mistakes in correcting the artworks.

It seemed possible, if unbelievable, that Johan's father had indeed been there, yet as soon as he started to feel persuaded of this possibility, he realized that such time travel was an insane idea. Johan could not imagine any rational or physical way it had happened and why. He knew the theoretical possibility of time travel, but he also knew it was science fiction. He was left with the conviction that all these thoughts were delusional, but that Pablo could not have been wrong about the additions to the painting. The extra thin lines, the fuzzy gray stripes and the mysteriously floating hat were drawn there in the sketch and Pablo seemed to be sure of who had left his marks there. Then of course, someone else could have done it. The idea was nothing new to Johan, the skeptical theoretical physicist, that any observation can have several alternative explanations, and even more so in this improbable situation in which he now found himself. He began to give in to the hopeless situation, unable to produce any rational and trustworthy explanation that would include the assumption that he had not lost his mind. He was again frustrated, realizing how little if anything he knew about art history. He'd never seen *The Saltimbanques* before, not even a photo of it, never in his own real, future life. He did not know the original at all.

Pablo waved to Johan and Maurice to join him, as he started towards the water fountain in the middle of the plaza. Johan felt his heart take an extra beat when he realized with Pablo and Maurice, he was about to repeat something his father's drawings had depicted. The fountain was not only a source of water, but a classic work of art, dark-green in color with signs of oxidation here and there. It was perhaps two meters high, shaped as four women figures holding a dome above their heads, with water flowing under it. The women covered the water basin from the falling tree leaves and the dust in the air. Pablo, Maurice and Johan gathered around the fountain, all admiring it, silent.

Pablo broke the silence.

"Look at this, Johan, seriously, and you too, Maurice. You might think it's just a simple object of beauty and practice, in our world, a place to visit when thirsty, to enjoy a refreshing drink. You might even have objective drawings of it, by the sculptor or by the engineer or whoever constructed it. But look at it, take a very good look and touch it. Can you ever come here, even with dirty feet like you, Johan, without being aware of its beautiful form, the charming women holding the decorated dome? Can you drink its water without being aware of its beauty or the ugliness? So, what is reality? Is it only about banal functions?"

He did not wait for an answer, continuing, "I make art that *is* the reality. I don't try to replace the rational world by art or make everyday things nice and beautiful. I build the reality, just as nature builds it! Art is more real than anything else we have! Don't ever make the mistake of believing that it's only an alluring overlay on the world, a decoration at home, to make it a comfortable place to live and die!"

Pablo's powerful talk, or improvised lecture, made both Maurice and Johan obediently touch and feel the fountain, and walk around it, side by side, in the early afternoon sunlight, every now and then looking at each other, exchanging curious facial expressions of admiration when sensing the delicate forms of the fountain, even of the women figures. It was a pleasant, warm day, no one else was around, the sun reached only parts of the fountain, and colored it with a few bright-white spots of light. The metal was wonderfully cool to the touch.

Pablo, glancing at Johan, said, "Correcting someone's work of art, as you did, is altering the reality, not the art!"

Johan was surprised by Pablo's sudden, passionate way of expressing his relation to the world, with such an unmistakable resemblance to his own thinking and experiences. Johan used different words and concepts, perhaps, and yet in essence he too felt the power of art as creating reality. This was something he had learned to be silent about in his academic circles, even among the best of his colleagues, and especially when talking to his physicist friends.

"I don't disagree with you at all, Pablo. I'm as enthusiastic as you are about the problem of the material world and the images of it. You see, to me, the world is but something that touches our senses. It's the only real reality we have, I mean *real* reality. This sounds almost funny, but it's the only knowledge or belief we have, on which to build everything we can and will ever know—about the world, science and art! Even our physics…"

Johan tried to continue, but the muting aphasia was getting at him again, blocking the intended expressions coming from the knowledge of modern physics. He felt a mild pain like a sting of a needle on his forehead, a deflating feeling from being unable to share his own earlier learning experiences, for instance his childhood research into the colored lights on the ice rink. He had no way of explaining to his friend Pablo the remarkable development of physical measures and physics.

Pablo's words had deeply moved Johan. It was the first time since Stanley that he had met someone who initiated this kind of enchanting discussion, presenting a serious and extremely difficult intellectual challenge to him as a physicist. He was amazed and delighted to receive the challenge from an artist. It was unexpected, and he forgot his aphasia when he tried again.

"Some like to believe that through perception and measurements we learn, better every day, to know what the world is like, or the 'reality' as they say. I'm not an artist, but to me, as a physicist, your art is an inherent part of the real world, as much as any machine and building is part of it. We just don't have sticks to measure your strange works. A measurement maniac might use the meter stick to characterize it, but eventually people would see such efforts at measurement as the work of a lunatic, doing more harm than good. Funny enough, the other domains of life and the world, where the meter stick is used, are not at all easier than your art, and the meter is still used as an unquestionable truth. Besides, as I know all too well, the meter and the ambitious science community establishing it as central, have hidden the fraud behind it."

Now it was Pablo's turn to be astonished. He stared at Johan without moving, his gaze suddenly warm, when he started speaking slowly, in an unusually soft tone.

"There is so much everywhere around us that appears to have a fixed structure and form. It's an illusion. Everything has a primitive and deformed origin! Just take a fresh look at a simple object on your desk, consisting of several parts, a book for example. You can take it apart, rip it if you like, transform the order and arrangement of the new components, to create something new, any possible way you like. And it is not only the order of the objects, colors, and surfaces, it's also the rhythm, the way of combining the parts. And it is the surprising collage of their parts, within the space supporting this collage, that makes the new object in the world. Once you have the components rearranged on your desk, you have changed the world and the way we see it, permanently. It's not a book and it is the book, the potential of it! That's what my paintings do. Beliefs and mechanical measurements make us blind and kill the creativity of perception!"

Pablo approached Maurice and Johan, spread his arms around them both, hugging them tightly, as he said, "My view of the whores, at the atelier, is all about that. It's a new kind of world, not least thanks to you, Maurice. But Johan, for the first time you make me wonder, why are you not an artist? You think like one! What has led you astray?"

Johan felt overwhelmed by joy and relief, able to share his thoughts with his friends. Without the slightest hesitation, fear of muting or of embarrassing himself again, he tried to express his view, which would make him look like a fool and a psycho among academics.

"Your painting of the *Whores* is a reality to me, different from anything I've experienced before. It offers gateways and invites me to a new dimension in a more realistic way than any formulas have ever made possible."

Pablo nodded.

"I know, it almost took me to unknown realities."

Chapter 20
Aphasia for the Future

Johan had spent three weeks at the Bateau, counting the days, and had slowly, without noticing it, been losing the sense of being in another, unknown world, with a forbidden future: he could not share his own reality with his friends, it had become the future of Maurice, Pablo and others. He had embraced the new, colorful lifestyle with its informal daily rhythms, the necessary and frequent interaction with people to get access to the simplest things, to accomplish a task and to coordinate meetings at the cafés and restaurants. The days were filled with routines of simple living and everyday necessities like carrying water in and out, finding cheap groceries, making sure he had money to support himself. He learned about all the new and relevant practices of life, and how to be prepared for any surprises. All this was not possible without a connection with his new friends, neighbors, and even the acquaintances at bars and cafés. The practical networking took all his time and occupied his mind.

Maurice had first tested Johan with simple probability calculations, and when he was convinced about his computational skills, he arranged simple bookkeeping tasks for Johan to do, in order to earn the little money, he needed. At first it was difficult to work with the large handwritten data sheets and the amount of extra work caused by even the smallest mistakes in calculating and tabulating the data. He learned quickly to be extra careful, to double-check his every result before writing it down in ink. Only rarely was he faced with the muting when trying to use and explain simple statistical analysis for Maurice.

The evenings Johan spent with his friends at the Lapin were always surprising and lively. He understood quickly that the visits there were not only for fun, they were a practical necessity of daily routines, a way to keep connected with the people and to follow the news from Paris and the world. He often thought of the Lapin as a hub or a platform, like the future internet, but it was impossible to use such words and concepts to explain this notion to his friends.

At the Lapin they would hear about the latest works and trials of the fellow artists and writers or about the family troubles of the working men who came there to relax and rest from the hard work. When people wanted to find a job or sell property, they came to this café; it was the best place to start. Rumors were frequent, about art, war and business. It was a new experience for Johan to notice how the best — if not the only — way to find out about the world, public or private, was simply to talk to a myriad of people, and especially to listen to them. But it was impossible to do that without joining them, getting to know them, and earning their trust. It was necessary to learn to live with them.

Then there were the women of the night, young and old, some of them charming, even inviting, and always flirtatious, living their lives not far from what Johan could see in *Les Demoiselles*. He could not understand their choice in life at all, and only over time did he find the courage to ask and talk to some of them. Then he would grow confused and somehow delighted, as he discovered that his way of looking at the women and listening to their stories was growing closer to how Pablo spoke with them and painted them. Every day he was less afraid of them.

One evening in particular transformed the way Johan perceived the women of the Lapin and the women figures in the *Les Demoiselles*. He had arrived alone. Pablo had a meeting with an art dealer at the Lilas and Maurice had to work late but promised to join him later. It was early evening, around eight o'clock, when Johan approached the restaurant from the Bateau, walking slowly in no hurry down the hill along rue des Saules; he stopped every now and then to admire the scenery opening above the darkening roofs of Paris. Already from afar, he noticed a young woman, Camille as he had learned to know her, sitting alone at the terrace table of the Lapin, leaning against the wall, relaxing. She was smoking and waved Johan as if to say, "Welcome."

In Johan's eyes she had always been the most charming and nicest looking girl there. As a waitress, she was lively, full of energy and joy. Johan had gotten to know her kind character in how she treated the clients and talked to them even when they were drunk and noisy. She had an unusual way of being soft and strict, as needed, and never rude. Often Johan had noticed her disappearing with a man, any one of the clients.

This happened almost every evening when there were only a few customers left and the place was about to close.

He did not know what to think about these women, "the whores", as Pablo called them when he referred to *Les Demoiselles*. To Johan the mere word "whore" sounded distasteful, and he felt sorry to hear it; he would never use it himself. At first, he was astonished to notice that Camille could disappear with a man during her shift, only to return to work again. Sometimes Johan would try to read her face, like looking at the faces of the women in *Les Demoiselles*, after such visits to see if there were any expressions or signs of the aftereffects of the — to Johan — disturbing professional encounters. Only rarely, did he think that he noticed a temporary sharp line to her mouth and an uneasy gaze, but typically she behaved in her characteristic lively and kind way, continuing her work, full of energy.

They had never talked, even though her lovely figure, the blue, lively eyes and fair skin, the slightly reddish hair, had caught Johan's attention when he first saw her. Her delicate face made Johan think of Yvonne, although Camille had curly, dense hair which she wore tied up and partly hanging on her left shoulder as a wild, bushy ponytail. Her red, thick hair and blue eyes were conspicuous among the typically dark-haired, brown-eyed women. She was always dressed nicely in a tight-fitting, white blouse and a long black, fluted skirt, that emphasized her slim waist and barely revealed her ankles.

On this evening, Johan walked straight towards her, delighted to end up in a situation where he could not avoid joining her. For an instant, he felt something similar to the intimate experience he had enjoyed at the Grévin when getting close to *Les Demoiselles,* before passing through the wall. She gazed up at him, her smile bright, and she motioned him to sit down.

"We don't have any clients yet. I've always wondered where you come from. You certainly are not one of the locals!"

Johan could not immediately decide how to answer. After hesitating, he returned her question. "I'm from the far north, as you can guess. What about you? You don't look like a local either?"

"I come from Brest in north-western France. We both have Viking forefathers, your relatives I would guess!" She laughed, but then became serious. "I came here to be married, but my fiancé found someone else. I was lucky to get work here. It's not easy, you know."

Johan was unprepared for such a direct, personal comment from Camille, and sensed she was trying to explain why she worked there. He had observed her having fun and spontaneously flirting, and had learned to see her as a natural part of the life at the Lapin, almost like a lively human form of furniture or decoration, making the place alive and welcoming to its guests. Now he felt uneasy about her sudden soft and personal approach, and did not know what to say. For the first time at the Lapin, he had a momentary taste of her real life.

Camille noticed his confusion. "I know what you think! Don't worry. I can handle myself. This is my work, like dancing. I have a small boy, Claude, to take care of; he's only four. Besides, many of the clients I entertain here are good men and they support me, Pablo included. That's why I'm here. I know them all. Foreigners can be different, but if I get into trouble, my regulars will help me."

Her soft and surprisingly natural tone broke Johan's resistance to her startlingly direct account. He was thoroughly embarrassed, and blushed; he was unprepared to face such an intimate encounter with Camille as she revealed her life story. Prostitutes were not entirely unknown to Johan; he had witnessed Pablo's behavior and in his real life, he had seen them on the streets of Amsterdam, Barcelona, and even Helsinki; however, it was the first time he had come so close to a person like Camille. They sat alone, intimately, face to face, and Johan could not escape the situation. There was no way to label her as one of "them", to span a safe personal distance.

Camille looked observant as she gazed directly into Johan's eyes. Leaning over the table to tap him on the shoulder, her eyes shining, she said, "I'll fetch a glass of wine for you. Relax for a while!"

She jumped up, disappeared for a brief moment, and returned with a full glass of red wine. Placing the wine in front of Johan, she surprised Johan by sitting close to him, holding him by the waist and leaning softly against his shoulder.

"I guess you are more alone here than I am," she said. "This is my home and I can take care of my son. I've often seen you stay quiet, alone, even sad; I can notice these things here; it's part of my job."

Johan tried to resist the disturbingly warm feeling of gratitude arising, realizing that Camille, in his eyes in her own desperate life situation and in need of help, was actually offering her support, to help him survive his own moody thoughts.

"Aren't you afraid of the consequences of what you do?" he asked.

He did not dare to call it her profession. The word "whore" used when talking about *Les Demoiselles* flashed through his mind. For a second, he imagined her work and blushed, ashamed. Suddenly he imagined the women in *Les Demoiselles* as mothers, and felt an uninvited guilt about something he did not know what it was.

As soon as he asked the question, Camille stared at him sharply. She took a little time to answer his question, and then she spoke, now with a low, almost fragile voice, reminding Johan of Yvonne's habit of speaking with a low tone when serious or worried.

"Of course, I am. We have a friend, Pablo knows her too, and there are others suffering from a deadly disease. Surely you know about it, but what else can I do but work?"

Johan turned toward Camille and hugged her, touching her hair gently, and taking a firm hold of her waist. As they drew apart, they stayed close, without saying a word. Both were smiling, yet Johan had a sad look in his eyes. Camille noticed his reaction to her situation, and broke the silence, recovering her vivid, energetic tone.

"There is always a way! Don't think I'm helpless; I'm pretty, and I have my clients; it's my blessing. I can make sure my son gets an education. Besides, one day I might get married. Don't think I haven't been asked already, but I'm wiser and more careful now!"

She moved to the other side of the table to face Johan, extending both of her hands to Johan; they felt cold in his own warmer ones.

"You think the men are using me. Well, of course they are, but that's not the point. What matters is that I can take care of my son, and when it becomes possible, I'll leave this to do something else, something safer. But even though it is this now, it won't remain a *cul de sac*! Don't you have any such problems in life, where you cannot change everything just like that?" She snapped her fingers. She stood up, getting ready to work.

Johan had to fight not to start crying openly and shamelessly, looking at Camille. He felt his own problems fall apart into insignificant fragments and pieces of the academic life. It was impossible to explain to Camille the problems which suddenly had lost all their monumental power to threaten him. He could only sigh, stand up, and take Camille by the hand, with a firm grip, so hard she had to warn him.

"You are hurting me!" she said, but she was not angry. They sat down, again, side by side.

Johan, startled and profoundly exhausted, touched her hair and tried to smile. "You amaze me and make me feel ashamed of my own weaknesses. My problems are nothing, but they've been too much for me. There is so much I cannot tell you!"

Camille kept staring at him, silent, smiling softly, and did not ask anything. Instead, she started talking about her daily routines and sharing amusing stories about her clients. Johan was embarrassed at first to hear the intimate details, even about the men he knew were married and visited the *Lapin,* but soon he was at ease, laughing heartily, often in tears of joy with Camille, as if her stories could be simply a natural and fun part of everyday life and living there. They continued their chat, Camille shining and showing her pride when talking about her son, the way he was growing and learning to read.

It was dark already when the first clients started to arrive. She left Johan by kissing him on the forehead, saying, "You could visit us and see Claude. He's a wonderful and clever boy. You could even teach him something!"

Johan felt so moved by her suggestion that he could not at first respond. Camille had already turned her back, and was opening the door to the Lapin, when Johan could finally utter, "Thank you, thank you!"

He was thoroughly shaken, in a mild state of shock, for a while unable to move from the table. Finally, he stood up, slowly, and went inside to find a table in a distant corner, where he stayed for three hours, silent and alone. Every now and then, he would go outside for some fresh air. He could not stop thinking about Camille and her son. She had been totally transformed in his eyes. From the entertaining waitress, one of the women of the night, she had become a charming and gentle, witty woman, a mother. Johan felt a new kind of compassion, and he wondered if he would experience this feeling in the future, every time he saw *Les Demoiselles.*

Maurice did not appear, and when it was getting close to midnight, Johan started home. On the way, climbing up the rue des Saules, he could not stop comparing his own life with Camille's as he tried to understand why the problems at Stanley and Helsinki had gotten such a devastating grip on him, why he did not have the same, amazing resilience Camille had shown. She saw new opportunities instead of obstacles, even in the middle of the worst problems and crises of life.

At the Bateau, Johan did not hear any noises from Pablo's atelier and went directly to bed. Unable to sleep, however, he lit a candle on the small table beside the bed. The talk with Camille kept reverberating in his mind, now aware, in a new and fresh way, of his own weakness and fragility. He kept thinking, "Why did I almost kill myself over such insignificant problems?" He could not forget the terrible experiences; they remained disturbing, yet this new insight was equally disturbing. He could not find any explanation for his fatal and utter helplessness.

Johan thought about Yvonne, the way she had saved him, first at the railway crossing and then by arranging a new opportunity in Paris. The gratitude and the guilt of having left her in uncertainty haunted him. He had become accustomed to the temporary aphasia regarding his own reality, but every now and then it became a heavy burden to carry, especially when something intimate happened, as with Camille. It made Johan feel he had failed or even cheated his companions, when it was impossible to share the deepest and most significant problems and encounters with them. Often it happened at the Bateau that he was unable to share and talk about the painful topics of his own reality. The most wretched pressure arose from the necessity, his personal *force majeure*, to consciously avoid the matters of utmost importance to him, his childhood and the subjects he had spent all his life studying.

The mysterious muting episodes reminded him of a physicist colleague, Markus Ravi from Helsinki, who had suffered a serious brain stroke and aphasia, causing severe problems in expressive speech. He was hemiplegic on his right side, fully able to understand speech, but unable to produce any fluent verbal expressions, typically uttering a few, often slurred and vague words. Markus was always extremely careful about choosing the words and expressions available to him, in order to speak and not stutter hopelessly. Over time, Markus and Johan could laugh at Markus' ability to use a couple of popular, strong swear words, in Finnish; he could even fluently sing parts of familiar pop songs, but speaking was extremely difficult. His sense of humor was the first sign to Johan that his friend-"was still there".

Johan had learned to be patient with Markus, to wait and not to hurry, not to show frustration about his slow and cumbersome speech, to give him plenty of time to express and formulate his restrained thoughts and ideas into a spoken form. Johan had learned not to help and interfere by finishing the sentences even when it would have been easy to do so. Instead, he let Markus do it, in his own way. The most remarkable lesson to Johan had been the observation and finding that he could assume his friend still had a full intelligent and creative capacity, and it was only a matter of formulating the ideas into comprehensible speech. For Johan, the benefits of doing so had been the delight to realize, unlike many of his colleagues, that Markus was still an insightful and clever scientist who had a serious, specific handicap in speaking and writing. Johan had learned to listen; that skill was also most useful for him at the Lapin. He had realized that Maurice and Pablo had the same accommodating attitude towards his muting, the momentary blocks, and felt deeply grateful for it.

Once, during such a long and tedious conversation with Markus, on a controversial finding from CERN, Markus had again been thoroughly frustrated when trying to offer his clever interpretation of the new data. He had put his left hand on Johan's shoulder, and gazed at him, with an anxious look in the eyes. Forcing Johan to listen, he had made a great effort to tell him something, extremely slowly. It took almost two minutes to finish the simple sentences, one word at the time, in a way Johan could never forget.

"Imagine what it would feel like," Markus said, "if someone asked you to describe what the word 'fluffy' means and you had to explain it to a group of eager listeners, in as colorful and expressive way as possible, but with your hands tied behind your back. This is how I feel with every inspiring thought I have and want to express to someone!"

They both laughed, while tears of joy and relief flowed. Laughter was easy for the aphasic and made it easy too for Johan to receive the message.

Markus had suffered from Broca's aphasia, and when in a light state of mind in Paris, Johan could now jokingly diagnose himself as suffering from what he called the Bateau's aphasia —a subset of Broca's, as he privately labeled it, limited to the verbal — written or spoken — formulation of any thoughts, knowledge and memories about the future he knew to be true. Johan's Bateau aphasia, unlike Markus's constant and indiscriminate aphasia, was dynamic, appearing in the middle of any conversation and baffling his intentions to express what he knew to be true.

Once Johan tried to joke about his Bateau aphasia to Maurice, who wanted to know more about it, but again the force prevented Johan from explaining his own humorous diagnosis. An awkward silence followed and made Maurice visibly uneasy, as he tried not to complete the sentences Johan had begun. The memory of Markus convinced Johan he simply had to adapt to the uncomfortable inner block. He had learned to recognize the risky situations, and to avoid them, but the adaptation had its price. The symptom had become increasingly disturbing, more every day, although it was easy to forget that he had this handicap, during the intensive discussions with his friends and the inspiring artists and writers at the Bateau or at the *Lapin*. He was alone with his true future.

For Johan, his new, modest life was full of creative energy and insights. Almost daily he was delighted by the sense of sharing with Pablo and Maurice, the most challenging ways of questioning the relationship between the reality of the world and its images. The views of the artists, especially the way Pablo presented them, were new to Johan, but in contrast to what he had previously thought, they were not unscientific at all; quite the contrary. To Johan these experiences were like an insightful, intellectual continuation of what he had learned on the skating rink with the colored lights, but only now he himself had a true education of a scientist. His artist friends had the capacity to change the way he saw the world, its colors, forms and light.

Johan could not imagine better companions to face the fascinating problems. There was no meal, long evening at a restaurant, or relaxed stroll along the narrow streets near the Bateau and Montmartre in which these topics did not arise in one form or another. It was like the everyday wine they enjoyed. At Stanley and in Helsinki it had been practically impossible to find company willing to immerse themselves in these puzzles of the arts and sciences, the problems that never ceased to inspire him. His colleagues were too busy with their labs, experiments and scientific writings. In academia, Johan had felt his spiritual questions and his stance already damaging his reputation as a serious empirical scientist. At the *Bateau* it was exactly this problem, crossing and breaking the borders between the art and sciences, that was always at hand and relevant in the discussions, a source of inspiration and joy. Introducing its various forms had now become Johan's natural asset, not a weakness, in inciting his friends into lively conversations. It was a wonderful source of intellectual joy for them all.

Sometimes Johan could even wonder if the future aphasia was a blessing, a boost to his creative thinking, as when the well-formulated knowledge was not available for him to repeat in the discussions; he had to come up with original arguments grounded in the present reality of his friends. It taught Johan to pay respect to his companions and their world views, not by giving up on their misunderstandings, but by trying to help them understand what he knew to be true.

The inhabitants of the Bateau rarely rose before noon. Every artist there worked hard, despite the wine and sometimes even drugs consumed. For some of them, the drugs were the fuel that kept them going all through the night until the early morning, and then in the evenings visiting the cafés and restaurants when they could afford it. The intense intellectual and creative atmosphere was not at all different from what Johan had first felt at Stanley and CLASH: everyone worked long hours, often alone and then joined others for a moment of diversion or to bask in the feeling of accomplishment and share the excitement of new challenges and discoveries. Passion for new and transformational ways of thinking about visual arts, literature and often even science was the driving force for everything now. It was ever-present, coloring and guiding the heated discussions at the Lapin, the men and a few women sitting at the terrace or inside when taking cover from the cold evening, or a rainy day. Nobody felt the need to control this flow of energy that simply emerged and whirled among the diverse, passionate souls.

Often the late evenings ended up in loud shouting at the Lapin. Johan had seen Pablo throw his wine glass against the wall, while cursing and preaching at Guillaume, Maurice, Johan or whoever happened to be nearby. Frequently Pablo had a true artist audience there. They were not only the art-agnostic pimps, women of the night from Montmartre or other societal outliers, but also art traders or devoted painters like the Italian-Jewish Amadeo Modigliani. Pablo always got into ferocious arguments with him about art, sex, drugs and Cezanne, who had passed away a year earlier and whom they both respected, in their own incompatible ways. Sometimes they were joined by the problematic Maurice Utrillo, who had begun painting rather late, but was now fascinated by the urge to present the life in Paris, especially Montmartre, his home. Suffering from alcoholism and mental instability, he was no exception among the clientele at the Lapin. During the crowded and noisy weekends, it was not rare to see abrupt fights emerge between the visiting artists and anarchists. They were quickly interrupted by the peace-seeking clients or by the respected owner.

For Johan the Lapin became his surrogate Epi Café, less cool and calm, but a forum where creative minds could meet, a place for innovative thoughts to emerge, mix, and be shared, for ideas to flourish or to be discarded, but with a remarkable difference, as Johan came to realize. The artists and workers at the Lapin were much alike, typically poor, living side by side. A painter or a poet did not expect any direct economic benefit or fame from sharing his — typically his not her — ideas, discoveries. This mutual openness occurred even while the artists remained extremely selfish and creative in their ambitions, often in a shameless, aggressive manner. Pablo, for instance, could lose his temper whenever someone challenged his works and style. Johan was astonished to learn that Pablo even tried learning boxing to manage his encounters with men, typically those much taller than he was. There was no promotion visible for any of the artists, no funding available, and nobody, perhaps with a very rare exception, who had the power to promote anyone. The poorest of the poor were supported with what little there was to help them to buy a glass of wine or a cheap soup. Luckily, Au Lapin was not an expensive place to eat and drink.

Chapter 21
A Mystic History

One early Sunday morning, Johan had woken up in the quiet Bateau after a long evening at the Lapin with Maurice, just the two of them, and now his mind was buzzing with the after-effects of the wine and the cigar-smoke, thoughts about the simultaneous, multi-dimensional representations of space-time in Pablo's paintings and the idea of what that kind of art might make possible in sculpting. He sat up in his bed, in the morning darkness, and stepped on the floor, careful not to kick the invisible bucket, moving slowly towards the door, stretching his hands up in the air, above his head, scratching his hair. There were various insects, including fleas, at the Bateau. He was happy on this morning that none were inhabiting his thick hair.

Johan opened the door to get some sunlight and fresh air, extended both of his hands up, yawning, taking hold of the wooden frame above the door. Stretching his back, hands up high, he stayed there by the door, looking to see if anyone from the rooms was awake already or walking by, but it was quiet. Only a distant snore echoed from somewhere upstairs. Then, hanging by both hands, he tried to extend the enjoyable stretch down to his lower back muscles, when he felt something on the rough board. It was too dark to see it against the bright-white light coming from the corridor, but it felt like an engraving in the wood. He moved his fingertips carefully over it, trying to avoid getting splinters in his fingers. He located the lines and corners of the engraving and started stroking them, smoothly, again and again, like reading braille in the dark.

He could not believe what he felt, but there was no doubt what it was he sensed under his fingers. It was the sign of his family, the bowtie ⋈, about four or five inches wide and two inches high. The observation almost threw him off balance. He stepped inside the room trying to see the sign, but it was in a dark shadow. The sunshine in the corridor blinded him and he knocked over the bucket, spilling something on his feet, but did not stop to worry. Instead, he rushed from the room, climbed upstairs to Pablo's studio to ask for a candle and matches. Without bothering to knock on the door, he entered the dark room, where there was no bed, only a mattress on the floor. He almost stepped on someone he thought was Pablo.

"Pablo, do you have a candle and matches? I need them now!"

It was silent in the room. Johan heard a light snore and repeated his question, when a hushed female voice from the bed answered:

"They are on the table, near the window."

He found the candle, lit it and started to leave the room, when he noticed the blonde, naked, slim young woman on the mattress, not bothering to cover herself. Quite the contrary, she raised herself up to a sitting position, and smiled at Johan.

"Hi, I'm Ann; we met at the Lapin, Pablo and me, I mean. I was modelling here last night." She giggled.

"Nice to meet you!"

Johan did not stay. He hurried out, muttering to himself on the way, "Really nice to see you," when suddenly, arousing images of Siiri flashed in his mind. He rushed down the stairs, back to the closet.

Under the candlelight Johan could only verify what he had already felt and recognized. It was the family sign. No one, he could not imagine anyone else, nobody, except for his father, could have left it there, especially there, above the door. He stood silent, remembering the visit to the old barn on the Snakefields, getting inspired and confused. The only way he could imagine the symbol could have ended up there was that his friends had lived there with his father and somehow, for a mysterious reason — what it was, he could not understand — his father had carved it there. It was evident that his friends could not see any difference between Johan and his father. Then he realized, the future aphasia had probably concerned his father, too, preventing him from describing where he had come from and who he was. At his first meetings at the Bateau, Johan remembered, that sometimes he could not be the first one to say his own name, "Johan," but once Guillaume had used it, he could use it, too. But all this was now too complicated. Why didn't he notice any language problems there? Why did everything seem to work as if the language did not matter at all?

"I'm out of explanations for this, what is happening and why. It's just impossible!" Johan thought.

He stepped out of the room, climbed up the stairs and sat down on the doorstep. Sighing, with his head down on his knees, looking at his filthy feet, he had the urge to talk about this discovery of the family sign with Pablo and Maurice, but how?

Johan had been sitting there for some time when Pablo came out.

"You met Ann! She's a wonderful model. We met at Au Lapin. She said you are quite an exotic and charming giant!"

Johan hesitated. How could he find the words that would communicate his situation to Pablo?

"What's wrong?" Picasso sat beside Johan. "You smell like a pig again, what have you done? You have shit all over your feet! Why don't you go and wash yourself!? Get water and come back so we can have a decent chat here when you smell better!" He tapped Johan on his head and took hold of his shoulder with both of his hands, like waking him up, a broad smile on his face.

"Go now!"

Johan was confused. As he stood up and started on his way to fetch water from the fountain, he said to Pablo, over his shoulder, "I've found a strange mark. It's my family sign!" but Pablo did not react to his comment in any way, as if he had not heard it.

Carrying water from the fountain, Johan came upon Pablo sitting on the entrance stairs. Relaxed and with his face held up to the bright sunlight, Pablo was enjoying the day so much that for a while Johan forgot his strange discovery. He washed his feet without a hurry and they both stayed quiet for a minute or two. Johan dried his hands and turned to Pablo.

"How simple life is," Johan said, tapping Pablo on the shoulder and laughing. "Art, wine, sex, and voilà! You wake up happy!"

Pablo pushed Johan like a boxer.

"Stay away with your shit!" Smiling, eyes closed, Pablo continued his encounter with the morning sun. Opening his eyes for a moment, he added, "Draw me the sign you are so excited about!"

Johan put down the water bucket and sat down beside Pablo, picking up a little wooden branch from the ground. He drew the bowtie mark in the sand, in front of Pablo, who slowly turned his gaze down to see it, as he listened to Johan.

Johan was excited. "It's an ancient sign or signature of my family. They used it to sign documents and mark any valuable family property. It was the time when only a few could write. I found it carved above the door to my cave!"

Pablo gave Johan a sharp look.

"Of course, I know it; it's been there for some time! Have you forgotten it?" He looked puzzled.

Johan, confused, did not know what to say, but remained quiet, as he started to dry his feet. Soon Maurice joined them.

"It's your outdoor recreation day again, Johan. What a wonderful day!"

Pablo and Maurice shared their good humor, as they watched Johan.

Maurice asked, "What has happened? You seem worried, Johan?"

"I found my family..." Johan began, showing the sign on the ground, but then the force prevented him again, and he could not continue. Instead, he tried another expression.

"I found an engraving in my room. It might interest you!"

Maurice threw a quick glance at the drawing.

"I see, that one. It's quite simple, but could be a projection of a complex geometrical figure, remember?"

Johan did not know what to say. He had to take it as given that his father Sten had, somehow, been in old Paris and had appeared to look just like Johan.

"This is not a scientific problem. I don't have any means to even formulate it," was Johan's thought. He felt anxious to know more about his father's visit, but was feeling totally helpless, unable to plan or even imagine a way to initiate any enlightening discussion on this conundrum with his friends. Any reference to the future muted him, making him look silly or even psychotic.

That night at the Lapin, after a cheerful and elated gathering, Johan again several times tried to refer to his own life. He became so frustrated about the strange aphasia that he drew a timeline from the year 1907 to 2016 on a napkin to explain, without talking, to show visually to Maurice and Pablo where he came from. The timeline was easy to draw, and he could continue it as far in time as he wanted, but when trying to write the word "me" beside the year 2016 his hand did not obey but instead drifted around over the napkin. He tried it several times and could only draw haphazard, thick lines here and there. He had no control along the timeline and his hand moved wildly, even tipping a glass of wine on Maurice, who became visibly worried and frightened.

"What in heaven's name is wrong with you? A holy moon disease or something? Should I take you to a doctor?"

Pablo did not seem astonished at all, only frowned as he said, "I had the same feeling when drawing the lines of a sketch of the Brothel, explaining their meaning to an art critic and his artist friend visiting me. They thought I could not draw! Then some months later, reading the comments from the same critic, I knew it was he who had lost his mind, not me!"

Johan was confused, leaning his head against both of his hands.

"I wish I could tell everything to you. There is nobody else now. Sorry, Pablo, I'm a fool!"

He turned silent, thinking, "I'm Markus here, making a fool of myself with my aphasia. It's my turn now, to pray every moment they have mercy on me and let me express my own thoughts!"

He realized that not only did he suffer from a mysterious aphasia for the future, but he also had a serious *apraxia* and *agrafia* for future-referring gestures and expressions. Having studied Markus's symptoms carefully when trying to find out how to best support him, he knew that in reality, such future-related syndromes do not exist, in the sense that there was no description of them in the neurology handbooks he had so intensively studied. Finding that he could not even draw or write about his true life had made him feel as if he lived in a perfect cage of time with no way out.

Chapter 22
Arts and the Power Game

One Saturday afternoon Pablo took Guillaume, Johan and Maurice with him to visit Gertrude Stein's home on the Left Bank, at 27 rue de Fleurus; it was the first time for Johan to visit her. On the long walk there that took an hour, Johan noticed their route ended up close to the rue de Vaugirard and the building where the metre plate, the standard, was attached. He felt a pressing, teasing urge to go and see what it was like *now*, to touch it again or before, as he thought, smiling to himself, thinking about his new time and to see if the mystic wall would again appear there, in front of the massive gate to the Palais du Luxembourg. He did not try to mention the gate to his friends, who already had their fuzzy and bad memories of it, especially the disappearance of Johan's father; to them it was just Johan and the mysterious, paranoid stories they had heard of the Metre. Johan could not get rid of the thought it was only five hundred meters from the Stein apartment. It would keep coming to his mind throughout the evening.

The Stein salon had achieved a not only remarkable, but also disputed reputation as *the* hub of modern and progressive art, literature and poetry in Paris. People, typically men — writers, painters, poets, playwrights and bizarre avant-garde artists — blessed by invitations, were validated as *the* meaningful, successful or promising individuals in their modern artistic endeavors and circles. Johan had not asked about the salon and its visitors in any detail and thought he would only be paying a visit to a peculiar kind of, but no doubt, higher social class home. He had never heard of Stein or the Steins.

It would not be a new experience to Johan, to go to a gathering of such figures. He wondered if it would be different from the formal gatherings and receptions among scientists. Often as a graduate student and later as a fledgling researcher, Johan had been invited to the parties his professors arranged in Helsinki. At Stanley too, he had had the chance to meet prominent, visiting scholars and other renowned academics. Johan had learned the social rules and the significance of the *academic hubs*. Like all his young scientist colleagues, Johan too had been eager and full of vibrant enthusiasm to meet the international celebrities, and to be given the rare chance to talk to them in person, after having read and admired their famous scientific articles, and to celebrate the achievements of his own research community as well. It was a joy to join these informal settings, free from the everyday pressures at the lab. Being a member of such a community was a privilege and a symbol of success and recognition.

However, after about half a dozen disappointing experiences, where Johan had repeatedly found himself a total outsider, he had quickly realized how the parties were not what they appeared to be. Often, they were not social calls at all, their core purpose was not to join in the joy of science, and not everyone was equal there. Contrary to what he had expected and imagined, he had attended parties which did not have much to do with the spirit of the ideal university and science. Something else was hidden behind the welcome champagnes, the fancy dinners and the colloquial talks. Decisions were prepared, attitudes tuned, introductions made, rumors spread; the parties were the hidden generators of the academic power fields. At first Johan blamed himself and thought it was his personal problem, his defensive suspicions, coming from such a modest and problematic family background as he did. He was socially inexperienced, yet after a while he realized that his observations about the way hierarchy and power worked on such occasions were accurate.

Over time Johan had made another, alarming observation: that to be accepted as a true member of this community and to be treated as a real scientist there, a visitor had to accept the golden chains offered with no option to refuse. The chains would bind the hands, feet and soul. The sad insight made Johan distance himself even further, especially when he understood he did not have any real friends there among the academics. He could only share the social space and move on the power field with these scientists.

One such occasion had become a revelation to Johan and in effect, liberated him from the uncomfortable social pressures he had originally experienced. It was a dinner party arranged at Calle's luxury home near

Kaivopuisto, perhaps the most prestigious neighborhood in which to live in Helsinki. Johan had been seated at a side table, far from the main guests, sitting together with the wife of a visiting Russian scientist who himself was not present at the party, and their thirteen-year-old, charming but visibly bored daughter, Nadia, whom Johan every now and then tried to cheer up. It was easy to see this was not her first time in an academic party like this, to be seated with someone who could not speak her language. She had short, curly hair and lively brown eyes. Her charming slim appearance made Johan think she must have a background in sports or in dance. The mother, perhaps not yet fifty, with somewhat gray and pale looks, and a quiet appearance, was open and kind to Johan. Later Johan understood she was an architect, but she did not speak English very well.

One of the guests, a local professor, walked with his gin and tonic from the bar, passing by their table in the crowded room. As he tapped the girl on her head, he commented, "What a charming little girl you are!" and "How do you like it here?" not stopping to talk to her or wait for any comment. He clearly did not realize that the girl did not understand English. The mother followed the chap with a sharp gaze up to the main table, then she turned to look at Johan, rolling her eyes. They both laughed and Nadia joined the fun.

About twenty guests had been seated at the central dinner table, covered by a bright white tablecloth, and decorated with miniature roses and candles, whose light created an atmosphere of a classic, traditional feast. Calle sat in the middle, opposite to Peter and Peter's beautiful, young wife. After the dinner, Calle gave a speech vividly praising his team, the equality of its members, and their shared successes together. Extending both of his hands, and looking up and down the table, he proposed a toast:

"Let us all stand and raise a toast to science!"

Everyone stood and extended their champagne glasses towards Calle, smiling. After a few seconds of an almost disturbing silence, everyone sat down, gazing nervously around. To Johan the atmosphere was a reminder of the scene in *The Last Supper* painting, with Jesus sitting in the middle of his disciples and everyone observing the painting knowing, it's not about a feast at all.

Calle remained standing and continued his speech about how everyone shared a passion for science. He thanked the team for helping to create the breakthrough of his and Peter's new model. Sitting at the side table, with no colleague to talk to, only the nice lady and her daughter, had at first been annoying to Johan, but now, after exchanging the eye roll with the woman, he could smile at it. He spent some time starting a sign language game with Nadia, her mother helping them every now and then. The girl was glad to have a break in the awkward atmosphere and was visibly delighted by the simple games and the attention she received from Johan.

Once he had started to have difficulties at Stanley, Johan had often looked back at that evening in Finland, smiling to himself as he entertained the amusing idea, "I was probably the Judas there, only that I wasn't even close to Jesus and no real threat then." He had remembered the old Swedish saying by which his father used to warn about the dangers of attractive social connections: *Gyllene bojor är också bojor.* Golden chains are chains, too.

It had dawned on Johan during this dinner that his main role there was to be one of the obedient members of the audience, not an actor, to make sure there was a reverberating echo chamber for praise, a scene without which Calle would have had to talk alone, in an empty space. All this was crystallized as Johan said his goodbyes and left the party. To his surprise, a sudden, disturbing emptiness filled Johan's mind while he walked slowly back home in the dark and empty city. He wondered if everyone at the party had experienced the same disturbing after-effect of meaninglessness and a feeling of having been used. As he walked, he also remembered the inspiring ideas in his own work and the fascinating research problems being solved, the absorbing articles written with his colleagues. From that night on, similar social situations bothered him less, as he learned to live them and to follow the emerging social drama during each party more from a safe distance, reminding himself of what really had value in his life.

The two worlds — one of research challenges and one of fame — were like parallel, but unfortunately not exclusive universes, and Johan realized there was not much he could do about this disturbing connection between these worlds. From that evening on, every time he visited an academic high-class home or party, he was eager to participate, to observe what was really going on there. He even adopted a private habit of conducting simple social experiments by testing where he was welcomed and where not. On one of these occasions, he had met Siiri, for the first time, noticing how she was trying to avoid some eager scholars and professors who approached her. Despite her conspicuous height, her odd, full-white, powdered face, dark red lipstick, and her thick eyeliner, which almost masked her eyes, her beauty was not hidden from the visiting male celebrities that had crowded around her. Johan admired her personal looks and thought of her as a modern, educated Goth.

Johan hoped that this salon at the Steins' would be warmer and more humane than a dinner like the one at Calle's house. For some reason, Johan thought of Siiri, and wondered what was it like to be a woman among the bands of male scientists and artists? Even Siiri, who was herself a scientist, had to constantly protect herself. Pablo had spoken nicely about Gertrude Stein, who was strong when needed. Johan had learned that despite her harsh behavior, she could be a graceful support and a mentor to both the visual artists and any writer she thought had potential.

At the Steins', Johan became, for the first time since his entrance into the world of the artists at the Bateau, aware of the familiar atmosphere, the biasing and annoying power fields and the drama that now was governing the difficult life of the poor artists. At first, being a novice to the art world, he could not exactly pinpoint the source of the atmosphere, but the disturbing social ether, the carrier of social power was definitely present there, familiar to Johan. It surrounded everyone in the salon. The art collectors, influential critics, and their use of money made it all happen, pushing the poor artists here and there, as they drifted on the power fields. Not one of the power generators was unknown and everyone's background mattered.

Johan was struck and surprised by the strong, penetrating impact the social ether seemed to have on these creative souls, his new, creative friends. He imagined how the deformation of the artists' space by the power figures visiting the salon was the same as what he had seen happening at Calle's and other academic elite parties. Later, observing the social code of conduct at the Steins', the way arts and artists were displayed there and the way the hosts and the invited art critics and agents behaved and talked to the guests, he understood what it was that so much bothered him, what was so similar, almost identical to his own experiences in academia. It was the familiar, ever-present dynamics of social power, be it art or science. It was a real, tangible threat, not far from a nightmare.

They had arrived early, and Gertrude had come to welcome them, with a loud greeting and a wide smile, full of energy, like a dynamo as Johan immediately thought about her. Although Picasso had claimed to think of Gertrude as a good friend, Johan did not experience her as charming at all. To him she appeared a rather robust person with a heavy character, not only in her physical appearance, as she had dressed to look more like a man, or a worker. She had a protruding, narrow nose, and simple, unkempt hair; the overall sturdy attitude emphasized her sharp, critical, even negative gaze.

She embraced both Guillaume and Pablo, and told them who were present, but she barely said hello to Johan and Maurice. Once Gertrude had heard Pablo's introduction of Johan as a Nordic physicist, she did not invite him into a discussion, and did not ask about his work, only flattered him, without a smile, for his tall, blond looks. She quickly turned her back then, to talk to Pablo and Guillaume. Maurice had noticed this momentary, awkward episode and came over to Johan.

"Do you know," he said, "Miss Stein has studied under William James, the famous American psychologist, who has most interesting theories about human vision. She too must have some scientific understanding of the visual arts, and I know she and Leo, her brother, have talked about James' work with Pablo."

"I don't see any human psychology in that behavior," Johan commented, winking at him, smiling. He did not confess that the name James was totally unfamiliar to him.

When Gertrude asked Pablo about Fernande, his mistress or "girlfriend", as Johan had put it in a conversation with Maurice, Johan realized he had not seen Fernande at the Bateau apartment. Pablo had mentioned Fernande a couple of times by name, but with such a tense tone that Johan had not wanted to ask more. It was news now to hear

Pablo commenting briefly that she was traveling, but he did not explain in any detail.

The other guests were expected to arrive after six o'clock, so that the band of early visitors had plenty of time to talk to Gertrude and Leo, who were both American-born and passionate art collectors. Gertrude was a writer and poet. No doubt, the Steins shared a profound understanding of the art business and trade.

No one disturbed Johan, who was free to walk around the impressive flat and make his own observations about the arriving guests, the way people greeted each other and found their places in the art-filled room, among the other guests. There was an inviting but empty armchair near the fireplace; the visitors had found other chairs and tables to form discussion circles and immerse themselves in exchanging experiences, ideas and events in their lives and the arts scene. Dozens of oil paintings and other forms of visual artwork crowded every wall of the flat, from floor to ceiling, creating a peculiar kind of a closed artistic universe, as Johan thought about it, a place where no one present could hide from the space-time the modern artworks spanned for them.

Listening to Pablo talk with Gertrude, Johan was surprised to notice Pablo's submissive tone, an unexpected change. Even Guillaume had become mysteriously muted. His colorful, sparkling and dandy-like personality had lost some of the bubbling edge of his wonderful, critical energy, as he behaved instead like a well-taught schoolboy when Gertrude or Leo lectured about the future of the arts.

Johan could only use a metaphor in his interpretation of what he saw. To his physicist eyes, the artists had suddenly turned into poor particles in the game, sliding on the power fields, until upgraded or integrated with larger masses in arts, to become something graceful and valuable material with impact. This would happen only by being accepted and blessed by the power generators. Gertrude Stein was one of them and there were others present whom Johan did not know. He pondered the scene and her looks and stance, the guru-like behavior and the impressive chair that she had reserved only for herself, making it the center of gravity in the salon. He felt a disturbing embarrassment for his friends, noticing how they had adopted their submissive roles immediately upon arrival and unlike at the Bateau, how unable they were to find their own, independent pathways there, to scatter around freely.

It was natural for Johan to compare what he had observed in the salon with his own position and scientific work for Calle and Peter, promoting *their* fame and influence. Doing this, he had ended up being chained by the golden bonds while they had obtained the position, the capacity, either to push him out of the science field or to pull him towards a wonderful reputation and fame. Despite his vague knowledge of art history, Johan was keen to notice the parallels: what it must mean to Pablo to see his works there, in the famous salon, hung side by side with the paintings of Gauguin, Renoir, and Cézanne, the famous names even Johan knew. No doubt, there loomed the potential for a total destruction of an artist's reputation as well, had Gertrude wished it.

It became clear to Johan how vulnerable even Pablo Picasso was, in the face of this mighty gatekeeping. Had the Steins wanted to destroy Pablo's career or harm him, so that everyone would know it, they could have done this easily. It would be as easy for them to hurt a revolutionary like Pablo as it had been for Calle and Peter to hurt Johan. All the Steins would have had to do would be to remove Pablo's works from their salon walls. The unspoken message would be that his works are suspicious, he has lost his touch, or is simply not doing real art any more, and that would be the end of it. They would never be caught for a lie. The only risk would be an economic one, if someone else would guess the value of Pablo's work in the future and leave them without an investment. It could take decades, however.

"Who would take the risk against the dominant thought leaders, the kings and queens who know the trends?" Johan thought to himself. "What a shame I cannot talk about the future I know! I should try to write or draw something about it."

During the salon visit Johan remained mostly silent, exchanging a few comments with Maurice. Every now and then he quietly conducted his private experiments by joining the small groups engaged in vivid discussions, and noticed how he was easily left out, even excluded from them, especially when he introduced himself as a physicist. It did not bother him much, as it was also a relief from the continuous awareness of his personal aphasia. Johan was relieved to avoid making a fool of himself as the mute Nordic, or the awkward physicist among the progressive artists.

Moving about the main hall, the dining room, and other open rooms, he tried to figure out the essence and purpose of the salon. "Why is this so important to even Pablo? He certainly does not lack self-esteem, but now seems to sell some profound, most valuable elements of himself. What is this he gives away, to these people? His freedom? Is it only money and fame? It's so familiar! No different from having my name hanging on the title page of a scientific article, together with the famous colleagues from Stanley or from other prominent universities and research labs. When they drop me, as Calle and Peter are probably doing, I'm nothing in the world of science; it does not matter what I think and what I have done and accomplished. I'm no different from Pablo, because he's nothing unless his name is hanging on the Steins' walls. It's the name that has value, not his paintings, which of course are a necessary condition to get the name Picasso hanging there, too. Without the name, the paintings would be worthless."

It was close to midnight when Maurice came to Johan, asking if he'd like to join them to walk through the city, over the Seine and then see if the Lapin was still open.

"Pablo and Guillaume are quite drunk already. It would be wise for us to leave before they start anything. I've seen it happen here, too often, and it's not good for them."

They both looked around to spot their friends and noticed how the two were indeed visibly recovering from their submissive styles, full of energy and audibly aggressive towards two art critics they had found there. Having loudly voiced what they thought about the critics' lame and conservative views, they had moved on to another victim to attack.

Pablo and Guillaume started pushing a short, well-dressed man in his fifties, wearing round, metal-framed eye-glasses. They were shouting at him, in a distant corner of the dining room, preventing him from escaping. Maurice knew the fellow was a well-known art agent whom the two attackers blamed in a visibly hot-tempered manner for treating the artists like slaves and for his cruel habit of buying art with a shamefully low price when the helpless artist could not resist the greedy offer. Suffering from serious malnutrition and a lack of money, even unable to buy the necessary colors, paintbrushes and canvases, the artists could only take whatever the agent would give.

Pablo was the first to push the man against the wall, with both of his hands, so hard that everyone heard the thump when the fellow hit and fell against the wall, sliding down on the floor, just below a large oil painting. When the victim was barely able to stand up and was desperately trying to find a way out from the corner, Guillaume gave him a shove. The poor agent fell on the floor again, sitting there, looking desperately around as if asking for help, but did not say anything.

Nobody seemed to react to the scuffle, but when it started to look dangerous to the helpless man, Johan interfered to save him, and was thoroughly surprised by Pablo, who started pushing him and calling him a stupid Viking, staring at Johan with his flaming eyes. The situation started looking ridiculous, when Pablo, who was almost a foot shorter than Johan, tried to push him as he had just done to the agent, but nothing happened. Johan just stood still, looking down at the angered Pablo and smiling his kind smile. He then laughed aloud, so that now even the guests noticed it.

Maurice tapped Pablo on the shoulder and said, "You can paint, but you cannot grow. Please leave our friend alone! He's just trying to save the bastard — and you."

Pablo breathed heavily, turned around and rushed to Gertrude, who sat on her throne.

"We are leaving! There are people here who kill my inspiration!"

He turned around, took Maurice by the arm, and started towards the door; Johan and Guillaume followed at a fast pace down to the dark street, where Pablo stopped in front of the entrance to say, "Fresh air, finally!"

Smiling at Johan, Pablo appeared to have completely forgotten the episode.

"Why did you get so angry there, even at me?" asked Johan.

"I'm just fine," said Pablo. "I'm fine! Nothing has disturbed me. Is something bothering you?"

Guillaume joined them, looking nervous, but not ashamed. Stepping in front of Pablo, he said loudly, "They are the parasites. We are their gourmet food!"

Chapter 23
Pablo and the Future

Johan felt it wise not to comment on the disturbing incidents any more, and instead tried to talk Guillaume, Maurice and Pablo into joining him on a visit to the Metre.

"I know you have seen it already, but we can walk to it first, and head for home then. It's quite near here and I really would like to see it once more. It's only a few blocks walk on a beautiful night."

He felt a strange, warm rush of emotions, realizing that he had used the term "home" for the first time when referring to the Bateau and the modest room he had occupied there; it would be one month soon. None of the guys was eager to comment on Johan's suggestion, but then Pablo stepped in front of him, looking up at him, scrutinizing his face first and then, making Johan abashed by the intimate move, coming very close to him, only a few inches, staring at him, eyes flaming, the way Johan had seen happen every time Pablo got seriously excited or agitated. However, there was a new, unusual, soft aspect to his gaze, a delicate nuance Johan could not interpret.

Pablo remained quiet and only after a half a minute of intense staring and silence, which felt an uncomfortably long time to Johan, did he begin to speak.

"I don't know what it is in you that I'm afraid to lose. Maybe you are the ghost of Carles. I felt his painful presence the last time you left us. It was like losing a friend, losing Carles for the second time, forever. You two gave me an intolerable grief by disappearing from my life; it took me by surprise, you are not anything like an artist, and for Heaven's sake, I barely knew you, I would not even flatter you as a good amateur. You showed disrespect to us and to our art by smudging my works, my sketches. Still, there is a mysterious link between us that I love; it connects your physical delusions with my artistic facts!"

Johan wanted to interrupt Pablo's accusation and confessions, to defend himself, but Pablo put his left hand firmly on Johan's chest, letting it stay there at first, and then moving his right hand smoothly, in a mesmerizing way, over Johan's chest, as if painting something on it, all the time talking in an exceptionally calm and kind-sounding tone. Johan had not seen Pablo so vulnerable, struggling with something unusually soft and sensitive on his mind. It was clear he wanted Johan to seriously listen to him and he was telling it by speaking and painting with his hands, formulating his story on Johan's chest, over his heart.

"You and Maurice are the only ones who almost understand the spirit of the *Brothel* and its space-time. I mean, the way I see it, although you only have your rigid mathematics and the complicated dimensions, you understand the spirit and mystery of this painting. I've noticed that for some time already you have been obsessed by the curtain-doors in it. You must have realized by now that they are not there by accident. They are not only symbols of a space-time gate; they are real doors, they are art as a wonderful reality, passages to the past or to the future. I don't know which and I don't care."

He continued without a break, did not give Johan a chance to step back, move away or respond. Johan understood how serious Pablo was about his own art and creativity, especially as it was reflected in the *Demoiselles.*

"Your amazing painting, the..." Johan intended to say *Les Demoiselles,* but was muted and immediately realized the name of the work had not been born yet. It was *The Brothel* or *The Whores.* He tried again.

"Your amazing painting, *The Whores*, has a special significance to me; I'm sure you have noticed it and Maurice knows it, too. The critics can say what they want, and the future will decide, not the past! I've had my lesson on this painting — it's about mathematics, but it's also about humans. And it makes me wonder: have you ever thought or imagined that the women could be mothers?"

Pablo looked astonished.

"What do you mean that they could be mothers? How can you know that? Of course, I have, I *knew* them!"

Johan thought of Camille at the Lapin but did not want to explain his confusion about her profession, only sighed.

"I think I saw something like that in the painting."

Pablo nodded, had a momentary, sad look in his eyes, as if he knew what Johan meant. He kept his left hand on Johan's chest, moving it from left to right, left to right, as if an indicator of time passing.

"They are not only whores," he said quietly, and then he simply changed the sensitive subject, and continued. "Everybody here, the artist and art critics alike, have a futile relationship with what is to come. Some fear it, some try to guess it. But that is not all. They have their selfish ways to twist history to benefit them, either in money or in fame. Then they want to build on this and behave like the best visionaries, poets, and painters of the future. It's impossible; nothing comes out of it, but they talk and talk and suddenly…" He paused, and continued.

"They are taken as visionary heroes! Without doing anything real, visible, or tangible! I cannot understand it, but you are the only one among us, in addition to me, who always remains silent about the future, and you hardly mention our past, as if you knew of something that is inevitable, something that you need not talk about. I have that same feeling every day when I wake up to a new day, in joy or in sadness. Without that empowering, that explosive feeling, I would just draw nice lines, repeat what has been done already. I would create nothing. I love the awakening and emerging tomorrow, but I hate to talk about it. I get bored with the talk of it; it makes me blind. I want to make the future happen *now*, and I try, again and again, to express this burning in me, to project it on canvas and make it visible and tangible with any possible material. It's not a future vision; it's not a vision at all, I simply force it to become visual and even visible because I'm the best artist to do that. I have something inside me, a world without words, a world without pictures, something I try to reveal to you all. I cannot talk about it. Words kill it. I don't want to do that!"

Pablo had not moved an inch from the spot where he stood. He had not shifted his gaze from Johan's eyes during this monologue. It did not embarrass Johan any more, even though he was not used to such a closeness; he was moved by the unexpected and unguarded show of affection and trust. He was struck by the observation that what he had considered as a strange aphasia, even apraxia for the future, was a source of creativity for Pablo. Hearing Pablo's moving story of losing a friend,

Johan had an inescapable urge to speak from his heart, to find a way, even an indirect one that would allow an access to his own reality.

Yet the only thing he could say without stuttering was, "I have come…" and this time he felt like fainting and suffocating, so much that he had to grab Pablo by both his shoulders in order not to fall.

Pablo did not move and remained quiet and calm in front of Johan. He did not ask anything, just let Johan rest and lean his chest against Pablo's head, Johan's hands resting on his shoulders, peacefully, neither of them feeling any hurry to separate.

Finally, Pablo broke the silence. "I know that state, and when it conquers me, I go to my canvas, choose my colors and paintbrushes. I forget the future and my tomorrow, and then, from the first stroke on, when I produce my thoughts on the empty white space, I breathe again with all my power. It is then I can see my mind turning into visible things and can work with them for hours."

Pablo pushed Johan lightly on his chest, not too hard, as if waking him up. Johan regained his balance and began to breathe freely again.

Pablo took the first step.

"Let's go and see your Metre!"

He smiled at Johan, who remained quiet and pale, standing erect again, slowly recovering without understanding what had hit him.

Johan felt dizzy, taking the first staggering steps, with care, trying to follow Pablo, who was again full of energy and soon walking far ahead of him, without looking back. Guillaume and Maurice had noticed Johan's insecurity and stayed near him, watching carefully that he would not fall or hit himself against the trees, parked carriages, or other obstacles left on the dark street, where only a few feeble gaslights provided a faint, bluish light.

Walking towards the place of the Metre along the rue de Vaugirard, they passed by a lamppost where two lanterns of gaslight hung from a high, ornamented metal arm, shining a soft light on the street and on the gray-brown walls of the house abutting the Jardin. On their right, some fifty yards ahead, they saw the façade of the building hosting the entrance gate to Le Jardin du Luxembourg. It was the gate where Johan had seen a curtain-like mask and a youngish man moving behind it. On his left Johan could barely discern the row of pillars and the arcs between them, belonging to the dark archway where the metre plate should be attached.

Pablo was already waiting for them at the end of the archway. He stood in front of the Metre with a lit candle in his hand.

"Well, you seem to be properly prepared for the night!" Johan commented, laughing. He realized quickly that carrying a candle was not magic, but simple, reasonable behavior from Pablo. Johan had already noticed that many of the main boulevards were well lit, but the peculiar parts of the city Pablo preferred, especially in the middle of the night and even later, were dark. Pablo was prepared and sure to have a light source, a candle and matches whenever he moved around.

The Metre was there, looking almost exactly as Johan had seen it, but not quite. It was dirty, covered with black dust or soot, full of traces left from the hands of the eager visitors, perhaps measuring their own sticks against it, or just curious to touch and caress it, exactly as Johan had done when visiting the place in the future.

Pablo was the first to ask Johan about the message of the Metre.

"This is serious now, Johan. It's your turn to explain why on earth you want us to be here with you again, and in the middle of the night? We could be enjoying wine, the charm of the women and the discussions at the Lapin. Instead, you practically force us here, hardly able to stand erect, and then want us to admire this dead plate, which, by the way, is terribly ugly!"

He lifted up the candle toward Johan, who could not help smiling.

"It's a wonderful symbol," Johan said, "controversial if you ask me, but you must know its meaning and value in Paris."

Pablo shook his head. "To me it's the worst possible symbol owned by hardened conservatives. It's their disastrous standard, a dirty sign as it appears, stiff and oppressive. It has only one message to tell us: comply and do not change anything, ever! Do as we tell you!"

Pablo was waving his hands vividly in the air, almost extinguishing the candle.

"Think about this, Maurice, what would *Le Bordel* look like if I had worshipped this dead Metre of the citizens? I'd be painting exact copies of the whores in the brothel of Avignon! Why would I copy them when I can visit the real ones?"

Johan laughed from his heart, the quiet archway echoing from his joyous voice.

"You mean, you don't actually like it, the Metre plate?"

Suddenly, Guillaume became excited and began to dance in the darkness, making pirouettes, with his hands raised high, and singing something in a strange language or a dialect Johan did not understand. It was the first time Johan did not understand a language he heard during his visit and wondered why it was so, but he forgot the thought when trying to observe Guillaume's dance. After bumping against the building walls a couple of times, Guillaume stopped the hilarious performance and started to chant his favorite incitement in words Johan could again understand.

"Empty the Louvre, what is it worth? Tear it down, bring it to earth!"

Johan was again puzzled as to why he had not understood Guillaume's language at first.

"Let me come closer, I want to see the Metre..."

Johan tried to calm his friends and was about to say "again" but felt the strangling grip of the muting force getting him. This time the muting was about one word only, that "again". Pablo moved the candle in front of the plate, making the golden letters of the word 'METRE' gleam.

"This is French history," Johan said. "I don't know if you have heard about Méchain and Delambre, who both worked hard to collect the meridian measurement data needed for defining the metre. They were brave heroes like you, true scientists. But then the power of the system got hold of Méchain, who not only cheated his good friend and colleague Delambre, but who also deluded the whole science community! He could not be open about the mistake he had made in one of his arduous measurements. He was after the fame and praises of the science community in Paris and all over the western world! Fame became more important to him than the truth. Maybe it was just the fear of shame among his colleagues, but it makes no difference. The error carried over the years and has cheated us all."

Pablo was agitated and excited, moving his hands and body so much that he extinguished the candle.

He continued in the darkness, "Exactly! Science is no different from the arts! The critics are afraid to lose their status as visionaries by failing to be the first ones to report on a new genius entering their market!"

Johan was surprised to hear Pablo's comments on the art markets, remembering how submissive he had been at the Steins. It was as if he lived a double life. This meekness in Pablo, in front of art critics and buyers, was a mystery to Johan, who had learned to appreciate Pablo's mental strength, even arrogance, and he tried to figure out an explanation for the evident paradox. As he thought to himself, "He must know there is a price to pay when entering the art saloon, but as soon as we got out from there, he seemed to forget it. It's similar to the science salons. Then on the other hand, perhaps I just have a subconscious picture of Pablo as it is in the media of my own reality, in Pablo's future of success. There he is strong, extremely strong."

Increasing the pitch and volume of his voice, Pablo said, "The agents fear for their reputation and money if they bet on the wrong horses. Artists hide their mistakes and claim they are natural-born revolutionaries who never make mistakes! What has cursed these people? Is it a shame or greed, or both: shame-greed, greed-shame?"

Pablo lit the candle again and started moving back and forth in front of the Metre plate, scrutinizing it by bringing the light close to it.

"I make mistakes all the time, and Johan, you have seen all the tens of sketches of *The Brothel* and *The Family*, in your cabin. Each of them is a mistake and a proof of my stupidity! No wonder then that you wanted to correct them, but you made your mistakes too. I don't hide my failures. Hiding them would make me even more stupid next time! I work and work and let you see what I've tried, how stupid I have been and what a failure. Then, sometimes, I don't know why, I have found something new! It's like the darkness here: we don't see anything when I extinguish the candle, but I know there are walls, I know your magnificent Metre hides there somewhere. I can hear and sense it. Someone must provide the light, but it's not enough. Someone must have a good reason to light a candle in places where we still do not know what exists there. I'm such a reason and I carry my candle with matches!"

Johan was impressed by Pablo's colorful insights, but before he had a chance to comment, Maurice interrupted.

"But, Pablo, listen! We need solid ground under our feet, don't we? Otherwise, the world will shatter, and no science can survive that. Every scientific and everyday measurement would be specific, an instant only and it would have no connection whatsoever with other measures and even less with any theories. We could not share our knowledge of the world, only our haphazard measures of it. It would be like Babel, crowded with local opinions and rumors, supported by the obscure instruments and the eager power- and money-hungry priests and savants using them. We would be lost, not only at sea, but everywhere!"

Pablo laughed as he shook his head vigorously and continued to gesture with his hands. Again, he almost extinguished the candle.

"But think! What if the standards are bad and even wrong, Maurice? What if they only imprison us? Besides, it was you, Maurice, who introduced the new way of thinking about space and its dimensions on my canvas! It was you who made me imagine what it would be like to have them all at the same time in *The Brothel*! Had I followed the citizens' stupid geometry, I would have the whores nicely depicted there, lifeless copies. Now it is about their life and our life, here and elsewhere, yesterday and tomorrow. Even the invitation is there! It has touched Johan in a mysterious way. Do you mean that only in arts this is possible, but in science you must remain obedient to the elite, to the one and only metre? Do you get your standards from some infallible, visionary and beautiful angels? I could paint them for you!" Pablo was excited by his own energy, smiling excitedly. The flickering candle exaggerated his facial expressions.

Johan felt the pain of the future aphasia again, his mind full of pressing, whirling thoughts and arguments. He could not express his own or comment on Pablo's challenging thoughts. It was everything he knew about quantum mechanics, the relativity and quantum gravitation, distortion of space-time, the quantum entanglement, the phenomenon even Einstein would soon call "the spooky effect" exactly because of the mysterious connection between particles over large distances. It was something no one could explain, in terms of exactly *why* such a phenomenon extends over the distance of several miles. To Johan it had become a most profound and natural question to ask: what is a distance standard in its deepest sense, and what would be the best way to define it in physics? Is it the same to the human and a frog, or to all aliens in the universe? No one in Johan's future and in his world of science knew the answer to this either. Asking it had invited curious looks from his future physicist colleagues, but Johan now admired the way Pablo posed the question, to question the simplest reality, just as he himself had so often tried to do.

Johan knew Pablo was right about the risk of misunderstanding the message of the Metre, but he could only talk to himself. "It is like the 'standard model' of particle physics: when mentioned, the uneducated listener is expected to pay respect to the theory that encompasses and explains almost every known phenomenon in particle physics. In real life it is like any incomplete theory that works well often, but not always. It is a shared truth — because there is no better one — among the scientists, and it will be discarded, piece by piece. It is meant to change, always, as long as scientific curiosity and work can prevail. In science, the standard model is taken as a reference against which new discoveries become possible. It is no more a forever-fixed standard than the metre should be."

In front of his Parisian friends, however, Johan was speechless. He could only show his silent excitement, waving his hands in the darkness, walking restlessly back and forth in front of the Metre, unable to express his passion verbally. He already knew he could not draw it either.

Maurice interrupted the silence.

"We need something solid; otherwise, we have no power. Archimedes knew this when he said, *'Give me a place to stand and with a lever I will move the whole world.'* To me, the metre is a lever. Without it, we would move only ourselves!"

Pablo's voice was sharp and aggressive in the near-darkness.

"I don't need the metre. I have my eyes, hands, and nose! I can move the world with *them* when I forget the metre! You can see this in *The Brothel* and you will see it in my sculptures!"

Pablo and Guillaume then launched into an intense discussion about the nature of Pablo's art, and disagreed in loud voices about how it should be defined, if it even could be defined. Johan could not follow the discussion and did not recognize the names they mentioned. Instead, he took a few steps into the dark street.

Chapter 24
Curiosity and Pain

On the opposite side of the archway Johan observed how the two lanterns, hung at the height of about three meters and flanking the entrance gate to the Jardin du Luxembourg, donated their light to both sides of the gate, as if welcoming any late evening guests. There was no one around, however, except the temporary *bande* of Pablo, Maurice and Guillaume, making their noise in front of the Metre. The street was unlit and the door itself appeared even darker than the surrounding night, giving it the appearance of a massive opening to an urban cave. Seeing it, Johan began to feel dizzy and weak again, but remembering the earlier encounter there he could not resist going nearer to the gate.

For a passing moment, standing in the middle of the dark street, where the light from the lanterns did not reach him, staring at the gate, he became aware of a sudden, peculiar tremor under his feet. First it was like a barely noticeable undulation of the ground, and he thought it was caused by his dizziness, but then the sensation changed, becoming stronger and causing his calves to shake and tremble in rhythm with the increasing and decreasing vibration under his feet.

He realized that the waves under both feet vibrated in a manner that reminded him of the scary wall at the rail crossing in Palo Alto, only that these vibrations were not visual in nature. They felt like the same pulsating waveforms, but now on the ground where he stood; he could only feel the waves passing by under his feet, as if he were standing on a wavy lake. Johan had only once experienced an earthquake, and he imagined it to be something like this.

In the dark he could not see any waves under his feet. The ground appeared stable and he was unsure if there was anything visible or real happening or if this sensation was a delusion. He tried to move his feet, to take careful steps and touch the moist street surface with both hands, but the vibration did not occur only under his feet; it felt the same everywhere, although it remained invisible. Standing up, he could sense slight but systematic differences in the timing and in the form of the waves touching the soles of his feet. The waveforms were developing a strangely familiar pattern, something he had studied already as a student, the domain of two-dimensional, wavy signals, and the various ways of generating them. It was like a sheet fluttering in the wind, but he could not see it, only felt it with his feet steady on the ground.

In Johan's mind's eye, the waves were being produced and sent by strange local sources, like when throwing a stone on a calm lake, perhaps two of them at the same time, sending their own wave fronts towards him, from somewhere near to him and then interfering under his feet.

He could imagine other more complex source configurations for the waves he was sensing under his feet, and which together could generate the same perceptual effect. He was aware his feet were the only two measurement points, but the idea of only two sources felt like a natural alternative to consider. "If I knew how these waves were produced, if they were real, I could exclude irrelevant alternatives." He was puzzled to notice how the experience was not scary at all, and a familiar, calm feeling of curiosity, similar to what he had encountered at the Grévin, got hold of him. For a moment he forgot his friends under the archway.

Johan's only earthquake experience was from Japan; when he visited Tokyo, he was awakened in the middle of the night in a hotel, in total darkness, shocked, feeling the bed tremble, the whole room swaying slightly, hearing the glasses tinkle in the mini bar and the mirror on the wall making noises, trembling on the wall of his small hotel room. This one in Paris was different. The waveforms did not feel threatening at all; instead, they felt harmonious and inviting, in an innocent, unexplained way, not forcing him to do anything, just to stay there and let them create their mystic wavy impact, as if softly carrying him along a power field, to somewhere unknown.

The harmonious feeling made Johan remember Pablo, who was still engaged in a vivid argument with Maurice and Guillaume; they were barely visible in the dim candlelight under the archway. Only a moment ago, when they had left the Steins', Pablo had explained how he could make invisible, unexplainable things visible. Johan now wondered, "Is this something he kept telling me, a world without words, not visual, not even physically measurable, but which is definitely there, and can be made visual, by a master artist? If I could do it, there would be an infinite number of ways to visualize what I now feel and perceive — with my feet!"

Trying to shout to Pablo, Johan was caught by a total aphasia, being unable to utter a single word or expression. He did not understand at all why it happened now; he was not trying to speak about the future or rely on his own reality. It was as if he were being carried on the crests of the strange, undulating waves, and he started to feel desperate to make or maintain a connection with Pablo and his friends. Then a new kind of fear hit him: fear of permanent separation. Muted, he imagined Pablo's painting of the dead Carles in the darkness.

The vibration stopped, abruptly. Johan saw the familiar, silky curtain descend and open in front of the gate and could see through it, in better detail than the first time in this same place. The scene behind the scrim was not static, and it showed as bright daylight. There were people moving, walking, and talking to each other, mostly people whose details he could easily discern, their simple dresses, hats and shoes, reminded him more of people out on a Sunday stroll than in a workday rush. Johan was astonished to notice that the bright light did not blind him at all, although he was observing the scene in the middle of the night. He wondered again, "Could it be that this is not real light at all that I see? Perhaps it's something I only imagine? Imagination does not blind!"

Then he forgot the problem, as his curiosity took over. The world seemed to extend farther than the screen, and the white light beyond it made everything clear and vivid. The scene looked like a well-lit cave, but urban in nature, with real, classic buildings in it. Johan could not decide what kind of architecture it was, but it reminded him of the buildings he had seen earlier and during his visit in Paris with Yvonne. At the far end of the cave scene, there was an oval opening leading to somewhere out of the cave, and a bright light radiated behind it. There were no visible, distant details; it was like a part of a cloudless sky, a faint, bluish hole in the urban cave.

For a moment Johan wanted to fetch his friends to show them what he saw, to confirm he was not hallucinating or had not totally lost his mind, but he could not call to them or move toward them; it was impossible to return. The siren calls of the vibrations under his feet, the mystic screen and its allure, the mystic promise had an irresistible hold on him and he stepped even closer to see better.

Standing at about fifteen feet from the silk-thin screen, Johan could observe the whole scene opening in front of him. He felt guilty about something he could not explain. Perhaps it was because of neglecting the friends he had persuaded to visit the Metre, or because of peeking into another life or leaving one without permission. The thin, grayish-brown, translucent curtain separated him from the people, the scenery, and the life behind it. The fabric of the curtain made everything appear slightly fuzzy, as if held within a mild, but kind fog. He could still see all the details sharply; this coincidence of fog and sharp detail was a paradox to Johan.

The first look at the scene was so inviting that Johan failed to immediately notice that the view of the scene was wildly distorted. There were several perspectives visible at the same time. When he gazed at each four-story house from the ground up, he could simultaneously see their roofs, as if viewing them from above and behind at once. This variation in perspective felt quite natural. Looking around, he saw the same distortion, as he perceived both the facade of each house and the area behind all its distant corners. The only thing he could think of was the way low-frequency sound waves bend around a corner, making it possible to hear the bass drum and tuba of an approaching band in a city before seeing the marching musicians rounding the corner. He knew how people just have got used to this auditory phenomenon. This scene before him, however, felt purely visual, and he did not remember ever having seen anything like it.

Suddenly one of Pablo's painting sketches came to his mind. Johan had been puzzled by the sketch but had forgotten to ask Pablo about it. It depicted a scene that extended nearly to the horizon of a beautiful, harmonious village, perhaps in Spain, with typical gabled countryside houses but all in a happy visual disorder, each of them tilted left or right, towards or away from the observer, looking as if they had been haphazardly dropped on the spot from the sky. The observer could see their walls and roofs simultaneously, so that it was possible to scrutinize any house wall, facing any direction. Nevertheless, the visual set-up, consisting of distorted single houses made the group of houses look like a real village, having an architecture with its own spirit, perhaps after an earthquake or some other force of nature that had mercifully left the houses undamaged.

Johan had never understood why the painting had been drawn like that. "The mystery hides in the details," he had thought to himself. "It lies in the way parts of objects of a scene can be thrown all over the canvas, without any natural logic or metric, even simultaneously, viewed from any possible angle, and still together they make a village, a real place for people to live and enjoy each other's company! I don't understand this at all; there is no problem in physics that would come even close to such a complexity, but the painting makes perfect sense!"

Johan could not imagine any formal way of describing what he saw in the charming village paintings. In the same way, the fragmented scenery in front of him felt real and full of life.

On the left, behind the curtain, he recognized a familiar-looking figure, a man he remembered having seen when visiting the Metre for the first time. The fellow was standing alone in front of a three-story building, carrying a black-brimmed hat in his right hand and a suitcase in his left, but he had his side turned towards Johan, so that he could only see the person's profile.

On the right, another man was approaching, coming out from the ample inner yard, through an elaborate, massive, five-meter door that was flanked by a fence with gilded spearheads. The door looked almost exactly, the bluish color included, like the one leading to the Jardin. The approaching man was somewhat shorter than the other one on the left, and perhaps he was a few years older, too; he had a mustache and was dressed in a smart black suit, white shirt and a bowtie. Clearly, it was not winter any more, perhaps early spring or summer, the same as on Johan's side of the curtain.

Johan started slowly walking from left to right along the screen, going nearer at first, but then moving back again and continuing, at a distance of about four meters, towards the right-most edge of the screen. He did not know what to do, but could not help walking back and forth, following the episode he was peeking at. He felt increasingly guilty about it, but he could not stop. Only once did he close his eyes for half a minute, which felt like an extremely long time, just to see if the vision would disappear. When he opened the eyes, the scene was still there with the same wonderful bright clarity.

A third man in the view had been sitting alone, on the last stairs leading to the massive gate. He was about the same age as the fellow on the left, rather slim in appearance, with thin hair and a high forehead, dressed in a modest, dark-green jacket, and black trousers. He wore round metal-framed eyeglasses, and he looked grave, and not healthy at all. Johan thought he saw a bluish-pale tint in the color of his face. From the stairs, the fellow was keenly watching the two men who had now met on the left of the scene, greeting each other and talking, only ten yards away from where the lonely man sat.

The vivid scene triggered an irresistible craving, an urge to approach the urban cave-world, the unknown people there, and join them. Johan did not know what was driving him; it was unusual for him to spontaneously socialize like that. He did not worry about meeting the men, while at the same time he became fully alert, remembering the incidents at the wax museum and in Palo Alto.

Johan had no rational logic or explanation to turn to. He became aware that what he was experiencing could all be real life or else it was a massive, pathological delusion. "I'm crazy enough to be — or imagine that I live — in the year 1907, and I don't even know if I can ever return home. What could be even worse, facing the wall again in front of me — I could be a hopeless schizophrenic here, becoming a schizophrenic there, too! What can I do? What should I do? Did father go through this?" He breathed heavily and his hands were trembling and cold.

Johan tried once more to shout to his friends, but it was impossible. Despite the worry of neglecting Pablo, Guillaume, and Maurice, he did not want to leave the wall, which had now totally engulfed him. It was not threatening; instead, it presented its kind call to enter somewhere unknown. Johan knew that whatever choice he would make, it would be impossible to predict the outcome; he would be taking an irrational risk. "Physics is easy," he thought. "At the lab, I can always try to see what happens. Now I don't even have a relevant theory or a hypothesis. I have only one try, and I don't even know what it is!"

Johan smiled at himself, feeling a misplaced amusement in front of the monumental, scary challenge. It was a new kind of enjoyment to notice how impossible it was for him to get rid of his scientific mind and analytical ways.

Then, after a short hesitation, perhaps half a minute, not more, without thinking, Johan rushed towards the right-most edge of the screen. He did not feel any resistance when reaching it; there was no feeling of touching it, and he was caught in an accelerating fall through the silky, extremely thin wall. He could just barely shout: "Pablo! Maurice! Guillaume!" this time with no aphasia, but he could not know if they had heard him or if he had only imagined shouting.

The fall was fast. Johan felt a slow, increasing grip of a force taking a holistic, whole-body hold of him and his soul, a peculiar kind of pain of separation he had never felt before. For a moment he had a memory flash, remembering his father and the way he had suffered from the psychotic fits. "Is this what he went through? All the current dimensions of life shattering and fragmenting, falling somewhere, to the unknown, with no solid ground anywhere, alone, leaving everyone behind, with nobody to understand it?" Johan could only perceive an overwhelming, physical-psychological disorder, as in the village painting in Pablo's studio, but this disorientation was not only visual. His balance, bodily senses and hearing appeared to be totally separated, each sense independent of the other senses, as if monitoring its own separate world, from all directions, simultaneously. The only experience remaining similar, invariant, in all his perceptions was the internal, emotional pain from breaking the bondage to and friendship with Pablo, Maurice and Guillaume, and their unselfish care.

Johan became aware of the permanent detachment from the difficult but enchanting living he had with the artists, a separation from something genuinely new he had met at the Bateau; the connection was broken with the men he knew were laying the foundations for revolutionary arts. Without knowing why, he was convinced they would never meet again. The world outside, what he had taken for granted, at least for a while, was shattered; the world inside was about to recreate its next form and content. It was to become the home of a new hope and perhaps pain, too. Johan groaned with the pain of permanent separation, and the sense of guilt, the same he had experienced when his father had died. This time it was about giving up on Pablo and on their — perhaps his father's, too — friendship.

A vivid image of a painting shone for a short moment in his mind. It was Pablo's painting describing Carles, his dear friend, on his deathbed, a visible wound of a gunshot on his right temple, the suicide. Johan could not escape the guilt of having intentionally hurt Pablo, the way Carles had done.

After the rush through the silky wall, the fall itself did not require any physical effort. Johan felt like an astronaut, escaping from his home base, the spaceship, floating in a multi-dimensional, fragmented mental-physical world, collapsing or transforming into an unknown, a new one or new ones. During the passing few seconds, he could not know if the fall would ever stabilize, to span a solid ground under his feet again, a world that would make sense. A vague comfort and mild relief were that he had been able to call to his friends at his moment of departure, something he had not been able to do with his mother and father when they had passed away. He had made the impossible decision to leave the life he had at the Bateau, and without hesitation, to throw himself on the mercy of a total uncertainty. Amid this freefall, he entertained the faint and floating possibility, to be able, once again, talk about his real life and join his friends — just as his father had probably felt after his mysterious journeys.

PART V

Chapter 25
Crowding at the Collège

The wooden, sturdy park bench, brown in color, felt comfortable to Johan. He sat relaxed, leaning against the backrest, facing a classic courtyard, ten by twenty yards, as if nothing peculiar had happened. Surprisingly, this was not the place he had observed through the silk screen, although the style of the building in front of him was similar to what he had noticed, perhaps more decorative in character. He was fully awake, not worried or scared, with an unexpected clarity of mind, not even puzzled by the change of place and the mental transformation. Despite the total uncertainty about the time and place, he had the same calm and composed feeling he had when he moved from the Grévin to Pablo's atelier at the Bateau.

It was daytime now, perhaps early afternoon, and he felt like an invited guest, but not knowing where. He still had his jeans and a blue checkered shirt on; the weather was not cold at all. Opposite to the bench he saw an old brownish stone wall displaying three small, arched insets, each one hosting a black bust of a man. The building was old, as were the busts, but the historical heritages did not hint of their era in any way.

Johan could not recall exactly how he had ended up here, what the route had been or if there had been any. A vivid image prevailed in his mind, about leaving his friends, the strange passage through the silky wall, entering a new space. He still recalled the grief and guilt of his quick farewell, but there was no pain any more. The style of the buildings he saw around him reminded him of Paris, but he could not decide what it was that created that comfortable sense of familiarity. There were no objects or signs visible to reveal the date or even the year in Johan's new world.

The lack of any worry about the strange journey surprised Johan, who thought: "Joining the life with Pablo and friends must have taught me to be ready for these unpredictable incidents, to adapt to them, to take risks if needed." He imagined any possible, rational reasons for his unexpected reaction, thinking about the unbelievable travels through the walls, but it was impossible to understand what had happened and why. Then he became, again, aware of the looming possibility that he would have a destiny like his father's, disappearing to his frightening journeys in the world of a schizophrenic, its time and space unknown — with the feeling that it was natural. But even that did not disturb Johan's momentary peace of mind. It was like a swift trust emerging when it was needed, allowing Johan to observe his new environment as he tried to orient himself anew.

On the left he saw a large statue, apparently of an eminent scholar, judging by the serious appearance and the classic academic robes the character was wearing, and the book and scroll he carried. He looked like a man of academic success, but he was someone Johan did not recognize. Further on the left, behind the statue, there was a bridge-like, impressive architectural structure, three high arcs each one supported by a pair of five-meter-high classic pillars, the arcs reaching up to a height of thirty feet. Under the center arc there were four steps leading to the entrance deck and to the building on the right, where a large double door was open, welcoming the arriving guests.

A crowd of well-dressed men, typically in dark suits, most of them wearing a tie, arrived from the left and continued to the building through the open double door. Only a couple of women accompanied them. Observing these people, it was evident to Johan that this could not be the twenty-first century. Based on the clothing and appearance of the visitors, it was difficult to judge what era or year it was, but people did not appear much different from what Johan had seen during his stay at the Bateau, only that these were now representatives of the higher divisions of the society. In his eyes, coming from the recent, modest way of living, Johan could notice how most of the arriving visitors had an aura of authority and wealth. The Bateau and the Stein salon had left their marks on Johan's way of seeing the world. Observing the manners of the guests entering the building and following the obvious order in the crowd, he could recognize the familiar, social patterns, something he had seen at the Steins' house and many times in Helsinki. "It's like Calle's parties, different clothing, the same soft smiles, hierarchies, a strange kind of crowding around power, silent distances between individuals here and there, the mutual, visibly selective and submissive acknowledgements. They must be academics!"

Johan tried to peer through the double doors on his left, to look for any information about the date. He saw two small paper posters attached to the doors and was about to go and read the notes on the doors, when the two men he had seen through the wall, arrived from around the corner, walking side by side, apparently following the crowd. Looking at them Johan thought the younger one of them was about forty, but the other one appeared more senior, already in his fifties, perhaps.

They stopped in front of him, greeting him in a friendly way.

"Are you joining the physics lecture? We will start in half an hour! There will be a fierce fight, a true academic struggle for seats, so please hurry!"

They both laughed and gestured to Johan, who was surprised by their unexpected, welcoming attitude. Again, he had noticed, immediately, for a reason unknown, he could understand their language without any effort.

As the older one of the men came closer, Johan quickly said, without thinking or worrying about the language difference, "Hi, I'm Johan Ek, theoretical physicist from Finland. I just arrived from…" he tried to say 'a visit from Paris' but instantly he felt a new kind of muting that he immediately recognized. He perceived that in this new place and time he would be unable to mention his recent history at the Bateau, but he could mention his own name. Despite the uncomfortable lack of words, he continued, reformulating his expression.

"I have studied…", wanting to say something general about his work "particle collisions" but as soon as he intended to utter this phrase, Johan realized his mistake. The familiar aphasia for his own, real knowledge of physics had not disappeared either. Confused, he blushed, when the man who had greeted him, dressed in a chic suit, apparently a person of significance at the occasion, laughed, a kind and loud laughter, introduced himself and they shook hands.

"Nice to meet you! So, you are a physicist as well. I'm Professor Paul Langevin, experimental physics. I invited Albert to give the talk here; it will be most interesting. You are not the first one to go crazy with our guest and for what he will tell us. Let me introduce to you Professor

Albert Einstein. He's about to commence his lecture here in a moment."

Johan had not recognized Einstein, who in his eyes was about forty then. Utterly amazed, Johan realized, knowing every detail of Einstein's work, he must have travelled to an epoch of the early twentieth century but clearly after the year 1905 or 1907, but which year? He did not dare to ask and wondered, amazed, "Could this be the meeting at the Collège? It's not possible! But it's Langevin and Einstein, it cannot be anything else!" In his liveliest dreams, he had never imagined what it would be like to meet the genius and guru, to face one of the rare gods of modern physics. The totally unexpected, even impossible situation felt unreal and amusing to Johan: to meet the hero of the theory of relativity, the meeting taking place in a space-time he actually new — and after what he had experienced. His hands started sweating and his feet trembled, as he realized he had no idea what to say, how to behave and speak. In fact, he was speechless, not only because of the strange aphasia but because of the shock.

He just shook hands with the smiling Einstein and did not venture to say anything, fearing he would make a total fool of himself. Finally, after an awkward silence and sighing, moving restlessly, Johan managed to utter one word, using a rising intonation to make it sound like a question.

"Relativity?"

Einstein spoke in a soft, almost melodic voice.

"Yes, the title of my talk here is 'On the Theory of Relativity'. A simple concept at the outset, but quite demanding to explain. I will do my best, so that we can have a discussion and not only a long monologue, right, dear Professor Langevin — Paul? The world can be changed in two hours, but it may not be enough today. Not here anyway."

He glanced at Langevin, lifting his eyebrows slightly, flashing a quick, curious smile at him before turning back to Johan.

"By the way, I know a physicist from Helsinki. Is he familiar to you, Doctor Ek? Professor Gunnar Nordström?"

Johan noted how he pronounced the names Nordström and Gunnar surprisingly well and accurately, as if he had learned the right accent from a Nordic person.

Before Johan could answer, Einstein said cheerfully, "I understand he will be present here, too. We have met and exchanged letters. He's a very, very clever scientist, a rare and real visionary, I would say!"

Johan was astonished to hear such praise from Einstein about his own compatriot, a Finn. A wave of shame caught him: he did not want to confess or indicate in any way that he had never heard of Nordström and had no idea who the fellow might be. Johan did not know the history of Finnish physics too well and this was not the right moment or company to reveal his ignorance.

"You should keep in touch with him! He is one of the best scholars to understand the nature of relativistic gravity. We met in Vienna, some years ago," Albert continued.

Johan felt surprised by this suggestion, and had to confess, "Unfortunately, we have not met."

Johan wondered if his imagination or the mysterious travel were playing tricks with him. "How can I know if there really has existed any Nordström, a famous and unknown physicist in Finland? This is weird!" he thought to himself. It had been one thing to know so little about art, but now Johan felt totally unprepared to face the same ignorance in his very own field, theoretical physics.

The name Nordström was intriguing to Johan. He should at least know the prominent names of Finnish physics. "My mind must be playing tricks with this," he thought. "I don't get it; how could the real Einstein know a famous physicist from Finland if I have never heard of him? I don't have the faintest idea of the fellow." Johan glanced at Einstein. Trying to be polite and not to stare at him in confusion, he thought, "He does look like the young Einstein I've seen in the historical photos."

Albert Einstein and Paul Langevin continued the friendly conversation, and Johan, thoroughly shaken by the occasion, adopted his well-learned way of being on guard, reserved, careful in how to comment on any of the topics discussed. During their conversation that lasted only about fifteen minutes, he managed to comment on the early theoretical basis of Special Relativity, the field and some of its amazing consequences he knew from the heart: the special role of the speed of light, the relationship between mass and energy and the problem of simultaneity. Now it was a real puzzle to him, what he could talk about freely, because he knew exactly how Einstein's theory had been confirmed and used in modern times. He remembered how he had experimented in his conversations with Maurice, when discussing the topics concerning four-dimensional geometry. This was a new, unexpected situation; there were probably new, hidden obstacles. The two men seemed to enjoy the conversation and stayed with Johan for a while, showing no signs of hurry. Johan's confused way of speaking did not seem to bother them at all, and Johan was encouraged to try again, to mention 'gravitation' in his comment.

"I'm aware of Professor Poincaré's ideas, already from 1905 about the gravitational waves, traveling at the speed of light. I've always thought of it as the very transformational idea in the theory. Perhaps we can hear more about that during the talk."

Paul looked astonished, remained silent for a while, glancing at Einstein first and then at Johan.

"I'm glad to hear that," Paul said. "When you follow the lecture, you will find out you are not the only one stuttering with this topic. My guess is that Albert will, even with his extremely polite way, offend some of our leading philosophers, who have their educated ideas about the nature of time and gravitation. Besides, there will be journalists and even a few celebrities who most certainly will be totally perplexed by Albert's argument that there is no absolute space! Add to that the way light propagates and what it means to the way we must think about the nature of time. It's going to be a mystery that will tease them, guiding them to accept the idea that the length and mass of an object are dependent on its relative speed! The journalists will probably think it's some sort of modern sorcery or metaphysics Albert is talking about. No surprise some newspapers have already described it as witchcraft. But it is physics, in its purest form, experimental and theoretical combined, using new generation mechanics to address the real and experimentally verifiable world. You will see, I'll try to keep order in the audience!"

Johan tried to find a way to comment on this short lecture as he thought about it, but could only say, "Yes, I know."

Paul continued, "We will have a dinner after the talk. Would you like to join us and perhaps find your Finnish colleague in the audience?"

Johan was delighted and worried.

"I'd be glad to. I hope I can recognize Professor Nordström. Perhaps he is one of the blond Finns like me — somewhat rare here, I guess?"

"I have never met him personally," Paul said, turning to Albert, who gave a short description.

"He is about my age, not a blond, shorter than you, and probably wearing his eyeglasses."

As Paul started leaving, he said, "We have to go and see that everything is ready for the talk. We will commence in ten minutes, so please hurry to find a seat!"

Johan followed Paul and Albert, realizing that now the mystic aphasia constrained both his real life and the recent experiences from 1907 Paris. "It's a shackle of time that locks me up. How can I talk to these colleagues if I cannot take up anything I actually know and believe about physics? And why has Nordström left such a significant impression on Einstein?"

At the entrance to the lecture hall, Johan noticed the poster on one of the doors. It displayed the title of the talk, "Theory of Relativity", and a short description of Einstein, plus the date and time: *Friday, March 31st, 5 o'clock, Amphitheatre VIII.* Reading further down the announcement, Johan noticed the year, 1922, and felt his heart pounding, almost stopping. "So this is it, the meeting at the Collège!"

Talking aloud to himself, he said with a wide shining smile, "It's 1922, I can go and see Pablo and Maurice again and surprise them if they are well and still in Paris, what a joy! This is crazy! It's been fifteen years! Pablo will never forgive me. I must be seriously insane!"

Excited, almost euphoric, he entered the hall, where the thrilling atmosphere, the sense of vibrant expectations and the buzz of reverberating conversations in the cramped room embraced him. It was a paradoxical feeling to join the energetic, academic crowd, like entering the Lapin with his artist friends, but now with scientists, many of whom were his historical colleagues. The auditorium was a classic university lecture room, overwhelmingly pompous to Johan's eyes, even compared to his own academic world, and especially to what he had experienced at the Bateau. The wooden benches and impressive walls made of brown hardwood framed a special place for science. A blackboard and an empty speaker platform in front of the hall were awaiting Einstein, who would give his talk. Johan was amused to notice the parallel: "It's not very different from the Lapin, when Pablo was getting ready for his presentations in front of the noisy and eager audience. There is only less visible struggle here; people are better dressed, too!"

Johan scanned the audience, trying to locate someone looking like a Finnish Nordström, but saw too many men with dark hair. Nordström could be any one of the younger ones, most of whom appeared to be somewhat poor academics. Even their proper dark suits could not mask their familiar, less prosperous background. In the back row, he saw a couple of young attendees, almost boys, who must have been students. A few men, probably guests of honor, had found their places at the front, accompanied by two charming-looking, elegant young women, dressed in what to Johan's eyes appeared like extremely fashionable clothing that was not academic at all. No one in the hall had blonde hair. All the seats were taken, every possible corner and passageway was occupied; it was going to be a real show of science in front of the excited, visibly charged audience. Johan could not help but notice, however, that not everyone seemed expressly happy with their expectations. He remained standing by the door, with an excellent view to the blackboard and to the platform where Einstein would face the well-prepared audience.

Einstein entered with Langevin, both guided by an elderly man, perhaps in his seventies, dressed in a stylish, dark-gray suit. The attendees rose and applauded enthusiastically at length, celebrating the genius who soon would receive the Nobel Prize for his studies on the photoelectric effect, not for his current subject matter, which was to shatter the world of physics. Johan knew his theory of relativity had already started the revolution. The host commenced the event by introducing himself simply as Mr. Croiset. He bowed to the audience of the Collège and to Einstein as he welcomed him. After that, Professor Langevin briefly introduced Einstein, everyone sat down and Einstein took his place at the front.

When Einstein spoke his first words, thanking the hosts and the Collège, Johan was again surprised by the quiet and calm tone of his voice. Later during the talk, when introducing the basic concepts and thought experiments explaining his original thinking about relativity, Einstein had an extremely clear, almost simplistic way of describing the utmost complex phenomena. Doing so, he made it easy for the listeners to follow him and even accept his strange, but well-founded arguments, which slowly became more and more demanding and astonishing as his talk progressed. To Johan it was like a perfect, dream-like introduction to his passion, to everything he had learned and studied during his academic career.

All the intellectual defenses and reservations Johan might have had because of his own knowledge of the field were abolished, and he did not feel any need to rely on his real knowledge. It was like re-reading an exciting but true novel. He knew what was to come in modern physics, and he was attending something of a live history in the making. In the talk there was nothing new to Johan, but the way Einstein presented and introduced his thoughts was like a totally new story of physics. Remembering Pablo's passionate and often aggressive habits to make his case, eyes aflame, making everyone quiet by the sheer power of his expression and charisma, Johan realized how different the two revolutionaries were, but they both had an immense impact on others.

The talk lasted for two hours; the audience followed it in earnest silence and only now and then relaxed when Langevin, who was well aware of the variable backgrounds of the attendees, helped Einstein to clarify some of the expressions and equations he was using and drawing on the blackboard. A murmur swept over the hall every time Einstein took up some of the most compelling descriptions and interpretations of space and time and the mystic, moving clocks, or when he softly mentioned, as if an insignificant sideline: *"The time of a philosopher cannot be different from the time of an experimental physicist,"* and then continued, without explaining it in detail, expecting that everyone had already seen it. Occasionally Johan could observe how some members of the audience shook their heads, exchanged skeptical looks, or made nervous moves; however, they all remained silent.

The session ended with a standing ovation. A small crowd eagerly gathered at the front of the hall around Einstein, Langevin and a couple of other apparently eminent figures, all of whom were men. Johan tried to move slowly towards the platform, but the crowd was too dense, so he stayed at a distance, still looking around, trying to identify Nordström. Then he felt a tap on his back and turning around faced the man he had seen through the wall and sitting at the stairs, just before he had rushed against the screen-wall.

The man had a bluish pale color on his thin face; he was shorter than Johan, with darkish hair and a high forehead.

"Do you happen to be from Scandinavia? I'm Gunnar Nordström from Finland and noticed you are the only one here with a Nordic appearance?"

He did not smile but behaved in a polite and kind manner.

"Well, yes, indeed, I'm Johan Ek, a physicist from Helsinki. Where do you come from?"

"I'm from Helsinki too, but I've been to Göttingen, working and studying. I decided to come here, to see and listen to Albert. He is a great scientist; we have met and exchanged letters. I just arrived last night."

For a moment Johan was uncertain what he could say, but then he commented, "Me too, I arrived last night. I've been at Stanley." Feeling relieved to be able to mention that, he added, "I'm here for the same reason as you. I was happily surprised to find this wonderful meeting here. I even met Einstein and Langevin right before the session started. They asked me to find you and join them for a dinner, which should start soon. I was delighted and quite surprised to be invited. I don't actually know them. You must have made a major impression on Einstein."

Gunnar did not answer, only smiled lightly, nodding. Johan was puzzled by the aura of a strangely peaceful tranquility around Gunnar, as he thought of it.

After gazing around, seeing the dense crowding near the podium, Johan suggested, "Let's wait here. I'll try to signal them that I found you. I'm taller and can see above the fame-hungry crowd there."

For a moment Johan imagined the ways of cumbersome and risky traveling in the present world of the early 1920s. He admired the scientists taking the trouble to work with the right people and communities in science, traveling over long distances. He spoke to himself: "We are quite alike. To me Stanley has the same meaning as Göttingen probably has for Gunnar." Then he remembered one of his physicist heroes. "For heaven's sake," he thought, "Minkowski worked in Göttingen!"

Gunnar frowned, looking at Johan. "What have you been working with? I have not seen your name before…"

Just before he had to answer something, Johan was lucky to see how from the middle of the crowd Langevin was looking at them, smiling and waving vividly as an invitation for Gunnar and Johan to join him. The timing was perfect for Johan, who could evade answering and getting muted by trying to be truthful to his own story.

"We should try to join them but look at the crowd! This is extraordinary, such celebrities, and now, what a wonderful and kind invitation!"

Johan smiled at Gunnar, who only nodded. They still had to wait for nearly fifteen minutes. During this time, they did not talk much, only commented on the audience and the atmosphere, nothing on physics, Johan especially tried to avoid talking about his work and changed the topic when he felt it was necessary. The hall was still full of people when Langevin finally waved to them once more as a sign to leave, and Johan and Gunnar started slowly, through the crowd, to approach the band about to go out to dinner.

The small group had gathered outside the entrance door. Einstein, Langevin, and Croiset, whom Johan now knew. Another man he did not recognize had joined, dressed in a nice, dark suit, wearing a bowtie and vest; he was perhaps in his fifties like Langevin, and with a well-groomed, dark-brownish beard. All four were immersed in a vivid conversation. When Johan and Gunnar approached, Langevin was quick to greet them, which again thoroughly confused Johan, but he was delighted as Langevin introduced them both by name to the other two guests. Einstein stood slightly behind the other men when it was Gunnar's turn to be introduced.

"Mr. Croiset, this is Professor Nordström from Finland. You have probably just heard of his work from Albert, on gravity; they know each other."

Croiset and Gunnar shook hands politely, and for the first time Johan saw Gunnar smile, as he made a polite, deep bow, saying, "I'm honored to meet you, Mr. Croiset."

Langevin turned to the other man who had just joined them: "Professor Nordmann, this is Professor Nordström from Helsinki." Johan remembered that it was this Charles Nordmann, the French astronomer, who had written the lively report from the meeting he just attended. He had read it several times. Langevin added, "Do you think you might have a shared history in Scandinavia? I wonder where the name Nordmann comes from? It sounds quite similar to Nordström?"

"Well, my name actually refers to Norway, but I was born in Switzerland," the man said. Addressing Nordström, he said, "Your name is Swedish, Professor Nordström, isn't it?"

Johan joined the conversation and answered before Gunnar could. "Professor Nordström and I both have Swedish names, although we come from Finland; Swedish is our second language and we both speak it. But it may not be too useful here!"

Everyone laughed, and Einstein stepped forward, saying, "No more useful than Finnish as far I'm concerned. I've seen some strange Finnish words, totally beyond my comprehension, in the letters I've received from Gunnar. Nice to meet you again Gunnar!" They shook hands.

Next, Langevin made the same introduction of Johan, using "Doctor" as his title, starting with Croiset.

"Mr. Croiset, this is Doctor Ek from Helsinki. He's an experimental physicist like I am."

Croiset seemed spontaneously curious and eager to hear more.

"Wonderful! You know, I'm Maurice, the *administrateur* at the Collège, my real background is as a Hellenist, which helps to understand the origins of everything in western civilization, sciences included." He laughed heartily, and continued, "I'm always curious to know our visitors. Perhaps you can tell me something about your work at the dinner?"

Johan blushed, remembering his friendship with Maurice and Pablo and felt a momentary grief at their separation. He had an almost irresistible need to say, "I have a close friend…" but knew he couldn't, and then just nodded.

"I'll be glad to! Part of it is about gravity and it's somewhat complicated."

He sighed, glad to be able to say this much without triggering the frustrating aphasia.

Langevin turned to Nordmann and made the same introduction to Johan, and then before any more conversations emerged, said, "Let's walk to the restaurant. It's just on the right of the main stairs, a short walk along rue des Écoles, soon after the small, tidy park on our right."

Johan was relieved to have succeeded so far in these introductions, but he worried about how to manage the dinner without failing totally, due to his embarrassing aphasia; he also realized he had no money and he was not properly dressed. Listening to the way these scientists addressed each other Johan paid attention to its formal nature, something he would not have expected from the colleagues of the same age at Stanley and even in Helsinki. He knew he had to be extra careful not to make fool of himself.

Langevin led the relaxed, short stroll, which every now and then was interrupted by Croiset, who stepped in front of them, and turned to the group to explain the history of the surroundings. He described the small park with particular enthusiasm:

"This looks like a modest park, but it's actually a garden and a meeting point. It's been a place for wonderful minds to meet for decades, possibly centuries. Even Voltaire, or his statue, at least, was here."

When nobody asked for any further details about the park, the merry group continued towards the restaurant, only two blocks from the park. Langevin led with Croiset, as Einstein and Gunnar walked immediately behind them. Johan and Nordmann followed them, a few steps behind. Gunnar remained silent, walking on the left of Einstein, who every now and then said something to him, but he spoke in such a low voice that Johan could not hear what it was. Johan had become curious about Gunnar's arduous, slow way of moving as if something hindered him. "I wonder what makes him so sluggish and silent? Perhaps it's just his nature, not untypical for some of us Finns. Perhaps he is just tired from the travel."

Chapter 26
On Champagne, Science, and Comedies

It was an unusually soft, warm evening for the end of March, and after a relaxed, slow, and short walk, they entered a restaurant. It had a simple terrace bordered by beautiful roses and other flowers; a few tables outside were placed under a red awning; the entrance door was at the corner of the building. Inside, the waiter came smiling to greet and welcome Langevin and Croiset, then shook hands with the others, and guided them to a table at a distant, quiet corner by the window. Four round, thick white columns separated the table from the rest of the restaurant making it a comfortable, private space. Croiset was quick to notice these, apparently familiar structures:

"As you can see, the columns don't have much to do with their classic ancestors, but they provide a modern frame for us!"

It was a soft, relaxing welcome, and brought a smile to everyone's face. They were ready to begin the dinner as the table was set and covered with a white tablecloth and an abundant arrangement of red, blue, and white fresh flowers.

Langevin seated the men, took Einstein by the arm, and offered him, with a warm-hearted smile, a seat in the middle, on the side of the table facing the room and the pillars. He remained standing behind his chair.

"We will celebrate you and your work now, and I welcome our guests, too." He glanced at Johan, as if guessing his situation, saying, "I will pay the bill, if that is acceptable to you?"

Johan blushed, realizing Langevin had accurately noticed his uncertainty. He tried to hide his embarrassment and remain calm, painfully aware of his jeans, the modest shirt, feeling the flatness of his empty pockets on his thighs. There was not a single franc there and he had no idea where to get money. Einstein remained standing behind his chair, nodding at Langevin first, and then addressing everyone.

"This is a most extraordinary gathering of ideas and thoughts about gravitation. I wonder if there is anything in it we can agree on, except that it exists and helps us to swallow our delicious French wine and food here?"

After a momentary silence, the group burst into a light laughter.

Langevin offered Croiset the next seat on the right of Einstein, saying, "You two have a specific agenda to discuss on all the possible practicalities of the coming days, I know, but please leave us and gravitation some rhetorical space! And Gunnar, would you please take the seat opposite to Albert so that you can interrupt with your scientific comments if the two fellows become too immersed in the world of bureaucracy, which can cause a devastating gravitation, in itself!"

Next Langevin guided Nordmann to the seat on the left of Gunnar, and to Johan he offered the chair on Gunnar's right, moving finally himself to stand at the chair to the left of Einstein. Everyone was still standing, as Langevin asked for the waiter to bring the champagne. The waiter arrived instantly and began to expertly fill each glass.

"We will begin with a glass of champagne," said Langevin, standing straight as he raised his glass. "I'm sure you are all as happy as I am for what we have just experienced: a historical talk at the Collège, and having Albert with us! This is something from our own champagne house in Ludes, and Mr. Croiset has been kind enough to select the best one for us."

All the guests clinked their champagne glasses and murmured their thanks and congratulations before their first sip.

Einstein turned toward Langevin, raising his glass again.

"Let me express my humble gratitude to you, Paul, and to the Collège, for inviting me. I'm well aware that in the eyes of some journalists and even philosophers you will now share and suffer from my reputation as a meta-physicist, but why not? In no time, what they have believed to be metaphysics will turn into a physical reality! Let's toast to that! Experimental, not only experiential physics!"

After a second round of clinking glasses and sipping the champagne, the scientists sat down, everyone relaxing and enjoying the light and friendly, collegial atmosphere. Johan was especially relieved, now that he knew he did not have to pay for his dinner. One at a time, everyone present took the chance to stand up and propose a toast, to thank Paul and to congratulate Einstein. After some casual comments from Croiset, a lively discussion followed, mainly on Einstein's recent travels and plans.

Finally, encouraged by the informal atmosphere, Johan was brave enough to thank the hosts himself in a short speech. He had had been planning it already on the way to the restaurant — what he could say without being embarrassed by the muting, how he could express his thoughts and knowledge, but especially, show gratitude and respect for being invited to join such special, distinguished company. He was confused by the surprising turns and events of the day, but what worried him most was the recurring, specific aphasia. He still did not understand its exact nature, the aphasia for the future, that this time extended to his recent, new past.

Standing up and speaking in a low voice, Johan said, "This is a most astonishing event to a totally unknown foreign colleague like me, coming from the North. I've been delighted to meet Gunnar here and hear about his contributions. Paul — Professor Langevin — I cannot thank you enough for the kind and very unexpected invitation. I only wish we could have the company of Professor Poincaré with us. Then I could enjoy the gathering of all the best gravitational minds here, you all. It would be a center of mind-gravitation in Paris! Let me thank you for your kindness! I'm sure I speak on behalf of Gunnar, too. Let's toast to the—!" He was so excited, remembering Poincaré's ideas about the gravitational waves, that he forgot his carefulness and automatically tried to say, "to the discoverers of the gravitational waves," when the aphasia muted him for a passing moment. He quickly reformulated his wording, with the simpler phrase, "to the gravitational waves!"

He threw a quick glance at Gunnar, who smiled and nodded. It seemed to be his way of expressing agreement and presence. Everyone stood up, lifting their glasses; they did not seem to notice the aphasia. Einstein remained silent, just frowning slightly. Langevin gave a deep, audible sigh, finishing what Johan had started.

"Poincaré, indeed!"

To Johan, Langevin seemed somehow confused, perhaps even moved. There was a transient sad look, a shadow in his eyes, which only slowly gave way to joy when the men lifted their glasses, smiling and looking at each other, nodding. Johan did not understand what this sorrow was. The guests did not seem to pay any attention to Langevin's worry; they were eagerly tasting the champagne, expressing their enthusiasm about it, as they sat down again.

Then Croiset stood up and said, "You may not know that I have a special scientific-cultural interest in the history of the Athenian comedies, which I have studied for quite some while. I'm sure that you, my distinguished scientists, do not see there much in common between your work and the ancient comedies. But think again!" He raised his both hands high up, trying not to spill his champagne, looking at each of the guests, and raised the volume of his voice.

"The Athenian comedies were influenced by political events, customs and the way the society functioned. Consequently, the comedies had an impact on the very essential aspects of human and social life, not at all unlike today, what happens in your objective science right now! The comedies had the power to move people and their lives." He lowered his hands, leaning against the table, becoming serious.

"What we have witnessed today made me think about the similarities, especially looking at the way our yesterday's newspapers wrote about the event, the excitement and repulsion I could sense and see in the audience, and then surely our distinguished guest Mr. Einstein is aware of the uncertain political atmosphere. Science and society cannot be separated. It is up to us to carry the light of independent science! Let us toast to free science and honorable scientists!"

Everyone applauded. This strong, emotional speech about the importance of art and science within society surprised Johan. He felt that Croiset had made an exceptionally powerful political statement. Silently, Johan cursed his poor knowledge of history. "I wish I had even a hunch of what he means by 'uncertain political atmosphere.'"

Next, Langevin, still moved, stood up, thanked Croiset, and then turned his gaze towards Johan and Gunnar.

"You, Johan, wondered why you have been so welcomed here, right? I knew about Gunnar's work in Helsinki, and then meeting you outside the lecture hall and during our short discussion, hearing your, pardon me, stuttering comments, I was struck by your scientific spirit and insight. Something made me curious about the silent knowledge you kept to yourself. Perhaps we can hear about it later. It was a real surprise to hear you mention Poincaré, and I realized there may be a mysterious connection between you and the work of Mr. Nordström. I'm astonished you have not met each other before coming to Paris! This is not bad company in which to get to know each other!"

Gunnar was amused, smiling at Johan, who realized he was getting into a tight spot; eventually he would be forced to explain his work to the amazing guests. Langevin paused briefly, looked at each of the guests, separately, and then at Einstein on his right.

"As you could see during the talk, there were plenty of admirers of the Theory of Relativity among the attendees, perhaps as many opposing, but there are only few who can contribute to it."

He bowed towards Einstein, with an expression on his face as if he wanted to ask about something sensitive but was trying to be careful not to hurt his guest's feelings.

"You are our guest of honor today and during the coming days here and at the Sorbonne. What do you think happened during your talk?" He sat down, sighing.

It was Einstein's turn to talk. Rising, he spoke in a low, but very lively voice, and Johan was surprised by an unexpectedly formal tone, as he slowly, almost word by word, stretched each word in a peculiar way.

"I'm sorry if I have brought you, distinguished Professor Langevin, a reputation of an experimental metaphysicist who works with ghosts! I know that in the eyes of some journalists and physicists my poor clocks were just too much!"

Everyone laughed at the well-timed joke, as they saw it. He continued:

"I hope to have better chances for serious scientific discussions next time here, perhaps already at the Sorbonne. I did notice a few reserved, or could I say even hostile expressions, and some people who only nervously shook or scratched their heads when I — as I thought about it — was politely and in very broad, general terms criticizing mathematicians who do not understand what exists in the world and who only trust their computational skills and imagination. The theory of relativity is about real life, a real world! It is not a formalism only, but experimentally verifiable, and a genuine part of our physical reality, of our real existence. We must experiment and experiment; it is only in this way that we will gain from the best analytical tools and methods. Some in the audience did not seem to like this view. Then I believe I saw some, perhaps philosophically motivated, people who restlessly squirmed in their seats when I suggested that we must discard the hypothesis of absolute time. But I believe it was time for them to reconsider."

Everyone at the table smiled at the pun and Langevin commented, in good humor again, "The right space-time for them to change their thinking, for the local philosophers at least, I'd say!"

Einstein added, "Overall it was a wonderful occasion, to be received with such strong support and enthusiasm at the end of my talk. I hope your students became interested in these matters."

Nordmann had been quiet, but now spoke up. He did not stand up, when Einstein had finished, but simply sat in his seat as he confessed, "I hope you don't mind, but I have taken some notes about this exceptional dinner meeting. I had already taken some at the talk."

Johan saw only friendly, agreeing nods, and a lively, spontaneous discussion followed, lasting over the whole menu they enjoyed. He realized he was witnessing the birth of the document he would read in his own real life. After the food he had enjoyed at the Lapin Agile, and the sushi, Asian and fast foods in Palo Alto, Johan was overwhelmed by the delicious duck he had chosen: braised duck breast with figs, star anise and cherry-port sauce, with some Bordeaux Graves wine he did not recognize, from the year 1900. The delicious dishes and wines were all new to him. The Finnish and Californian experiences in campus restaurants had not introduced him to the world of gourmet food.

Perhaps it was the wine or just the awareness of the exceptional chance to discuss the most exciting problems of physics and even metaphysics, with the best minds of modern physics that encouraged Johan to take up 'the problem of the metre' as he often called it, the same question about which his fellow scientists in Helsinki and even at Stanley had mostly laughed. He did not feel any risk in talking about it in this company.

Standing up, Johan began, "Honorable and distinguished colleagues, I hope you don't mind if I take some of your time to get advice from Professor Einstein about a problem that has bothered me here and there.

Actually, I've never got rid of it or found any real solution to it either. I hope it's not meta-metaphysics." He smiled, glancing at Einstein.

Langevin was quick to encourage him, and Einstein nodded, looking relaxed:

"Please feel free, I'm convinced we will all enjoy hearing about it!"

Johan continued. "Professor Einstein, the question puzzling me, actually two of them, but related, is this: in the general theory of relativity, you deal with accelerating bodies. But how can we know what acceleration is?"

Einstein interrupted immediately, without waiting for Johan to continue.

"Of course, we all know that in the theory it is just another side of gravity. Surely you are aware of that?"

Johan nodded, politely, and said, "Let's try a thought experiment. If it was impossible for an arbitrary, theoretical observer, an unknown alien, for example, to ever perceive motion or a location of an object in the way we humans do, how could it know what acceleration is and how could such a creature develop a theory of relativity? I mean, there could exist such aliens, or perhaps they are non-aliens and we are the aliens. They could live somewhere in the universe and be totally unlike us."

Einstein commented, in a mild, soft voice, "My dear friend, now you are questioning the basic assumptions of physics as we do it and the empirical observations behind it. We all know how the physical measures of motion have developed ever since Galilean and Newtonian mechanics. You come very close to metaphysics here, I'm afraid, and you might burn your fingers or at least measurement instruments!"

Johan was not embarrassed at all and continued, without hesitation. "But if the observer could not see motion, how could this observer develop anything like Newtonian mechanics? How could he define acceleration at all unless there is a God who sends his design documents about it? It's like the problem with the assumption about absolute space. Surely, we should not assume an absolute observer either?"

Langevin took the chance to join the discussion.

"In other words, Johan — Dr. Ek — you are talking about the theory of the observer. I don't know how you see it, my friends, but to me the observer is always a normal, healthy human being, preferably an educated man, lunatics excluded!"

Everyone laughed. Even Johan understood the humor, and was not offended, but he could not restrain himself from adding, "In my thought experiment, I imagine an observer who is unable to see or feel any motion or location and because of that, he cannot know what acceleration is unless there is an outsider, like a human physicist who informs him. Only then, perhaps, he could use mathematics to develop his theory further, to make it similar or even comparable to ours. Now, about my serious questions: 'Are we, as human, physical observers nothing but the prisoners of our own human senses, forever? Is it possible to think that there is another kind of physics, built by observers different from us?'"

Once Johan was seated, a momentary silence followed, after which Einstein stood up to speak.

"Dear Johan, that is a wonderful viewpoint of a person who reaches beyond what we call science. To think like that is brave, to have an open mind and heart to the possibilities of the universe. I'm a religious-minded agnostic, if I can use such an unusual expression. I don't think there is a fellow God or a heavenly bureaucrat in the heavens advising us, with his design plans as you say and who defines the laws of nature. But I do believe or trust that there is a deeper essence in the universe we can try to discover. At the same time, we cannot escape our senses, but we can extend them with mathematics and empirical sciences, with our instruments. What you are suggesting, Johan, is that we return to the origins of science and define our physics anew. But how could we do it? We only have our minds and senses, and the merciless world, no matter what we do. So, my answer to your two questions. First, there is nothing wrong with the idea that our senses constrain all our physical theories of the world and the universe. But when you ask that question seriously, with the aim of doing something with it, please make sure you do not introduce theories that cannot be tested empirically and made true empirical ones. I am afraid your suggestion is not testable. Second, I don't know what the real nature of acceleration or gravity is. Gunnar and I, we are only describing them in a formal way, but keeping in mind that our theoretical descriptions must be open to experimental tests."

Johan was moved, realizing that Einstein did not, at first hand, deny the philosophical value of his problem, which had made him so often embarrassed. The scientist, whom he admired over any other colleague, did not ridicule the thought experiment, but was serious about it.

"Thank you for the understanding and the wise words!" Johan said. "I can see that if I ever try to construct a theory of a general observer, even of an alien, I must make it testable, one way or another. But still, don't you think that I can build a theory that I cannot test empirically? Maybe an alien might be able to do that for me, one day! And well, why not a representative of a future-generation physicist?"

Everyone laughed, and Croiset turned to Johan.

"A comedy on earth might not be a comedy to your aliens; it could be dead serious to them when they enter our earthly theater! So, beware, you might hurt their intelligence and sense of humor!"

The evening continued in a lively and pleasant atmosphere and Johan's speech, together with the delicious wine, had loosened their academic tongues. Although metaphysics was clearly the most used term in the discussions following, Johan felt he had touched on something valuable in terms of physics too, at least for his own scientific development. The problem of the metre prevailed and he felt empowered, his thoughts connected to Maurice and Pablo and their discussions at the Lapin Agile and by the well.

When they were finishing the dinner, enjoying the cigars and Calvados, Einstein stood up once again.

"Dear Paul and dear friends, I have been touched by our inspiring discussions. This dinner and the meeting will always have a special place in my heart. It has indeed been the most impressive gathering of minds sharing the passion for understanding the theory, or should I say the theories, of relativity and gravitation, even aliens. I could not have had a better company for this. And Gunnar, it has been a special pleasure and joy to meet you again and exchange all the wonderful ideas you have introduced and to know your devoted and intelligent colleague Johan. We are all the next generation physicists, who will change the way we, as humans, see the world and the universe!"

Gunnar remained silent and pale when Einstein continued, "If you remember, Gunnar, after our exchange of letters, it was your theory I thought was the only serious competitor to me and what I had been developing as my general theory of relativity. But my thoughts had an impact on your theory as well. This is how science works. It is wonderful; we are never alone with our puzzles!"

Gunnar did not comment on that either, and it was at that moment, perhaps as Johan noted the melancholic silence of Gunnar, that made him realize why he had not heard of Nordström. Despite what Einstein had just said, and despite the fact that the two men had known each other for years, Nordström's name had not occurred in the related and most important scientific writings Einstein had published.

Johan knew especially well the article from 1916, published in *Annalen der Physik* by Einstein, and which Johan's professor Engström had told him and his fellow doctoral students in Helsinki to read and then re-read and re-read again. Johan knew everything about it, having even studied some German language in order to comprehend it properly. According to the professor's words, it was the most stimulating paper ever written for future physicists, far beyond Einstein's own time. Johan knew exactly to which other scientific articles Einstein referred in his famous text; there were only three references, and one was to Einstein's own 1915 article. Nordström was not among them.

Johan became restless about his insight. He did not know what to say and did not want to disturb the friendly atmosphere. Noting Gunnar's pale face and his continued silence, he nevertheless decided to take the risk of being impolite and to ask what bothered him, to talk to Gunnar when they leave the restaurant. At the same time, he realized he had no place to stay and it was already getting late. As the other physicists continued the intense discussion, Johan and Gunnar remained silent, only following the others' exchange of ideas, and every now and then glancing at each other.

After a while, Johan could no more resist his nervous urge to find out about the references to Gunnar's work and simply made up his mind to ask Einstein about this. He was fully aware of the risk of shattering the relaxed atmosphere and the celebration of science. Nevertheless, he thought, "Every scientist deserves credit for what he has done. Even if he has been wrong in his theory and interpretations, if he has significantly contributed to the way his followers can continue and learn, not to make same mistakes, and to think and develop their own theories? It is a common journey. This is what the phrase 'standing on the shoulders of giants' means in science; even Newton said it." He remembered then Pablo's furious talk about his mistakes and how important they were for his development as an artist.

Thus, Johan plunged onward, interrupting the discussion Einstein was having with Nordmann.

With a slightly nervous tone, he asked, "Professor Einstein, I do hope you don't mind if I ask you why you didn't mention Gunnar's work in the *Annalen der Physik* article from 1916? He is not mentioned as a reference or even by name. I think he would have deserved it and you said yourself that he had made a significant impression on you? However, you do make a reference to Hilbert in that article?"

Einstein was visibly surprised by Johan's blunt question and his poorly disguised accusation, which seemed to be totally misplaced in the relaxed context of the dinner. Einstein's gaze wandered among the guests. Everyone had heard what Johan asked, and they waited in silence, following what was to come, when Einstein slowly and seriously responded.

"David Hilbert and I had an intense interaction. We had a lot in common and exchanged several remarks and comments on the wave equations. I think his contribution to my thinking and even to some of my equations has been so remarkable that I felt comfortable mentioning it in that paper."

Johan did not give in, and was even more curious, continuing, "I understood that Hilbert also corrected some of your mistakes?"

"No, it was not like that at all! David and I have a mutual admiration, I believe, but we had different viewpoints."

Now Einstein seemed annoyed, and Johan felt it would be better to back up a bit. He decided to leave it at that, not to continue, only commenting, "But you do agree that Gunnar's work has had an influence on your thinking, and he did present an early version of the theory of relativity, didn't he?"

"Yes, he did, of course, but unfortunately there were problems with it."

Now Gunnar stood up, turning to Einstein, speaking politely in a quiet voice:

"As you know, my theory of gravitation from 1913 was indeed a predecessor of the theory of relativity, and there were none similar that would have used the same geometrical methods." He stopped and sat down, exhausted, and then he continued, "I'm not feeling well; I have been sick for some time."

Johan was worried and remained puzzled, but after he realized that Langevin was staring at him in a meaningful way, he said, "I'm sorry to be so simple-minded, but I believe these are important aspects of our work as scientists and as a community. I hope I have not offended you, Mr. Einstein?"

"No, not at all, I understand your eagerness and admire your honesty. Perhaps you have similar experiences from your own career as well, where you share ideas with your colleagues, develop methods and try to solve problems and then one of you sees the light. It is difficult to say who has been the first one to get the process started and especially who finalizes it."

"I did not mean that," Johan thought, but saw it better to mute himself.

Langevin stood up to leave, evidently trying to prevent the situation from deteriorating. The others followed quickly.

"Let's go and have a drink at Albert's hotel," Langevin said cheerfully. "It's an elegant place with comfortable chairs in a private alcove"

Chapter 27
The Tower of Eiffel

It was already dark outside, still warm, but with subtle signs of the nightly chill. The atmosphere among the diners recovered from the momentary turbulence and was good again. Langevin pointed them in the right direction and they walked back along the rue des Écoles, Langevin ahead with Einstein, followed by Croiset and Nordmann. Johan felt relieved that his comment had not spoiled the spirit of the dinner. He stayed with Gunnar and got up the courage to ask him a question.

"When I arrived at the Collège," he said gently, "I saw you sitting alone on the stairs there, but you did not approach Einstein or Langevin, although you must have seen them there. Why was that? Are you, all right?"

Gunnar stopped walking. He looked intently at Johan, his face pale.

"I respect Einstein and even nominated him for the Nobel Prize last year, also this year. Let's see what happens. But I'm not particularly happy about the way he has treated my works and neglected them in his writings. I assume I had a significant contribution to his thinking and to the final emergence of his theory. He admitted it in our discussions and said it openly in one of his talks in 1913, in Germany. Of course, I know I had to change my views, based on what I learned from him and Hilbert. Yes, the disappointment still bothers me. It's about research ethics. Alas, there is not much I can do about it now, and Albert is a great mind. Besides, I am ill and need to quiet down a bit, so that is why I did not want to join them immediately."

Johan felt sad, realizing why Gunnar had appeared so distant and slow.

"What is the matter, Gunnar? Is it serious? Have you been to a doctor?"

Slowly, Gunnar started walking again, saying, "I'll be fine. It's severe anemia; I should take better care of myself."

He did not return to the topic, appearing almost depressed and slow in his reactions again. Johan did not want to disturb him with further questions about his health.

"I have an idea," Johan said then. "Why don't you write a summary article of your own, and describe the history of the relativity theory as you have seen it? You have enough sources and knowledge for that!"

Gunnar stopped, and looked into Johan's eyes. Johan could see a spark of hope in Gunnar's eyes.

"I do have something in preparation, which I hope to finish this year. I have some colleagues as well."

The other men were already a hundred yards ahead and had reached the place where the stairs led to the entrance of the Collège. It was dark, about eleven p.m., and Johan saw Langevin standing under a lamppost, waving for them to follow. Gunnar continued his slow walk and did not hurry at all. Johan felt sad to see this and became quiet, walking slowly, thinking, "How come I never heard of his work during my studies and work in Helsinki? No one mentioned him even when the gravitational waves were detected and celebrated. It's shameful for such a marvelous and respected scientist among all the colleagues, including Einstein, to be overlooked. I have not seen a single article or historical document of him at the department, let alone in my textbooks to describe what he has done. There must be a reason he has been treated like that, almost like an outcast. It cannot be only that he has written some of his papers in Swedish. Surely the Finnish academics should have been proud to celebrate a star like him and make Finnish science known to the world? There must be more, something I cannot understand, an internal mafia at the university doing this, perhaps professors who have been against his and even Einstein's work, keeping him out of the limelight? Could it be the same sad power game Calle and Peter are playing against me, even though I have no recognition, nothing to compete with them! Maybe I have missed something, being too much focused on my own work? I wish I had studied history! This is insane!"

The group was standing at the Collège stairs, waiting for them, and when Gunnar and Johan were still a few yards away from them, Einstein asked the approaching Johan, in a surprisingly loud voice, "You seemed to have a lively discussion, is it still about David and Gunnar?"

Johan was astonished by Einstein's tone, and the sharpness of his question. He felt ready to defend Gunnar further, in the face of this situation. As he approached Einstein and the others, Johan thought, "Everything speaks for Gunnar; he should be recognized for what he has achieved in leading the way to the first version of the theory of relativity, at home and elsewhere. It's not a weakness to be wrong in innovative thinking that leads to better discoveries."

Then it struck Johan; he had been so moved by the explicit unfairness that he had totally forgotten it was the past he lived in now; it was 1922, and he stopped abruptly, standing on the street.

"Damn it, what do I think I'm doing here? How could I change the future to be fair to someone! I'm blind! Of course, my aphasia and apraxia have prevented this all the way, guiding and binding me as it has done from the beginning of my visit here and at the Bateau! But how, then, was it possible to question Einstein in the straightforward way I did, using my knowledge of what is to come of his work? Does it mean that I'm not alone with my ethical worries? What if the disturbing knowledge about Einstein's neglect already exists here somewhere, perhaps even documented, but at least in the minds of these people? How else could I have asked for an explanation the way I did without the strangling grip of my future aphasia? It did not prevent me from expressing my worry, even being blunt about it. Maybe what I said was nothing new or wrong in this world in the first place; maybe it was just a repetition of what already exists as a shared but perhaps not public, silent knowledge, hidden somewhere? Is it possible that the awareness of this unfair process will be transmitted to future generations, even to my own times, by someone like me? Or I'm just insane."

Johan did not answer his own silent, mischievous questions, and Einstein continued to stare at him, puzzled and apparently restless. Both men remained speechless for such a long time that Gunnar looked uneasy as he observed the mutual silence. He looked back at Johan, signaling to him to come join him again. Then he surprised Johan by turning to address Einstein with a small smile.

"It's nothing new. We were just going through the development steps of your and my theories. Let's go, Johan!"

Johan joined the group and Croiset took the lead again, continuing his spontaneous role as a late-night tourist guide, pointing to the direction ahead.

"Let's walk towards the Pont Neuf. Albert's hotel is somewhere behind the buildings on your right at rue Dauphine, a nice, traditional place, about one kilometer from here. We can all walk him there."

Langevin took Einstein by his left arm, began a vivid discussion, and together they followed Croiset. Nordmann joined Gunnar and Johan and the incident was forgotten; no one gave it another thought.

Nordmann was in good spirits as he said, "I have the most extraordinary material from the talk today at the Collège and the dinner! I will continue reporting the forthcoming meetings with Albert. It's quite historical, don't you think so?" He was full of energy and did not appear to expect any answer. Turning to Gunnar and Johan, he asked, "Where do you stay, are you at the same hotel? I live near the Boulevard Saint-Germain, north of Le Jardin du Luxembourg."

Johan remained quiet, uneasy, as Gunnar answered, "I'm staying at a modest, small hotel, south of the Jardin."

Johan saw the chance to ease the moment; he had no idea where to stay.

"Then I'm quite near to Gunnar. I'm heading towards rue des Ursulines, we can accompany Albert to his hotel and Gunnar and I can then continue our discussions, getting to know each other. It's quite a surprise to meet a countryman and even a prominent colleague here in Paris, a miracle indeed!"

It was close to midnight, still a comfortably cool but not chilly evening for the nightly promenade, when they arrived at the crossing of the rue Dauphine and turned towards the Seine. Einstein's hotel was on their right, just after crossing the rue Christine, not more than about two hundred meters from the Seine. They stopped outside the hotel entrance; a thin, chilly spring mist, floating above the river, reached them at the hotel entrance; the nightly wind embraced the friendly group, extending its moist touch, almost by surprise, from the dark Seine. It was the first distinct sign of a cold night, making Johan uncomfortably aware of not knowing where to stay overnight.

It was time to say a quick goodnight, to exchange polite thanks and expressions of mutual respect and gratitude. Croiset and Langevin made sure the practicalities for the following days were clear to Einstein, who thanked them once more and then turned to Gunnar and Johan.

"I hope to see you both at the Collège," he said, "when we can have a more open discussion. It's the day after tomorrow, but if you cannot make it, there will be one after that as well. I've enjoyed our discussions, even the tough ones with you, Johan."

Johan did not know what to say. Einstein had already turned his back, as he quickly entered the hotel lobby.

Langevin smiled at Johan. "You made an unusual impact on him, Johan. But don't think you are the only one who has had similar thoughts about Gunnar's work! You are not alone, although you had the straightforward Nordic way to express it, or was it a purely Finnish style to declare your worries? There are ways. I have to admire you here, right now, but this time I'm the host, you see, and we work together with Albert." Johan nodded to Langevin, who seemed to confirm his earlier thoughts that the truth can come out in one form or another.

Croiset and Nordmann laughed aloud, tapping Johan on his back, but Gunnar remained silent and serious. All of them walked together, away from the Seine. At the crossing of the Boulevard Saint-Germain, Langevin stopped.

"It's time to say goodnight! We will continue from here with Charles and Maurice. Johan and Gunnar, our paths will now diverge. If you can, you are welcome to join me for a lunch at the Collège tomorrow, but if you cannot make it, we will see you at the next talk!"

They all shook hands and Gunnar and Johan took the rue de l'Odéon towards the Jardin and Odéon Theâtre d'Europe, which was faintly lit and visible far ahead, at the end of the street. Croiset, Nordmann and Langevin had turned to the right, continuing along the Boulevard.

"You look sad" Johan said to Gunnar, immediately after they were alone, adding, "What do you think about Einstein's behavior? Do you have the faintest idea why he has not publicly given you written, documented credit, just like he has done to Hilbert? It is evident he appreciates your work and your contributions to the theory of relativity. You two had some kind of a collaboration going on, if I understood it right? Was it productive?"

Gunnar walked slowly, without looking at Johan, just staring at his feet, and for a minute or two they just walked in silence.

"I did meet him twelve years ago in Zurich," Gunnar finally said. "That was where we had serious discussions on how to represent the sources of the gravitational fields. I'm convinced he benefited from the interaction as much I did, but he is also a rare and competent scientist and has progressed a lot since then. It's quite possible that he's the kind of a person who just does not think about these matters of fame."

Johan interrupted him. "On the other hand, Albert does make references to his own works, so he's not blind to his own achievements, and he must be aware of the logic of our work as a scientific community, just like Newton was when he referred to the shoulders of the giants?"

Gunnar had a curious smile on his face. "Well, perhaps Albert just takes me as a pygmy."

Johan was happy to see him smile, something he had not seen during the evening stroll. But he did not leave it at that.

"It is so easy to forget where the crucial triggers for new ideas actually occur and who contributes to them. I have met scientists who simply steal ideas from others, whenever they can, even admit that, bluntly, at least when drunk. This is not that kind of a case, but it keeps me unhappy to notice how your contribution has been treated. It will find its right place one day."

Johan wanted to tell his own story: how Calle had tried to destroy his scientific career and how the real skills and contributions did not matter at all in the hands of such malevolent actors. It was impossible to say all this, as he well knew, so he did not even try. Instead, he approached the subject from a different angle.

"We do not work in isolation, Gunnar; I'm sure you'll agree with me. Science is a social play, a drama. Remember what Croiset said at the dinner, about the Athenian comedies? Funny enough, but science is not different from a comedy. The difference is that it's serious in nature and sometimes almost as true as the comedies. Like science, the comedies have their impact on individual and social life. You said you've suggested that Einstein should receive the Nobel prize. Imagine what happens to any person receiving such an award! Surely you do not think that they do not care or that the society and people can easily neglect that kind of a glory? Einstein is no machine either. After such fame and celebration, nothing remains the same in the society and in the mind of the awarded hero!"

Gunnar remained sober and silent, letting Johan continue his preaching.

"What I mean is that if you have done something worthy in science, even tried it the hard way, sweating and being lost on the way, being honest to science, not hiding your mistakes and bad results, you deserve the glory as much as those who have made it."

Johan realized he was giving a lecture or speaking like a manic priest, almost like Pablo used to do, but he was still annoyed by the thought of Gunnar having missed the public respect from Einstein that he would have deserved. He continued, in a loud voice echoing from the walls along the dark street ahead.

"I'm disappointed and even angry for you. In this case, there is no doubt about it. I mean, you deserve it, and don't you ever forget it! It's the simplest law in science: we do it together, we cannot build it alone, even the most stupid of us! What is a genius worth without willing pawns?"

Johan tried to make fun of the frustration he experienced, and they continued the slow walk, in silence. A faint smile arose on Gunnar's face and every now and then he nodded to Johan, who was slowly calming down.

They entered the plaza in front of the Odéon Théâtre, a beautiful classic building with an impressive row of pillars, eight of them at the entrance. Its style reminded Johan of the House of Parliament in Helsinki, but he did not know if this similarity was just an accident or a purposeful decision on the part of the Helsinki architects and leaders. A few people were gathering under the streetlights in front of the building. Some were sitting at the stairs leading to the theater, enjoying wine. Johan noticed a line of horse carriages, even one — to him a historical — car parked near the entrance on the left, apparently offering transportation, waiting for customers. It was less chilly there and they both sat down on the stairs near two young couples who seemed curious about Johan's blond and tall, good looks.

A young man next to Johan commented, "You look like a lighthouse here with your blond hair! Where do you come from?"

"I'm from Finland," Johan said in a polite tone, and was not at all surprised to hear the response.

"Is it in Europe?"

"Yes, it is, in the north. The Russians are our eastern neighbors!"

"Well, good luck to you, then! I'm from further east there; we ran away only a few years ago, but in time!" Johan was amused noticing the man did not know that Finland is part of Europe, but was not surprised by the ignorance, and did not comment in any way

They looked around at the plaza, observing people coming and going. Bars and restaurants were closing. Johan, curious about their habits and clothing, commented to Gunnar on what he saw, but Gunnar did not show any interest.

Instead, Gunnar turned to him and said, "Now I hope you can finally explain what kind of research you work with. I haven't had a chance to hear about it!"

Johan had noticed a food stand nearby, lit by several candles. Hoping to avoid Gunnar's inquiry, he suggested they go there to fetch something to eat and drink.

Gunnar stood up and stretched a little. "OK, let's first go there and see if they have something to offer. I confess, I'm a bit hungry again. Once we eat, let's continue this conversation. I really do want to hear about your work in physics. I am surprised I have not heard of you before today."

There were two booths, side by side, each one with a table, the size of about three by six feet, one selling fruits and vegetables and the other one offering souvenirs.

Johan remained standing at the stairs, feeling glad to observe Gunnar hurrying to the stands, energetic again. Stopping by one of the booths Gunnar waved to Johan to come and see the offers, explaining to the approaching Johan: "Look at the towers on the table, there must be a hundred of them or more and they are either right side up or upside down, in an apparently random order! There is something peculiar in this arrangement, something systematic, the way each tower has found its place and orientation, but I don't see what it is!" It was a curious arrangement of dozens of miniatures, wooden *towers Eiffel*, each about four inches high. The towers had been laid on the table in a visibly haphazard order, each one painted in one color only in the colors of the French flag: blue, white and red.

Coming closer to the stand, looking at the young woman behind the table, Johan had to take a second look at her. She was a young woman, who looked to be in her early twenties. All Johan could think was, "My God, she looks so much like Yvonne, her dark hair and cheeks and her roundish eyes." For a second, he thought there were faint stitch marks above her right, curving eyebrow.

Johan tried not to stare at her eyebrow, and then he got puzzled remembering Yvonne's poster of the Eiffel Tower, which she had attached upside down on her apartment wall. She had never explained why she had done that. "I must be dreaming," he thought, "or else I'm not seeing properly. It's so dark here."

Gunnar stood over the table with the Eiffel Towers, still curious about their arrangement. He studied them for a minute or so, and gestured to Johan as if to say, "Look at this!" Johan stepped forward, looked briefly at the set of towers and immediately, without any effort, recognized their apparently haphazard order.

"Aha! Yes, a clever arrangement of these little trinkets. Don't you see, Gunnar, there is only one tower which is both blue and which is upside down! All the French flag colors have been used but only one of the towers is different from all others, the one that's upside down and blue! Perhaps there is something conspicuous about it, I mean the colors have symbolic meanings, I think; I hope it's not one of the *Liberté, Égalité, Fraternité* themes that is upside down!"

Gunnar shook his head a little and kept gazing at the table. He carefully counted the different color classes of towers, until he was convinced Johan had seen it right.

"How in Heaven's name can you do it so fast, count all the color and position combinations, just like that, with no effort whatsoever? I had to do it one by one, really count them!"

"I don't know. I've always had some kind of a fast, visual capacity, but I don't see everything so fast; this is a specific case, I guess. I do have an excellent reputation as a mushroom hunter, though."

Gunnar laughed, tapped Johan on his back and suggested, "Can I buy you that special one, the blue and upside down one, for you, as a unique souvenir, to remember our visit here? I'm still amazed by your visual capacity!"

"Wonderful! Thank you! I don't have any money, however, so I cannot pay it back now. I'm sorry."

Johan, still curious, asked the woman, "Can you please explain why you have made that unusual, compelling arrangement of the towers? Was it your own idea? Is there a reason only the blue one is upside down? Is there a message in it? It really works! It's a wonderful idea indeed. I bet not too many of your customers notice anything special in it; they might even think you are somehow careless with your stuff?"

He tried again to see her face, especially the details of the eyebrow above her right eye, but it was too dark, and the candles produced strong shadows on her face. She had a kind way of speaking in a soft, slightly low voice, that again reminded Johan of Yvonne.

"It's a lure," she said. "You cannot guess how many interesting customers I get by this! Usually, they don't immediately see my system and most of them are annoyed by it. Then they are intrigued, and finally try to find a system in it. It takes time and it is good for my business. You were the first one to do it so quickly and effortlessly. That's quite amazing!"

Gunnar picked up the blue, upside-down one, handing it over to the woman for packing, when Johan said, "Please do not pack it. I'll be happy to carry it like that!"

She looked Johan in the eyes, a friendly and warm look, as she handed the tower to him. The moment Johan touched the tower and her extended hand, the faint marks above her right eye, almost lit up in Johan's eyes. There was no doubt they were the stitches in Yvonne's eyebrow. He did not have any time to think about what he saw when a flash of bright light occurred and a transparent, grayish-brown wall, like silk, ten by fifteen feet wide, extended between him and the women, who now looked exactly like Yvonne. Despite the weak light he was now sure there were small dots, the marks of the stitches on her right eyebrow. There was no texture, a pattern or any figure drawn on the screen; again, it was a smooth, soft and slightly undulating screen of silk. Behind it Johan could now see two human characters, Yvonne on the left and Siiri on the right. He tried to say something to Gunnar, pointing at the screen, but was totally muted, and could not utter a word. Gunnar looked astonished and said something Johan could not understand.

Now Johan was scared, his heart pounded. It was the first time during the strange adventures in 1907 and 1922 he was in such close touch with his real life, only that both Yvonne and Siiri were now visible and behind the wall. He was afraid to lose the connection with them, to miss a chance for return, forgetting his surroundings totally, and could hardly finish his thought: "I cannot wait, I have to act... now!" and he rushed, with all his physical power, towards the booth and the wall, on the right, thinking of nothing but the connection and a possible return. He chose to move toward Siiri.

PART VI

Chapter 28
Choices of the Future

Johan stood, mesmerized, in front of the entrance to Les Ursulines, the modest brasserie he immediately recognized, remembering the celebration of his first moments of freedom in Paris, with Yvonne. It felt like very early morning, misty and chilly, only a few people, not a crowd yet, busy passing by, hurrying to work. The first thing he noticed was the humming background noise from the traffic. He did not see many cars in the crossing of the rue des Ursulines and rue Gay-Lussac. Nobody paid attention to Johan. Everything — the house facades, the few cars, the asphalt surface of the street, the way people were dressed, the traffic lights and electronic devices here and there — told their modern story. He felt the spontaneous connection with this world, as if it was the scene of his own, real life in Paris, far from home, but it felt like *the present and a home.*

Through the cafeteria windows Johan could discern the bar, its small tables, and a few clients, typically alone, enjoying breakfast and getting ready for the day. The sun was shining low from the east, lighting the rue des Ursulines, and blinding his eyes, forcing him to turn his gaze away from the bright light. Looking around, he tried to figure out what year, month, and day it was. He did not feel perplexed, frightened, or scared at all, but hoping he had finally returned home to Paris. It was like a most natural thing to enter the new, less unknown world than he had experienced, a new space-time as he thought and hoped. Johan recognized the familiar, paradoxically calm and tranquil feeling he had experienced entering the Bateau and the Collège. It had been a mystery to him before, ever since the first strange shifts or transportations in his personal space-time, carrying from the real world's artificial compartment at the wax museum to Pablo's lively and inspiring studio, finding himself sitting on the floor there, meeting the new friends, totally unprepared, but not worried at all about what had happened and what was to come. The same, kind psychology of transportation had captured him at the Collège, but this time it was different. Rushing towards the wall he had been desperate to find the presence he knew, the place and time he wished would free him from the muting aphasia.

At the Odéon, Johan had met his moment of choice and sensed the pressure to make the decision, to reach for his own, real space-time life with its open past and the hidden, but possible futures. He had dreamed of being able, again, to give his best, to share, with his friends and colleagues everything he had learned, imagined, and knew, to live on the mercy of the unknown and exciting future, while trying to create something novel, something of significance. This was what he was after now, to rid himself of the strange forms of future aphasia and apraxia. It was like a craving for a recovery from a long-lasting journey, not an illness, dreaming of a chance to be his genuine self again. Johan realized how the possibility to join his own true, full reality was a call more powerful than it ever had been to escape it.

Johan could not understand why he had chosen Siiri over Yvonne, but the choice had been spontaneous, without a whit of hesitation and colored by an instant hope. Trying to explain the choice to himself, he thought, "Siiri is from Finland, from my real home; it's more than a physical place to return to; it's everything I am." Remaining still, standing at the street crossing, he turned around, slowly, peering in all directions, searching for any conspicuous signs of the exact timing of his new presence; he was thinking about Siiri and Yvonne.

Suddenly an overwhelming attack of bodily pain struck him, like a burn through the whole body, hurting like flames of fire, so much that he was forced to bend down to stand it, trying with both hands to find and press the spots of pain in his body and head, to ease the ache, but he could not locate its source. He remained squatting for almost a minute, and then, as suddenly as it had hit him, the grip of the pain was over and he could straighten up his body again. It was the attack of grief from having left Gunnar and failed Pablo and Maurice, their worlds, their time, their space, their life; it was not only the immediate awareness of the separation that hurt him, it was the loss of the life they had momentarily shared, the way of the difficult and creative life. Johan recognized his agony arising from the instant, almost like a temporary death, while at the same time being re-born in the familiar world, knowing what the past was like, difficult to grasp and understand, but ready and willing to meet the unknown future.

A young girl, who looked like a typical university student to Johan, perhaps under twenty, with elegant, raven-black hair tied into a long ponytail, dressed in black long-line blazer and light blue jeans, had stopped by Johan, touching lightly his right shoulder, asking something in French Johan could not understand.

He only said, "I'm sorry."

She switched to English, a sign to Johan that he was again in a world of languages.

"Are you all right? You had some kind of a fit! Do you need help? Are you going somewhere? Do you want me to call a taxi for you?"

Johan smiled at her. "I'm OK. I'd just like to know what time it is."

The girl looked at him, puzzled. "It's about seven-thirty."

"But what day is it?" Johan continued without thinking.

"It's Tuesday."

He went on. "Which month?"

Now the girl smiled, took a step back, hands on her hips. "You seem quite OK. Are you teasing me? One more question and I'll be on my way!"

"Which year and month is it?"

The girl laughed. "That was two, but you don't sound or look like you're seriously lost! OK, this is Paris, 2016, April 19th. You are not from here, are you?"

"No, I'm not. I just arrived. Thank you for your help. I'm a bit confused, but fine now, thank you."

The girl said goodbye, hurrying away, her ponytail swaying, like waving goodbye and a welcome to Johan, who stood still, trying to figure out what had happened:

"I've been away for two weeks, but I know I spent three with Pablo! It's like father's disappearances, not very different from that, not at all, the times don't match. I have to find Yvonne."

He hurried to the narrow entrance gate, with the familiar, inviting writing of VILLA GAY-LUSSAC arching high above it, in a metal font, at the rue des Ursulines. He was eager to see if his apartment was still available, if everything was as it had been. He didn't have the key to the building and had to ring the doorbell at the gate. The concierge, Bernard, he had met earlier, answered immediately, greeting Johan who felt his heart take several extra beats:

"Well, there you are! I'll open the gate for you! We have been searching for you. Your friends have been worried and desperate, having heard nothing of you for two weeks! We have kept the apartment for you. Yvonne never lost the hope you will return. She did not even think about giving it away. Come in, do you have anything to carry?"

Entering the building Johan was relieved to meet the familiar fellow, a reliable, promising sign of the past as it had been. He wanted to find more evidence for the new, hopefully safe reality as he wished it to be, to make sure he knew where he was and what had happened to him, to be able to talk about anything. To have a home.

"Great to see you, Bernard, I'm so glad to see it's you who welcomes me, especially today. No, I have nothing with me now, I'd like to rest for a while and find Yvonne."

"You have a guest."

Nothing surprised Johan. He did not even ask who it was, only rushed upstairs to the third floor, exclaiming to Bernard:

"He will then let me in."

"It's she!" echoed the answer from the downstairs.

Johan knocked softly on the door and only after a painfully long-lasting moment, did he hear the familiar voice:

"Just a moment, please, I'll open the door in a minute!"

Almost five minutes passed before Siiri opened the door, giving way to the surprised Johan to enter the room. He could only sigh "Siiri!" and try immediately to hug her and say something, but she stepped aside, as if to avoid any physical contact and interrupted Johan, staring at him from a distance, her head slightly tilted, with a look, annoyed and curious at the same time, when she spoke in Finnish:

"You assume it's just fine to treat your friends like this? Have you forgotten what your father did to your family and you? Have you lost your marbles, too?"

She had short blonde hair now, with a straight cut across her forehead; she looked boyish, dressed in black jeans and a bright green sweater. Her pale make-up and the bright red lipstick gave her that familiar, edgy appearance. Clearly it had taken the extra five minutes to prepare. Johan did not know what to say, feeling the relief of being together with someone so real while bothered by the increasing guilt for the trouble he had caused. He could only guess what it had been like, the seriousness of it. He could not figure out why Siiri was there now, apparently involved and why he had seen and chosen her on the screen at the Odéon Theâtre. Johan was puzzled, wondering if it had all been a coincidence, a dream or something else.

Johan sat down on the coach in the small living room and noticed all his stuff on the coffee table in front of him: his mac, wallet, mobile phone, the keys to the gate and the apartment, a pile of papers, mostly receipts he remembered having had with him when visiting the wax museum.

"Where did you get all those?"

Siiri walked back and forth in the room, but she did not look at Johan.

"They returned them from the Grévin where you left them. At the Villa, the concierge took care of them, the guard found them on the floor at the museum, near the Picasso. They had no idea what had happened to you. Then we called the police. You can offer your explanation now! We've done our share."

Johan was curious to hear more. "Where exactly did they find them?"

Siiri did not comment on this. "Go see for yourself! We have done enough. You can talk to the concierge here; I don't care a bit."

Johan blushed. "I understand your feelings. I'm sorry for causing whatever trouble it has brought to you. Why are you here?"

She did not answer the question, instead simply said, "I can leave, now that you are back and apparently safe. You can go on living your Parisian life with Yvonne! I've done everything I could. There were no signs of you in any of the networks I went through. I was of no help! Besides, you smell like a pig. Haven't you had a shower at all?"

Johan was embarrassed but getting irritated by Siiri's harsh accusations and her attitude. Her style of critical behavior was not new to Johan, who knew it well, and he tried to calm her down, but did not know how and what to say, how to tell her about his experiences and how to explain. It was like the aphasia and apraxia again, what he had suffered during the journey, but now when he could speak about anything, he did not know how to tell the truth without making a complete fool of himself. Then he realized he was in serious need of a shower and became aware of the possibility of getting a reasonable diagnosis of being psychotic, like his father. He tried to continue the discussion:

"I have to check that I have everything. Yvonne is a good friend. I'd better call her if my phone is still working."

Siiri stood in front of him, looking grim. "So, you think we have not properly taken care of your stuff, is that it? Before you touch anything here, go and take a shower, please, there are clothes on the chair for you!"

Johan had to smile at Siiri, who had every reason to be mad at him, and still took care of him.

"OK, I'll do it, thank you, thank you!"

Johan tried to hug her again, but she only pushed him away, took a hold of her nose to make sure Johan understood he'd better shower first.

Johan enjoyed the warm and comfortable shower, a luxury. He tried to relax and calm down but was losing the tranquil feeling he'd had on arrival, realizing the problems ahead if he would try to explain what had happened to him during the two weeks he had been away. He knew he just had to live with it and accept Siiri's frustration. Yvonne's possible reaction was another puzzle. He realized now how his father had felt and why, after his disappearances, coming back to the real, and hopefully kind world. Typically, he had behaved like nothing special had happened. It was easier now for Johan to understand why his father had been like that, having left his friends somewhere in the past, and then being met with the hard criticism and conflicts at his arrival. It had made life extremely frustrating and Johan remembered how his father was muted in front of his mother: "No wonder he did not want to explain his experiences."

The wonderful freshening experience eased his worry and he sat down on the couch and called Yvonne. She answered and sounded exhausted; she could only speak with a very low voice. Johan could hear she was profoundly excited and moved:

"Where are you? Where are you? It's finally you! It's finally you!"

"I'm at the Villa with Siiri, could you please come here, and I'll explain to you, or try to do it, what has happened. I need to eat something, we could go to the Les Ursulines with Siiri. Why don't we meet there?"

"I'll leave immediately! I'm at the lab. Where have you been? What has happened to you? Are you OK? Are you OK?"

"I will explain then. Please come there as soon as you can! Love you! Bye!"

"Bye!"

Siiri's presence made Johan stop the call too soon, feeling uncomfortable to explain his intimate thoughts to Yvonne in front of Siiri. He realized having automatically used his American expression "Love you!" to Yvonne, in a way Finns never do unless they are deeply and romantically in love with someone. In Finland, it's not a typical wording to express a warm family bond or care; it's practically always about serious love. Johan was confused about his own motivation, noticing the dark-cold look in Siiri's blue eyes. Johan thought she had made her Finnish interpretation of the "Love you!" On their way down the exit stairs, Siiri went ahead, did not look at Johan and only talked to the stairs:

"You are not healthy. You need a shrink and a shock or both!"

Walking to the restaurant, only one block away from the Villa, Johan did not have much time to think and decide how to explain his adventure and how to convince his friends he was not insane or a schizophrenic. The familiar choking feeling caught him, the pain he remembered from the aphasia at the Bateau and at the Collège for his real life, for his friends' future and how desperately he wanted to tell everything he knew and believed in physics and then the pain of muting, with Pablo and the Bateau friends, and then again with Einstein and Gunnar. He decided to tell everything exactly as it had happened and how he had experienced it, no matter what. Now he could talk about anything he saw relevant and interesting. "I have to try it; if I cannot trust Yvonne and Siiri, then I have no friends at all."

They found a table in a quiet corner of the Les Ursulines, the same one they had used with Yvonne, left from the door at the back of the room, a somewhat cramped place, but separate from the other tables, a typical old-fashioned bistro table for four, a rounded settee, with a brownish-violet, artificial leather covering. Johan insisted they take the seats there, side by side, Siiri on his right, but she refused and took the seat opposite to Johan who then faced the door, eager to see when Yvonne would arrive. A place was reserved for Yvonne on Siiri's right.

"My story is so strange and unbelievable that I don't want any extra ears near me."

A waiter, a man of about Johan's age, with a welcoming smile came to meet and serve them; Siiri looked up at him and ordered a Salade Ursulines, "Without any meat, please," she said in English.

Johan felt tired, as one does after a long trip, and was ready to enjoy a proper steak to recover, so he ordered the Steak au Poivre, and Grand Marnier crêpes as a dessert, a half a bottle of red house wine, and mineral water for them to share.

"You do drink wine?" he asked Siiri, jokingly, trying to touch her hand, but she did not answer, withdrew her hands from the table. When the wine arrived, she did not resist the waiter serving it to her.

"Where should I start? It's going to be difficult for you to believe."

Johan observed Siiri, tried to avoid upsetting her, to find a way to approach and make a soft connection, but he could not see any opening in her powerful psychological defense. It was still a mystery to Johan, why Siiri was there. Johan was also puzzled that she wanted to spend any time with him, after how she had spoken about the incidents and his disappearance. Then he made up his mind, convinced that this was the right thing to do, not to lie, not to twist the truth as he had experienced it, to test the limits of his reality and to enjoy it after the muting experiences. He began with what he felt was the most unbelievable, true story to tell:

"I've spent several weeks in 1907, it was summer, with Pablo Picasso, living in a small closet, in the same house where Pablo has — or had — his atelier at the Bateau Lavoir. I had a most remarkable time with his friends Guillaume Apollinaire and Maurice Princet. I cannot tell you how much I miss them, especially Pablo and Maurice; I've never felt a pain like this, being separated from my friends!"

Siiri only uttered a short comment, almost a sigh:

"You did not miss your friends in this world? That's something."

She became silent, only kept looking Johan in the eyes, as if she was searching for something.

"Then I moved to the year 1922 and met Albert Einstein, and, strangely enough, a Finnish colleague, Gunnar Nordström, a physicist from Helsinki, whom I had never met before. It all started at the Grévin where I saw the wax-Pablo and then a mysterious silky screen and Pablo's wonderful work *Les Demoiselles d'Avignon* painted on it, appearing in front of me, out of nowhere, like a window inviting me to another world, and then I took the chance and went through. I don't know why, but I just could not resist it."

Siiri remained silent, but her eyes were wide open. She was about to say something when Johan stood up, electrified, as he had seen Yvonne arrive, and rushed from his cramped seat to meet and hug her at the entrance. On the way, he almost spilled Siiri's half-empty glass of wine. Reaching Yvonne, he could not say a word, only held her close and tight when they hugged, looking into her eyes, scrutinizing the small scars above the eye, and could not stop sobbing, a shining flow of tears on his cheeks. He turned his gaze from Yvonne, feeling ashamed, trying to wipe away the teardrops and recover from the expression of affection. Yvonne could only say, with a very low voice: "It's you! It's you!"

They walked slowly to the table and sat down, Yvonne on Siiri's right. Siiri greeted her, smiling and kissing her on both cheeks, not looking at Johan at all. Yvonne placed her order with the waiter who had quickly noticed her arrival and she ordered the same as Siiri had done, and then turned to her:

"I'm so grateful to you for being here and for the connections. I did not know what to do. Without you, I would have lost all hope!"

Siiri was quick to respond in a soft tone that to Johan's ears was in a marked contrast to how she had spoken to him:

"At last, you can stop worrying about his whereabouts; however, you will face other weird kinds of problems when you hear his version of the universe."

Johan blushed, felt irritated, and sighed:

"OK, let's begin again," he said as he repeated the story, he had already told to Siiri, remembering to mention that his only choice now was to stick to the absolute truth of what he had experienced.

Now it was Yvonne's turn to remain silent. The two women staring at him, both puzzled, speechless. Siiri spoke first with her edgy comment:

"Like father, like son. Can you agree with us that your story sounds like a hopeless confabulation, a dream world of a psychotic? Is it at all different from what you father used to tell you when he abandoned the family for weeks and then returned as if nothing had happened?"

Johan was hesitant to respond, knowing how right she was, but he did not alter in his decision to tell and stick to the truth in everything he would tell Siiri and Yvonne:

"My father had been with Pablo, some years before me. I'm quite sure about that. I even found traces of him and my relationship with Pablo was partly built on this. It made possible a swift trust among us and friendship for me. I was received like a good friend and a member of the community I had never met before; they did not see any difference between me and my father! It all happened so fast and felt most natural."

Almost a minute of silence followed; the women stared at each other and then at him. They were like twins in their disbelief. Johan continued, realizing the impossibility of the task. It was going to be difficult to convince them about anything he would tell, but at least there was no aphasia to stop him.

"I want to stick to the truth, I have to trust you, you are the only ones I have for this, here. There is no other way. If I start hiding my reality from you, it will be like the muting aphasia I experienced with Pablo, even worse; I'll be a schizo in your eyes. During my stay with him, it was impossible for me to mention or discuss my own, real life, about what I have learned, know and think, about anything that was *their* future; in fact, I could tell them nothing about you. The same thing happened with Einstein and Gunnar. I could not even make gestures or draw anything that referred to my life here, in *their* future. I don't want this illness of muting here; it was my oppressive disease there. I'm here in my own life now, with you! Can you understand it? If I stop telling you what my reality is, I will be an aphasic, for my real past in this case, a real psycho!"

Johan felt still strong enough to stick to the unbelievable truth, but a new kind of an urge, an itch, started bothering him and he asked for paper and a pen from the waiter.

He drew a timeline, marking the years 1907, 1922, 2016, and 2017 on it, explaining to Siiri and Yvonne what he had seen at each epoch and what he imagined would happen next in 2017. But he could not stop, and instead continued, as if under a compulsion or a spell, possessed and then started drawing *Les Demoiselles,* above the 1907 mark, and so large that it extended to the edges of the paper. First, he drew an overall sketch of it, and then added features, again and again. He corrected them and added new ones and corrected them again until the paper was crowded with details, drawn with the blue ballpoint pen, in excessively strong lines. He was not very good at drawing, but the outcome bore a fair resemblance to the *Demoiselles*, to its overall structure and the details of the women in it.

"What is this?" Yvonne asked, pointing at the *Les Demoiselles* sketch, with a worried look on her face, embarrassed for Johan's manic behavior with the drawing.

"It's Pablo's cubistic work, *Les Demoiselles d'Avignon.* I don't know where it is now, but he painted it in the Bateau atelier. He called it *Le Bordel.*"

"Is it about France, I mean Avignon? What are these women there?"

Johan hesitated for moment, but continued as he had decided:

"No, it's actually from a brothel in Barcelona, *The Brothel of Avignon on Avinyó Street,* in Barcelona. The women in the painting are the local whores. One of them used to be the mistress of Carles, Pablo's good friend, who killed, shot himself. But that's not the point. This painting, the rightmost part of it, was my first door to the world of Pablo's and his friends!"

Johan knew he was using the word 'whore' in a way he did not like himself, but wanted to be as open as possible, even blunt, despite the risk of making things worse.

Siiri looked astounded. "Is that the place where you have lived, in Barcelona and not in Paris, with the whores? What else have you been doing or imagining? Did Einstein have whores, too?"

The last comment was so funny to Johan that despite the seriousness of the situation, he laughed aloud, relieved for a second, and even Yvonne joined him and threw him a quick smile.

"No, Einstein was clean, and I lived in the same house with Pablo as I told you, at the Bateau Lavoir, in Montmartre. I had a small closet to sleep and rest and my father had left his sign there. It's quite possible the studio is still here in Paris, I don't know. We could go and see it, and Le Lapin Agile as well!"

"Yes, it is here and so is *Lapin Agile*," Yvonne added, with her remarkably low-pitched and whispering voice again. She looked worried.

Johan could not stop drawing while speaking to his astounded friends. The compulsory drawing felt like an after-effect of his apraxia when now he was finally free to draw anything he wanted and could not stop before the whole page was full of the blue lines, marks, and drawings. The paper was extremely crowded, sometimes extending to the tablecloth; most of it was related to *Les Demoiselles*. He had drawn a dozen of the bowtie signs framing the whole page with them.

When he began to write down the equations, Yvonne commented: "That is about your work at Stanley, what is it?"

Johan did not answer, but just continued a series of equations, breathing heavily.

Yvonne and Siiri looked at each other again, anxious and worried; they observed Johan's emerging strange behavior in silence, first following his fast, drawing hand, and then his strange facial expressions.

Finally, Johan said, "I just had to see if I could write them down again. I can. You see?"

They did not smile.

Yvonne asked, "Why did you think you couldn't? Why?"

They sat in silence and only a few words were exchanged during the rest of the lunch. Neither Siiri nor Yvonne wanted to question Johan about his experiences. Every now and then, and while eating, Johan could not stop making small changes, improvements, in his drawing and re-writing the equations. When they had finished the desserts, Johan was already moving restlessly on his seat, embarrassed by his compulsive acts. He felt he wanted to escape from the awkward situation and from its strange grip.

"Let's go and have a walk around the Jardin," he said. "I need to relax and have some fresh air. My recent experiences and memories keep haunting me. I know my father had the same symptoms, and I don't even know if this is any different from it, but now I do know, if he had experienced the same things I did, he was not a madman, and neither am I. Or we both are. How can I convince you that my story is real, and not the imagination of a madman?

"I don't think you can," was Siiri's blunt comment.

Johan stood up, grabbed the drawing and headed for the door with Yvonne following him. Siiri remained seated.

"I'll stay here," she said. "I'll take care of the bill. I have something to work on and will be at the Villa. We have to share the room for some time, Johan, but you can have the couch, unless Picasso has a room to offer."

Johan was confused by Siiri's cold comments and her rejection of any of his positive approaches. He did not know what to do and how to react, and started regretting the decision to tell his own truth in all the unbelievable detail.

"OK, see you then. You don't know how much I'll enjoy a sofa, even alone, but in this time and space!"

He tried to laugh, but it became only a muffled grunt.

"We, or I, will be back in a couple of hours."

Siiri threw a quick glance at Johan. "Are you sure?"

Yvonne waved goodbye to Siiri, silent, and they entered the street, taking a left along the rue des Ursulines, heading towards the Boulevard Saint-Michel and the Jardin.

First, after having walked a few blocks, stopping every now and then to relax and look at the garden, in front of them, on the other side of the Boulevard Saint-Michel, Johan stepped closer to Yvonne, hesitantly, aiming to take her by the hand. He had not done that since the incidents in Palo Alto and the visit to the Stanley Hospital. Before he could touch her, Yvonne had already taken a firm grip of his right arm, leaning her head against his shoulder, looking down first and then slowly lifting her gaze to Johan's face.

"I don't know what to think of you, but I was afraid you had lost your mind somehow. I still don't know what to make of it all. I hardly know you; it's just impossible to understand your story, but I learned something about you when you took care of me. I can try to trust you. I have my own world, too."

Crossing the boulevard, they turned right, towards the Sorbonne and along the Boulevard and then left along rue de Médicis, which would take them to the Odéon Theâtre. When he got sight of the Odéon, Johan started feeling anxious, a mild nausea, sensing the presence of the wall he had met at the Odéon and the Metre, further on. He remembered the tower of Eiffel and stopped.

"I'm afraid I cannot go further this way. Let's turn back! I need time. I don't want to go to the Odéon or the Metre either. I cannot take the risk of vanishing again! Not now!"

They walked to the Luxembourg RER entrance, stopped there, and remained standing in front of a poster attached on the metal fence, an old re-colored photograph, a scene with a young couple posing in front of a horse carriage in Paris in the early 1900s; the hazy, slightly orange-colored silhouette of Sacre Coeur could be seen in the background.

"You know, I had a strange experience, a mystic incident, just before I returned to this time. There was a young woman, running a sales booth, who looked somehow very much like you, selling small, colored models of the Eiffel Tower. She had many of them and they were only in the colors of the French flag: red, blue, or white. Only one color had been used to paint each of them."

Yvonne got pale white on her face, visibly startled, her brown eyes fully open as she listened, but did not say anything.

"Then I noticed that only one of them was upside down, and it was blue. When I picked it up — Gunnar wanted to buy it for me as a souvenir — it was like an immediate, a most powerful trigger, a switch to transport me back here! Then I found myself in front of the Les Ursulines and I was not scared at all! It felt like any everyday move from one place to another, only that I wasn't sure where I was, hoping to be at home, with you!"

He did not mention Siiri, whom he had actually chosen when he rushed against the wall, and continued:

"I did experience a momentary, most painful grief, for having left my friends."

"Upside down? The French flag?" Yvonne asked, taking a step away from Johan, staring at him, with a puzzled expression on her face, almost shaken.

She seemed to know what Johan would ask next and interrupted him.

"I have never explained to you why I had the poster upside down in Palo Alto and you never asked. Please don't ask now. Please!"

Johan did not know what to think about her unusual, almost scary reaction, what was this about, but asked, without a hesitation, trying to smile, "Well, why?"

"It's nothing suspicious, but please don't ask! I cannot tell. I cannot tell."

She looked away, sighed and stared at the pavement. Only then, hearing the familiar worry in her voice and the repeated answer, did Johan realize how serious Yvonne was, and decided to leave it at that, to wait for a better occasion to ask again.

Yvonne took Johan by the hand again when they continued their quiet walk, continuing back along the boulevard. Johan felt uneasy, yet he was curious to visit and see the places where he had been with Pablo and Maurice, walked with Gunnar and Einstein, to the sites of the mysterious walls opening to him, at Grévin, the Metre, and Odéon, but was afraid to go.

"I'm trapped here in this very part of Paris, I've had the most wonderful and scary experiences of my life. I don't know where I can go without going astray again and losing my real presence and life — and you! It's the northern, north-western side of the Jardin that haunts me. Living at the Villa I have Stein's apartment close by here. I didn't tell you I visited the Steins, too! Then there is the Metre and the Odéon Theâtre looming just around the corner. I cannot live my life by constantly avoiding the world around me, to stay away from something I've actually loved. It's worse than a new version of apraxia or aphasia I already experienced. Now when I'm finally able to talk about these events and places of importance, nobody believes me. I could visit all the places, but I'm afraid to do it. This must sound like a psychotic talking, doesn't it?"

They stopped for a while, silently observing the people walking in the Jardin on their right.

Yvonne broke the silence. "When you first mentioned the tower, it made me think — it is possible that you have just imagined or confabulated it, having seen my poster and your psychotic mind has done its tricks, something over which you have no control. But then you mentioned the colors of the French flag."

She was silent for ten seconds.

"My poster was in black and white, if you remember."

"So, what about the colors, then?"

"I can only tell you that to me the colors represent a community that grows out of the old system in France. Surely you know where the colors of the flag come from? Have you seen Kieslowski's three movies, on the colors blue, white and red?"

"No, I haven't, and I don't have the faintest idea of the color history. I'm a physicist, for God's sake!" He felt the familiar shame of ignorance, having always loved the problems of color vision, ever since his experiments in the skating rink. This was, again, one more sign of a black hole in his historical and cultural knowledge. He could only continue the questioning.

"But why do you think the colors are important in the tower I had? By the way, I don't have it with me, it must have disappeared! Why did the colors make you rethink? Why, suddenly, you seem to believe that I've not lost my marbles?"

"Please don't ask any more! Please, don't ask any more! I have to think!"

Johan was still hesitant, eager, and curious to know more. He tried to make a joke.

"Everything in France is upside down. In some of Pablo's works you don't even know what is up and what is down! I've seen them at the Bateau and on Stein's walls!"

Yvonne's alarmed appearance made him serious, realizing it was better to accept her anxious wish and not to tease her too much. Knowing Yvonne, he was convinced it must be something of importance, perhaps even dangerous somehow. They continued their slow and quiet walk along the green and already colorful, flourishing Jardin, back towards the Villa.

The worries about Yvonne triggered his own, gloomy memories of the depressive and murky suffering, the threats, the fear, the accident or the attempted suicide and its disastrous consequences in Palo Alto, and then the worry of and gratitude to Yvonne who had saved him, hurting herself in doing it. Glancing at her, he could still see the small dots, the signs left from the stitches, above her right eye. He was struck by the strong premonition that Yvonne had run into trouble and suddenly, he felt a powerful and vivid urge to fight for his own recovery, to gain a new balance, a relief from the present pain, to support Yvonne, whatever she was going through.

It was already early afternoon when they arrived at the Villa and knocked on the door — although Johan had the key. Siiri opened the door and welcomed them with a smile, hugging Yvonne and waving her hand to Johan:

"Welcome to our temporary home, Johan! I've made up my mind to stay here for a week, so you better get used to the arrangements! I've made everything ready for you!"

She turned to Yvonne.

"Could you come with me for a second? I'd like to talk to you outside the room."

Yvonne threw a quick glimpse at Johan, who could not hide his astonishment, and then she followed Siiri out. Johan checked the room, the closets and drawers and found all his belongings, his Mac and back-up disks there, the shirts and trousers even ironed. "It must have been Siiri!" he sighed, remembering some of her Finnish neatness.

Johan sat down in the comfortable, soft armchair with scarlet upholstery, and gazed out the window, quietly observing the closed curtains on the windows of the classic old Parisian house opposite the Villa. An endless series of open questions whirled in his mind. "What is happening to me, arriving at a place, like coming home, but knowing I'm a total stranger here? What was it I wanted to gain and re-gain when taking the decisive leaps, first to Pablo's world, like a madman, an insane risk, and then to Einstein's, driven by the insane curiosity and then, finally arriving here, when I even chose Siiri, for God's sake! What was it I was after, except for a home? Why do I miss Maurice and Pablo so much, their arduous life, my cramped cabin there? What can I do now, here, and with whom? Damn it!"

He stood up, walked a couple times around the chair, remembering: "Yvonne had even arranged a few lectures for me. What has happened to them? Have I missed them already? Are they ready to listen to a psycho? What if Yvonne reveals my story to her colleagues?" He had a painful flash of memory about his father's problems at the university.

Johan became restless and started his Mac to see if it worked. As he browsed his short list of private mails, Siiri and Yvonne arrived, laughing.

"The collider in CERN is a children's toy compared to what you claim your walls have done to you!" was Siiri's first comment when entering the room. She did not show any signs of aggression and smiled at Johan.

"You need to see a shrink or someone who can figure out what is happening to you. We have friends who can find a psychiatrist you can trust and who has treated quantum physicists before. He can understand what you talk about!"

Yvonne stayed in the background, gazing at Johan, raising her eyebrows slightly, so that the small stitch marks became briefly visible in a friendly sign that Johan could not interpret. He was puzzled by the evident friendship between the two women.

Johan stood up. "I've said it before: I don't need a psychiatrist or their treatments! I've seen enough of that!"

He was delighted and surprised to notice that Siiri did not get agitated by his comment, but instead approached him calmly and at ease. She asked him to relax and sit down, and surprised Johan by touching his shoulder lightly, and looking him in the eyes, and then, talking in a soft voice Johan had not heard for a long time.

"Now listen to me, and you know me, this will be good for you, and for us. You will not lose anything, but if all goes well, you might learn something. It's not about your psychosis; it's about your life, about us, the way you relate to the world. Think about your own work: would you refuse to analyze novel and intriguing data that could be the key to unprecedented knowledge, only because it is unbelievable at the outset? I guess you would be more than excited about such a possibility. This is no different; it's only that you are the data source now! Aren't you curious to find out about yourself? It's no different from your collision data analysis!"

Johan remained silent. He did not want to be rude and reject Siiri now that her behavior had changed, and her approach was kind and persuasive. The disturbing memory flash continued bothering him: the disappearances of his father, the anxiety shared with his mother when they, for the first time, heard his father talk about his strange worlds, the metallic, manic tone of his voice, like trying to convince them about the true reality of what he had experienced, the manic drawings, and then the crushing and final diagnosis of psychosis, the terrible suicide as the final ending point showing that there was no way out of his suffering, no way to remain in the world of his family. It was too much, too painful and Johan felt unable to accept the offer. He needed time to think, to escape the *cul de sac* of his present state, the dead end, literally.

After a half a minute silence he could only say: "I have to think about it, to know more. I need to sleep on it; it's just too much now!" He felt himself chill and turn deathly pale from fear.

Yvonne approached Johan. "I'll leave you here. You'd better just rest and sleep today. Please consider what we suggested. I could send our friend to see you here. Please think about it. Think about it!"

***

For three days Johan was not ready to receive or talk to any "shrink out of this world" as he called them, sometimes trying to joke about it. He did not ask Yvonne or Siiri for any details of the particular psychiatrist they wanted him to meet. He had been restless to sleep in the same flat with Siiri, who behaved as if it was a most natural arrangement and moved spontaneously around in the flat, preparing breakfast and working, in good spirits and appearing in her long, black, silk nightgown, though never without having prepared her trademark— the white-pale, strong-lined make-up.

On the first night, Johan woke up believing he was still in the closet of the Bateau, carefully stepping out of the bed in the dark room, trying to avoid what he thought was the bucket at the end of his bed, when Siiri spoke to him from her bed:

"Try to sleep, please; I've listened to you talk to Maurice and Pablo about a Metre, the bucket and something about a white and blue light, over and over again. Then you were sobbing. You can come and sleep with me, if you would feel better and safe that way; I don't mind."

Johan wiped off the traces of tears from his cheeks. His heart took a couple of extra beats, when for a moment he felt the urge, a warm rush of emotions through the body, to accept her unexpected and exciting invitation. He took a few careful steps towards the bedroom and stopped. He walked back to the couch-bed, sighing.

"I miss them so much, I miss the light! I have to clear up my mind alone, I'm sorry, but thank you, Siiri!"

Siiri had been up early, silent, getting ready to leave for work. She did not tell Johan where she was going or what work she had to do; she had already fetched croissants and fresh bread from a bakery and prepared a delicious setting on the table, but she finished her own breakfast quickly, stood up, and waved goodbye to Johan, who was slow to respond; she had already shut the door behind her.

The same silent process was repeated the next day, making Johan nervous, as he wondered what was going on, but despite his inquiry, Siiri did not give him any explanation as she once more left early in the morning and returned late.

Johan spent the whole day intensively with his computer, reading everything he could find about Pablo and *Les Demoiselles*, looking at the old photographs taken from the familiar atelier, the Lapin and the Bateau. The old black and white photos of the people reminded him of what he had seen and met but there was something disturbingly artificial in them: they did not carry the atmosphere, movement and engagement among the people there, or the vital power of life he had experienced with them. He did not recognize any of the clientele. Most of the photos appeared artificially arranged, as social set-ups. Perhaps they were just that: the photos bent the rays of history just like gravitation bends the light rays in space, making the real light source displaced. Johan had not seen anyone take photos during his visit.

It was painful to accept the fact that his friends, all of them, were dead now, having led their very different and colorful lives, becoming the amazing, prominent figures in art history. Johan could not stop the tears when becoming properly aware of their amazing success and then their deaths. It was a short time he had spent time with them, but the impact had been immense. He had to fight his surging emotions to get used to browsing the hundreds of photographs he found on the Internet, scanning them without getting upset every time when recognizing the familiar faces and characters. Especially Guillaume's tragic fate touched him: he was the father of the terms "cubism" and "surrealism", and always full of imaginative, colorful and encouraging energy. Then World War I muted his best creative powers, and he fell to an early death. "What a light source he was, to us all, especially to Pablo, perhaps to Sten, too. Even in the darkness and difficult times, from the first moment I met him. Where can I find such wonderful people and colleagues now?"

Johan felt a painful, familiar awareness of how little he knew about the history of art, and especially about Pablo, his exceptional life and work, the creative struggles he had and then suddenly, the wonderful future that opened to him after 1907. Johan realized he knew better Pablo's everyday manners and ways to think and talk about art than he knew his contributions to art. It didn't take any effort from Johan to return, in his imagination, to the old world: "It was my reality, as real as this. How exciting it had been had I known their future world better, to understand what Pablo was accomplishing by breaking all the rules of arts. Even with my muting, it had opened my eyes to all possible details in his work and thinking. So much to learn, so sad and in a weird way amusing to realize how much I know about my own field and to see, it is only about that. In the world of Pablo and Guillaume, I was a blind man dancing, with a sharp eye for my own world, for a world which had very little to offer to their art. There was nothing valuable I could say about arts to them — nothing. Maurice was different, but I could only blabber away and confabulate about my narrow but sharp reality. What a shame and what a scale of ignorance! Why were they so kind and close to me, despite my aphasia and ignorance?"

Johan could not stop reading about his friends, spending hour after hour, under a spell and compulsion, skimming through Pablo's work, any photos he could find of him, searching for any articles and other texts about Guillaume and Maurice. When Siiri came from work, he just continued, only briefly saying hello or responding to her suggestions for dinner.

From the Net he found only superficial history data about Maurice, but not a single photo of him. "No wonder he used to describe himself as the unholy outsider of the Le Bande; he was even ashamed of his work as a mathematician, and being a clerk helping the well-off people, his employers, to make more money and keep what they already had, while seeing how difficult the life of the artists was. He was a spontaneous and benevolent contributor who simply enjoyed helping his friends, without getting any immediate fame for it. And still, his views were crucial to the birth of *Les Demoiselles*. A strange and kind character he was, the super-intelligent mentor of the creative band, but why is he not known for it? Why are there no traces of his contributions? Is it again the same story as with Gunnar?" Johan felt sad to realize the parallels in the fates of Maurice and Gunnar.

After a thorough reading of the huge amount of material Johan came to a promising source, from 2006: *Maurice Princet. Le Mathématicien du Cubisme* by Marc Décimo. He could not read French and sighed to himself: "That's the title he deserves! What a treasure, I must find it and see if there is a photo of Maurice in it!"

Then he read about Gunnar, and found out he had died of pernicious anemia, at the age of forty-two, only a year and a half after their meeting at the Collège. This was too much for Johan who suddenly realized what was the extreme pain he had experienced when arriving at the present Paris and leaving his friends, Pablo, Maurice and Guillaume first, and then Gunnar. He felt as if he had been responsible for their deaths when he entered the present time! He did not know what to think; there was no way to deny it, and he could not imagine a way to be free from this burden. It was the deepest form of guilt he could imagine and realizing that he was shocked.

When Siiri returned from work, she found Johan lying on the sofa, looking miserable, visible traces of tears on his cheeks. He started immediately explaining to Siiri why he felt so bad, and they spent the whole evening talking about the strange dark aspect of time traveling, neither of them able to find any relief for Johan. Johan was astonished to notice that Siiri did not doubt his stories now and listened carefully to what he had to say. Johan began to slowly recover from the depressive angst, and Siiri tried to cheer him up by joking:

"The bright side is that you could indeed be a schizophrenic, and there is no need to worry then."

Johan did not laugh, but felt better as he enjoyed Siiri's company and support.

"I'm so glad to have you here, Siiri. I'm not alone with this; it's too much!"

Friday, the following day at the Villa was better for Johan who tried to relax, even prepared an early breakfast for Siiri before she got up, fetching croissants and juice from the Les Ursulines. She only wrapped herself into and under the quilt, telling Johan to close the bedroom door and then, after a while, rushed towards the bathroom in her silky nightgown. She covered her face with both hands, on the way, hitting herself slightly against the doorjamb. After five minutes she came out, in her full make-up, and sat down with Johan to enjoy the breakfast. She smiled at Johan as she relaxed in her charming morning outfit, this time a bright green, silky morning gown.

"Please try to live this world, Johan; you cannot keep on suffering and living with your lost friends."

Johan could not help staring at Siiri, grateful and being amused at the same time. She just stared back, with a surprisingly soft look, without saying a word, enjoying the breakfast delicacies. Johan could see she did not want to delve into his problem any longer, and was trying to help him forget it, too, to regain his balance. He was fully aware that it would be difficult if not impossible for him ever to forget the pain completely, but Siiri's energetic presence helped him focus on the present. He stared at her, thinking: "Some paradox you are! You paint and hide your beautiful face, but not your wit and charm." He imagined what a wonderful model she would be for Pablo, and immediately he felt a quick sting of jealousy.

Johan sensed the mental friction in trying to recover from his depressive thoughts, and tried his best to clear his mind. He asked Siiri about her connection with Yvonne:

"Something has changed your attitude and it happened rather recently, or perhaps even after you talked to Yvonne, when you left the room, remember? What was it?"

Siiri chuckled, looking directly at Johan. She was quiet and touched his hand softly, which startled Johan and he blushed.

"I've been waiting for you to ask. I wonder why it took so long, but I cannot tell. You will find out when you talk to the shrink, I mean, when you agree to meet him. I could make the call now for the appointment, any time you are ready for it." She was persistent as ever, but again with a kind tone.

Johan was now better prepared and did not get immediately agitated by the mere thought of a therapy session.

"You know what I think about this. Of course, I could meet him, just out of curiosity, there are worse things in life. I don't have anything to lose unless his diagnosis just makes things worse for me. How do I know that it will be of any use? Is it you who want to know something? I'm not ill. I just lived through something unbelievable and difficult. How do you know I won't jump out of the window immediately after his wonderful treatment? Or buy a gun? I've seen people get crazy *after* the therapy!"

"This is different, trust me!" She sounded assertive and stared at Johan, calmly:

"I've been to it and so has Yvonne. We both had our reasons, not as insane as yours but good ones, believe me. We got to know each other — at a distance — after the sessions. It is not about making a specimen or a guinea pig out of you, but connecting you with others, to make you alive again, to enjoy your world of work, and rejoin the connected life of science."

Johan was confused by the new aspect of Siiri's explanation, a comment he did not understand. He knew he would not get a straight answer from Siiri, to any direct inquiry, so he tried another approach.

"A connected science, what's that? Isn't that the essence of science? It's always been connected. Disconnection is impossible, just like Kant said, and I know it by heart, remember: *Without community, each perception of an appearance in space is broken off from every other, and the chain of empirical representations would have to start all over again with each new object...* and so on. You have heard this from me a dozen times in Helsinki? It's all about the community, including its rotten fruits like Calle and Peter!"

Johan sensed his pulse accelerate.

Siiri grew serious and asked, her eyes suddenly in flames, so much that Johan forgot his own worries. He had seen Siiri get excited in heated discussions before but was astonished to see her act and appear like a female Pablo, full of fire.

"Do you think this is true in the modern scientific practice, crowded with novel phenomena you can read from the best journals like *Nature* and *Science*? What is novel there? I mean novel novel? Do you think it is still new, even though your geniuses hide what they know, as long as they can, before anyone is allowed to know about it?" She stood up and started walking around the room.

"How do Calle and Peter fit into this? What are they after? Sharing the best available human knowledge with the community and their best colleagues, helping mankind? Don't make me laugh, Johan; I could weep, having seen what they did to you. They want to share the awards and pride, at any price. Science and knowledge are secondary! Do you seriously think they give a thought to serving the scientific community and its knowledge creation when they destroy your future and prevent you from contributing to their field?"

She approached Johan, coming very close, standing in front of him at the breakfast table, so near that Johan was overcome by her sweet fragrance.

"Remember what happened when you wanted to know what Calle had done with his method? You were a dead man! Besides, what was this collision data and the simulations you were working with, the Monte Carlo methods? You think you were doing simulations for them, but you were simulating science life, don't you see! It was plain slave work for them, to build their reputation! Why did you devote all your time to it? Was there anything in it you had discovered by yourself? Or do you think you are simply so stupid that you are unable to produce anything truly novel, something that is genuinely your creation? These men, and they are not the only ones, and I bet my makeup there are similar women; they love to seed such fears and cast dark shadows around their miniature empires. What a foolproof way to build an intellectual shelter, preventing any surprises and revolutions, to shine without fear of the slightest intellectual threat! How and where are these Jesuits connected? Is it a secret society of their own, the one they define and live on, serving them? We've attended their hierarchical feasts, remember? Through their power they can kick you out, torture and punish you and other problem cases, any time they want. Ask a question and you're out. Why would you offer them the right do this? Is *that* your science?"

Johan was speechless and thoroughly startled. He wanted to explain to her how much honest and devoted collaboration there was among the physicists, but was muted when he realized how Siiri had gathered the essence of all his terrible experiences at Stanley, re-arranged and interpreted them and gave them a painful, eye-opening form, so vivid and real that despite the gloomy picture it painted of the scientific practices, he saw no way to oppose it. The image she sketched of Johan and of his frightening experiences was like any of the cubistic portraits Pablo would have painted of Johan's present life and his academic situation: everything, every part and compartment in it was true, but the perspectives were totally new and expressive. She was not finished yet:

"They took several intentional steps to destroy you the very first day you asked two simple questions: 'Is everything OK with what you have done? Is there something I should know?' Your friend Kant would have gone crazy with such a community of psychopaths in science! You are lucky they only have the peer-driven guillotine at their disposal, with no real blade! Surely, they are our current heroes, not unlike the French revolutionaries were and they too hail *Libérté, Égalité, and Fraternité* as long as it serves them. But disagree with them openly and it's the peer-Guillotine! Just as it happened to Lavoisier, if you don't know how low, exactly, to bow to them. Well, the lucky Lavoisier does have his name on the street here in Paris, close by, if you noticed, even an Institute. But he lost his head, for Heaven's sake! Their way of tricolor sounds beautiful, but it's a perfect recipe for the selfish and cruel destruction of the soul of science. Their science tricolor has no space reserved for the word *Responsabilité!*"

Siiri sighed deeply, her shoulders falling. She took Johan, who still sat at the breakfast table, by both hands, looking at him, down, deep in the eyes, still sharp and passionate, but now sad, with a tired gaze. It was a touching surprise to the unprepared Johan, who tried his best to hide his affections, to prevent tears from flowing but could not. Johan had never heard such powerful talk from Siiri, or seen her so strong, yet vulnerable at the same time; Siiri's passionate way of supporting him was totally unexpected and utterly confusing to Johan. She sat down, quiet at the table; the coffee was getting cold. The short moment of silence felt like minutes for Johan, who did not know what to think about Siiri, about his own situation and how he should react to Siiri's suggestion, to go and see the shrink.

The sudden, amazing outburst from Siiri caused a deep sense of gratitude in Johan, when he realized the scale of her sincere and devoted care, something he did not expect at all and could not grasp why she had such a critical stance towards science and even his career. For a reason he did not understand, images of his friends at the Bateau rushed into his mind.

Johan stood up, slowly.

"I'll prepare another coffee for us. I don't know your role in this, Siiri. I only know you helped me and something has been going on behind my back. You are right, no doubt, and there are things I should have thought of, like what I've been seriously trying to do in science and why. But I don't see the connection here. How is this all, what you say, with such passion, related to a visit to the shrink?"

"It isn't and it is. Just go and see him!"

Johan did not have a faintest idea what she meant by the cryptic expression, knowing there was no use in trying to ask for more details. He was curious. They finished the breakfast, without saying a word, Johan staring at the table surface; Siiri's passionate talk had made him ready to comply, slowly, to see what may come out of it. Finally, after a several minutes' silence he lifted up his gaze towards Siiri, serious:

"OK, it's one more wall for me."

She remained quiet for a moment, then stood up, abruptly, her gaze lively again:

"I'll prepare myself, make yourself ready in ten minutes, I'll take you there!" She was full of energy, immediately, as if there had been no gloomy monologue at all. Johan was puzzled, unprepared for her quick recovery and offer, and squinted at her:

"You knew it all the time, didn't you? That I would end up saying yes? I'm more predictable than the proton collisions, is that it?"

Siiri flashed a smile at Johan, kissed him on the forehead on her way to the bedroom, and closed the door behind her.

Chapter 29
The Shrink

Passing through the gate of the Villa, they entered rue des Ursulines. It was still a lively rush hour, people hurrying past them, on their way to work, and cars making their busy noise. Johan could not wait any longer and asked, "Where are you taking me? I thought you wanted to call someone? A shrink?"

Siiri pointed ahead, on their left.

"It's very near here, just across the street, and it is no accident. I called him yesterday evening, telling him you needed one more day. He will receive you there; it's number 10, Studio des Ursulines. It's actually in a special kind of a movie theater; even your friend Pablo was known to visit it!"

Johan was amazed to hear her mention Pablo and his connection with the movie theater, without a slightest reservation in her tone, but he didn't have a chance to comment on it. Siiri was already hurrying across the street, waving at him to follow. He observed new expressions of excitement in Siiri's behavior, in her voice, her agile movement, as she practically rushed towards the theater. It was an ordinary looking, simple, classic entrance to a movie theater in an old, typical Parisian building. Two smaller, dark wooden doors with brass knobs flanked the double door in the middle. The text above the entrance read "STUDIO DES URSULINES" in capital letters, each word written in a different color. The doors were closed.

Johan joined Siiri by the entrance. He tried to read the two bulletin boards on the outside wall, but they were in French:

"What did you mean about Pablo coming here? What is this place?"

She did not answer, and before he managed to repeat the question a young man with dark hair tied into a long ponytail, wearing strong eyeglasses with a black frame, opened the door, inviting them to step in. He looked barely twenty-five, dressed in worn blue jeans and a white t-shirt with *IoB* written in black font on the front. The man's style and looks of the young made Johan immediately associate him with many of the young colleagues at Stanley, the stereotypical nerds, and he tried to figure out who he was: "A nerd, for sure, but I wonder what his domain is, in a place like this?"

Johan did not ask anything, however, as he followed Siiri into the small entrance hall. She acted as if she had been there before and felt clearly in charge now.

As soon as Johan came into the entryway, the young man greeted him.

"Welcome, Johan, we've been expecting — in fact — we've been waiting for you! I'm Michel!"

Johan's first impression was that Michel spoke excellent American-style English with only a slight, soft French accent. Johan introduced himself as a Finnish physicist, silently enjoying the possibility to speak freely after the muting visits. He did not mention Stanley, saying only that he was visiting Paris for a short time for work. A sweet wave of shame for the voluntary muting about Stanley made Johan aware of his vulnerability.

"I know, Siiri has kept me informed and called me yesterday to say that you might visit today. Is everything OK?"

Johan did not answer, only smiled politely, and they remained standing, just the three of them, with no one else around, in the middle of a small, cozy entry hall leading to the movie theater. It was a classic room with a kiosk, a place where normally the eager audience, especially children, would get their candy, and wait for the doors to open and invite them to the world of the movie. The program advertisements seemed to include quite a few children's movies. From the signs outside the entrance, Johan had understood that the theater did not open for films before early evening. He was struck by some of the announcements he saw, referring to gatherings and events he thought were related to psychoanalysis. He was worried about them but could not fully understand the French description of events under the title *Théâtre et Psychanalyse.* He had no idea of the nature of the theater and its programs. Siiri had never mentioned psychoanalysis.

"Why are we here? You seem rather young for a psychotherapist, let alone a psychoanalyst."

Michel smiled. Siiri was quick to speak up before he could answer.

"I'll leave you two here, and Michel, please call me when you are ready. This will probably take a few hours, I guess, if all goes well. We could have a late lunch together at Les Ursulines whenever you are ready, right, Johan?"

Michel nodded, but Johan spoke up nervously. He felt annoyed, unwilling to lose control of the situation.

"I'm sorry, but what is this? I'd like to know now! I should know."

Siiri turned around towards the door, and just before stepping out onto the street, she turned towards Johan with a bright smile, waving goodbye to him and Michel:

"If this place was fine for Pablo, it should be a paradise for you!"

She was out in a second and closed the door behind her. Johan was muted, standing there confused, feeling uneasy and embarrassed.

Finally, he turned to Michel to ask, "Did Siiri tell you about my strange experiences?"

"Yes, she did. I know all about it, I mean what she told me. Let's go upstairs, there is nobody here and we can have a chat and a nice view of the screen, from there. I'll explain what I want, and you can decide if you agree. If you don't like what I suggest, you can just leave; this is not Hotel California!"

Michel's enigmatic smile made Johan stare at him, puzzled. He was surprised by the comment on the "mantra piece", as he used to call the Eagles song. Michel did not react to Johan's staring; he simply guided him upstairs to a classic, charming theater balcony. There were two rows of comfortable-looking seats, with bright red upholstery. They sat down in the middle of the first row, Johan on the right of Michel, getting increasingly curious. He leaned with both hands against the balcony railing, slowly recovering from the confusion caused by Siiri's quick disappearance and his futile inquiries. He grew alert again.

Sitting alone with Michel, side by side in the empty theater, made Johan feel awkward. He had paid attention to the unexpected joke by Michel, who apparently on purpose, had revealed private knowledge about him — the Eagles song and what it had meant to him. Michel knew something Johan thought nobody could actually know unless someone had been spying on him. He did not remember telling Siiri or Yvonne about his habit of singing the old lyrics. All he could think was, "One of them must have heard me, but where?"

He turned to Michel, saying, "How do you know about this song? You know I've had a habit of humming parts of it when I feel seriously troubled or depressed? It was my father's favorite. He passed away already some years ago."

Michel did not explain his knowledge. He simply nodded, with a serious expression on his face.

"I know," he said. "Let's start." He looked at Johan and continued, "I have two important questions for you. Please consider them carefully, because everything depends on what you think about them. You can do whatever you want; we are not pressuring you in any way, and if you don't like this conversation, you are free to leave immediately, and no harm comes to you or to us. You just continue your life as best you can."

Johan wondered why he was repeatedly using the word "we" and not "I" or "me." This did not feel like talking with a psychiatrist; it felt more like sitting in a movie theater with someone wholly unknown to him, an audience. He could not figure out why they were there and what Pablo had to do with it.

"So, what are your questions then? Before you ask me, please tell me what Pablo has to do with this? Is this place somehow linked with psychoanalysis? It's not my favorite — perhaps you already know that? I'm sure Siiri has mentioned *that* detail!"

"This is the place where Dali's and Bunuel's famous movie, *Un Chien Andalou — An Andalusian Dog,* had its premiere in 1929. It's a strange movie. We are not going to watch it, but the story might appeal to you. It has no explicit plot and things just happen there; each episode has its own logic, kind of a local logic in each episode, but arranged so that time and space do not constrain the story. Any change of place, space and time is possible. This must sound familiar to you; surely you know the film? It's a classic, and quite fitting to your recent life as well, right? Some of the scenes are brutal. Have you seen it?"

"Unfortunately, I've never heard of it, but what you say about time and space is similar to life I recently experienced with Pablo in 1907, and then with a Finnish physicist, Gunnar Nordström and even with Einstein

347

in 1922. You've probably never heard of Nordström. Sorry, I know I sound like a psychotic in need of therapy."

He felt ashamed to mention these names, knowing he must sound seriously insane, and explained, "I don't know film culture at all. I've spent all my academic life with science and in the labs, sorry!" Johan felt abashed about his ignorance.

Michel continued, without seeming bothered or surprised at all.

"Yes, I do know Nordström's work. That's another story. In the selected audience here at the premiere, there were a few known artists of that time present: Dali and Bunuel, of course, also Cocteau. And Pablo Picasso was one of them."

Michel's comment that he knew about Nordström threw Johan completely off balance and he did not know what to say. He found himself even more perplexed than when entering the old worlds of 1907 and 1922. Too many questions filled his mind simultaneously.

"I'm finally in my real world, but now I'm totally confused!" he thought and could only say, sighing, "So, what does it have to do with me?"

"There was nothing mysterious about the historical audience, it's a different story," Michel said, "but two things made us take you seriously when Siiri and Yvonne contacted us. I will tell you about them later, but now to my questions, OK?"

Johan's impatience grew and irritated him like a bad rash. The meeting had taken a turn he had not expected at all, and he started fidgeting in the chair, scratching his head, as he tried hard to concentrate and keep his mind calm. He was still making an effort to resist the pressure to try this "cure", but the comments about Pablo and Nordström had affected him, and, intrigued him enough to give Michel a chance.

Johan asked, in a slightly ironic tone, "OK, you ask your questions and I'll think about them. Is it about my personality or childhood or about my father's illness?"

Michel did not react to the style of Johan's inquiry. Calmly and directly, he said, "Would you be ready to work in science, provided it was possible to make a reasonable living with it, but with the risk of never getting your name on the first pages of scientific articles? In other words, without immediately receiving personal fame from it?"

The first thing that came to Johan's mind was that there must be a plot against him, but then he remembered Maurice and his unselfish way of helping the artists at the Bateau. He could not stop the automatic, blunt comment, uttering to Michel:

"That is a strange question from a shrink!"

The implied message in Michel's question bothered Johan, who recalled the irritation he had experienced at the dinner arranged by Langevin. He had practically lost his temper, scolding Einstein for not giving the undoubtedly well-earned, written credit to Gunnar, even when knowing and respecting his theoretical impact and praising him at a conference. Of course, Gunnar should have had the opportunity to enjoy the fame as a skilled, original theoretician and a physicist. "That was the way the science community works, or how it should work," Johan thought, "and he had put all his life at stake, to work for science, helping others to progress, but then dying young without the deserved fame." He remembered Siiri's emotional monologue, just an hour ago, and continued, becoming passionate about the problem himself.

"What are the Nobel prizes for? Who would work for science if it did not offer a chance to enjoy the fame of success and even prosperity after hard work?"

Michel did not say anything, and Johan remained silent as if waiting for him to answer, to take a position on his pressing question. Johan was surprised, even slightly annoyed, to notice how the silence did not seem to bother Michel at all. He started thinking about his father's repeated complaint about the frauds in science, especially Méchain's, who hid his own measurement errors. It was nothing more than a matter of fame and prestige. The researcher had not hesitated to cause trouble for his closest colleague in doing this.

Neither of the men broke the silence, and then something made Johan think about artists and vivid images of the life at the Bateau and at the Steins' house came to his mind. Perhaps it was the atmosphere of the theater, making him wonder, without saying anything to Michel: "Are scientists at all different from artists?" Johan seized up, as the lifelike images of Maurice, Pablo, and Guillaume came rushing and flashing to his mind, along with the dirty, shabby rooms, his own, small, cramped closet, the primitive sanitary conditions, and the unusual community of

349

artists, workers, and their nightly visitors. He could not stop laughing aloud as he recalled his first bucket episode, and how Maurice helped him when he sat down outside the Bateau, cleaning the disgusting mess from his feet and trousers.

Michel looked at him with surprise, interrupting him. "Is this a laughing matter? I would not think so."

"No, no, by no means, no, sorry! It's a urine bucket matter, an incident I had at the Bateau, my first night or morning there. Please let me think for a while! I'm sorry if this sounds crazy."

Michel showed a reserved smile. Johan could not help observing the slight sway this caused in his ponytail, as if to express the first wavy sign of understanding.

"I'd better tell you my whole history with Pablo and the Bateau, OK? Otherwise, you will think I'm a lunatic, and after hearing it, I'm sure you will be convinced of it!"

Michel nodded, his long ponytail again adding its approval. "Please do; we have time."

Johan began with the first encounter with Maurice and Pablo at the atelier, without mentioning the Grévin incident, and then continued, describing their first evening together at the Lapin Agile and the midnight meeting with Guillaume in front of the Bateau. It took almost an hour to describe the modest way of living there, the way he experienced the poverty and shortage of everything, from food to living premises and clothes, and in the middle of this, the incomprehensible kindness of sharing what they had, without making a fuss about it. All this was happening among the men, mostly men, but together with strong women, laying foundations for the most amazing revolution in the visual arts. Johan explained that he had no money during the mysterious visit, but was never left alone, hungry or suffering; there was always someone around: Pablo, Maurice, and even Helen, the young charming woman at the Lapin, were all there to share the very little they had and to help when needed. A couple of times Johan had suffered moments of hunger together with Pablo, but there were always ways out of it, either with the support from Maurice or Guillaume, who was never unable to move ahead and get things done. Twice he had been lucky to enjoy the Saturday meals at Gertrude Stein's house, when she offered her evening delicacies.

At the Villa, in his recent reading about art history, Johan had found out and knew now, although it had not been clear when he stayed at the Bateau, that it was the beginning of better times, even fame for Pablo, who had told Johan about the difficulties when he had arrived in Paris with Carles, whom he then, very soon, had lost. Telling all this to Michel, Johan was struck by the pain of the guilt for having had to leave Pablo, knowing it was going to hurt him as Carles' suicide had.

Trying to escape from the pain, Johan moved on in his story, to the intense discussion about the fourth dimension, the possibility of representing it in paintings, and how Maurice had not stinted in his efforts to describe and explain it, again and again, to the artists, even drawing detailed sketches to make it understandable to them and the rest of the audience present.

"Think about this, Michel. Do you know who Maurice Princet was?"

"No, I'm sorry, I don't."

"Today — nobody remembers Maurice and his name is not in the famous catalogues of arts. But surely you know who Guillaume Apollinaire was and what his role was with Pablo, and with me, too?"

Johan was not surprised to hear that Michel knew about Guillaume, who had become a famous writer and poet, a colorful figure in the history of French art. Johan had been astonished to discover that simply putting Guillaume's name into Google search gave almost half a million hits, whereas for Maurice he got barely seven thousand.

It was difficult for Johan to tell the story without stopping every now and then, wiping the unstoppable flow of tears away, trying to calm his stuttering. He was not ashamed of his emotion, being fully aware how he was now able to talk about everything and anything he wanted, what he had experienced, how it felt, and what he thought about his life and the future, what he had learned. He could become muted temporarily by the power of his affections, but this was now natural.

"I miss them so much, my friends, these guys, the companionship and their creative presence. I don't have better words for it. The separation has been difficult to stand, even though I know they lived in a different world and I made the voluntary decision to return, to leave them there, by the Metre. Knowing that they are all dead now makes me feel unbearably sad; it's as if I had killed them all! I feel like the life with them happened only yesterday, and it's happening again tomorrow. I don't miss their fame, I miss *them*! I'm sorry, Michel, this pain is a mystery to me." He became quiet for a minute, sighing and turning in his chair.

Michel did not interrupt or hurry him. He only stood up, took a few steps, and returned to his seat, giving Johan time and space to relax and continue. Finally, Johan was calm enough to return to the episode at the Metre, where he had taken the decisive choice to leave his friends, despite the pain, while at the same time experiencing the mental imperative to leave. It had been paradoxical to live as an incomplete person in the world that otherwise had so warmly welcomed him.

"The exit did not lead me home, but instead took me to the year 1922. It's another unbelievable story. So, you can perhaps understand that if I said 'no' to your question I would fail Maurice, Guillaume and Pablo and everything I learned and enjoyed with them at the Bateau. I know, Pablo became famous for his mastery and his transformational work, but that was not the first thing to worry him then. There was no visible future for him. No one knew what was going to happen, except perhaps for Guillaume, who was a creative visionary. Of course, Pablo demanded to have his signature on his own works of art; he would have been mad at any suggestion of not doing so. He did not work in a social, or even an economic vacuum. He had to make a living and signing the works was a way of building his personal life as an artist!"

Johan looked at Michel, trying to see if anything in his facial expressions and gestures would reveal a reservation, possible thoughts that he was listening to a crazy maniac talking, but he was surprised to notice that nothing hinted at such a response.

Johan took a deep breath and continued. "Stein was Pablo's door to a reasonable living when she bought his works and helped him to his fame, too. There is nothing wrong with the fame when it follows naturally, whatever that natural could mean — naturally good for mankind, I guess. I really don't know."

Johan was tired but relieved to be able to explain all this to Michel.

"Your question is a tough one and perhaps unrealistic, too. Its timing couldn't be better, though. Having learned about the bright side of the art community at the Bateau, I would be stupid to stay out of the world of scientific knowledge building and not to leave my own trace and hopefully, one day, enjoy some form of fame. Telling this now, I don't know what I would like to gain by having fame, what it would mean to me, in the end I mean. Then again, remembering the artist friends, I'd like to believe there are, or at least there should be better ways. I hope I'm not disappointing you with this complicated answer. Besides I'll be out of money soon, like Pablo and Guillaume."

Johan smiled at Michel, amazed by the abrupt change in his own attitude towards this person here to help him somehow. He sensed an emerging trust between them, in this strange situation, having told his weird story.

"I hope I have answered your question somehow. I think when fame is deserved, it should come to someone. I also feel that — in the case of an artist like Pablo — just to do the art is better than any fame. Community is important. I will not forget the life and its lessons at the Bateau Lavoir. What is your next question?"

Michel sat quietly, staring ahead, down at the theater hall and the movie screen. Then he turned slowly towards Johan, who was astonished to notice that Michel did not demand a more precise answer to his first question, but instead asked a new one.

"You did not mention Professor Roos, your supervisor from Helsinki, nor did you say anything about your visit at Stanley. Why? This is not the second question. I just want to know."

Johan was not surprised at all that they — whoever they might be — already knew about Calle and the visit to Stanley. As with Siiri and Yvonne, he decided not to hide his own feelings and interpretations of the difficult and stressful times, but instead to be as truthful as possible, with whatever risks it might bring.

"I can see now that Siiri has been in touch with you," Johan said. "She not only hacked Roos and Professor Jason, Peter. I guess she also informed you about me and my affairs? But why?"

Michel avoided answering, again.

"Yes, she kept us informed, but she was not alone. After your accident, I mean disappearance, Yvonne got in touch with Siiri and they provided other information about you. They wanted to help, but please continue before we move to the second question."

The early, secret connection between the women was a surprise, with a shade of mild disappointment for Johan, who paused, determined not to ask about it now. He returned to his story, having learned not to press Michel, since it did not seem to have any result.

"I worked hard at Stanley. I really tried my best to help Calle in his striving for making a breakthrough with his model. I ran a number of simulations, reported everything I learned back to Calle so that they could use the data I provided. I never let them down. There was only one person with whom I spoke critically about the model, but I cannot reveal the name, not to you."

Michel interrupted him. "But wasn't that unethical, to disclose your supervisor's ongoing work to an outsider who might steal the idea?"

Johan became annoyed by this hint of his possible unethical or unfair behavior.

"I didn't reveal anything sensitive to this person, who was more active and critical than I could ever have been. I just passed along the worries about potential problems in the model. I have not looked at it since, do not even know what they are doing with it, and I don't care now. I think."

Michel gazed at Johan, over his round eyeglasses.

"Who was that person you talked to?"

"Why do you want to know? Why do you think I would reveal the person to you? That, if anything, would be unethical, especially now that I'm here and after what I've gone through. Is that what you want? The person wanted to help me and took a great risk in doing that!"

Michel did not comment on Johan's forceful answer and his facial expressions did not reveal any emotions when he said, "This is not the second question either, but don't you think it was unethical to use Siiri's hacked — illegally acquired — data to attack your supervisor, to benefit from it personally? Did you also try to blackmail Roos?"

Johan stood up so quickly that he stumbled against the balcony railing, angry.

"I never said anything to him that would have been blackmailing, far from it, I was devastated that he was doing that to me! What do you think of me? Why do you ask anything like that?"

Michel said calmly and gently, "Please sit down and try to

understand. I want to learn to know you. I'm not hurting you; this is between you and us."

Johan sat down, leaning back, extending his feet toward the railing, trying to relax.

"Who are you, that 'we and us' you keep repeating? Is it that 'IoB' on your t-shirt, what is it? What is it?" A vivid image of Yvonne flashed on Johan's mind and he blushed.

Michel stayed calm. "Did you send or give classified data or texts about the Roos project to your secret partner?"

Johan was now better prepared, ready for anything, and answered in a cold tone, looking away, gazing around the theater.

"Never. None. Go on!"

A silence followed, and then it was Michel again: "How do we know what has really happened to you during these past three weeks?"

Johan continued in his indifferent, chilly tone. "You don't. You can't. I can't. I have no proof. It was just my life. Call me crazy if you want!"

Then Michel surprised him, by taking a sheet of paper and drawing the bowtie sign ⋈ on it, smiling mysteriously, as if openly teasing him.

"Do you know what this is? Have you seen it?"

Johan was taken by a total, unexpected surprise. He eagerly leaned forward to see and make sure of what he saw, unable to utter a word.

"You look like you've seen a ghost, Johan! Why?"

Now it was Johan's turn to avoid answering.

"Where did you get that?"

Michel looked at Johan.

"It is a strange coincidence. I'll explain it to you later, but now to my second question, actually a series of them."

Johan was frustrated. The bowtie took all his attentive resources and he was desperate to know more. He could barely follow Michel, without interrupting him, when Michel stood up and turned around to face the astonished Johan as he sat down on the low railing.

"If you would answer yes to my first question, would you be ready to make everything in your scientific work, your scientific behavior, your thinking, reading, writing, experimenting, problem solving, talking, coding, and worrying — everything you do, even your intentions to do something in science, fully open and available for a community of other scientists and students working with the same or similar problems and topics?"

Johan's spontaneous reaction was to reject such a complete loss of privacy and ownership. Like most of his colleagues and others protecting their intellectual property rights, he had discussed the privacy issue dozens of times, worried about the current trends like disinformation, manipulative sharing of data and straightforward lies, hacking, everything he had seen happening in social media and even politics.

"Never. I know about open science, but it's totally different from this. I would never let someone own my identity and play with it. How could I know what they — anybody who would control my data — would do with it? It sounds like a criminal hacker's wet dream. How can you even think about such an arrangement or offer? Is Siiri somehow involved with this? I'm ashamed of having gained the disastrous data of Calle's behavior by illegal hacking, from Siiri. But I don't regret it!"

Michel did not move or seem nervous at all and continued, strongly stressing his message.

"Note what I asked. It concerns only your scientific activities and behaviors, even intentions, whatever you do in the name of science. You would be joined by other scientists, researching the same or similar problems as you are, sharing their activities with you. And finally, they would not need to know your identity, who you are or where you are unless you specifically want to disclose that information somehow, to somebody, but it would be your decision."

Johan was puzzled, listening as Michel elaborated the concept.

"It would not be different from what you have done during all your career. Some might even think it would only be more open, honest. The difference is that today nobody, except for those with whom you intimately work, can exactly see or know what and how you work with your science problems and other activities. Of course, you know the powerful ethical code that works for all genuine scientists and makes them do the right things. It's like a benevolent Big Brother, an immaterial spirit if you like, watching over you so that you don't fake or fabricate your data, don't steal from others, don't give false statements of others' scientific work, pay respect to what others have already done and when you solve any problem at hand you do it in a best possible way accepted as a good practice of the scientific culture and community. And you are supposed to help others to be even better than you are."

Michel stood up from the railing, moving slowly in front of Johan, who now saw that Michel was serious and excited about what he was telling. Johan remembered Wolle's words in San Francisco describing the way science is done: "It's insane!" He wondered if Wolle was involved with the strange scheme Michel clearly was part of but decided not to mention it.

"You do know, of course," Michel added, "that nobody would be watching you, what you do, but you would still follow the code. When you write a research article, based on your data and theory, a peer, typically unknown to you, reads and comments on it in a truthful manner and decides whether it is good work, good for the society and for the scientific community, whether it should be published or not. You assume that he or she does not play any games against you, he or she does not have bad or unhealthy motivations towards you and the scientific community you represent. When you then go to a conference and describe what you have done, your findings and thinking in a scientific form, everybody gets to know, or at least assume, what you have achieved. You don't tell and explain every detail of your work and the whole process, and everyone will assume and believe you did not fool them, you did not do anything wrong, on purpose."

Michel had been walking back and forth in front of Johan but now he stopped in front of him, staring at him with a sharp gaze, pointing his hand toward the back rows of the empty balcony, as if wanting to share his conviction with a wider audience:

"Unfortunately, both the conference talk and the publishing of your findings will take place very late. As you know, sometimes it can easily take two to five years, even a longer time, from your actual work to the time it becomes published or you tell your colleagues about it. We would make this whole process visible from the very start. Imagine what a benefit it would be for your community."

Johan was silent, trying to think how that could be possible without serious ethical and even practical problems.

"I find it hard to follow you. Besides, some scientists do work

357

together from the beginning already now. Are you talking about something real and different? Is this a vague vision or a wild confabulation of a world to come, one day? Is there anything real in it? I know there are initiatives where scientists are asked to use specific IDs, so that everyone would know who has done what, but that's a simple matter of identifying scientists. You mentioned my intentions? How could someone know them when even I don't, especially now, in my messed-up situation, as you must know?"

Michel was quick to respond. "Every scientist has personal — some of them very concrete intentions — just as we all have, even the craziest ones of us. In the case of scientists, it would be most valuable knowledge to be shared, it's a special kind of knowledge indeed, more precious than any big data or machine learning analysis can ever be. But even the most modern representatives of the knowledge revolution rarely think about this."

Johan nodded, but remained puzzled while Michel explained.

"Imagine what would have happened if Einstein had known, from the beginning, what Nordström was intending to work with, what he was thinking, and how he progressed with it on paper, at home and in his laboratory in Finland, and then the other way around? The whole scientific process would have been totally different and so would be the emergent theory of relativity as we came to know it. Nothing would have been the same. Einstein could have avoided some mistakes and he might even have ended up with better ideas. We cannot know exactly, and there is no use guessing now; it's too late. But we could do better."

Johan had to agree with Michel. "Well, indeed, Nordström would have left his mark and Einstein could not have left out his name from the classic works! It could have been the other way around, even."

Then the sarcastic thoughts and frustration got Johan again. He laughed drily, asking, "If I tell you I intend to create a new theory of the origins of the universe, what use is it? Any lunatic can express such intentions and indeed some seem to do so. Nothing comes out of it. Or what if I share my humble intention to stop drinking wine here in Paris, and let you all know this wonderful idea? You can be sure the probability it will happen is practically zero!"

Michel was not offended at all and remained patient and calm with

Johan, who thought he had the nerves of an elephant.

"There are intentions and intentions. Some expressions of personal intention have no value at all. But some, and we should know them, are most valuable, even precious. They can have a very high predictive power and extensive consequences. That's something that interests us. If you tell me that you intend to study Maurice Princet in the near future, I'd be one hundred percent certain that you will indeed do it! This is not useless knowledge, believe me, especially if you are not the only one doing it!"

Michel began to walk back and forth along the railing again.

"Let's take a thought experiment. Imagine you are working with the quantum theory of gravitation and you have a challenging time with some mathematics related to it. If you now let — I don't know exactly how many there are right now — one thousand, of your most skillful colleagues, all over the world, know exactly the problem you are working with and what you are doing with it every moment, wouldn't it be wonderful to share this knowledge with them, and even get their immediate professional help and support, if they are willing to offer it and see a good reason to do so? Think about the direction of communication here: they know what you are working with, you don't have to search for a colleague who would possibly be interested in helping you and have time for that when you need it. You could know it and you would get the best information and guidance exactly when you need it. You can provide your help to a colleague or a student working with a similar problem at the same time with you, sometimes in the same second? It's not such a long time ago that the *Physics Today* journal estimated that there are close to one million physicists working in the world, right now, and new ones are joining this distributed community as we speak. We don't have the faintest idea of the intellectual potential hiding there! In China alone there are forty thousand members of their Physics Society. Then there are the cross-disciplinary fields, research and development, students, the emerging and unknown geniuses and others, the whole intellectual community, and its global potential for humankind. The numbers and the capacity for knowledge sharing are huge and increasing, fast! What if one hundred of them were specialized exactly in some parts of the work you do, even better than you are, and available when needed? You could be working for weeks with a detail of a problem that someone will solve for you in an hour!"

Johan's first thought was, "Why would people be ready to help each other like that, without getting a due reward for it?" but then a vivid image of Maurice flashed through his mind, again, like a reminder of something valuable, telling the story of his motivations at the Bateau and Johan became silent, looking at Michel, puzzled.

The massive and amazing vision had surprised Johan. He realized the potential scale of possibilities and remembered his own practices, to work alone, every now and then searching for a knowledgeable partner and help from a supervisor or other professionals on his field, experienced in the problem at hand. It was not impossible to find personal help and comments, but it was often difficult and extremely slow, because any published document reflected the work already done, and much of the underlying activities and thinking were hidden somewhere. He remembered the seminars and workshops at Stanley where he could easily discuss almost any relevant scientific topic, but even they were more like social gatherings and forums for exchanging views, not so much to get direct personal help and support. The colleagues were always busy, following their own ambitions.

Michel sat down on his seat, looking tired. Johan stood up.

"I'm sorry to be so critical and negative. I don't have the faintest idea why you are so patient with me, as if trying to ask me to join something I know nothing about. How can I know it is real what you talk about? You could be one of the loud and idealistic clans of the network world? Siiri and Yvonne are already members, I assume? I do realize the immense possibilities in what you explain, if it's real, no doubt. I must admit you surprised me, totally, totally; I never imagined such a huge number of opportunities as you describe. It's a condensed or boosted form of science if it works. I can see a plethora of limitations and obstacles, even misbehaviors, yes, but also a chance to improve what we have today. It's true that the scientific process of today is slow and problematic, and not only because it must be reliable, but also because it's simply old fashioned. It could be improved. Accomplishing that would make our work more engaging. What you say sounds ethically viable, unless I miss all the hidden, dark forces behind it. Don't forget types like Calle, I mean Professor Roos! I don't think any system would stop them!"

Michel gazed at Johan, grinning.

"So, what are your answers? And by the way, the idea of this model originates from a colleague of yours, a psychologist, can you believe it, but not a psychoanalyst!" He flashed a wide smile at Johan, being energized and ignited again.

Johan yearned to know more, but asked for time to think, till the next day.

"Why don't we go for a lunch with Siiri?" Johan said. "I'm tired, and so are you, as I can see. This is simply too much to decide so soon. What I've heard is a major surprise, too big to handle just like that. I was not prepared for anything like this — if it is real. I was expecting to meet a psychoanalytic shrink; you must know that? But OK, I'm serious now with one condition: that you can prove to me you are not making things up. I want to make sure you have accomplished something real and that this is not a delusion or a wild vision. I'm not too eager to go after anything like that, not after what I have experienced. I've lived in two or three worlds, difficult to comprehend. I don't need one more of them."

Michel's visionary and compelling story had confused Johan. The disturbing experiences with the walls, at the Bateau and at the Collège, vivid in his mind, reminded him again of the uncertainty of what is the real world and what is imagination or even worse: what is a delusion. He could not help thinking about his father's illness, again.

Michel stood up, tapping the worried-looking Johan softly on his back: "It is fine with me, but there is one thing I want to show to you; it's an old photograph taken from here, at the premier of *Un Chien Andalou.* Let's go down; I'll show it to you. It made me re-think your story."

Chapter 30
The Signature

Michel led Johan down to the lobby and then downstairs to the cellar floor corridor, which surprised Johan by its modern style. It had the clean appearance of a modern office, brightly lit, with a couple of modern chairs lining the wall of the ten-meter-long space; all the doors were closed. On the end wall of the corridor, a large poster caught Johan's eye. It was almost two meters high and one meter wide, a framed collage of about a dozen photos, containing still frames, each twenty-by-twenty centimeters, of the movie, including the famous episode where the eye is being cut by a razor. Johan felt sick looking at it.

"I don't get that kind of art," he said. "It makes me nauseous, even ashamed somehow!"

Michel nodded.

"It's from the time there was a premiere here. We don't know the exact date of the collage. It was found from among the old furniture stored downstairs. Take a good look at it. There is one special photo in it, in the lower right corner. Unlike the other frames which are black and white photos, this is in color, a miniature painting, painted over a black and white photo. It has nothing to do with the movie. In fact, it's a sketch of Picasso's *Les Demoiselles*, a painted postcard."

Johan felt his heart beating faster when he knelt in front of the poster, to see the minuscule details in the photo. Looking very closely, he recognized the image he knew so well and cherished with all its complex details. One specific feature startled him so much that he blinked to make sure of what he saw. It was an extremely small bowtie symbol, perhaps only five millimeters wide, drawn with black ink, a very thin stroke, barely visible against the uniform, skin-colored surface of the lower back of a woman on the right of the painting. This symbol appeared precisely on the spot where Johan, at the Grévin, had aimed his jump through the large curtain having a barely discernible image of *Les Demoiselles*. He remembered one late night at the Lapin, trying to describe to Pablo the incident at the Grévin, exactly as it had happened, but the muting had made his story bizarre, when he tried to refer to the importance of the "inviting door" in the bottom right of the painting. Pablo had ended up staring at him silently, visibly moved. Johan had sensed a change, a new change in Pablo's attitude towards him, but in the noisy environment he never got a chance to ask why, and then he had just forgotten it.

Johan remained kneeling down, on all fours, in an awkward position, trying to find a suitable distance to the photo, to properly discern its various details, hoping to discover additional signatures or other familiar signs within the small image. Every now and then he glanced up at Michel.

"How is this possible? How did *you* know about the sign? Do you know what it means to me? This is just too much! Do you have a magnifying glass?" Michel smiled at Johan but did not answer, only nodded.

Johan was too excited to wait for an explanation and sat down, collapsing on the floor, sobbing, holding his head with both hands, raising his eyes a couple of times to Michel, as if pleading for help, and then again staring at the miniscule sketch, the guilt hurting him again, as it had done so many times. There was an extra, acutely painful mystery now.

He could only exclaim with a sigh, "Not again! Why do I see these things, these signs?"

Michel did not answer or move. He waited for Johan to calm down. Slowly, Johan began to breath normally and he stood up slowly, visibly shaken.

"This is insane! I cannot prove anything to you, Michel, but that sign, it's the symbol of my family, and my father had carved it on the doorframe of my room at the Bateau in 1907, and now it's here! Can you believe that? I can't!"

Michel did not look surprised at all, only nodded, again. Johan stared at Michel, feeling anxious because of his silence, but then the puzzle of the signature took his attention again.

"It's meant to address me, one way or another," Johan added. "It's the only reason for it to be exactly where it is, in that spot. There can be no other explanation for that kind of an extra mark to exist in the photo. I've never told anybody, I mean anybody here, about that special location. A similar sign was used in the ancient Viking documents, but this has a special meaning, it is not one of them, it's a sign of my family. It cannot be an accident! Unless someone is playing tricks on me, or my mind is doing it to me and I'm living a delusion in a world of shadows!"

He stepped back to see the whole poster properly, wondering aloud, "I just don't get why the bowtie has been put there, as if someone had known or thought that I'd be around here, at this studio. Pablo and Maurice knew my sign. They *knew or guessed* I stayed in the Villa. I tried to explain it to them one day, after I found the sign above the door to my room, the closet, but I got muted. Who else but Pablo could have left that mark on his own work? Maurice? He would never, never touch Pablo's work, but my father could have done it. He was there before me, I know, but what if he was there after me, after me! This is impossible!"

Johan turned quiet and pale, experiencing the strangling feeling of the muting; it was not the aphasia for expressions, but simply the sense that he was out of any reasonable explanations, unable to generate any viable theory of what could be hiding behind the mystery, except that he had lost his mind. There was nothing he could say about it. Nothing reasonable.

Finally, Michel spoke, explaining, "We have an enlarged version of this image, and we do know it's been painted on the color sketch itself, not on the photo, though. The photo can be dated back to the time around the movie premiere in 1929. It's not a forgery of any kind; it's an original. Of course, you must know that Picasso was an active photographer and loved to play with the camera and create unconventional photographic effects?"

Johan interrupted him. "How do you know of this? I mean about the signature and its meaning?"

"We got connected with the work of a skilled art historian from Norway. She had discovered the extra feature, the sign, in a copy she had been studying some years ago, but had no explanation for it, and it had remained an intriguing puzzle for her. Then we got in touch with her through our system. The symbol had been a mystery for us too, until only two days ago, when Yvonne shared, in our network, her acute interest in it. She was curious to see if anyone was or had been studying it, and our contact person from Norway explained its background and the findings about it. Yvonne told us you had repeatedly drawn the sign, as if driven by a compulsion, on a napkin on a piece of paper at *Les Ursulines*, remember that? Some coincidence, don't you think?"

Johan was pale, feeling shaky and ashamed of his strange behavior at the café. He was exhausted and totally out of rational explanations, unable to find any reasonable solution to the puzzle, no way to deal with the enigma, while, at the same time, he felt an empowering connection with something of crucial importance.

He stared at Michel. "How did Yvonne know whom to ask? This is not some everyday topic to discuss, and I doubt there are too many publications about the symbol, especially on a sketch by Pablo! How did you find your Norwegian connection? I couldn't be more confused! I have no idea what to think about this. Seeing it here is painful enough, but it's a sudden source of relief too. Can you believe that? You can think of me whatever you like and speculate about my mental health, but this is a true relief, a connection, a mysterious but solid bridge over time. I may sound stupid, but I don't care!"

Michel laughed and started moving again; he had been standing motionless all the time Johan had been scrutinizing the photo and explaining his amazed and paradoxical feelings.

"I'll tell you later," Michel said, "if we can come to an agreement. Believe me, I'm not a candidate for the new age lunacy farm, and would not even speculate about Everett's parallel, possible worlds where anything can happen and everything possible does happen. But this was such a mystic coincidence, something I could not explain either, in any rational way. So, I just had to take the mystery seriously until we could find an explanation. I must admit I became really, really curious about it. There is always the possibility that someone is playing games with you and us."

Johan nodded, thinking about the other alternative that he'd lost his mind. He was surprised and relieved to notice Michel's calm and curious attitude; he looked Johan in the eyes as he continued.

"We don't know where you've been and whom you've met and to whom you've told your bizarre story. It was only two days ago that we discussed the mark on the photo with our Norwegian friend. After I heard it was a genuine part of the old sketch, I just could not skip the occasion to take a deeper look at it. We did some background checks as well and are ready to take the risk with you. I'll tell you more if we get that far. You'd better rest and think about it. We should quit now. Why don't you talk to Yvonne and she'll let me know if you'd like to proceed? OK? We are good friends. You should thank her."

Michel started towards the stairs, and Johan followed him reluctantly, looking back when leaving as if to make sure he would not lose the connection with the image containing the bowtie symbol. He wanted to remember and to be absolutely sure of what he had seen. Michel guided him to the bright sunlight and locked the door behind him. Then he extended his hand to say goodbye.

"I'm sorry I cannot join you for the meeting with Siiri and Yvonne. I'll be hearing from you, after the weekend, I hope."

Johan stood on the street in amazement at this sudden goodbye, reacting so slowly that he barely had time to say "OK." He did not even thank Michel, who had already turned his back, on his way towards the rue Gay-Lussac; apparently, he was in a hurry to get somewhere.

Johan remained standing in front of the studio, turning his face towards the sunlight, enjoying the gentle light warming his skin. He grew aware, slowly, of the possibility of a connection, or connections, with something that could relieve him of the burden of pain and guilt, the fear of delusions. It was the same unexpected, calm state of mind he had experienced when entering the Bateau through the wall at the Grévin. There had been no fear then, despite the unexplainable episode and his new, strange environment and situation. The world continued to appear as a mystery, just as it had been at the Bateau and at the Collège, yet now again the mystery felt natural. The depressive reality, the history in Palo Alto and Calle's threats did not bother him now. It was as if he had returned to a new world with its own but kind walls, and now with a personal history that felt real and natural, despite its mysteries. It was a graceful paradox of a simultaneous recovery and mystery unsolved. Now he knew. He would say yes to the questions Michel had presented, come what may.

"It's Friday now. For once I'd have time to think, but now I don't need to."

PART VII

Chapter 31
A Memory Lane in Arts

At the Villa, Johan met Siiri, full of energy working at her PC and welcoming him with a bright smile.

"I already heard from Michel," she said. "He was quite impressed, but wondered what you will decide? The bowtie is some mystery!"

Johan had already grown so used to the small, frequent surprises that he did not even ask how she knew.

"I saw something I just cannot understand. Unless I've been in the parallel world of a psychotic, lost and unaware what I've done and where I've been. As you know, I do have vivid memories of it all and I don't doubt a bit where I've been. It's Pablo. It's Maurice. It was Gunnar and Einstein and my colleagues and friends like Guillaume and all the wonderful people. They are real to me now and they will remain so!"

Johan sat down, opposite Siiri at their small kitchen table, to get her full attention.

"I cannot wipe them out from my memory, and I don't want to! I have not talked about the bowtie to any of you in the real world, here, I mean. You and Yvonne did not know about its meaning to me? Or have you seen it in my articles, I used it as my *ex libris*?"

He stared at her, hoping to get a rational explanation, but she did not answer, just shook her head, silent. Johan continued, shaking his head.

"I should study history! I've been so mesmerized by my own physics research that I've just neglected it all. I've become a total ignoramus when it comes to art and cultural history. I cannot understand how it was possible for Wolle to be a real professional ballet dancer, to do something so different from physics and then become excellent in physics, too. I don't even know my friend Pablo well and whatever has happened to him. I don't know where he is buried, for God's sake! What a shame!"

Siiri looked up from her PC, stood up and took two quick steps towards the unprepared Johan, kissing him on the cheek so abruptly that he could not even try to hug her before she was already sitting on the couch, smiling.

"Forget the grave and deaths now," she said cheerfully, "you are alive; you are learning! I'm so happy you met Michel, getting prepared for a better future and no walls, please! You cannot go on like a lunatic wondering about the walls and what has happened to you. At some point, you must give up and admit you just don't understand it all. I certainly don't! This is as good as any time to do that, find a life, maybe even a lab. Have you decided what to say to Michel?"

Johan stepped in front of Siiri, looking at her. He wanted to sit by her and take her in his arms, but he did not have the courage. He felt confused by her kiss.

"I'm all for it now, but I promised to ask Yvonne to tell him my decision."

For a second, Johan thought he saw a glimpse of darkness in Siiri's eyes but was not certain whether it was his own interpretation. He felt a soft breeze of guilt, invoked by the mention of Yvonne.

Siiri jumped back to her PC, not asking Johan about his comment.

"I'll send Yvonne a message right now. Done! You are free now until Monday!"

Johan sat down on the couch, silent. He did not know whether to laugh or to blame Siiri for managing his private matters, not bothering to ask for permission. He decided to stay calm and relaxed, entertaining the amusing thought,

"I wish I knew my own intentions, now. I do know I will go forward with this, whatever it is, with you and Yvonne and Michel, but I don't have a faintest idea what I will want next, I really don't know now. It's a mess!"

Siiri looked up from her PC, turned back to Johan, and looked him straight in the eyes with a sweet understanding smile.

"Why don't you go to Picasso's museum, here in Paris, and see his works? They have some interesting sketches, even some of his belongings have been preserved there. It could do you good. Go and see the original *Demoiselles* there, I mean as it is now, if you dare. I'm sure they have it; it's one of the leading Picasso museums in the world. It could be therapy for you to see it and all the Picasso's stuff in your present real life, now, in this world. I guess." She forcefully tapped the table surface with her forefinger as if to show Johan their shared reality.

The suggestion and Siiri's gesture silenced Johan for a few minutes while Siiri continued her intense work. Her idea was both frightening and tempting; he could go there, get in touch with Pablo's work again, and then, perhaps even go and see the Bateau and the Lapin, what they are now in the present reality, new to him.

"I'd better go and see the Bateau first. The *Demoiselles* can be too much for me. I don't feel safe to go there alone."

They did not speak for almost half an hour, neither of them feeling any need to talk; Johan rested on the sofa, enchanted and worried by the mystery of the bowtie in the miniature painting, unable to come up with any rational explanation for it. Siiri remained immersed in her work but then she suddenly stood up and took Johan by the hand.

"Johan, this is the real world. You need to get a good grasp on it!"

Siiri's energetic and encouraging attitude delighted Johan but was a new puzzle, too. He wanted to tell Siiri in detail what it was he saw in the modern studio basement, but was baffled by her knowledge about the meeting with Michel, about the photographs, the timing of the poster, and the mystic bowtie mark. The only thing that seemed to surprise her was the significance of the exact location of the sign. Johan realized he had never told or messaged about it to anyone else and he was not sure if he had even mentioned it to Pablo or Maurice, either.

Johan started making plans for his return to the Bateau, to its present version, a recovery journey as he called it, as if to make sure he wanted to stay in the present world and reality. Entering life in the Paris of 2016 had convinced him that despite the grief over his lost friends, he did not want to go back to see them now, but he was still curious and worried about his possible reaction, when seeing what had become of the world he had visited in 1907 and that had felt real and meaningful then.

"I'll pay a visit to the Bateau Lavoir and the Lapin, right now," he told Siiri, "and then over the weekend, I'd appreciate it if you could join me to see *Les Demoiselles*. I'm hesitant to go there. To tell you the truth, I'm afraid to go there alone. Grévin is out of the question. I'd rather not go there at all, not now, perhaps later, perhaps never. To meet a wax Pablo would be too much for me. Then there is the Collège de France, but let's see, one at a time."

"Of course, I will come with you, but please keep me posted on your visit to the Bateau, so that nothing unexpected happens. I'm here to help whenever you need it. Are you sure you want to go alone?"

Johan nodded, adding, "I want to walk there. I know it's a long way, but I like to know where I'm going in the Paris of today."

She seemed to accept it without a hesitation, showing only a mild sign of worry.

Johan assured her, "I'll take the same route I walked with Gunnar."

It was early afternoon when Johan began his expedition; he was excited. He walked along the eastern side of the Jardin, towards the Odéon Theâtre de l'Europé, where he had met the woman selling the Eiffel towers and faced his wall, the curtain of return. Already on his way he calmed down, sensing how different and safe everything appeared, as if he had been given new mental resources to perceive the world and its objects. The core of his being and the time in Paris were now profoundly different. There was no mystery hidden, to continuously challenge him. Everything felt somehow predictable, reminding him of the nature of classical physics and its straightforward laws.

Johan could spontaneously remember the Paris of 1907, as he walked through the city on this clear, present day. That earlier Paris was a colorful memory now, floating over the new, tangible reality but not attached to it. He recognized the geographically familiar locations, the busy and lively streets of Paris, but they did not carry the feeling of a hidden excitement. Everything, including the sunshine and the shadows, was different, somehow brighter, even overwhelming, without the subtlety he had perceived and experienced during the visits behind the walls.

Arriving at the square in front of the Theâtre was an instant disappointment, however, something that felt cold from the outset. The classic, roundish square appeared gray, almost desolate, although there was no explicit color gray anywhere. There were no sales booths visible, only a couple of Asian tourists taking photographs, no one was sitting on the stairs leading to the theater; there were no signs of a vibrant life. Then he noticed the lampposts, simple objects reminiscent of the past, two of them flanking the wide theater entrance, similar to, and perhaps the replicas of the ones he'd seen there with Gunnar. They had electricity now.

It was the first time since Johan's arrival that he felt such a distinct personal distance from the place he had visited. At the Villa and Les Ursulines, from the first moments of his arrival, he had felt welcome, as if he were coming home, to the graceful meeting point where departure and return are married. Entering the square now, Johan decided to go to the exact location where the last wall had appeared, in front of the booth, and where he had left Gunnar. Approaching that spot, he felt a spontaneous, momentary sense of grief, but this time it was not like pain at all; he could easily stand there and try to sense the atmosphere. What he felt was more like a yearning for friendship and a true companionship than an urge to go and meet those friends again. He was relieved to notice that the awareness of their deaths, the knowledge of the eternal separation, had not weakened the bond with them. It was stronger than with most of the people he knew. These deep, spiritual thoughts felt as if they came from a different world. He passively observed the tourist crowds passing by. The place and time did not matter now.

Johan remembered the peculiar, disconnected experiences of visiting a particular place, a quiet park by the lakefront in his home village, where he had spent time with a girl he had fallen in love with, the romantic first-love passion of a teenager. The girl had had left Johan for another, an older boy, causing him several months' despair, but then, after a few months, when the tangible and painful connection was over, the place had only its architectural and geographical meaning to offer, beautiful scenery, inviting other experiences to cherish, a trigger of some memories perhaps, nothing more, and the new reality, new friends, and girls had taken over. What he now experienced was not a recent love affair lost: the strong spiritual bond with the friends was preserved, untouched. "Perhaps it is mutual love, over time and space," he thought. Only the physical connection was broken now, and the plaza had none of its historical charms left. Turning his back to the Théâtre entrance, not looking back, Johan continued on his journey.

Walking along rue Dauphine, approaching the Pont Neuf, Johan noticed that it had not changed too much, except for the modern transformations, including two high-class hotels, one in the same place where the group of physicists had left Einstein. This hotel now had a refurbished facade and a style and an appearance inside that did not evoke any memories of the event or the chilly night there. It did not invite him to enter and he had no urge to stop and try to recover the events with Gunnar, Einstein, Langevin, Croiset, and Nordmann. He continued over the bridge, turning left after a while, then along rue de l'Échelle, towards rue Sainte-Anne and finally the memorable street, rue Ravignan, leading to the Bateau.

Walking uphill towards the Bateau made Johan aware of the familiar physical effort he had sensed when trying to follow Pablo and Maurice on their nightly walks from the Lapin Agile back to the Bateau; now the accelerating pulse and strenuous breathing reminded him of the psychological meaning of the place. The sense of distance from the men at the Bateau, the grief and grayness had a momentary grip on him again.

Resting for a brief moment, he observed the cars and the neat, clean streets, and he became aware of rumbling background noise from the traffic of modern Paris. There were no strong and uncomfortably sweet smells of the waste and urine or scents of food being prepared somewhere. Johan knew from his own experiences how a familiar smell could carry far on memory lane, to recall something like magic, even from childhood, something believed to be already forgotten. This time there was nothing like that — no scents to support his associations, his dear memories.

Passing by the old, traditional restaurant and its inviting terrace on his right, just before the square, he was reminded of his first visit there. The plaza had changed dramatically. Johan was astonished to notice how quiet it was now. The charming well, with its four female figures in the middle of the small plaza up ahead stood there alone, but it caught Johan's eyes first; it was where he had observed a sudden change in the way Pablo talked to him, a sense of camaraderie and care. Nobody seemed interested in it now. There was more free space to move about than during the time when cars were a rarity. He realized that people had spent more time outside, talking and strolling together; it had been a social necessity, with no phones and especially no mobile ones, and no cars rushing here and there with single passengers. The world had been more communal. "There were more reasons then, to meet people face-to-face than there are in the modern communicating world," he thought and remembered the valuable, and often surprising meetings he had had at the Lapin.

Johan easily climbed up the wide stone stairs, and there it was, on his left: the Bateau Lavoir. It was now completely different, with its well-painted greenish facade and its modern window. The color of the window frame reminded him of the famous classic sports car green; it had nothing to do with classic artists. A nice entrance door had replaced the old, smaller ones. It was too modern, too much altered for Johan to recall any of the significant experiences there. It looked like a different building. He did not want to go inside, not now, and found a comfortable place to observe the Bateau from a distance, in the middle of the modest plaza.

Sitting there on a park bench, under a tree, he observed how people, mostly tourists, quite different from those he had used to see there, walked by, not too many stopping to admire or wonder about the Bateau. Then a funny thought caught him, and he smiled, remembering the first bright morning there, after the bucket incident: "If I sat down now at the entrance, cleaning my shitty feet and trousers, half naked, I'd probably wake up even the most ignorant tourists and invite a couple of strange looks, some interest at least, perhaps even from the police. In Palo Alto I wouldn't have a chance of surviving that." He smiled, a relaxed and easy smile. The looming grief was slowly drifting away, giving way to a soft joy of return.

Everything — the newly built, modern façade of the Bateau, the square, and the buildings he saw surrounding the plaza — appeared much smaller than in his memories. Even imagining Pablo, Maurice, and Guillaume on the spot where they had had their first late night conversation, in front of the Bateau, did not make the place look the same in scale. But the scale of the warm emotions, the feeling of friendship, and the longing for his new, but past friends, had not diminished; quite the contrary, it had remained spiritually magnified, almost overwhelming. Johan had recognized the same asymmetry between reality and his memories when he visited his father's home village and met the old man, Alex, who had showed them the bowtie symbol. The village, its roads, fields, and small country houses had appeared almost like miniature structures to Johan, who wondered how such modest places could have carried and hidden the monumental feelings of attachment and love taking place there.

Johan felt he could begin to accept the historical and permanent distance, the separation from the world he had experienced and lived, but he had not yet found a new way to perceive and receive the new, real Paris as the home of his mystic past and the wonderful and touching experiences. As he contemplated this new possibility, he realized that it would take time to build a new relationship with this city from the inside of his mind. He stood up, turned away from the Bateau, aiming at the hilltop slightly to his right, and then he took rue des Saules down towards the Lapin to see, feel and hear what it would be willing to tell him.

Immediately, when walking uphill, he again had the vivid physical memories of the frequently experienced strain in his leg muscles, sometimes after too much wine, sometimes just from the pure exercise of climbing the hills up and down in the dark. It was the genuine feeling of physical strain that had made him believe the life at the Bateau was real and not just a psychotic dream. The visual environment and its spatial scale felt different and separate from the sensory memories he felt in his muscles, as if the muscle sense was the only real connection left. As he said to himself, "Pablo and the guys must have had excellent stamina; they never complained about this when I was already exhausted. There were no taxis and buses to take them to places."

Already from the distance of about one hundred and fifty meters, high up on the hill, looking down the street towards the bright city horizon, he saw the familiar profile of the Lapin, its name on the old and worn end wall, now an orange-pinkish color. The modest building had the appearance of a modest country house or rather a pub from the outside; it did not appear like a real house at all. Walking down the street, coming closer, Johan saw it was closed and would open later in the evening. Standing there, in front of the simple, dark-colored main door, touching its surface softly, Johan remembered the vitality of the clients there, the noisy crowd, the everyday mixture of workers and artists, even dogs, people moving in and out of the main building. The terrace was now empty, clean, and lifeless. Johan remained standing near the wall in the place where the kind Camille had shared her life story with him. There were no tables or chairs, and everything, the terrace space, the entrance door and the windows, felt surprisingly small, as if from an insignificant, miniature play-world. On the door, there was an announcement of an evening show. Johan could not imagine what the show would be like, when the tourists would come and fill the artificial place with no historical heroes, his friends present. It felt impossible to attend the virtual life of Lapin.

It was late afternoon, not yet dark, and he saw only a few busy locals and slowly walking tourists passing by, up or down the hill, some glancing at Johan. This place seemed to have no external interest to anyone without a reason to visit it. Johan remembered how the people at the Lapin would perform anything when they felt like it and without an invitation. Often the crowd was persistent enough, asking the artists to sing, play an instrument or give a speech. Some of them used to bring their paintings, writings or even statues to pay for the wine, women, food, and their old debts. The Lapin Agile had no sense of agility left now, not for Johan. It was less than or not even a museum to him.

On the way back to the Villa, Johan decided to pass by the Bateau once more. He stopped in the middle of the square in front of it, in between the densely branching trees, exactly on the spot of his memorable encounter with Pablo, Maurice, and Guillaume, from where he could observe the entrance to the Bateau. Standing there, quietly, gazing up at the treetops, he realized one of the trees could have seen him visiting the Bateau then; the other trees were clearly younger. Turning around slowly, he scanned the high houses surrounding the square, with their modern, well-kept, even luxurious facades and window frames and the few dark-colored entrance doors. None of them seemed inviting. Johan did not see anyone go in or come out. No shops or booths were visible up on the hill.

The moment of silence turned into one of peaceful enlightenment for Johan: "This is a new world, another space, another time; it's not the place to enter the Bateau, the original; it is not here to be reached. The true entrance is in *Les Demoiselles*, hidden."

Johan approached the well, remembering the gatherings around it, admiring its style and the beauty of the female figures. Walking slowly around it, stopping every now and then, he slid his left hand along the edges of the statue base, softly touching the feet of the female figures.

He stayed there for a while, eyes closed and then turned away, stepping down the stairs, walking slowly, not looking back until he reached the Seine, crossing over it, along the Pont Neuf and then around the Jardin, this time on its west side and up to the rue d'Assas, and then passing close by 27 rue de Fleurus, Gertrude Stein's salon. He did not go to see the historical plate in front of its entrance. Finally, he stopped by the front gate of the Villa, and stood there for a moment before entering, as he thought to himself, "I must learn to love these gates that don't lead anywhere."

Chapter 32
Les Demoiselles Lost

It was noon on Saturday when Johan and Siiri arrived at the impressive, classic, four-story building, Hôtel Salé, hosting the Picasso museum. Although it had been Siiri's idea to visit the Picasso museum, Johan could not ignore his fuzzy feelings of guilt, for not asking Yvonne to join them, but Siiri's powerful presence and support made him soon forget about that.

They had enjoyed a quiet, hour's walk, only occasionally exchanging mutual gestures and signs of interest when observing the people and the city scene on the way. Siiri had a natural habit of sometimes, even in busy company, remaining quiet for a long time, a mode that made her American and even French colleagues uncomfortable, as they tried to invite her into any possible discussion topic, a casual chat, often with no success. Her new acquaintances and companions had the false impression that she did not exactly follow what was going on in the discussions, or that she simply did not have any original ideas to contribute to the heated arguments. It was tempting to assume she either did not see what was happening around her, or that she just did not care. Both interpretations were wrong.

Siiri did not openly show her interests, but was a master of sharp and revealing observations, especially of people and their behaviors. Her specialty was observing *what was not said or what did not happen*: a lack of praise or smiles, people avoiding each other via small moves, gestures and body positions. With her Japanese colleagues, there was no such problem or prejudice. In their company it was always possible and easy to remain politely and mutually silent, without the slightest signs of discomfort or awkward social pressure to begin insignificant small talk. Talk had to be large for these Japanese colleagues, and for Siiri, to be initiated and in which one could become immersed. Many Finns, especially the older generation and country people, still share this social attitude and stance.

Walking towards the museum, Siiri left Johan to his private world of memories and expectations without disturbing his elation. She appeared to understand that he was getting both excited and nervous. They strolled through the historical district of Le Marais, along the rue de Thorigny, when the museum, the serene lawn, and the well-kept garden in front of it, became visible on their left, through a classic gold-decorated iron gate. At first sight the place looked like a high-class hotel or a classic old palace with its four-meter-high windows along its ground floor, and with the first floor facing the garden and the gate. The two upper floors were not so tall; a row of skylight windows lined the top floor.

At the sight of the magnificent building, Johan could not immediately accept the idea that Pablo's works would be stored and shown in a place like that. The impressive, extravagant style made it appear unreal, as vivid images of the Bateau, the shabby studio with its dark colors, and the vibrant, avant-garde atmosphere, even some of its unpleasant scents there started crowding his mind. He wondered why there were no people walking or even queuing in the park.

The spontaneous impact of the grandiose building on Johan was a feeling of disbelief, growing stronger when he tried to open the gate, only to find out it was closed. There was no entrance that way and he was confused, hastily looking around, as if searching for help, embarrassed like a guest arriving at a magnificent party without an invitation.

Luckily, Siiri led him to the entrance.

"We have to go around the corner. We can get in there."

At the entrance to the museum, soldiers stood in their green, camouflage army uniforms and machine guns. Johan and Siiri were asked to show their bags to one of the armed guards before entering and paying the fee. Johan stared at Siiri, lifting both of his hands in the air so abruptly that one of the guards turned towards him, ready to interfere.

"Imagine this, Siiri: when I took Yvonne to the Stanley hospital, we got practically the same treatment there as here, only that here they don't ask for our insurance or credit cards. Gun and arms check it is, in arts and care. Same fears, different motivations!"

Siiri did not answer, only waved her credit card high in the air, laughed and hurried to the ticket counter.

Inside Johan was astonished to find himself surrounded by the pure-white, brightly lit, spacious first hall and a crowd of stylish guests. He took a few steps and stopped at the center of the hall, turning slowly around, making a full circle, trying to reorient himself, taking time to accept the fact that it was indeed Pablo's life and work shown in this extremely white, almost clinical environment. The images of the original, modest atelier, its feeble, bluish light, the floors dotted with a spectrum of all possible color paints, his own narrow closet and even the image-like, floating memories of the uncomfortable smells there began to flash and flicker as lively memories, only to be attenuated when he sensed the first scents of the perfumes, the modern auras of the visitors around him. He could not help making a joke.

"One thing is certain here, Siiri. Now I can walk around without watching my step and spill the bucket. I'd guess they have not preserved that treasure here!"

Siiri tried her best not to laugh too loudly in the distinguished setting. Johan, though, could not prevent his own hearty laugh.

Siiri, in her usual careful, intelligent way, had made a detailed plan of how to walk through the museum.

"I'm sure you want to see the epoch when you visited your friends, 1907? And then *Les Demoiselles*, of course? I looked at the map of the museum and took this leaflet, so we can find our way. Strange enough, I did not find a note about the *Demoiselles* but you can ask them here."

Johan was surprised. "You mean you did not look up all possible information there is about *Demoiselles*?"

Siiri did not answer, smiled and asked, "Do you want to go alone? I'm fine here. You can follow the timeline-based, ordered collection if you want to travel in time. It should cover the beginning of the twentieth century."

Johan turned to Siiri, gazing her in the eyes, and took her softly by the waist.

"I'd like you to come with me," he said. "I don't know what I will do or how I will react if I see *Les Demoiselles*, or any of Pablo's belongings, if they have them here. Let's go. Please stay with me."

Siiri nodded, and they walked through the ticket checkpoint and climbed the stairs to the floor where Siiri knew the collection, including the early works, was shown. They entered a series of rooms arranged around the massive staircase in the middle of the building. All the rooms were full of Picasso's works, and in the glass vitrines here and there Pablo's handwritten texts and sketches were shown. The visitors were mostly quiet, and only rare loud sounds or exclamations of admiration were heard from people standing in front of the paintings or the vitrines. Johan could not help thinking that the eager visitors had been muted by the power of Pablo's art.

The extensive white walls and the large windows of the museum halls made each section of the exhibition a special kind of light trap, creating an extreme, pure-white, spacious and hazy atmosphere, almost unnaturally clean in nature, as in a notion of heaven, contrasting with what Johan had experienced at the Bateau. He vividly remembered how these paintings had looked in the modest, almost gloomy and dirty, but very real and exciting conditions of Pablo's atelier. Even at the Steins' the light had been weak and warm on those Saturday evenings, the floors and walls sucking away the feeble light rather than reflecting it everywhere, as happened here in the spacious white rooms. At the Steins', it had still been possible to feel and imagine the world where the works had been created, their origin, the studio, the models, and the way of life from where the paintings carried their messages to their enthusiastic audience.

At the museum, it felt like the paintings and the sculptures had been brought there on purpose, to give them a new life, to be placed under the bright, dazzling light, to be viewed in a safe and familiar social clinic, without the slightest hint of their past life, the hard life. Johan's first thought was that the intention had indeed been to hide the originality and essence of the paintings, to make sure they would be suitable or proper for any art buyer's prestigious, and surely well-lit house and collection. To Johan the extreme white appeared as if it had been meant to prevent any disturbances and uncomfortable signs of the simple life, the reality of the young artists, their tangible world, to erase the places where the masterpieces were born, lived their first days, weeks and months. Some paintings never made it this far but died away; no one but the artists ever saw or touched them. Johan remembered the amusing but serious confusion about the name of *Les Demoiselles* when he visited the Bateau. Pablo had called it *Le Bordel d'Avignon* and only later it became the *Les Demoiselles*, to make it more palatable for bourgeois patrons; it had to be the safe *Les Demoiselles* in any hushed, clean gallery.

The extreme whiteness made Johan think about the possibility of re-creating a real, original atelier by using modern lighting and virtual reality systems to show Pablo's early works and to show the life at the Bateau atelier. He started eagerly explaining the idea to Siiri.

"The white walls would serve as excellent projection screens. If they wanted, they could generate a genuine feeling, a virtual, but very similar Bateau or any other atelier Pablo used! People could see where the masterpieces were born and created and how they appeared *there*. That would be something, especially the first works! What a way to see the world where the art originated; people would not believe it! I could even consult them, but they would probably take me as a stereotypical art lunatic!"

Siiri smiled, did not say anything at first, looking around the room and its walls, then shook her head.

"I'm getting ready to believe you really *would* know the details!"

Walking through the first two rooms, only one painting among the many caught Johan's full attention. It was a version Pablo had painted about Carles Casagemas' death, the friend from Barcelona with whom he had, as a young and poor, beginning artist, come to Paris. In the painting Carles was lying on his deathbed: a greenish, yellow-blue-pale color dominated the painting and especially Carles' face, showing its pale expression of death, the mark of the bullet on his right temple. The painting had an irresistible power to invite and lure the viewer, safe and full of life and its sensory pleasures, to come closer to see it, to perceive death from as close a distance as possible, both physically and psychologically — and then run away from it.

Johan could only take a short glimpse of the painting as he tried to approach it. Thoroughly startled by the presentation of Carles, he took two rapid steps back, almost falling over. Then he closed his eyes and turned his head away.

"I'm sorry, I cannot look at this! I'm sorry! It so sad and terrible! It's like me and my own death! It's me crying my own death with Pablo at it! It's pure pain!"

He spoke, almost shouted so loudly that the young man passing by, a museum logo on his shirt showing he was a guard, stopped, looked suspiciously at Johan, but did not say anything. Siiri took Johan by the hand and guided him to sit down on the bench in the center of the room. She sat down beside him.

"What is it? Why are you so upset about this? I can understand that the painting moves you. There is something extremely real, the presence of physical death and a permanent departure, a human separation and loss. Even I can see it, but it's only a painting. Why is it so painful to you?"

Johan could not immediately answer. He did not know what to think and only breathed heavily. Leaning against Siiri's shoulder, he started slowly explaining the relationship of Carles and Pablo.

"The worst thing was that Pablo told me how my first disappearance had been like the dreadful loss of Carles, what his suicide did to him. Looking at the painting of the dead Carles, I can feel and imagine I have the same pain, Pablo's pain in myself. I don't know why he felt my, or my father's, disappearance so strongly, but there was a strange, unexpected and firm bond between us. I believe Maurice was connected through the same mystery when he tried to explain about the four dimensions to Pablo, a gateway to other worlds, why not even to the world of death. That's what I see in that work, the darkest of the dark dimensions, when going close to it, it almost sucks me in. It's more complicated than even you can understand, Siiri. I cannot explain it. The worst thing is I feel like I had killed Pablo and my friends by rushing back to the present time!" He sighed quietly, "They are all dead now."

Siiri looked very serious, nodding, encouraging Johan to continue.

"Please go on, you must talk about this. I want to hear."

"We would all discuss and remain inspired by these possible worlds, the imaginary dimensions, day by day, but Carles' death did not fit into it; it was incomprehensible, too much for Pablo. It's possible I replaced Carles for Pablo, to live with him at the edge of something revolutionary, something Carles never saw. I was there and Carles wasn't. Perhaps I helped Pablo to forget the pain, and by disappearing I hurt him again and openly. I believe he guessed I was living in a world different from his and his friends' world. I could never describe my world to him in words, I was muted, it was my aphasia, but I often had a feeling he knew or guessed something of it; he did not need words and sometimes he even explained it to me."

Johan stood up, feeling slightly better but still startled.

"I think we could just walk around, if you walk with me. I'm OK if we just get an overview here. There is so much of his later work to see, most of it unknown to me. I don't think I can look at anything he's written or drawn in the sketches. I'd better come here another time when I'm strong enough. I wonder, I have not seen *Les Demoiselles* anywhere here yet. I want to be careful with it. I don't want to rush to see it and fall against it, again. It's not good for me to be alone there. The image of Carles was already too much."

They continued walking from one hall to another, scanning carefully each of the four floors, and every time they met the works of some other painter or sculptor, like Giacometti, Johan was eager to approach them, scrutinize and comment on them in detail to Siiri. He would then observe each artwork from different distances and viewpoints, walking towards and away from it, to evoke any possible experiences from different viewing angles and distances. He did not appear disturbed or worried at all.

"I'm feeling better now, ready to see *Les Demoiselles*, finally!"

He smiled at Siiri, who had been patient, following Johan at a close distance, ready to help and interfere if necessary. She joined him now, remaining quiet.

"Fine. I have not seen it yet. Let's take a look at the time series of his works, the place in time where it should be."

Johan started scanning, again in temporal order, the early phase paintings like the *Carles*, and other paintings after that, but only noticed there was a gap in the collection, exactly in the place where the *Demoiselles* should or could be.

"I'm feeling really stupid now. This is no dream or confabulation. Why don't we see it here?"

Siiri laughed. "Maybe someone is guarding you or me. I'd hate to lose you and see you disappear through the brothel gate again! But, OK, let's find a guard and ask; it must be somewhere here. Are you ready to face it, really?"

Johan did not answer.

They walked almost a full circle in the halls, around the stairway, when they saw the familiar young man, the guard, with light-red, curly hair, a striped shirt, and a trimmed beard of the same color. He had paid attention to Johan's reaction by the painting of Carles and was now standing in one of the corners.

Johan approached him. "Excuse me, do you speak English?"

The man nodded, and he continued; Siiri joined them, but remained standing behind Johan.

"Can you please advise us how to find *Les Demoiselles* here? We did not see it, but it must be here somewhere. I hope it's not in storage or being repaired or something. I know it's the most famous Cubist work in the world."

Siiri remained silent.

"That is a very good question, especially now. You see, unfortunately, or fortunately to them, the painting is at the Museum of Modern Art in New York. I'm sorry. Does it have a special meaning to you? They do sell postcards, prints of it downstairs."

Johan smiled and burst into laughter, relaxed, lifting both hands in the air.

"You can only imagine! But it's good this way, for me I mean, the work has mysterious powers, it can move space and time, I know. Thank you anyway!"

The man lifted his eyebrows, smiling. Siiri thanked the man and joined Johan in silence. As they turned towards the stairs, Johan once more waved and thanked the guard, who now, his forehead wrinkled, observed their slow departure. They descended the massive stairs and continued to the boutique, where Johan immediately found the card, a small print of *Les Demoiselles*, the size of about ten by ten centimeters.

"These don't scare me. I can buy and live with these miniature walls, having the size of only about twentieth of the original. It's smaller than the one in the poster at the Studio. I'm surprised, Siiri, this is not at all like you, how come you did not know that the *Demoiselles* is not here?" Then it struck Johan: "You *did* know it's not here, you just played ignorant, to keep me safe!"

"You have made me adventurous, Johan!"

Johan glanced at her, smiling, knowing there was no need to ask more. She would tell, one day. He had regained his balance, relieved and relaxed. He paid for ten cards and they walked out, again passing by the soldiers guarding the house of arts with their machine guns. Johan was in a good mood and the impact of the painting of Carles was fading away.

"Good for us that these soldiers don't look like models of a Cubist work where everything is twisted. At least we can know where they are pointing their guns in our space! Had Pablo built their guns, we would be walking through a danger zone!"

Johan waited until they were outside the gate, out of sight, before he started to laugh aloud, exhilarated. Siiri followed him a few meters behind. Johan had recovered, being again lively and energetic in his movements, looking around, almost as if he were saying goodbye to the museum. He smiled at Siiri, and she smiled back.

Chapter 33
Strings of Science and IoB

On their way back to the Villa, Siiri confessed, without a bit of shame or apology, having been in touch with Michel again.

"We can go and meet him and some other people tomorrow, at noon, at the Studio. They have something to show you and a suggestion or an offer I cannot reveal; actually, I don't even know the details. It's not my business."

"Since when has my life *not* been your business? I'm getting used to you and Yvonne as a dark matter team, conspiring behind my back. Nevertheless, and strange enough, I do trust you two, even when you conspire. You can guess my trust is not self-evident at all, not after what I experienced with Calle and Peter!"

Johan took her by the waist, hugging her lightly.

"Yvonne will join us, too." Johan blushed and took his hand off her waist.

Siiri stopped in the middle of the sidewalk, so abruptly that a busy passerby almost hit her, and Johan thought she was offended by his comment about Yvonne. Instead, she surprised him, by turning towards him, coming unusually close, resting her hands on his shoulders, staring him in the eyes, with a serious but calm look.

"Johan... I'm grateful you never revealed my identity on the hacking of Calle and the Civil fund system. You suffered a lot by protecting me. I would have survived, but my life would have become difficult. I'd have had to disappear and continue working elsewhere. It's a small playground at home, as you know."

It was both an embarrassment and a reason to be proud for Johan to hear her praise his loyal behavior, although the comment sounded cryptic. He had no idea what Siiri had been working with in Finland and had learned not to ask about her job or about the hacking. The perfect timing of her hacking operation had puzzled Johan, knowing he had not told her anything about the problems at Stanley and that he had met Yvonne only after Calle's malevolent operations. Johan knew he would not get a definite answer to his curiosity and could only expect, one day, to hear about how Siiri knew so much about him, and what her projects involved.

"I'm learning to live with you, Siiri, in silence."

She threw her best smile, a wide and bright smile that lit her face with joy. Johan had not seen such a charming and lively expression on her face for some time. They started walking again, Siiri pushing Johan softly aside and looking back over her shoulder.

"You mean you don't ask any nosy questions? By the way, I asked Yvonne to join us for a brunch at Les Ursulines tomorrow morning at ten. She will be at the Studio, too."

Johan could not get sleep that night. He could not stop thinking about the bowtie, the family sign and the trip to the countryside with his father. He got up from the couch and back, three times, first at midnight, when — not tired at all — he switched on a small LED lamp he had for reading. Unable to read, he paced the small room, careful not to wake up Siiri. He tried to figure out what he was about to commit himself to, something secretive that Siiri and Yvonne already accepted, no doubt, or were participants or at least active members. He could not picture Yvonne involved with anything illegal, but he was not sure about Siiri. She had always been unpredictable, an extreme individualist. Then he remembered the night with her in Helsinki and was fully awake.

Siiri's behavior had remained a mystery to Johan, who had often observed how she followed a moral code of her own, a kind of a private ethic, as if she was sure and at ease with what was right and wrong. He did not understand her deepest motivations to do the right thing, and she never talked about it. Siiri had remained a mystery, both in her external style and in her private secrecy. She never spoke badly about people; she could be blunt and straightforward in her comments, but she always had an argument difficult to beat.

The location of the Studio had appeared like a coincidence to Johan, as it was so close to the Villa, but he quickly realized Yvonne had known about it from the start, and that she must have had a history there. The most amazing things were how and why the bowtie symbol had appeared in the poster and the fact that the Studio, so close to the Villa, had been visited by Pablo. Johan could not imagine any rational way to explain all these coincidences. Then there was something Michel appeared to be trying his best to hide. And why a movie theater? Was it a special place somehow? Johan spoke silently to himself, as he nervously fetched a glass of water. "Why can't I see any pattern in this," he wondered. "It could be a secret society behind it all, a mafia, but this is Paris. It must be connected with science, it must be, why else would they be interested in me and Yvonne too, for that matter? Maybe there is no pattern at all. There are too many simultaneous worlds for me to follow, the life with Pablo, and then the time with Gunnar and now again, present academia. Perhaps they are physically exclusive, as in Everett's ideas, with no real opportunity to move from one to another or even to send signals between them. But I have been in them all and then there's the bowtie. Nothing can explain it: it is either a hoax, or I've lost my mind."

He was already hoping Siiri would ask him to come to bed, but only heard her breathing, in a deep sleep. It was five o'clock when he finally fell asleep. When Siiri woke him up at eight, he did not immediately know where he was. His first thought was not to spill the bucket.

The breakfast with Yvonne and Siiri at Les Ursulines did not help Johan to solve the puzzle of the Studio. They were again seated in the small and cramped booth in the most distant corner, where they could talk, almost head-to-head, and not be heard. Johan tried a friendly approach and interrogation with Yvonne, as he asked her about Michel and the Studio and about a possible mafia behind it all. She only laughed, however, when he urged her to give him details. She glanced at Siiri and they both smiled at him. It was clear they would not reveal anything; his questions were received with a friendly, almost an amused, silence.

They were interrupted by the young man, the waiter who had served them on their first visit, approaching Yvonne and Siiri as if they were all good friends.

While the man was waiting for them to order, Johan asked Siiri in Finnish, "Do you know Jacques, that is his name? You seem like old friends?"

Siiri was quick to answer in English, "Place your order, Johan, let's have a proper breakfast! Please don't be jealous; it's time to calm down, don't you think?"

Johan blushed and tried to avoid eye contact with the waiter as he quickly ordered a brunch.

When the waiter left, Johan asked Yvonne, "Is this waiter a physics student? I saw him reading something when we were here the first time. Did you notice it then?"

Yvonne blushed. "I know he is studying. It's quite normal here to work and study, quite normal."

The familiar repetition of the last words in her comment made Johan smile at Yvonne, staring her straight in the eyes for almost half a minute without saying a word. She blushed and blinked. Johan was sure there was something hidden behind her reserved behavior, but then the waiter arrived, interrupting the sensitive moment, serving them smoothly, Yvonne and Siiri first. Johan did not want to embarrass Yvonne more and waited patiently until the waiter had finished his task. He thanked the man but could not help teasing the girls as he lifted his cup of coffee, pretending it was a toast of champagne.

"Let's toast to all the secret physicists!"

Now it was Siiri's turn to blush, although her white heavy makeup did not reveal anything. Her ear lobes were fully red, with the color of ripe tomatoes, however, so vivid and in contrast with her calm expression and her make-up that Johan could not hold back a heartfelt laugh.

"Siiri, you know we don't too often use the word 'love' in Finnish to express our feelings of affection, but now when I say it, I hope you understand the passion behind it: I love you both!"

A silence followed again until Yvonne broke it.

"It is difficult not to be able to tell you everything I, or we, both know, Siiri and me. Please don't worry, though! We are not against you, and if all goes well, there will be new things to share. Please believe me! Believe me!"

A lively conversation followed, and Johan could forget his curiosity. It was like a kind of soft muting, from a common decision; without saying it; they kept the mystery in the background, while all of them visibly relaxed. During the conversation, Johan began to realize that both Siiri and Yvonne had been under a distressing pressure during his disappearance, taking care of all the necessary arrangements during his absence. He had not made it easy for them and had not even thanked them enough.

They enjoyed the delicacies of the brunch, the vegetable quiche, croissants with cream cheese, smoked salmon and finally glasses of champagne. They toasted, this time for real, every now and then, to spontaneous topics like "To the Villa!" or "To the Studio!"

Finally, Johan lifted his glass to make a new toast: "To Pablo, Maurice and Guillaume. How I wish you had known them!"

He could not hide the tears, and both Yvonne and Siiri tapped him on his shoulders. After some time Siiri stood up.

"Time to go!"

She did not wait for Johan and Yvonne when she rushed to the bar and paid the bill. Johan could see her exchanging a few words with the smiling waiter.

Arriving at the Studio, they found the serious-looking Michel already waiting at the door to welcome the guests. He guided them inside straightaway, Siiri and Yvonne first, without further comments or small talk, to the balcony where Johan had been before. Siiri and Yvonne remained standing at the balcony entrance, silent, while the other guests found their place in front of the first row of chairs, having an open view to the screen and to the stall. An elderly man, in his sixties, with gray, almost white hair, dressed in light-blue jeans, a light-brown jacket and a white t-shirt, approached Johan, smiling. He had a graciously wrinkled, friendly looking face. He was rather tall compared to Michel, but shorter than Johan, with a sporty, agile appearance. He greeted Johan first.

"Great to see you here in person, Johan, finally. I'm Maurice Hecaen."

Johan was momentarily startled, hearing the familiar first name, but then relaxed. Maurice turned to the young woman standing on his left:

"This is my colleague, Marianne. She's originally from Cambridge, and she's working on social network dynamics."

Johan greeted Marianne, who had a somewhat pale appearance, brown eyes and dark hair, without any makeup, slim, about the same height as Yvonne, dressed casually in black jeans and an orange, cashmere sweater. She looked very young to Johan, whose attention was caught by her tiny, eloquent earring on her right ear. It had an implanted diamond on a miniscule oval-shaped silver plate, with some text on it. Johan couldn't help staring at it, but then greeted her, assuming she was still a student.

"Nice to meet you, Marianne, what is your field of study, may I ask?"

She had a serious aura, as if reluctant to talk to Johan, and answered shortly, "I'm developing a string-theory-based modeling of dynamic multi-layered networks. I'm a professor at Cambridge, at the Department of Computational Physics."

Johan was hit by the earned embarrassment, but smiled, lifting his eyebrows and nodding.

"Well, string theory has been my passion for years! I'm curious to know what you mean by the network concept in this context. Perhaps you can enlighten me later?"

Johan had once confessed to Wolle that the real reason he had applied for the research fellowship at Stanley was the work done on string theory there. The participation in Calle's work with the collision data was just an interesting necessity. Instead of asking Marianne for more details about her work, he turned to Maurice, glancing at Michel first, hoping to get his support.

"This is a conspicuous theoretical coincidence, but why am I here? I agreed, said yes, to Michel's two questions or a series of them, meaning I'm interested. I still think I need the chance to withdraw in case I don't like what I see, or if you are working with something that is not good for me or appears ethically unsound. You could be working with things I find suspicious. OK?"

He did not know whom to address, who was in charge of the meeting, so he tried to open his question to all of them.

Maurice said, "We will show you something first, to get you warmed up. It will get your full attention, believe me. We are serious with what we do and have already done and when you learn about it you can make your final decision to proceed. But before that, you should sign our non-disclosure agreement about what you are going to see and hear. By doing that you will be in trouble if you disclose anything of it to outsiders, or even let them know what you know about us, or that you have been in touch with us. If you decline our offers, you are on your own and can continue your life as if we did not exist."

He continued, looking grave, almost gloomy.

"It's of utmost importance for all of us that you sign this agreement. We need protection, too; surely you understand this? We are only starting this and do not want to take any extra risks. Fair enough?"

He handed over the NDA to Johan who sat down to read it. It contained only a few pages, including an introduction of the background, the important conditions to be met, Johan's full name and his address at the Villa, and then a simple statement that he would not disclose anything he would see in the mentioned presentation and would not even disclose having had contact with anyone related to the project and the presentation; then there was the date.

If he were to break the conditions of the NDA, he would be obliged to pay 543,210 Euros to the society indicated in the paper — a stipulation that made him exclaim, "A strange sum you have here. Besides, I don't have such money!"

Maurice waved his hands up in the air, as if confirming Johan's interpretation of a real threat and that they were serious about it.

"Well, you don't need it if you behave. The sum is easy for you to remember and it's a kind of a countdown if you fail us! You don't take any risk if you respect the requirements of our agreement."

The name of the society in the NDA, "IoB^s International, Paris" did not mean anything to Johan, but he remembered seeing the symbol on Michel's t-shirt. He turned to Siiri, asking her opinion about the NDA.

She stepped forward, towards Johan, nodding. "There is no trick in that. I've signed it, too, and you can understand why I've been so secretive about it. Read it! I suggest you sign it. Trust me! There is no risk if you just keep this to yourself. There is nothing to lose."

Yvonne was quiet as if she did not want to interfere, but Johan could see she was smiling and attentive, even excited. Johan knew that Siiri was always extra careful and he could trust her judgement. Everyone remained silent when Johan spent fifteen minutes, carefully reading the conditions again. It was a simple enough text, mostly free of difficult legal formulations and complex expressions. He was ready to sign.

"OK." He wrote his name on two copies and stood up. "I'm all yours, so far! Thank you, Siiri; I trust you!"

He noted a flash of a wide smile on Yvonne's face, but she turned serious when Maurice took the paper and said, "Fine, thank you. Let's sit down!"

Maurice asked everyone to take a seat, waving a remote controller in his hand. Marianne and Yvonne took their seats at the second row and Siiri, Maurice and Johan moved to the first row. Michel started towards the back of the hall, waving at Johan, "I'll take care of the projectors and lights.'"

"We'll start when you are ready, Johan!"

The lights went off, only weak, reddish-yellow, warm lights providing some visibility in the theater.

Johan was the last one to sit down, asking, as a kind of an opening joke, "OK, is this a movie?"

"You'll be surprised. You are in the leading, supporting role here!" It was joke from Siiri, and Johan could see her smiling profile. He did not understand what she meant.

There were no texts; only a black screen appeared. After a while, two timelines, one above the other, flashed on, with data and time tags. It was a typical representation of sound recording tracks familiar from audio apps. Then a sound signal was shown to start and progress, from left to right on both timelines. The loud and clear voices were easy to hear:

Track 1. *"I've been asked if our model has been already tested in a fair comparison situation with other competing models, Monte Carlos and others. I could not immediately answer and wondered if there are already some simulation runs and data, I'm not aware of. They would like to see the material and the test data having the promising outcome you described in the latest abstract."*

Track 2. *"They — who?"*

Track 1. *"A colleague of mine from here who worked at Cern with similar methods and instrumentation; knows the stuff really well, works for Clash now."*

Track 2. *"Cern? Who is he?"*

Track 1. *"I'm sorry, but I cannot tell. I promised."*

Track 2. "So, you want me to give you our confidential data, what we have under preparation, and you would then offer it to someone I don't know, is that it?"

Track 2. "Fuck you! Now listen to me, you can tell the guy to fly here at his own cost and see for himself! Who is he to doubt us? And if you want to continue there just stick to what you are supposed to do. You know that your funding is only one year at a time and it must be continued for the next year — next month is the deadline. Don't mess it up!"

Johan stood up in anger:

"That's me and Calle. I called him! How can you have this?" Maurice did not answer, only calmed Johan down.

"Please sit down and let me show all of it. We can discuss it then. It's a collage." Siiri threw a quick look at Johan, who sat back on the chair, with an audible slam and thump and failed to notice her soft smile.

Johan realized someone had recorded the whole conversation where Calle presented his first threat concerning the funding. He wondered how it had been possible for them to know what to record and choose the timing of the hack.

Maurice explained, "We received an inquiry from your friend Wolle, who had offered to check if you would be a potential candidate to join us. I've known Wolle and Siiri for some time already. They have my full trust; we have an extensive history of collaboration and would not have started anything like this unless it was hundred percent sure what it was about. Your friends have supported you, I mean they trust you, and backed up this meeting, too."

Johan was confused by the comment of "friends".

"What do you mean, were there others besides Siiri and Yvonne, and Wolle? Is that what you mean? Who are they?"

"You don't know them personally, but you've met." Maurice continued:

"Wolle was worried about a potential conflict between you and Professor Roos and suggested we take the case to see what's going on. We have more. It's all based on the relationship between you and Roos. Let's take a look at this."

Next, they saw a video clip of Roos having a Skype call with a Finnish colleague, a retired professor of physics, Seppo Manni, whom

Johan knew by name. Maurice lifted his right hand, pointing at the screen, throwing a sharp glance at Johan:

"Pay attention to the date, Johan, it's already the 5th of January 2016 here. We've translated it in the subtitles, but you of course understand it. This professor Manni was the head of the evaluation committee at the Fund."

The clip revealed that Manni was preparing the review of the evaluation and ranking of the applications they had received at the Fund. Maurice explained, "As the chair of the committee he introduces the evaluation data to the Fund and discusses it with the evaluators; he is practically responsible for making the decisions, although the evaluators have given their suggestions and ranked the applicants."

Roos opened the session with casual talk, and Johan grew increasingly curious and worried, wondering how these people had managed to hack this, but he did not say anything, only thought about Siiri, knowing she could have done it. Then he heard his name mentioned. It was enough to get him agitated, and he stood up again, nervous, following the hacked conversation, feeling his pulse accelerate, remaining muted by what he saw and heard.

Roos: "One of the applicants is my student, an excellent post doc. He's at Stanley and wants to secure the continuation for his funding. He's already got the first year and done an excellent job. But they have a lot of research money there at the lab, and my feeling is they don't really need this. I don't feel it right either that he would be competing with those in a much worse funding situation here."

Manni: "But you must know this is a fair competition; if he's done what he proposed in his previous plan, which we accepted, then we automatically guarantee the second year. Right? Surely you know our practice?"

Roos: "Yes, of course I know it, but this is a special case. I might even fund him myself if there is a risk he cannot get this or anything from Stanley."

Manni: "But he has not mentioned your or Stanley funding in his application, and you know the applicants are requested to declare all the funding they have or coming to them during the funding period. We are very strict on that."

Roos: "He must have understood the options, knowing my good situation."

Manni: "I'm still hesitant. I think he's presented a fair application."

Roos: "Of course you could move his application to the special grant group, where you have applications from all fields of arts and sciences. If he makes it there, he indeed deserves it. It would be a prestige, as you know; it's always big news. He's the best of our candidates to compete for that."

Manni: "You must know how difficult it is to make it to the top there? The decision criteria are more variable and unpredictable because of the spectrum of different fields — I'd say he has less than five percent chance if he's in that group. Artists and writers are not going to support him."

Roos: "That sounds like a fair alternative. He's an excellent candidate. But it is your decision, of course."

Manni: "OK, if you think he's really that good, then I'll think about moving it there."

Johan was shocked, hearing so many blunt lies. It was now clear why the continuation of his funding had been rejected. It was a fraud. He stood up for a second, and then sat down, exhausted and frustrated, but even the revelation of the misconduct by Roos did not prevent a worrying thought: "Why didn't I make it in that group? What am I doing wrong?" He remained silent, realizing that Roos had fully orchestrated the devious deception. The clip continued, and there was one more reference to Johan at the end of it, where Roos repeated his comment on what an excellent candidate Johan would be.

After the clip had finished, Johan turned to Maurice:

"He told me he doesn't have any money to support me! Do you have that hacked, too?

Before Maurice could answer, Siiri turned to Johan and commented, "Yes we do."

Johan continued. "How could you time your hacking like this, just on the right time to record the critical episode? How could you know that? I mean, you cannot have these people under your surveillance, just like that, all the time?"

Maurice smiled. "We didn't shadow them all the time. We know how to be on time when certain behaviors occur. Let's hear and see one more soundtrack and a video clip."

This soundtrack was from Johan and Roos talking. Johan was not surprised this time that they had recorded it.

Track 1: *"Do you know why I didn't get the continuation to my funding?"*

Track 2: *"How can you know that? It's not public yet?"*

Track 1: *"I just know."*

Track 2: *"Is this another secret operation of yours?"*

Track 1: *"I just want to know what has happened."*

Track 2: *"You must know, I'm not allowed to talk to you about this before it's public. What I can say is, there was nothing I could do; you had clearly the best application of all the candidates, and they moved you into a special group outside the normal one; it was open to everyone applying. I was one hundred percent sure you would make it there, and it would have been a better deal for you. Something must have gone wrong. It was a tough competition, tougher than I could expect. I know nothing about it."*

Maurice turned to Johan and tapped on his hand, calming him down.

"This is how the dark champions in the grant decision game do it: by always telling nice truths about their victims, so that they appear to be their benevolent patrons. Who could blame them then? When they want their own candidate to win the game, they just praise this candidate by referring to any possible quality criteria which they then don't mention at all for the victim, such as adding that 'they are equal candidates, but this one has...' and so it goes on. This works always when the competition is tough. There are always many excellent candidates; it's the name of the game today. Roos praised you, which made him look generous and fair to the chair of the committee, perhaps even to you? He behaved like a perfect candidate for the next funding committee, an honest and benevolent academic!"

Johan listened to Maurice's gloomy explanation in silence, trying to figure out why the chair and the officials did not see such things happen. Maurice continued.

"These crooks do lie and introduce suspicions or reservations, but only about things nobody can check, typically referring to an unknown, trusted third party or to something they have heard. In a scientific sense, it is strange that this works. If you, as a scientist, present a claim that nobody can check, you are lost in science and no editor will accept your story. But committee work is not science; it's social psychology."

Maurice, now red in the face with excitement, paused, as if inviting a comment from Johan, who could only add, sighing, "I know my Kuhn, but this is almost impossible! How can a scientist behave like this?"

"You'd be surprised how effective a negative rumor is when it is launched by a respected academic and scientist whose whole personal fame and brand is based on doing trustworthy scientific work. Roos sent the rumors flying and lied about your funding opportunities at Stanley and about his own intention to fund you. Who could claim that there is no funding available at Stanley, one of the best universities in the world? If faced with a serious risk of being disclosed, he even could have funded you to save his neck. It's foolproof. He could not be caught for having presented false negative information because he always spoke the truth, but not the whole and relevant truth he knew. How do you think the funding office representatives could discover such behavior? No way, only in extreme cases someone could begin a serious investigation, but it would be hard work and I've never seen it done. A person doing that would be taken as a troublemaker, believe me, I know. Besides if you ask the officials of the Fund what has been said and done, they turn you down and you are the problem case then. 'Confidentiality.' It's a jungle!"

Johan noticed that Maurice was becoming upset and angry, and he wondered if Maurice had been in Johan's position at some earlier point in his own life.

"We have more on this," Maurice said, in a calmer voice. "We also have recordings where Roos phoned three of your lab colleagues, not your closest colleagues, at Stanley immediately after the negative decision at the Fund. For them, the confidential story was that Roos had been shocked to hear someone at your institute in Helsinki mention you stole their research ideas and misused the funding in your earlier work. He put in their heads a suspicion about a scientific fraud, and that it was probably the reason your funding was terminated. Roos did not say that he *knows* exactly the nature of the ethical problems he had heard of, but he hinted at them, referring to unofficial sources without mentioning any names. He emphasized it was confidential information and something he was worried about."

Maurice paused again, and everyone waited until he continued.

"That's a clever way to implant distant suspicions and paranoia without a risk of getting caught for lying. How could your colleagues know whom to approach in Finland to check that the story is true? To whom could they turn? When the Faculty in Helsinki would then start the process against you formally, it would be proof of what they had already heard about you. Positive evidence, though. Your colleagues at Stanley could have approached you, but then they would have broken the promise of confidentiality and taken a risk with Roos. Wolle knows this disgusting strategy all too well, having lived and studied in Russia, but you can imagine he had to be extra cautious in the US. Roos played the good guy by warning your colleagues about talking with you about any sensitive research topics and advising them to keep their data secure. You can imagine the effect, and yes, of course you have seen or sensed the result."

Johan felt his hands trembling. He stood up and interrupted Maurice, grasped his hair, speaking in a loud voice as he looked around the theater.

"*That* is why they suddenly did not answer my calls and remained so distant! Roos should be prosecuted for this!"

Maurice nodded. "We have masses of material on this, and there is more, but the next one is about the system itself. Please pay attention to this now, it's the key to what we do and who we are. It's why you are here and more important than anything you have seen so far. Roos is just an academic deformity, an educated sociopath if you like. You are not his only victim, but he will be forgotten over time. Forget about the revenge. Don't paint your life with it, please. You don't need it!"

Johan was not relieved at all. Instead, he felt full of new, undischarged frustration. He wondered why Maurice tried to calm him down when it was evident that his own face was bright red from distress. Maurice paused again, this time standing up straight and breathing deeply, as if listening to his own suggestion to calm down. Johan sat down.

Next, a typical, connected network scheme, simple black and white graphics, appeared on the movie screen. It consisted of more than one hundred small, distinctly clustered circles, each one representing a unit connected to several other similar units.

Maurice announced, now more relaxed and enthusiastic, "This is our look at human behavior in networks. The units here are persons, researchers, for example, and the arrows between them show the connections between the units, that is, between people. The thickness of the arrow is an indicator of the strength or power of the specific connection and the direction of the arrow shows which way the flow of information or material occurs. You can imagine the arrows describing the amount of data flowing from one person to another or why not, how much money flows and in which direction, or whatever measurable human activity and behavior it may be. The configuration changes over time, of course; it's the result of the behaviors of these people. It's like me and you right now, the network connection between us is changing all the time, in both directions. In other words, this is a typical, standard, dynamic social network description, right, Marianne?"

Marianne nodded, but remained silent.

Maurice waved toward the screen. "The special case now on the screen is also a geographical depiction of the net in the sense that the separations between the unit-persons reflect the real geographical distances between them. The distances have been scaled to fit in the image, but they cover all continents, so this is a global social map of a selected set of people. As you can see, some people are well-connected locally."

Johan was still uneasy. "I'm not a specialist in these matters, but even I have seen hundreds of such networks; is there anything new in this?"

Siiri glanced briefly at Johan, looking grave, but she did not answer, and let Maurice continue. Johan's skeptical comment did not seem to bother Maurice at all.

"The network image is actually a video showing how the configuration develops over time. I have stopped it for one instant, so that you get an idea what it is. Look at this, Johan," and he pushed the button in his remote controller.

Now each unit had a title; sometimes it was the name of a person, or a set of key words related to the person, and some of them, a minority, included a face photo. It took some time for Johan to notice that there were familiar names in it and after a while, scanning through them, he found his own name, too. He started searching through the rest of the units and again felt his pulse accelerate and hands getting cold: Carl Roos was one of them and then there were Yvonne, Siiri, half a dozen of his teammates from the Stanley physics lab, and several unknown persons, some of them with a Finnish name. The face and name of Peter Jason was there too, but Johan did not spend time on him. Instead, he started eagerly tracing Calle's dense and abundant Finnish and other connections.

"So, you have collected data about these connections? What are they? Is it just a standard social network description I can get from a plethora of apps? I don't get it, there's nothing new in this!"

Maurice said, without the slightest change in the tone of his voice, "We can address any *behavior* occurring in this net, individual or collective, sometimes even an expressed intention, including what Roos was doing, and what you were doing. I guess you understand what this means? Marianne and Siiri will explain this to you. For example, I can rewind it back in time, like this."

The video started rewinding and the network became alive, connections changing and new units appearing until it stopped.

"This describes the detailed network activity during the week before the 7th of October 2015, when you had the phone call with Professor Roos; it was late in the evening at the park in Palo Alto. You were anxious about the funding and whether the problem with it was being solved. He assured you everything was fine with your application."

Johan knew this hacking was illegal, there was no doubt about it, but he was curious to know what they had.

"How in the hell can you have this data? It's illegal, of course."

Maurice was not alarmed. "Just take it easy and decide about it when you know more. Look at the net, please. I will forward it to the beginning of January, the next year, 2016, when the applications were processed at the Fund. You can see the cluster of four people with whom Calle has actively communicated, starting from the beginning of January and until your phone call, where you told Roos you knew about the decision. This continued until the end of February, before the publishing of the funding decisions. Two of his connections are the reviewers of your application and one is the chair of the review committee. You probably know them by name."

"So, Calle had been in touch with the members of the committee while telling me he did not know what had happened to my application, and then he was guiding the chair as well, all the way, with false information about my funding situation. What a crook!"

Siiri stood up and turned to Johan, shaking her head, and instructing Maurice, "Please run it to the 1st of February, and stop it there for a while. I'm sure Johan would like to follow Roos' behavior."

Maurice gestured to Siiri to continue and explain. She pointed to the screen.

"There are new clusters here. One consists of six of your teammates and the physics lab at Stanley. They are based mostly on phone calls, but there were emails and social media stuff, too. The other people include two officials from Stanley dealing with matters of fraud, for example, and the third new cluster consists of CLASH personnel. You probably know them all."

She sat down. Johan was still hesitant:

"This is serious spying, for Heaven's sake! But OK, OK, I don't have to repeat this!" He did not know what to think.

Maurice walked back and forth along the balcony railing as he said, "This would take too long for me to explain, but remember now, you have the NDA, so whatever I disclose to you, we have the deal. If you get tired or worried about this, you are free to go. I don't want to play with a reluctant victim!"

For the first time, Johan observed signs of nervousness in Maurice, who was getting pale again, and scratching his head. Johan realized he had to calm down, and said, "OK, I'm sorry, this just feels like opening my old wounds."

The network visual changed into a multi-layer version, viewed obliquely, like a deck of cards in a nice pile, sparsely spaced, half a dozen of them, each card showing a different network configuration: connections and clusters. There were also some vertical one-to-one and one-to-many connections between units in different layers. Maurice began to walk slowly back and forth in front of Johan.

"We have good reasons to use layered networks in our work. I will explain this in a minute, it's rather complex and extremely rich in its general nature. The number of layers could be about one hundred or so, but there is no limit; we can have as many layers as there are human behaviors, different in their content and dynamics. One layer of units — be it people, firms or any other actors — is reserved for their specific, professional behaviors, for example, and another one for work life, or friendship-related behaviors that occur among the actors. The units have copies in all layers, because all people, for example, have different roles, which guide their behavior. You could consider the layers as human or social role platforms if you like; people do not show the same behaviors at home and at work. We live in layers. Hence, also the meaning of the connections within each of them differ; they are layer specific.

However, unlike in standard networks each unit in these layers has multiple simultaneous connections with every other unit to which it is connected there. There can be any number of connection as we need, representing different behaviors, but typically no more than one hundred. It depends on what we want to do with the data. Think about people again, Johan. Think about Roos. You have many simultaneous behavioral connections with him: in one layer as a colleague, in another as a pro and in another one as a criminal. They are simultaneous, and always there. They do not vanish even when you deal with only one type of connection like we have done here." Johan felt his pulse accelerate and hands suddenly becoming cold wet, but he remained silent and did not want to disturb Maurice.

"Each connection represents a certain kind of behavior of the unit in question, and in the case of professional relationship, for example, it can reflect a person's specific collaboration activity with a colleague like writing a shared manuscript, exchanging thoughts and ideas, having a chat, or sending messages. Each connection can have any number of states, each state describing the status of the specific activity related to the connection.

So, the input data to each unit and its output data in one layer is typically, but not always, specific to that domain. Remember again, that a unit can be a person, organizational entity, even a computer or a hub of them. Each layer has a specific theoretical model to fit that layer. Mainly we are interested in professional layers. Of course, we are only building and testing the models we use, it's a huge endeavor. We are learning, all the time." He paused for half a minute and Johan remained silent, looking reserved, but eager to hear more.

Maurice continued, "But then, there are connections between the units located in different layers, as many as we need, and this is most interesting; it means we can model natural behavior in all of its complex and even spontaneous forms! After all, we never behave along one behavior dimension only, not when we display economic behavior and even less so in case of criminal economic behaviors. For example, if there is a money transaction from a unit in an economic layer to a unit in a friendship layer, you can imagine it having a number of alternative states describing the various meanings, from bribery to business, presents, and whatever. When we see such connections, it's our task to recognize them. It is a most useful form of knowledge!" Maurice paused and gazed at Johan, smiling.

Before Johan had a chance to comment, Maurice said quickly, "You are right, Johan, there are models, multilayered, even with multiple connections like this, but ours is different, as you will see; just wait!"

Maurice sounded relaxed again, sat down and asked Marianne to continue. She stood up slowly and moved from her seat behind Johan to face him. Now she had a soft voice and was hesitating. Johan could sense her excitement.

"This will take some time and it comes close to your string theory concepts, although it's an analogy only, so please don't take it literally; please be patient with me. You must understand our approach, so that you can see how we look at people's behavior in the net and what future potential this has; we have a lens on their behaviors. I was thinking you might even be interested in contributing to this. But let's see.

The multi-layer image you saw is a visualization of the kind of data we have. It's about real human behaviors. Each layer has its own behavior model, but in fact we deal with simultaneously active, parallel and interconnected behavior channels within and between layers, be they economic, social, psychological, or even political in nature. We are interested in how each unit — a person — behaves within his or her whole network, all layers included. OK? Life is multi-dimensional, as

Maurice said, every minute and in every context, you see? We never do or think only one thing at a time, Zen priests perhaps excluded." She made a funny face at Johan and turned to stare at the back wall of the balcony, without moving. Then she continued.

"In a simple, standard network you would connect two or more units sending data to one another. You can even have deep learning, a constellation of several groups of units, each group feeding to the next one and so on. The term 'depth' is only a popular way to say that there are several groups of units in the model. The mathematical model used describes how the input data is represented, how the connections change, how learning occurs, and the dynamics evolve in the net and what will be the network output, what it can do, as is the case in language translation, for example. In a sense the net behaves, obeying the mathematical model used. Researchers hope such a modeling would describe real-life behaviors. All social media apps use such an approach to recognize and predict customer behaviors, mostly to sell them stuff or spy on them. Some seem to think we would learn what is the nature of human consciousness by using such models. I don't buy that. It's a thin approach to life. We have more." Marianne glanced at Johan, and for the first time he saw her broad, relaxed smile. She paused, took a few steps, relaxed from her tension, as she turned to Maurice. "But that's another matter. There are dozens of models for that purpose, thousands of scientific articles published, some related to the way the brain processes neural information. Some are just computational tools. I'm sorry this is such a long story, but you need to understand it, Johan."

She gave him an encouraging smile for an instant before she waved again at the screen.

"This is how we are different. It relates to the string thinking. In our system, each connection between two units consists of a collection of several parallel, simultaneously acting channels that occur within or between the layers. If it occurs within a layer, it's about a certain behavior class. If it's between layers, it is about more complex behavior. Imagine the connection from one unit to another one: it is like a vibrating string having many potential, but unique states. In other words, each string has several possible and potential vibration states — meaning behaviors — please don't get me wrong with the vibes concept here. The strings in the model are capable of changing state as fast as needed for any practical purposes. It is like people — you and me — we have multiple connections between us, just as we have with our friends, colleagues and close ones. You thought I'm a student and it spanned a certain state of vibration in one of the strings between us, but it changed fast and now the state has changed between us. It's the same string, perhaps there are others, too we don't know yet, but its state can change."

The string concept sounded alarming to Johan, who interrupted her.

"Strings between us? That sounds strange to me. Do you really mean strings as we talk about them in physics?"

She smiled again at Johan, amused by his serious looks.

"Please be patient with me. I do talk about vibes, too. The vibes made only some aspects of interaction possible between us, too bad for you and me. Luckily, there are multiple, simultaneous channels active between two people engaged with each other, physically or virtually, so we still have a chance, and you have already changed our vibes. The relationship between two people is described by the activity profile and dynamics of these parallel, simultaneously active connection channels. It is a complex evolving process and it is fast. It is exactly what makes life such a wonderful process!"

Johan leaned back in his chair, trying hard to see how all this could be related to the strings as he knew them, their assumed dynamics and size, being extremely small and mathematically complicated. Marianne's concepts sounded far-fetched.

Marianne went on, "Each individual uses a set of behavior channels to accomplish a task, related to work, hobbies, love, hate, business and even religious behaviors. The channels are all there, to allow connection with people and the world, always available, never silent. Some may call part of this system the subconscious, but I'm not fond of that interpretation here. Our behavior *is* the outcome of all these channels — call them strings if you like — acting simultaneously. I'm tempted to say *life is* that activity. Each of us can try, and sometimes we almost manage, to focus on one channel at a time, to keep the rest of them quiet, to silence their vibes, but it is extremely difficult, if not impossible. Our individual, human characteristics and curiosity take care of that."

She turned to Siiri. "You may know this better than I do, but Zen meditation could be an extreme example of silencing the restless vibrations in all our strings, to build a well-defined focus. Some may think our personalities are defined by the nature of these string sets."

Siiri only smiled back, silent, winking at her. Marianne continued her presentation, facing Johan again.

"Take a simplified thought example like nepotism, where two channels or two different strings, one related to the private life, and the other to business, for example, are active at the same time. Together they determine the person's behavior in a decision situation. Often it is easy for us to keep one channel in control and the other one silent, but for some and sometimes for all of us, it becomes overwhelmingly difficult to do so. Imagine Roos, Johan! You assumed he acted on the science channel only, and that he would have silenced the channels representing his personal ambitions and needs, his anger. It would not be wise to assume that the mathematical models describing the two layers, private life and science business in his case, would be identical. They are very different, and we want to model them accordingly. To put it simply, it is life we try to model; the net is secondary."

Johan remained reserved but was slowly becoming curious about the compelling string analogy and the consequences Marianne had described. He lifted his hand, to comment, but then became quiet for a moment, trying to grasp the big picture of what he had heard.

He sighed and asked, "What about the scale? How do you define the scale or the size of the strings in your model? Surely you know we are talking about extremely small and hypothetical sizes, smaller than any particle we know of. Unless you mean that as humans and individuals we simply are moved around by the human gravitation, or what you might call it, attraction and our behavior is but a result of these unknown human strings producing the gravitation? This is complicated. Too wild for my taste!"

She looked at Johan alertly.

"Please remember that this an analogy, nothing more; it's a formal one, though. We don't have to worry about the scale of the strings here. They extend over any geographical or other distance if there are string channels available for a connection. This may sound unbelievable, but in this sense, we are all connected over any distance, whenever there is a mental connection, even over and after death."

The last comment startled Johan, making him think about the experiences at his mother's death bed. Then he remembered other connections of his own, the pain he still felt for leaving Pablo, something that did not disappear, even over time. Einstein, Gunnar and all the people he met were dead, but he did not feel like he had lost anything of the personal and spiritual connection with them. He started thinking about the Bateau and the possibility that his father Sten had been there, a strange link over time, and then the bowtie. He sighed, staring at the screen, seeing nothing, thinking about the strings that make our physical reality happen and not only to exist. Tears filled his eyes.

Marianne noticed Johan's serious silence and paused for a while before continuing, "For example," she said, "now that we know each other better, you have a connection with me, unlike it was ever before, right? Even if I don't have any direct way to know what this connection is, it exists. It will be there forever, even if you don't think of me, even after one of us dies. It's mystic, I agree, but I'm quite comfortable with this view. To be more practical, I don't claim we have a model or that we are even close to building a holistic model of a human behavior like this, but there is a lot we can do already. We have done it, too."

Johan watched Marianne, amazed. He was getting ready to accept the vague analogy, trying to match his physical-theoretical view on some of the string characteristics he knew so well. He realized how difficult it was, for a theoretical physicist, with his own specific knowledge background, to imagine what aspects of human behavior would, in the real world, correspond to any of the basic properties of the strings in quantum mechanics, even as an analogy. He felt a familiar lack of words, almost like the muting at the Bateau.

"I can see the value of your model and understand the analogy with how I think about the strings, if I'm very open-minded. If I'm really wild I can even think of some mathematical approaches here. But is that description of any real, practical use? How can you know what behaviors to monitor and record from your target persons, like Calle or anyone, and spying on me, for that matter? How could you have such models? Is this only one more version of big data analysis? What about your hacking?

Marianne, you sound like a female shaman talking when you say we have string connections extending even beyond death!"

Marianne flashed her open smile at him.

"The shamans are closer to your country than mine, I guess. But here is the second major difference, and this is now crucial. We have a method to address any behavior occurring within the active network entity and to open access to all data related to that specific behavior. This is a very strong and true claim. We have a saying: 'Identify the strings and their states between the people and you can learn to know them.' This is not big data analysis, which is a way to look at the rear mirror stuff, at the often, ill-defined data, as you must know. We monitor ongoing real behaviors. We call it b-data, to differentiate it from data, which is not necessarily behavioral in nature."

Johan still had difficulties in following all the behavioral implications Marianne was explaining, but he made up his mind to stay calm, to wait and see what he would learn, and then decide what to think about it all.

Siiri stood up and interrupted them. "The world is drowning in the new kind of behavior data, it's a Babel, as we all know. Soon there will be more behavior data than any other kind of data, perhaps it has already happened, but we can be prepared for it now. I guess you saw the symbol on Michel's t-shirt; its main element is *IoB,* which stands for *Internet of Behaviors.* This is again a surprise for you, Johan, like Gunnar was: there is a Finnish colleague of yours who introduced the string idea in this context, to be used for behavior analysis. With it we can identify and follow any behavior and then make use of any behavior data available in the net. We are not there yet, but have already achieved quite a lot. Maurice, please."

Siiri sat down and Marianne returned to her seat to let Maurice continue. He stood up and explained, "We are not afraid of the complexity and the multi-dimensional nature of human life and psychology; quite the contrary, our grounding hypothesis is that we need to consider all the simultaneous dimensions of behavior to understand the essence of even the simplest human thought and act, even death, as Marianne mentioned. We are at home with complex spaces, just as you are at home with your own work in quantum mechanics, Johan. The main idea of our model is first to define and recognize and then assign a code to any interesting-to-us, multi-dimensional pattern of human behavior. I mean any specific behavior, relevant to us, or to someone. Think about your own practical work and activities in physics as an example. You can solve a specific mathematical problem, dealing with tensors, for example, and interact with a colleague. Your work or the interaction always happens at several layers, simultaneously. Even the simplest task, like writing a meaningful symbol into an equation, always incorporates several dimensions of behavior. We want to know what goes into any behavior, and knowing that gives us tremendous advantage in supporting and helping people in what they do."

Johan was surprised to hear the comment "helping people in what they do" after all the problems with Roos they had touched and the hacking he had seen. He was getting impatient, wanting to know more, and asked, with an exceptionally high pitch in his voice:

"Once you are able to code a behavior, if I assume it is possible to do, then what? So what?"

Maurice switched on another video.

"I'll show it next, but imagine you can know, with a one hundred percent certainty, and in a sufficient accuracy, along the most relevant dimensions, when a person is behaving in a certain way. We don't have to think about the strings here, explicitly, but if you so like, imagine you know the relevant strings spanned between two people and you have a means to monitor and follow the string states and the way they evolve over the interaction. Think about you and Siiri, take one well-identified pattern of your shared behavior as an example!"

Johan could feel himself blushing.

"Once you have identified that specific behavior and assign a code to it with a coding system relevant to such behaviors and give it a label, then *voila*, the knowledge of that specific behavior with all its ingredients can be made available and used in the net, anywhere in the world, by anyone."

"As a banal example, you could have a device and every time you push a button in it, you tell the whole world, through the net and the mobile, without disclosing who you are, that you — a person X, somewhere on the globe — a physicist like you, is right now at this minute, working on a specific problem, with let's say some aspect of your proton collision data. As a further thought experiment, imagine a device which would reveal all the strings and their states spanned between you and your work environment, your colleagues, your immediate world relevant to that specific work. You would in effect provide full knowledge of your behavior to anyone who is able to read your device through the net."

"What you would, in fact, be revealing then are the strings activated at the very moment you work with the task at hand, even though you don't explain everything in words. As a result, anyone interested in your behavior, perhaps even working on the same problem at the same time with you, could join, be available, in the right time, follow how you proceed, help or get help from others in a matter relevant to him or her — and to you. A global network can be spanned around any specific behavior! It's like the Internet of Things, but this is about behaviors."

Johan smiled, silent and eager to hear more, eagerly nodding to Maurice.

"Can you imagine," Maurice added, "what a huge potential such a system can offer? Forget now that the world is not full of proton collision specialists, and there are even fewer specialists who have the same motivation and work style that you have, but there are many who do not interact optimally, as you know, despite the video connections and other real-time collaboration tools. The world is full of other specialists, professionals and gifted students who can, and some have already done so, develop useful sets of behavior addresses to make efficient collaboration possible."

He continued, now with a bright smile, eyes shining, "Of course we cannot spread such magic devices all over the world, and I doubt Calle would have been eager to push the crime button every time he made any of his clever moves against you! But there are ways to recognize and classify good behaviors, to identify the strings and their states. Scientific work especially is not haphazard. We have something going on in implanting IoB codes that are activated by scientific articles, books, and other materials when a person works with them. We call it 'science behavior', but it can be education, as well. This will evolve into a wonderful asset; think about the masses participating in MOOC programs and the way this could help coordinate communication and collaborative work and learning! Anyhow, I'll explain how we did it with Roos. That was a very limited, special case, the dark side, but an excellent learning experience. I'm not too proud of it, but Siiri made us do it and we trusted her motivation."

Maurice glanced warmly at Siiri, who only nodded and then turned at Johan who thought he saw her ear lobes reddening. The scale of the system was starting to open to him and he realized how ignorant he was about the psychological theories of behavior. Maurice gestured at Siiri.

"Siiri had her reasons and ways to read Roos' documents and the interaction on the project with which you were involved. She identified the relevant targets, the strings if you like, the relationships between people and objects. I mean she found the activities and the decisions to move your application to the special grant class and the negative decision that followed. It was exceptional at the Civil Fund to interrupt someone's research period as they did to you; hence, they discussed it in the reviewer meeting. Minutes were recorded and Siiri found a copy from Roos' PC. He was the vice chair. Then she called you. I'll explain how this happened. Be patient."

Siiri glanced at Johan, nodding seriously, but she did not say anything. Johan nodded back, lifting his eyebrows as if in a sign of acceptance and gratitude.

"Siiri wanted us to test our behavior coding on Calle, in your case, and was able to convince us with her documents that you were clean and that Roos' behavior was suspicious. You should also know you had risk-taking friends at CLASH, who took the risk to help you!"

"We launched a simple trial, first with only one behavior code, a very general one: 'Calle acting on Johan.' Very simple. The aim was to monitor the strings Roos activated in your case. It worked like this: Siiri implanted a logger agent that looked at Roos' activities with his PC, mobile phone and in the net, monitoring the occurrence of any of your ID data such as name, email address, social media codes, your address book contents and a few others, but not too many. It could have been more specific, but our assumption was that whenever these occur in his activities, he's doing something related to you and we were curious to see what this behavior, *C acting on J,* was and what information was exchanged in the process. Every time this behavior occurred, our system received a kind of an extended IP address — we call it IoB address through the net — which we used as a gate to all of Roos' communication and action channels and documents he would use, when this behavior occurred. Related documents were then open, a mobile conversation was ongoing and so on. We could even monitor the tone of his voice and sometimes the eye movements on the screen. Following what Roos was doing to you, we knew it was nothing good, and we were convinced our own activity was well founded. It was risky, and we knew it. That's how we got our sound tracks and the videos. It's like the Internet of Things operating on light bulbs having individual IoT addresses, for example, but we operate on behaviors, this time it was bad behaviors. I hope we don't have to do it again. Sometimes we deal with intentions whenever they have been expressed and can be detected.

Some things were simple to follow, like when Roos phoned or mailed you or people in your address book. Our voice recognition system is not as good as it should be, but we can isolate some words like names, an increasing number of topics and so on. Sometimes it's difficult with your accents. Because we address only specific behaviors, we are not drowning in irrelevant data. Of course, we sometimes recorded also an article you were included in as an author, but it only shows how effective the monitoring was.

We have learned more with every bit of b-data and don't have to do so much guessing, as is typical in many big data approaches. There are ways to converge our b-data accuracy by looking at events that happen within a close temporal or spatial proximity of a specific behavior. For example, for Roos we saw a cluster of phone calls and even a couple of emails and almost nothing else, immediately after you had told him on the phone that you knew about the negative funding decision. It made him act and sound nervous, which was shown in our voice analysis. It was ninety percent of real hits for us, and bad for you. You see?"

He sat down, glancing only briefly at Johan, lifting his thumb to Siiri.

Johan realized their data was a gold mine and it occurred to him that such information presented a tempting possibility to disclose Calle's fraud. He could clean his reputation and secure his future at Stanley and elsewhere. He became excited, telling Maurice,

"There are so many questions open, but one thing is certain, this is not legal. Despite that, I still wonder if we can use your data against Calle and make him confess what he's done, to withdraw the crazy accusations?"

Maurice was now serious and visibly exhausted.

"We could, but that's not the way we work. This is only for you and for us to know, it would be unethical otherwise. I'll explain to you what we do, what is our purpose of doing it. This was an exception and nothing more, the only time we've done it. It's not our business. We don't want to get involved."

Johan did not know what to think. He had become angry at what he saw, the hard evidence about the fraud, but he still did not know why Roos had done it. "This is so close. We could get him!" he said. Then he remembered Maurice's earlier words: "Forget about revenge. Don't paint your life with it, please." Color shadows on the ice in the darkening evening came to his mind.

Chapter 34
Internet of Science Behavior

The session had taken an unexpected turn, totally surprising Johan. He had to abandon his prejudices about the novelty of the approach, when shown the way it had been used to reveal Calle's actions. First, he had not been able to imagine how human behavior data could be injected into the complex model, but then he had been given a practical example. The creative use of his own specialty, although an analogy, the string theory, astonished him, and he could now see its use as the basis for the novel approach. What struck him most was the implication that it could have something to do with how science is done. He still had defenses left, but it was time to try to see the opportunities, not only the obstacles.

Maurice stood up again, addressing Johan. "Do you know how many professional physicists there are in the world? Yes, Michel mentioned your discussion; there are about one million of them, the same with physicians and medical doctors. How many professional mathematicians are there? Probably some hundred thousand if we could count the situation everywhere. How many software developers? At least twenty million and more; coders flourish everywhere and AI will boost their work. Add to that the students and the increasing number of people from all over the world studying these topics in open education forums, MOOC and Khan Academy and everywhere, even in Les Ursulines, and in the Villa, if you've noticed. Clever robots are coming to help us, if they can. The global knowledge potential is huge, but mostly inefficiently used, overlooked, especially in the underdeveloped countries, waiting for a chance to gain strength. The world needs it, desperately!"

Johan saw Maurice was now speaking from his own motivation, wondering what might be behind such a powerful attitude and persistence, but he did not want to interrupt the talk.

"We intend to improve this and that is why we have IoB^s, we call it the Internet of Science Behavior. It will build bridges between everyone working on any scientific problem, or studying it, so that as a scientist you are never alone, you don't have to guess what the best scientists in the world are doing and how they think about the problems in front of them and a lot more. It's about recorded openness as well. Besides, many excellent people cannot afford traveling to foreign labs and conferences."

Johan still wished Maurice could help him with Roos, but this wish did not turn off his curiosity now.

"Why do you do it? Don't you think there would be other ways to improve the communication among scientists? We do have open science movements already. Physicists work together, massively as you know from CERN. Besides, even scientists need to live somehow, to make a living and get a salary or a funding? They need positions and promotions."

Maurice was quick to explain, filled with vibrant enthusiasm. "Guess how much knowledge-based work exists in the world? It will hardly diminish, even now when the robots and Artificial Intelligence are coming everywhere. I assume you don't even know your own, true market value, I mean the people and organizations who would be ready to recruit you for a shorter or longer period or to benefit from your skills and competence when and at the very moment they desperately would need it. Surely you don't think Helsinki, Cambridge and Stanley are the only options?

"Well, I don't want to tease you more, Johan, but frankly, we've made good money with this, from organizations, individuals and through our own form of crowdsourcing. We've invested most of it in improving the system and making sure people who work within it find funding or a reasonable salary. There are risks, of course, especially at the start it was not easy."

Johan spoke up. "How can you be so sure of it? What happens when your efforts and community are discovered by others?"

"So far, we have grown, and the system is stabilizing. The growth occurs where it provides value, in one form or another. It can be an extra hand where needed, a very special skill or real working relationship. Indeed, it's a small wonder that we have not been discovered yet, but it's about trust, matchmaking with the right kind of people, doing it just in time and sometimes finding the right combinations of skill sets to solve complex problems. If the system benefits science, I believe it will survive, simply because there are no better means. The true professionals know their fields and the quality requirements."

"But it's a risk?"

"Yes, in a sense. But we already have a consultancy, kind of an international front, operating on the markets, a soon to be listed company and a successful one, too. We are here the back office, to put it mildly. There is a lot more coming, believe me. I can still show you something to convince you and then I think it's up to you how you see the situation. There are no real risks to those who join us. You will learn, whatever happens, and we won't spoil your reputation — quite the contrary! — if and when you perform. We won't impose any limits on your work. Everyone is free to leave, with a strict NDA."

Johan was now impressed. Suddenly he had a vivid recall of how Maurice Princet had tested his skills at the Bateau and then recruited him to do some bookkeeping. The memory made him think, "How many students are there in the world, whose skills we don't know? How difficult is it to find out who would be available and with what kind of skills and motivated? Talented people cannot use what they have and learn more."

Thinking about *the* Maurice at the Bateau, he smiled and laughed, embarrassed, knowing he could not explain the reasons for his amusement to Marianne and this Maurice.

Yvonne had remained in the background during the whole session. Only now did she join the discussion, addressing Johan.

"I've led a double life, including CLASH, sometimes as a university scholar and sometimes as a ubiquitous member of the IoB^s, but I've spent most of my time with relevant problems, even made a reasonable living on that. Michel's question about the motivation to work for science, even with the risk of not getting your own name on the front pages of the best articles, is a challenge. Nothing prevents you from becoming a member of research teams, as I've done, and benefiting from the background support you get from our network. But you will be bound by our ethical code of conduct. It's like invisible, ethically solid hacking for the best of science and humankind. If you act as an anonymous contributor, then of course you will not get the fame and your name on any scientific articles, but you will know, and we will know what you have accomplished and done. There will be records of your contributions of your strings, if you so like."

She paused for a moment and looked at Johan, who realized he did not know much about her true background. Now Johan was seriously puzzled about Yvonne, realizing he had been so focused on his own problems that he had totally neglected Yvonne. "I don't even know of her family situation!" He sighed, feeling guilty when looking at Yvonne, serious. Maurice continued.

"Our data is not about article references, it's more and detailed. It's much better than the survival trend of having your name, at any price, on the front page of any article. Today it's practically impossible to know what a person having his or her name on an article really means. What can they actually do or know? Our system will change that. We do have some interesting ideas on how to give credit to anonymous contributors, but that's another story."

Johan trusted Yvonne but could not imagine what IoB^s could offer him.

"Could you give me an example of what I could do?"

Siiri stood up, received the remote controller from Maurice and laughed, "Finally you asked! I'll show you a real-time video demo of what is going on right now on one of our member specialists. She's only eighteen. Let's call her Lisa, an exceptionally skilled young mathematician. We got in touch with her when she was fourteen. Her father is a medical doctor. I'm not a mathematician, but as far as I understand, what she's working on is called 'time-reversal, as related to dynamic systems.' You and Marianne might better know what that is about."

Johan nodded, looking at Yvonne with some puzzlement, commenting, "It's rather strange to see such a young person working with this. I guess it's related to quantum mechanics. There are colleagues in quantum mechanics working on it or on stuff related to it. I'm curious."

On the screen Johan saw a set of icons and photos of persons arranged in a mosaic-like arrangement, altogether about fifty or sixty images. At the center, one of them was marked with a red frame; otherwise, it was just like any collections of icons one might see on a computer desktop. Johan was impatient.

"So, what is that? What's going on there?"

Siiri waved the remote control. "I'll show you what they're working with."

Next the icons and photos on the screen were reorganized into miniscule images of different objects like text, graphics, book and article pages and something Johan could not discern in the small images. Then she changed the image so that only 2 x 2 images were visible. One was of an article page consisting of mathematical symbols and formulas; one was a graph; and the third and fourth were hand-written texts in real time, someone writing and drawing on a typical sheet of paper. Johan thought he recognized some of the formulas in the book.

"It looks like someone is working on Hamiltonian dynamic systems. Who are these people?"

Maurice explained, "Each of the fifty-six researchers have — for one reason or another — indicated that at this moment they are working on some aspect of the Hamiltonian systems. They use both an automatic and a human-controlled coding system, prepared and shared by the community, to indicate what exactly they are doing. For example, the behavior can simply be the writing of a manuscript with a specific content or a section of it, use of an analysis program, studying a topic, or working with any material object or a well-defined problem. They have made the IoBs address or a code of that activity available in the net so that we all, members of the system who know the behavioral meaning of the code and have the right to use it, can participate at the right time and with relevant content, in one way or another. We can have the role as a teacher, collaborator, or mentor or whatever we like and see useful. The person indicating her behavior can allow us to access everything related to her activity or the problem at hand, the materials, statistical and mathematical tools, handwritten text, everything. We can approach her via any available communication device. We don't need to know who and where she is, it's all about behaviors although often we do know the identities when participants think it is useful. It's almost, like a reverse MOOC, but the good thing is there are practically no drop-outs, in contrast to MOOCs where they are a major problem. This is a drop-in system!

We have designed a coding system for different forms of science behavior. They are behavior addresses for each community, specialize in something, to use. It's emerging and developed over time and now includes codes for the main topics in several problem areas. Of course, in most areas this is only a beginning and often it's difficult. Some fields have advanced fast, some have not. This is how Lisa got started and had the best available researchers to help and share their skills and best knowledge sources whenever they happened to be active on or eager to deal with the same problem. It was no surprise to notice how the best brains in the world were willing to help her progress. They are not teachers in the traditional sense, but rather partners or 'virtual parents' in science and education. We don't have a proper way to call them. In the future they can be intelligent, specialized robots, but even they must know what help is needed and where! I have to confess I don't like the idea of robots doing this; I prefer humans."

A moment of silence followed, and Maurice walked back and forth along the railing, until he stopped in the middle of the row of benches, now in a good mood.

"The scale of the willingness to support anyone devoted to learning science was somewhat of a surprise to us. Then on the other hand, we realized that it had always been like that, an essential part of healthy scientific culture. Did you know that in the first university in Bologna at the beginning of the tenth century, it was the students who hired the professors and could kick them out if they did not deliver what they expected? This is a modern version of that, and much more, but it is virtual."

Johan had now grasped the enormous potential, and a flow of questions filled his mind. He still did not understand what he could do, in his own, real life, and what the risks were.

"Assuming I join you, what could I do and how could I make my living? How do I know there is anything relevant for me to do? How many are enrolled in your system? What if I just waste my time?"

Siiri said, "There is just too much to go through here; surely you understand Maurice cannot explain everything here and right now. All I can say is that I make part of my living with it, and so does Yvonne. Is that enough for you? I'm happy to guide you to get started, and so is Yvonne."

Maurice joined in. "Yes, I agree, there is just too much. But Johan, please use your imagination here, try to see the opportunities! Wonderful things have become possible with the system, from teaching and learning to collaborative solving of extremely complex scientific and other problems. And don't think it's science only, since we have now artists and art researchers joining us. I know it can be dangerous, too. You saw how we handled Roos and his behavior with our IoB approach. We don't want this system in the wrong hands."

He glanced at Johan, relaxed but serious. "One more thing, and we can then finish. Nobody needs to know who you are or anything about your identity. Everything you do is driven by knowledge creation, only that. Actors do not need to know each other; they are profiled by the topic codes they use so that we can at any time see how many are active, working under a specific code, even right now, but not necessarily knowing who and where they are. There are identity risks, of course, but we will make a continuous effort to deal with them. It's all about the behavior, not about the identity of the participating person!"

Johan felt that he was at the start of a great adventure. "Can I ask for a favor, one more thing — could you show me how many people right now are working on a specific topic I'd so much like to know about? It's related to your name, too."

He smiled at Maurice, who looked happy to finally hear the unreserved, enthusiastic inquiry from Johan.

"I wondered why it took so long! Are all Finns so slow to warm up? So, what do you want to know?"

Johan explained, "I've tried to learn about Maurice Princet, who helped Pablo, I mean Picasso, to develop his Cubist approach and style. His help is clearly visible in the painting, *Les Demoiselles*. I've found it difficult to locate any accurate data about him or even photographs of him. I'd so much love to find more, find photos of him, but have only found one book or a booklet on him."

Marianne was eager to help. "Just a moment, you mean *the* Maurice Princet who was called Le Mathematicién du Cubisme? What do you want to know about him? Why? I need to know the topic or the theme."

Johan was astonished Marianne knew anything of Princet and felt embarrassed to explain, could not even ask how come she knew about it, and decided to be open again.

"I met him in my strange journey to 1907. I know it sounds like I'm a nutcase, but please forget that for a moment. I'd like to get in touch with people, historians or anyone who knows how he lived after being in such close contact with Pablo. I don't have the faintest idea if someone is working on him. Google just gives a limited number of documents and it is tedious to go through them all, trying to find out what they are doing or is there anything going on about it at all. Perhaps I'm the only one really interested in him?"

Marianne nodded at Johan, pointing at the screen showing a mosaic of icons again. "There you have the people in our network who, right now, at this very moment, have something going on related to Princet. I could show you how these people are related — if they are — but this is not the point here now. On the right you can see the list of IoBˢ codes or addresses they have decided to use and under which they work. The first code is *Maurice Princet's divorce,* meaning someone is researching that — it is not gossip journalism, these are serious people — then there is *Maurice Princet and the fourth dimension in art*, then *Maurice Princet and the painting* Les Demoiselles, and *Maurice Princet's life after the Bateau.* There are altogether about twenty themes active right now and seventy-six people actively working on them. But I can see that there are more than two hundred altogether who have declared these codes in their work but are not working on them at this very moment. Is this helpful to you? If I click on any of those themes, I have immediate access to various sources they use right now and the people too, if they are not anonymous. Is there something especially interesting to you? Some use time windows to indicate when exactly they are active with a denoted theme, even if they don't do it all the time. The window can exist from now up to one year or even longer."

On the address list Marianne showed, Johan had paid attention to a specific code evoking the vivid and familiar, painful memory on how he had left his friends. He could not figure out why someone would study a topic like that, something that was a compulsion to himself — *the Metre.*

The code was *Maurice Princet and the Metre.* Johan felt his heart pound and he had to struggle not to cry. Marianne noticed his reaction.

"I know, I've been surprised so many times. Sometimes it can be touching, especially when seeing what your colleagues, already passed away, have worked with."

Having seen and realized the immense potential of the system, Johan had forgotten all his doubts and wanted to dive in, as soon as possible.

"You mean these codes are actually addresses and if I have your application or the interface to use them, I can get in touch with the people working on this subject, or at least have access to every document and other material relevant to it?"

Marianne nodded. Siiri had been quiet for some time and now joined them. "Yes indeed, and, Johan, it's much more pervasive than that, no limits in the human behaviors on the globe."

She threw a soft, kind smile at Johan.-"It took some time for you to figure this out. And this is only the surface!"

Johan nodded. "I'm sure there is a lot of stuff on Picasso, but can I start working with this immediately?"

Maurice switched off the screen and turned to Johan.

"You are welcome, Johan. Why don't you talk with Siiri and Yvonne? They will get you started. It's a simple process to join the system, but you need to get acquainted with what is relevant for you. Then there are other processes we want to start, declaring you and your profile in the system so that you are known and have any necessary rights to work with it. There are a lot of details you need to take care of. I'll let you know whom to contact and how."

The possibility to advance, fast, made Johan excited, but one thing continued to worry him.

"I'm still in serious trouble with Roos and all the allegations. Joining you does not change anything. I will remain what I am right now, some kind of an outlaw in science."

Before Maurice answered, Yvonne joined in. "Roos will be the outlaw, trust me."

Then she reminded Johan about the deal with her doctoral students in Paris.

"Our seminar is going on and you can start there. At least you can cover your housing and get started with the system. Don't forget, you have people enlisted in IoB^s working at CLASH. I'd be surprised if they and I would just remain passive, knowing you have joined us. Roos might hear from them."

Johan did not know what to make of Yvonne's comment about Roos and the Stanley colleagues, but decided to discuss it later with her and Siiri. Everyone was leaving and just before stepping out from the lobby to the street, Johan remembered what he had seen downstairs.

He asked Maurice, "What's there, in the basement? It's not like a standard office or a store."

Maurice tapped Johan on the shoulder. "We have twenty-five of them now, in the US, Europe, and Asia, although none in the Nordic countries yet. After you have enlisted and have all the rights, we will introduce this one, our Paris hub, to you. Basically, it's a center where we monitor the ongoing activities, the active networks, and their outcomes based on our inquiries. It's a business center as well. Part of a consultancy we run in Paris."

"How can you keep it secret? Or can you?"

"It's dynamically configured with only one or two relatively permanent employees. In IoB^s we typically need special personnel and invite an optimal group, holding the required skills and knowledge level to work here for a week or two. Only occasionally it can be the same group of people, but all are members of the IoB^s. They live at the Villa; some work with companies at the same time, and the Villa supports that. Due to this constant input from colleagues, we have up-to-date knowledge of the progress in all the fields covered. We do have some reliable intention data, too, so that we know the plans and aims of the enlisted researchers and other knowledge workers, even before they have finished their exact research plans or grant applications. It's quite fascinating. We get a lead of about two to three years on those who are forced to rely on articles, applications, conferences, or infrequent lab visits. Mostly we are invisible!"

Johan thanked Maurice, as all of them reached the sunny street. He waved goodbye to Marianne and Michel, too, who had come to say goodbye to him. As he crossed the street with Siiri and Yvonne, he said cheerfully, "I can't imagine a better occasion for champagne! What do you think? Les Ursulines?"

He heard only a muffled answer, as Siiri and Yvonne headed toward Les Ursulines, almost running. Johan was about to cross the street and follow them when he was stopped by a familiar sight. Standing in the middle of the road, he saw the extremely faint, translucent, brownish silky curtain, spreading open and covering his whole visual field, fluttering softly, in beautiful waveforms, spanning in front of him. There were no women figures on the curtain, but he could vividly see Siiri and Yvonne behind it, hurrying, hand in hand, towards Les Ursulines. He was not worried at all. It was the first time he had heard them giggle, and he walked, unafraid, through the wall.

Postscript

I have called the genre of this story *fiction science*. It amends from exceptional, true historical events and even modern innovations, but of course, it is pure fiction. Unlike me, the protagonist, Johan Ek, is a theoretical physicist. Hence, in the spirit of fiction, I have taken several liberties in introducing the problems and work in theoretical physics, especially quantum mechanics, and I apologize for possible errors and misinterpretations. I have tried to show the respect I feel for modern physics and its heroes. I'm grateful to a number of beautiful books and articles dealing with arts, sciences and culture but have not listed them all. The famous quote on perception is from Kant, I. (1781): Kritik der reinen Vernunft. (Critique of Pure Reason up to the end of the Analytic), translation by J.F. Bennett. I believe it is easy to find the sources I have used on the basis of the information included in the story itself.

The error in the meter standard, ideas of 4D geometry, and Picasso's work captivate Johan's attention. He knows by heart the meaning of standards, especially the meter, for all physical theories. I had imagined what would happen if the protagonist, haunted by the problems and the documented fraud of the meter standard, would meet Picasso who is about to break all visual art standards and metrics in his works. *The Measure of All Things* by Ken Alder was my guide to the mystery of the Metre, and I was no less inspired by the observations in my articles: *On the construction of psychologically based, general theory of observation: an introduction* (Gestalt Theory, 2013) and *Hidden human variables in quantum mechanics* (arXiv.org).

From the marvelous book *Einstein and Picasso* by Arthur I. Miller I learned that Picasso had a friend, a mathematician, who informed him and his friends about 4D geometry. I came to like this curious person, Maurice Princet, and wondered about his motivations. There is a beautiful little book by Marc Décimo about him: *Maurice Princet, Le Mathématicien du Cubisme*. I'm a scientist, not an artist, but I have had the privilege to work with artists and theatre lighting, and feel at home with artistic contexts, often as a welcomed outsider. I recognized something similar in Maurice Princet but again, the story about his motivation is pure fiction and I have allowed my imagination fly. I hope my admiration for artists is visible in the story.

At the beginning of the story, the teenage Johan and his father meet a curious amateur historian, a blind man. The character and the incidents are a version of a true story: we were driving with my brother in the countryside of Evijärvi in north-western Finland where our mother's family comes from. The fellow, Aleksi Kultalahti, was standing in the middle of a countryside road, hitch hiking, and after some introductions and discussions he led us to the place, an old barn, where we found the historical bowtie symbol of our family, from the times people still could not write: ⋈. Aleksi was a wonderful character whose persistent work made it possible to preserve valuable historical knowledge and objects from his home village.

Einstein (1879-1955) was known to appreciate the Finnish theoretical physicist Gunnar Nordstöm (1881-1923), not well-known here, in his home country. In 1913, Vienna, Einstein gave a talk on the relativistic theories of gravitation, and publicly praised Nordstöm who was present at the meeting. This resulted in a "friendly and cordial relation" between them (H. Tallqvist, *Minnesteckning över Gunnar Nordström*, Soc. Sci. Fenn. III.1., 1924 [In Swedish]). There were fictional—and why not factual, too—reasons to make these great scientists meet with the haunted protagonist. I had read a well-written document about the talk Einstein gave at Collège de France, in Paris, 1922 and the occasion was just perfect for these characters to meet. The meeting is described in delicious detail in *Einstein in Paris* by Charles Nordmann (21st Century Science & Technology, 2011). I also included some of the real figures from the conference in the novel. I have tried my best to treat and meet these wonderful people with respect and honor.

Johan mentions an incident from a scientific meeting, the European Conference on Visual Perception (ECVP) in 1984 (31 August – 3 September), Cambridge, UK, where a prominent visual scientist, Professor Ingo Rentschler, had chosen to use some specific portraits of Salvador Dali in his image processing demonstration. I have often visited this wonderful conference and attended the interesting talk by Ingo. The photos he used in the experiments were from the *Burning Dali* (Salvatore brennt) by the Austrian artist Gottfried Hellnwein. As it happened, only a day before the ECVP conference, on 30th August, 1984, Salvador Dali had been in a fire and suffered from burns.

Writing the novel, I had included in it a charming Parisian restaurant, which I found from Google Maps, close to the conference site, where I imagined the scientists would get together after Einstein's talk, but which I had never visited. From the map photos I imagined its interior. Kiisa and I were eager to visit Paris and see some of the places occurring in the book and then in the autumn of 2017, when I had recovered enough, we had reserved a room from a charming small hotel *Relais Saint-Jacques*, at Rue de l'Abbé de L'Épée, where we had stayed earlier. Arriving there we found out that there was no reservation for us. The kind receptionist told us that there was a Hotel Saint-Jacques—without the 'Relais'— located at rue des Écoles. I had accidentally reserved a room at the wrong hotel.

We took a longish walk with our luggage from the first hotel to the one at rue des Écoles where we had the actual reservation. The 'wrong hotel' happened to be near to Collège de France where the famous conference had taken place. But that was not all. Tired, we climbed to the room, unpacked and I opened the window to see outside and was astonished: the restaurant where the post-conference meeting takes place in the book was just on the other side of the narrow street and we had a straight view there from our window! Of course, we visited it for a late dinner—I only had to move some pillars in the story to make the real place match with the imaginary one.

Another wonderful real-life experience inspired the episode on English pronunciation in the story. Our accidental lunch meeting in Palo Alto, in 2011, with linguist Neil G. Jacobs, an amazing professional, helped Kiisa and me to learn about our own ways to pronounce English. There were more 'coincidences'.

The compelling concept of the Internet of Behaviors (IoB), a use case of it, as engineers would put it, became part of the story. It is my invention and it is to human behavior what Internet of Things (IoT) is to artificial objects and systems. I introduced it in my gotepoem Wordpress blog already in 2012 and started searching for support from Finnish innovation funds and firms to develop it further. It was frustrating to meet the total lack of interest and motivation to understand it at all. I had continued writing about it but was already getting tired of the real-world struggles. Then I realized that it could have a compelling role in my book and I introduced it into the fictional world of Johan's, inspired to leave a fictional trace of the IoB. But life takes strange turns. Only a few months after I had sent the manuscript to Pegasus, I learned that Gartner, the world-famous research and advisory firm had listed it as the number one technology trend for 2021. Fiction was faster than reality.

I have borrowed the name of a good friend, Dr. Wolfgang Teder, Wolle as we called him, for the story. The fictional and multi-talented Wolle in the book is like his real model, who was a skilled guitar musician, brain scientist, and an electronic wizard, who loved to design and build ingenious guitar amplifiers and other gadgets. He passed away too early and I remember him now in the story. We used to tease each other and sometimes I called him the 'ballerina'—he was a tall and sensitive man.

Finally, my mentor, Fergus W. Campbell, to whom I have dedicated this book, together with Alec Aalto, was a famous neurophysiologist and vision scientist who had his lab at the University of Cambridge, UK. I was often invited to Cambridge and in addition to the collaboration with Fergus, I learned to know him as a friend and mentor, with the highest ethical standards in scientific work and his knowledge and respect for the history of physics. This made it a special pleasure to work with Pegasus Elliot Mackenzie Publishers—from Cambridge.

Siuntio 21st April, 2021

Göte Nyman